IN COMMON

A NOVEL OF LOVE AND SACRIFICE
excessive *undeserved*

NORMA WATKINS

Black Rose Writing | Texas

ISBN: 978-1-68433-923-5
PUBLISHED BY BLACK ROSE WRITING
www.blackrosewriting.com

Printed in the United States of America
Suggested Retail Price (SRP) $26.95

In Common is printed in Book Antiqua

*As a planet-friendly publisher, Black Rose Writing does its best to eliminate unnecessary waste to reduce paper usage and energy costs, while never compromising the reading experience. As a result, the final word count vs. page count may not meet common expectations.

PRAISE FOR NORMA WATKINS AND
THE LAST RESORT

"So this is a tale, first, of an enchanted childhood, then a murky drama of marriage and adultery, all played out against a background of bitter American struggle. I found it splendid in every way."

–Carolyn See, *The Washington Post*

"Norma Watkins, a rare, brave, and entrancing human being, has written a uniquely Mississipi story about coming to terms with family, state, and tumultuous times — and discovering herself in the process. It is a great read, pure and simple."

–Hodding Carter III

"*The Last Resort* reminded me of why I started reading in the first place — to be enchanted, the be carried away from my world and dropped into a world more vivid and incandescent. Norma Watkins casts her spell with exquisite sentences and unerring, evocative details. She is a writer of inordinate compassion and formidable intelligence. This unsparing and unsentimental memoir documents a woman's struggle for independence over the course of her lifetime and took great moral courage and ferocious honesty to write. And let me add that this book is so much more than personal memoir. It is an eye on history. Norma Watkins puts us there at the white hot center of the struggle for racial equality in Jackson, Mississippi, in the turbulent fifties and sixties."

–John Dufresne,
author of *The Lie That Tells the Truth, Deep in the Shade of Paradise, Louisiana Power & Light*

"What a book! What a woman! And what a life she has led...touching upon all the major issues of our time. I was riveted from start to finish. Brave, honest, and open, Norma Watkins is a born writer through and through. *The Last Resort* is an absolute must-read for all southern women — and men, too — as she shines a light into some of the darkest, most secret and sacred areas of our culture. This is one of the best memoirs I have ever read."

–Lee Smith,
author of *Fair and Tender Ladies, Oral History, On Agate Hill*

For Allison, who loved stories

IN COMMON

"It hurts to love. It's like giving yourself to be flayed
and knowing that at any moment the other person
may just walk off with your skin."
–Susan Sontag

"… nothing is worth having so much as something unattainable."
–Jodi Picoult

"Above all, be the heroine of your life, not the victim."
–Nora Ephron

1

Before dawn on a March morning in 1933, Velma Vernon, nine years old and already tall for her age, set onions behind Uncle Drew's tractor. South Mississippi stirred from winter. A mist hung over the low end of the field and the plow cut loamy furrows into the cold soil. Uncle Drew sang, "Life is just a bowl of cherries," his voice loud over the engine's growl. Velma sang along, straddling the row, stooping every six inches to place a baby onion, standing to pull another from her sack.

The singing stopped. Trying to turn at the bottom of the field, Uncle Drew had backed the tractor into the drainage ditch. Cussing, he revved the machine back and forth. He called to Velma. "Go get your Papa and tell him to bring me a couple of boards."

Velma skipped over the furrows, singing the second line of Uncle Drew's song: "Don't take it serious; it's too mysterious." The words felt ticklish on her tongue and she was glad for a break. It took 150 onion sets to plant one eighty-foot row. They had done ten rows so far and her hands had gone stiff. The sun rose behind the mist, turning it gold. Velma stopped to admire it.

Inside the dark barn, she found Papa sharpening an axe on the foot-peddled grinder.

"Gol-darn-it," he said. "Every year I remind the man to cut the furrows shorter when he gets to the bottom of that field." He scrambled through the used lumber pile and pulled out a couple of two-by-sixes. They headed back. When they came over the rise, Papa started running. Velma ran after him. The tractor lay on its side at the bottom of the ditch.

Papa shut off the engine. In the sudden quiet, his voice sounded strange. "Sister, don't come any closer."

Velma couldn't stop herself. The rusty red machine rested squarely on Uncle Drew's chest. His eyes were open. Pink foam bubbled from his mouth.

If she had run instead of skipping, if she hadn't kept singing, or stopped to look at the mist. Guilt and grief weighed on her. They filled a sack she couldn't put down.

For the first year, she dreamed the accident almost every night. She woke screaming and Mama would come. "Shush, Velma. It's nobody's fault. Drew made a bad choice, and every now and then one of them will kill you."

2

On Christmas morning in 1933, Lillian Creekmore woke filled with anticipation. Twenty-four years old, dark-eyed and quick moving, she wore her hair bobbed and possessed a petite, small-bosomed body, perfect for the flapper fashions she could not afford.

Dressing hurriedly in the cold room, she brushed her teeth and hair, and ran downstairs. The family hotel had closed for the winter, but the oldest wing, the Warm Part (though the wheezing furnace never made it so), rang with the voices of everyone Lillian loved.

"Christmas Gift," she called to her sister Maude. If you were the first to say it, you got the good luck. "Christmas Gift" to her sister Ernestine and sister-in-law Faye. "Christmas Gift" to Knox, Ernestine's sweet husband. You could not be depressed, even during a Depression with the people you cared for close around. "Christmas Gift," Lillian yelled to her brothers James and Leland.

"Christmas Gift, Angie," they yelled back. Angie was her nickname, shortened from Aunt Jemima, the pancake mix. As a child, she loved pancakes so much, James and Leland gave her the name off the box.

Lillian had a reason to be excited: her brothers had hinted at a surprise. From the secretive looks she'd seen passing between them, she'd become convinced they'd found her a car. She couldn't imagine how, but James and Leland were shrewd, maybe shrewd enough to pull off a miracle in the middle of these dark years.

Lillian was the baby, the youngest of five Creekmores, and people had been telling her how darling she was since she could remember. The boys at Ole Miss (where she would have stayed longer if a plummeting economy hadn't dried up the family finances) certainly thought so. It was harder to stay darling when you were poor and stuck in the middle of nowhere. She needed a way out, and maybe today she would get it.

She opened the swinging door to the kitchen. "Christmas Gift," to Lena, bent over the pink-hot wood stove. To Lena's son Johnny and his wife Flora May. To Ellis and Preston, the waiters. When the hotel closed for the season, the servants were sent home, but everyone returned for Christmas Day.

In the dining room around the big table, the family sat down to the traditional broiled quail and grits breakfast. Since quitting college four years before, Lillian had helped her brothers and sisters operate Creekmore Hotel and Spa. Most of their guests were older people taking the mineral water cure (a cure that promised to ward off everything from asthma to warts). Nobody with the slightest romantic possibility. Lillian knew how to charm the ladies and harmlessly flirt with their husbands, but as the years went by, she felt her chances slipping. She wasn't young anymore. She could still pass for young, but on February 11, she would turn twenty-five, and she didn't fool herself: twenty-five was practically middle-aged when you weren't married.

Ellis handed around a basket of hot biscuits. Lillian split one and buttered it. Maude passed her the dish of homemade plum jelly.

Their father died when Lillian was three. He had the brains for business, everyone said so, and the hotel thrived. With him gone, their mother took over. Just after Lillian turned sixteen, a doctor in New Orleans botched a simple appendectomy and her mother died on the operating table. The five siblings had been left to keep the place going. Creekmore was a seasonal hotel and needed to make enough money from May through Labor Day to carry them through the other eight months. They'd done it, and with enough left over to send Lillian to college, until the Crash.

Knox lifted his coffee cup in a toast. "Here's to us. We may not be celebrating next year if Hitler stays in power."

A murmur from the men, talk of the last war and worries about the next.

Ernestine tapped her water glass. "Adolf Hitler is a failed house painter. A country with Germany's deep culture will soon come to its senses. Let us not spoil Christmas." She paused, looking around the table. "The Lord will provide."

Lillian smiled into her cup: the implication being, if the Lord didn't, Ernestine would.

People told Lillian she had been blessed with a sunny disposition, but behind a cheerful exterior, she fretted. If she didn't find a husband soon, she would be stuck here, eleven miles from the nearest town of Canton, and thirty-five miles from the capital city of Jackson. She would grow too old to marry, working to keep this crumbling enterprise going. She wanted her chance and she wasn't asking for much: a decent man to love, a house of her own, and, please God, not to worry about money every single minute.

Ernestine was going on about the Lord again, how grateful they should be for His help in making it through another year.

Nibbling around a tiny quail leg, Lillian returned to her thoughts. She needed a way out, especially during the long, gray winters with the hotel closed. That meant some kind of independent transportation. She didn't care how old it was or how beat up, as long as it got her to Jackson for weekends with her former sorority sisters and single men. The friends fortunate enough to graduate had gotten engaged during their senior year, married soon after, and were already having babies.

Summers at the hotel were bearable. Lillian didn't mind hard work, and keeping the place running took all five of them. From May to September, with the sixty-six rooms filled, she ran from the moment her feet touched the floor in the morning until she dropped into bed at night, too tired to brush her teeth. Summers kept her so busy, she didn't have time to worry about the future, and there was always the possibility a handsome son might arrive to fetch his mother.

At the hotel, the price of a room included three hearty meals. During the height of summer, the dining room filled twice at lunch and dinner. Extra money came from shipping five-gallon jugs of Creekmore's famous (and evil-tasting) water all over the country. Additional cash was earned discreetly from a two-story building behind the Annex, where Leland oversaw cockfights in a pit downstairs, while James ran roulette, poker, and blackjack tables above.

Set ups were sold at the Fishes' Club, the "nightclub" at the far end of the Annex. Prohibition had ended in the rest of the country, but Mississippi chose to remain dry. People brought their own liquor and, if they didn't, a bootleg bottle could be arranged.

In a pasture behind the kitchen, Alan tended a large vegetable garden. Up the hill in the barn, they kept cows for milk, chickens for eggs, and pigs for sausage, bacon, and smoked hams. With all this, the five of them managed to pay the help who did the planting, cooking and serving, while keeping the place in fairly good repair.

Lillian looked around at the plates piled with tiny bird bones. Today felt fun, but come January, with the rooms empty except for family and one or two servants, she might as well be a monk. Her oldest sister Maude told her not to worry. Look at her at thirty-one, perfectly content without a husband. Lillian did not feel reassured. Maude was a saint, everyone said so, and saints were happy with whatever scraps fell off God's plate. Lillian wanted life to be a feast and if she ever figured a way out of here, she intended to find a place at the table.

Breakfast over, the family gathered around the fireplace in the big parlor to open gifts. Lillian tried to act nonchalant. She praised the satin slip from Ernestine and the red beret crocheted by Maude. She smiled as Leland and James tried on scarves she'd knitted them in Ole Miss's colors, cardinal and navy. Faye's son, followed by Ernestine's, ran in and out of the room, conducting aerial battles with the small tin airplanes Lillian had given them.

Lillian held off opening the lumpy package from her brothers until there were no more presents. Affecting a modest disinterest, she untied the red string and ripped off the white paper.

Out tumbled an envelope and the radiator cap from some kind of car. She'd seen a cap like this one, with a red-line thermometer that told you if the engine over-heated. *This was from her car.*

"I can't believe it." She leapt to her feet, dumping the wrappings on the floor, threw her arms first around Leland, then James. "You are the best brothers in the entire world. Where's the rest of it?" She slammed out the front door, looking up and down the graveled parking area. James and Faye's beat-up Chevrolet Coupe stood alone.

"Okay, you two," Lillian said. "Where'd you hide it? Is it in the carport?" She ran past them, headed through the dining room.

James called her name, puffing along behind. At thirty-two, he was getting fat. She did not stop to listen.

"Wait," Leland said.

She dashed through the kitchen and out the side door, racing along the frigid open porch and down the stairs by the family's summer quarters. Her brothers tried to catch up, but Lillian was thin and faster. The low open carport held the hotel's one and only vehicle, the battered 1925 Packard used for hauling guests and supplies. Lillian stood confused. "Where is it?"

"This was Leland's idea." James bent, hands on his knees, trying to catch his breath.

"Where's the rest of my car?"

"We knew how bad you wanted one, so we—" James trailed off.

"You didn't open the envelope." Leland handed it to her.

Lillian tore it open and found a twenty-dollar bill inside. Stabbed by disappointment, she flung the money and the radiator cap into the dirt.

"The radiator cap was sort of a guarantee." Leland said, "and the money is our first installment. That's all we could afford this year."

Seeing her brothers' forlorn faces, Lillian laughed through her tears. "I hate you both."

"Please don't be mad," Leland said. "We thought you'd get a kick out of it."

The red birthmark on her forehead must be showing. It blazed forth when she got angry. "Only you two would treat me this bad."

James tried to hug her. "We'll get you a car, you know we will, as soon as we find the money." He picked up the radiator cap and the twenty-dollar bill.

"When things get better," Leland said.

Lillian shook her head. "I'm not ready to forgive you."

James handed her the money. "Put this away and we'll add to it."

They looked like hound dogs, wet-eyed, begging for reassurance. She could not stay mad. Forgiveness was one of her best qualities.

Walking back toward the hotel, she linked arms with them. "Let me see if I have this straight. I'm getting this car one piece at a time." She poked Leland in the ribs. "A chunk each Christmas. By the time I have the whole thing, I'll be so old you'll have to wheel me to the driver's seat."

James pulled her closer. "You're our baby sister and we'll always take care of you."

She knew they would, which almost made up for being an orphan with no hope of escape.

After a late afternoon dinner of turkey and dressing, ambrosia and coconut cake, Lillian went upstairs to her room. Christmas had been splendid, but she'd had enough. She kicked off her shoes and crawled under the quilt in her clothes. This might not be the life she dreamed of, but it was not a bad life. How many girls had older brothers like James and Leland, and a sister as good as Maude? She might have no money or prospects, but she was rich with love.

A soft knock on the door. "It's me—Faye."

Lillian sat up. She loved James's wife. Faye was like a blood sister, only better because she wasn't.

Faye crawled under the covers next to Lillian and took a hammered metal flask out of her purse.

"This is why I adore you," Lillian said. "You're the only woman I know with a flask."

"Men shouldn't have all the fun."

Faye was six years older, tall to Lillian's short, and languorous compared with Lillian's energy. James married her when she was sixteen, so Faye had never finished high school, much less college. She gave birth to one baby, declared the experience horrible, and told

James not to plan on more. They named him James Junior, but everyone called the child Jimbo, after Jumbo the elephant. He weighed nine pounds at birth, and at twelve was twice as large as Ernestine's Knox III.

Lillian loved Faye for being pretty and lazy, and not caring what Ernestine or anyone else thought. James adored her. He called her "baby" and treated her like a precious, breakable object.

"Have a swig." Faye held out the flask.

The whiskey went down hot and Lillian shivered. She didn't really enjoy the taste of straight bourbon, but she loved the way it made her feel. "I'm going to be stuck at this hotel for the rest of my life."

"The boys would have given you a car if they could."

Lillian took another swallow. "I know."

"And you're not stuck. You're too cute to get stuck anywhere. If this were Ernestine we were talking about—" She poked Lillian and they laughed.

Ernestine was the most proper member of the Creekmore family. She knew the right way to do everything, and didn't mind correcting your manners or your grammar. It felt good to laugh at her.

"Ernestine's already got a husband," Lillian said, "even if he is short and nearly bald."

"You are going to meet someone so wonderful." Faye stretched her long legs under the covers. "I can feel it in my bones. All you've got to do is keep your eyes open and recognize good fortune when he shows up."

"What about love?"

"You know what I say."

"It's as easy to fall in love with a rich man as a poor one."

"Easier." Faye tapped a cigarette out of her pack of Pall Malls and offered Lillian one. Her lighter clicked and they sat back on the pillows, inhaling with satisfaction.

"But you love James and he's not rich." Lillian made a smoke ring and watched it rise toward the ceiling.

"Not yet, but he has prospects. I could see that in him, even at sixteen. You know he's been buying and selling cotton?"

Lillian got out of bed to fetch an ashtray. "I know he's spending more time in Canton than here at the hotel. Makes Ernestine furious."

"He's good at brokering cotton. It takes a knack and James has it. If this pans out, he'll be more help to you than working here. There's good money in cotton." Faye ground out her half-smoked cigarette. "That dinner knocked me out. I'm going to my room for a nap."

The door closed behind her. Lillian took a final puff, made sure both cigarettes were out, and set the ashtray on the floor. Faye thought she had a chance, which felt comforting. *Comforting under a comforter.* She closed her eyes. Nice to hear wood crackling in the corner fire place. This was her favorite room. Out there somewhere, a wonderful man waited. Behind her closed lids, Lillian tried to picture what he might be doing as they traveled toward each other in time.

3

Three months later, Lillian found herself in Jackson, invited by Hilda, her best friend from college. Hilda had graduated and married her high school sweetheart.

In Hilda's spare room on Saturday night, Lillian got ready for the spring dance at the country club.

Hilda sat on the bed. "You look adorable,"

"It's Ernestine's dress." Lillian adjusted the neckline. "She'll kill me if I spill anything on it." The dress was yellow chiffon over a peach taffeta slip, and cut tight across the bosom. It featured a lace panel from neck to hem, beaded in pearls. Lillian twirled in front of the mirror, admiring the sleekness of her finger-waved hair. She leaned toward the mirror to paint on a bow of scarlet lipstick, and noticed there was fraying at the neckline of the dress. She knotted a long string of fake pearls to cover the flaw and hoped for a dark ballroom. She was wearing Ernestine's shoes, too, which were a size too small and squeezed her toes horribly. Pain could be ignored. This was her first visit to the city in a year, and she was on her way to a dance.

The lights in the crowded ballroom were as dim as Lillian hoped and the air heady with perfume and cigarette smoke. Onstage, a Negro band played. Boys she'd known at Ole Miss, men now, waved. She spotted three already-married sorority sisters and they ran to hug her.

"We thought that was you."

"Don't you look darling?"

She hoped so.

Hilda's husband Troy introduced her to a man she'd never seen before, Will something-she-didn't-catch, good-looking, blond, blue eyes twinkling down into hers. Marty Lyons led her onto the dance floor before Lillian had a chance to make a proper impression. Carter O'Ferrall tapped Marty's shoulder and whirled her into a foxtrot. Lillian loved to dance. For the first time in months, she felt truly alive. The new man, Will, tapped Carter on the shoulder.

"Hello again," he said.

Lillian tried to keep the eagerness out of her voice. "We didn't get a chance to introduce ourselves."

"You're too popular. I'm Will Hughes. I haven't seen you at one of these dances before."

"Because I don't live in Jackson. I'm Lillian Creekmore and I'm an import." Looking up into his blue eyes made her feel slightly dizzy. He was the handsomest man in the room.

"Imported from not too far away, I hope."

"I live," she stretched the truth, not wanting to sound inaccessible, "out from Canton." Canton was twenty-five miles north and the hotel eleven miles north of that, plus another mile up a country road.

"That's not so far, Lillian Creekmore. Did I get it right?"

She nodded. "What do you do, Will Hughes?"

"I just finished law school."

"Do you plan on lawyering with someone local?"

"I'm an associate here in my father's firm."

His father has a law firm. Lillian's heart thudded uncomfortably. He sounded rich. She touched her pearls, worrying about the frayed neckline. "Which is—?"

"Hughes & Blair."

"I've never heard of it."

"Because you're not from here."

"But I've traveled widely."

He gave her a teasing look. "Have you now?"

They were broken in on by Vaughan McRae, whom Lillian could have cheerfully strangled. Did she catch a flicker of disappointment in Will Hughes' eyes? She hoped so. Seeing Will watching from the sideline, Lillian gazed at Vaughan with such a brilliant smile, the poor man turned red and stumbled.

When the band took a break, Lillian wandered close enough to make sure Will Hughes found her.

"Do you want to go outside for a cigarette?" She felt his warm hand on her elbow, guiding her through the French doors onto a veranda overlooking the golf course.

This might be the man, the one she'd prayed for. Except she was poor and Will Hughes obviously wasn't. She'd only finished two years of college and he'd gone to law school. Not to mention her advanced age. He probably wanted someone nineteen, not twenty-five, an educated girl, maybe a doctor's daughter. If this was the man, she needed to work to make him care for her, without seeming to work at all. She was finding it hard to breathe right.

Lillian pressed a hand to her chest. "Stifling in there."

Will lit her a cigarette, then his own. His hand brushed hers and she felt a shock of connection. He felt it, too; she saw it in his eyes.

"Too many people in a small space," he said.

His voice sounded normal. She didn't want to over think a touch and come across as desperate. There was nothing men feared more than being pursued. She would take Ernestine's advice: When you have nothing to say, say nothing. She gazed across the golf course, hoping she looked moody, maybe ethereal. When the silence had gone on long enough, she said, "Isn't it interesting the way the trees seem to outline the night sky?"

Will Hughes studied the horizon. "I'm not sure I see what you mean."

Not a poetic man, so what kind?

"Tell me about yourself, Miss Creekmore."

An opening. She could talk about herself all night. "I live in a house with sixty-six rooms." Laughing to show she was teasing.

"How many?"

"It does have sixty-six, but only because it's the family hotel. I help run it."

The eyebrows over those amazing eyes went up in a questioning way.

"You've never heard of Creekmore Hotel and Spa?" she said. "We're famous for our nasty healing water."

He shook his head. "I've been away at school since the sixth grade."

That meant he'd gone to a prep school. "Were you such a terror they had to send you off?"

"My father wanted something better for me than the local schools."

This spoke volumes. His family would look down on the Creekmores. To get to public school, the five of them had caught the banana train from Way to Canton. She could make it into a funny story: *We rode to and from school on a train that carried bananas from the port of New Orleans up to Yankee-land.*

The music started and Will led her inside. Lillian saw Marty Lyons heading over to claim another dance. "It's been very nice talking to you," she said. As they parted, she gave Will Hughes what she hoped was an irresistible smile.

"Maybe I could give you a call," he said. "Where are you staying?"

Lillian held Marty in place with one arm while she spoke to Will, hoping she didn't look as gratified as she felt. "With Hilda and Troy Burns."

"When do you have to go back?"

"Not until Monday morning."

On Monday, like Cinderella, she would put on her rags and catch a ride back to Canton in a wholesale produce truck. Ernestine would meet her when she came in to get the week's supplies. No need to mention any of that.

"I'll call," Will said.

She let Marty Lyons sweep her away. "Another conquest, huh? Our Lillian hasn't lost her stuff."

"Shut up, Marty." She smiled to make up for the harsh words. Will Hughes might be watching.

When she got back to Hilda's, Lillian's feet hurt so bad, she had to sit on the edge of the tub and soak them in hot water. Examining her blistered toes, she realized Faye had been right: she'd kept her eyes open and met someone wonderful. Faye claimed men were like fish.

You played one until he got tired of fighting and then you reeled him in. But the fish must never become aware of being played. Lillian thought she was pretty good at man catching, but she hadn't had much practice since college. What bait might work on Will Hughes?

4

She woke expecting Will's call, and waited nervously through breakfast. Nothing. She went to church with Hilda and Troy and to lunch with Hilda's parents. If Will called now, she wouldn't be there to know.

They sat in a sunny dining room. Lillian played with her silverware.

Hilda said, "Why are you so jumpy?"

"Am I?" She put her hands in her lap. "I'm sorry. I dreamt my toes were run over by a train." She smiled at Hilda's father. "I wore my sister's tiny shoes to the dance last night, and I'm being punished for my vanity."

He shook his head consolingly and continued chewing.

Hilda's mother took a forkful of congealed salad. "Never mistreat your body, dear. You'll pay for it later."

"Yes ma'am." Lillian looked more closely at the salad: a leaf of iceberg lettuce topped by a jiggling green square, inside which floated baby marshmallows and maraschino cherries. Ernestine would close the dining room before she let the hotel serve this.

At two o'clock, when Hilda called her to the telephone, Lillian had given up and laid down for a nap. Will asked if she'd like to take a drive along the Natchez Trace.

Lillian did a brief jig of joy, then calmed her voice. "What a good idea. Give me twenty minutes." Refreshing her makeup in the bathroom, she gave the mirror a practice smile. She was not playing this fish; he was playing her.

Will opened the door of a sky-blue roadster, exactly the kind of car she'd wished for at Christmas.

"What a darling car."

"A pile of junk, really. I drove it all the way through college."

Lillian tried to imagine how much money it took to finish college and law school with a car of your own.

He started the engine. "Do you mind it if we keep the top down?"

"Not a bit." Lillian prided herself on possessing the kind of hair and personality that enjoyed being windblown. She wanted this man to see a girl who was undemanding and carefree, not a fretter, no one who might turn into a nag.

They pulled away from Hilda's. She liked the look of his long fingers on the steering wheel. He drove with one hand and each time he shifted, his hand neared her knee.

"Let's hope we make it without breaking down." Will Hughes gave her a smile that made her breath skip.

The engine did have a ragged sound. "I'm totally confident in your mechanical abilities."

He laughed out loud. "Don't be. Mother says it's lucky I have a good head because I'm useless with my hands."

She could think of a use for those hands. He quoted his mother. Lillian smoothed her skirt, glad she'd borrowed Hilda's suit, a wine-colored linen that suited her dark hair and eyes. It had a short flouncy skirt that kept blowing up to show her good legs.

Will headed north on State Street. "Have you ridden up the Natchez Trace lately?"

"I haven't." The Trace was halfway back to the hotel, but Lillian would never ask for a ride home. She'd rather jounce home tomorrow in a delivery truck than have him think her needy or, worse, poor. Besides, she didn't want him to see the hotel in the middle of spring-cleaning with all its shabbiness on show. When she'd left on Saturday morning, Maude, Ernestine, and the help were dragging the worst of the furniture out to be scrubbed and painted. When she got back tomorrow, she would help them put things back in place.

"That's my house." Will pointed to his left. Sitting back on a grassy rise, a two-story mansion with fluted white columns.

"Golly," Lillian said.

"It just looks big. There were five of us. You said your house has sixty-six rooms."

"There are five of us, too, and none of the rooms are fancy."

"I'm the youngest," Will said.

"Are you? So am I." Lillian found this an amazing coincidence, practically destiny. "That means we're both spoiled."

"I'm not spoiled." Will sounded almost defensive.

"It's about the handsomest house I've ever seen." She didn't mean only the house.

Will's pleased look made her face feel warm.

The engine coughed and he adjusted the choke. "I'll need to get a respectable car soon. I don't look like a serious lawyer in this one. Can't have a family in a two-seater."

Her heart dropped like a stone. "Are you getting married?"

He gave her a teasing smile. "Someday. Aren't you?"

She gazed ahead. "When the right man comes along."

"How old are you?'

"What a rude question."

"I'm twenty-four," he said.

"I'm twenty-three." She glanced sideways, watching his response. Winning Will Hughes would not be easy and she didn't mind lying to do it. Having lopped two years off her age, she began changing dates in her head, from birth through high school graduation. She did a quick run-down of friends who might accidentally tell him the truth. Now that everyone was out of school, it wasn't a likely subject, and she could warn Maude and Ernestine. Ernestine disapproved of lying. She'd need to find a way around that.

"You're quiet," Will said.

"Enjoying the scenery." Which *was* lovely. They had turned onto the narrow Natchez Trace. The trees were dressed in bright spring green.

"I like a girl who's not a yapper."

Lillian made a note of this. Most people would say she *was* a yapper, and she wondered what else Will Hughes didn't like. She was willing turn herself inside out to be what he wanted. Plenty of time to be herself—after she became Mrs. Will Hughes. She erased the name from her mind; rotten luck to even think such a thing. She shivered.

"Are you cold?" Will said. "I can put the top up."

"No, everything is perfect."

5

Two months went by and Lillian didn't hear from Will. Getting the hotel ready for the summer rush, she went over and over their afternoon together. Where had she gone wrong?

"This was fun." That's what he'd said when he dropped her back at Hilda's. A comment that could mean anything. She opened a box of newly printed stationary. Long distance telephone calls were ruinously expensive, so he wouldn't call her, and a proper young woman did not telephone a man. Or so Ernestine pointed out, along with her other rules of deportment—keep your knees together, don't laugh so loud, listen instead of speaking.

The new postcards had arrived, hand-colored photographs of the hotel, the rose garden, and the pool. Lillian slid them into a rack on the wall.

A week later, an envelope appeared in the mail with the law firm's return address and what Lillian assumed was Will's large and sprawling handwriting. Her hands shook tearing open the flap.

Dear Lillian, he wrote. *Enjoyed spending time with you. Hope you can make it down to Jackson again soon. Let me know when you're coming. Best Wishes, Will.* At least he'd written, but signing a letter "best wishes" was like saying, "This was fun," a response you'd give your aunt.

She made herself wait a week and wrote back on hotel stationery: *I enjoyed our afternoon. I wish I lived closer, but we are in the height of the season here at Creekmore. My brothers and sisters would murder me if I asked*

*for a weekend off. Perhaps you'd like to drive up for dinner one evening?
We're famous for our food.*

She issued the invitation with trepidation, thinking of the white-columned mansion and seeing, as if through Will's eyes, the hotel's threadbare carpets, the exterior in need of a coat of paint. She signed her letter *Best Wishes*, too, and dropped it into the outgoing basket.

Inviting him to dinner might be considered bold. She hadn't consulted Ernestine about the etiquette, and wasn't sure if Will approved of girls issuing invitations. Still, she'd gained a point by not racing back to Jackson.

"Your young man called." Ernestine reported this casually, looking up from posting the day's receipts. Two weeks had gone by since Lillian sent the letter to Will, and she had watched the incoming mail with something close to hatred.

"Will Hughes called?" Lillian grimaced, tugging her hair in frustration. "Why didn't you come find me?"

"You were not in reach of the telephone. Quit pulling at your hair like a dime store heroine. He said you were kind enough to invite him up, and his father had granted him a Sunday afternoon away from the law. I told him he should come for tea."

"Tea? You invited him to *tea*? He drives thirty-five miles and that's all we give him?"

"We will have a very nice tea."

"I invited him for dinner."

"It will be a tea much like dinner. We'll do it in the garden. It's never wise to offer a young man too much in the beginning."

Another of Ernestine's cloaked warnings: don't offer them dinner and don't offer them anything else. Her sister had graduated from Sweet Briar, a finishing school for young ladies, and found herself a husband. Lillian didn't quite dare and laugh off her rules.

On Sunday, as soon as the lunch rush finished, Lillian retreated to her room and darned the worn spots on her pink linen sheath with tiny, almost invisible stitches. She washed her hair and set it in waves to dry. She had worried Ernestine so often about the menu, her sister threatened to serve Will Hughes rat cheese and crackers.

He was due at four. Maude offered to give him a tour of the place and Lillian agreed. Maude told funny stories; Ernestine filled her tours with "Father did this," and "Father thought that," waving her arms about and pronouncing "father" as if they'd been raised in England.

Lillian warned them about the age change. Ernestine said, "Don't be absurd," causing Lillian to weep.

"This might be my main chance," she said, "and if Mother were alive, she wouldn't make a liar of her youngest child in front of the most promising man in years."

Ernestine relented, saying she would never knowingly tell a falsehood, but Lillian's age probably would not become a subject of conversation. Maude said if age did arise, she'd shove a ham biscuit down Ernestine's throat. James and Leland begged off, which was just as well. Their idea of hospitality consisted of manly back thumps and offers of whiskey. Lillian wasn't sure what Will would think of her brothers.

He arrived ten minutes before the appointed hour, a plus in Ernestine's eyes. Lillian tagged along on the tour. Maude told about the still their father hid in the woods, and the homemade whiskey he aged with charred oak until it turned into something resembling bourbon. Will Hughes told them about lodging with an eminent judge during law school, and trying to make beer in his room. He'd hidden the bottles in his closet, where they exploded one after another while he was downstairs having dinner with the judge and his family.

Things were going swimmingly. They met Ernestine in the garden and ate at a table under the pergola with the white climber rose providing shade. Ellis served, winking and nodding his approval behind Will's head. The tea was lovely: ham biscuits, cheese straws, shrimp remoulade in lettuce cups, and lemon curd tarts for dessert.

Lillian decided in advance not to be a yapper. She smiled at Will Hughes over her cup, and rolled her eyes when Ernestine went on about the history of the hotel and the Creekmore family. At least her sister refrained from claiming their ancestry went back to Charlemagne, which she sometimes did. Ernestine accepted the young man's compliments on the food as if she'd made everything herself.

Lillian walked Will back to his car.

"Wish we'd had more chance to talk," he said.

"Me, too." Secretly pleased. Twice now she'd appeared hard to get. "After Labor Day, I may be able to get down to Jackson."

"I'd like to return the favor. You can meet my family."

What a terrifying thought.

He did not kiss her, not in daylight.in the hotel parking lot, but he did squeeze her hand. She stood waving until the blue roadster drove out of sight, hoping she looked fetching in the rearview mirror.

Every week or two, he wrote her a funny note on the law firm's letterhead, and she wrote back on hotel stationery, printed with Knox's drawing of the well house in green.

She invited him up for the hotel's closing ball on Labor Day, but he said his father had him working six days a week plus Sunday afternoons. A shame, but she understood; she'd been too busy to see him for practically the whole summer.

With the hotel shut for the season, the unheated wings stripped of linens, and the lamps unplugged, Lillian was free to leave. Hilda said to come down any weekend, so she wrote Will and took the train to Jackson. They went to a movie Saturday night with Hilda and Troy, and out for a ride on Sunday. Still no kissing, which Lillian told herself meant Will didn't think she was cheap. He asked when she might be coming back, and Lillian said she would let him know. No mention of dinner with his family. A relief, but that also might mean he wasn't serious. This was different from the idle flirtations she'd conducted at college and she wasn't sure how to recognize progress.

6

She waited a month to go back to Jackson. "Restraint," Ernestine advised, which was not Lillian's best quality. This time, she and Will went with Hilda and Troy to a nightclub outside of town. They danced to a Dixieland band and drank bootleg liquor. Will wasn't the best dance partner she'd ever had, but he was the handsomest man in the room and told hilarious stories about practicing law under the eye of a stern father. Listening, Lillian suspected these events weren't nearly as funny when they happened, but the man was a good storyteller. She was not, and she appreciated the ability in others.

Back at Hilda's, Will leaned against the car, taking Lillian's hands in his. The other couple went inside. *He was going to kiss her. Finally.*

He cupped her face, his lips soft against hers, then urgent. Lillian laughed at girls who talked about swooning, but that's how Will's kiss made her feel. As if her legs were melting out from under her. When she withdrew, she felt lightheaded.

Will Hughes studied her face. "Mother asked me to bring you to Sunday dinner tomorrow." Casual, as if the invitation were nothing.

"Tell her I would love to come." She tried to sound nonchalant, but she'd brought along an extra outfit just in case.

Their first kiss *plus* an invitation to meet his parents. Lillian lay in Hilda's spare room, hugging herself, unable to fall asleep. She needed to be restrained tomorrow while working to charm Will's parents. Not a yapper, but not so quiet that she faded into the wallpaper. She had to keep in mind her new age and the changed years that involved. She almost wished for Ernestine. Her sister had never met an awkward silence she couldn't fill with something uplifting.

Entering the Hughes's large dining room with its dark wainscoting and gleaming chandelier, Lillian decided the house was every bit as awe-inspiring on the inside as it was from the street. Will's father was tall, taller than his son, bending toward her in a courtly way, brown eyes smiling into hers. Will's mother had a soft face and a comfortable body, but behind her spectacles, sharp blue eyes took Lillian's measure. Lillian had worn a gray wool dress of Ernestine's with the long strand of fake pearls, hoping to look demure.

There was a cream soup. Lillian sipped it out of the side of her spoon. "Delicious," she said. Ernestine would have recommended more salt and a touch of nutmeg.

Growing up at a hotel, Lillian knew how to talk to strangers. She mentioned the church service at First Presbyterian where Hilda and Troy attended. Mrs. Hughes touched on several points of the day's sermon at their Methodist church. An elderly male servant named Eli took away the soup bowls and brought in the roast beef. Will's father appeared to look upon Lillian kindly, but he had probably seen a lot of young women at this table. None of Will's sisters were there. After Mrs. Hughes served slices of the roast with rice and gravy, Eli came around the table offering a bowl of green beans.

Will's foot nudged hers under the table. Lillian smiled at him and complimented his mother on the centerpiece. "We grow roses at the hotel, but ours never look as beautiful as these."

"'So interesting, running a hotel," Margaret Hughes said. The way she said "interesting" made it sound suspect.

Lillian said, "A summer resort really. In the late nineteenth century, the original owner was a widow from New Orleans. She dug a well. The water tasted vile, but people who drank it began claiming cures from whatever ailed them." Lillian ignored the skepticism of Mrs. Hughes's raised eyebrows. "People started dropping by on Sunday afternoons to fill their jugs. At the time, our father worked for the railroad. He and his father-in-law bought the place as an investment. Father let guests stay in the main house, but as more arrived, he kept adding rooms."

"Sixty-six rooms," Will said.

"Mercy." Mrs. Hughes raised her pale brows. "That must be difficult."

"Difficult" as in low class? Lillian went on. "We're closed for the season now. Closing the place isn't hard. It's opening it that wears us out. One year while I was away at college, the servants were doing the spring cleaning (She wanted this formidable woman to know she had gone to college, even if she hadn't graduated.) A couple drove up looking for a room. Nobody was there but the help. They were all filthy from hauling mattresses out to air and scrubbing floors. Everyone tried be welcoming, Flora May told us they were curtseying, smiling, talking fancy. She said those people looked around, saw nothing but black folks, and just flew out of there. She said, 'You should have seen the look on those white folks' faces.'"

Will laughed. Mr. Hughes laughed. Mrs. Hughes gave a small, tight smile. "How fascinating."

Fascinating was one of those words that could mean inappropriate. In this family you probably weren't supposed to tell stories about colored people. Lillian responded with care. "When things go well at Creekmore, you feel like you are part of a big, smooth-running machine: rooms cleaned, meals served, people checking in and out, everyone smiling and having fun on vacation. But when things go wrong—" She made a face. "—it can be awful. The plumbing fails and you can't find the trouble. A delivery doesn't arrive and you have to improvise meals for a hundred. One year, someone put soap flakes in the swamp cooler, and halfway through lunch, the dining room filled with bubbles."

Mr. Hughes was still laughing more than his wife. Maybe Will's mother didn't have a sense of humor…or perhaps Lillian was yapping.

"You must be a very smart young woman to be able to handle all that," Patrick Hughes said.

"My sisters Maude and Ernestine are in charge. I just help out."

"Is there much—" Mrs. Hughes paused delicately. "—drinking?" Will had warned Lillian that his parents were strict Methodists and his mother belonged to the Temperance Union.

Lillian lied without hesitation. "We don't serve alcohol." This was not a complete falsehood; people brought their own liquor and the hotel provided the set ups. "And you can't touch a drop if you're taking the cure. Alcohol turns the sulfur water black. But people will drink. They bring whiskey in their baggage and—" She tried to look dismayed. "—we are forced to deal with the situation."

For the first time Mrs. Hughes looked sympathetic. "How do you handle those—*situations?*"

"My sister's husband usually takes care of people who, you know, have too much. One night, this man checked in and went to bed drunk. Nobody realized. Every morning, Preston, one of the waiters, delivers the healing well water around to the rooms. When you're taking the cure, you're supposed to drink two glasses before breakfast, and the stuff is not quite so nasty tasting if you drink it fresh out of the well." Was she yapping? They looked fascinated. "Most guests leave an empty pitcher outside the door the night before. But in case you forget, Preston walks up and down the halls at six in the morning, yelling." Lillian put her hands around her mouth. "'Waaaaa-tuh. Waaaa-tuh.' Giving you time to jump out of bed and hand him your pitcher."

Will's father was already laughing.

"Well, the poor man who'd checked in drunk must have waked up feeling dreadful. He took Preston's yelling as long as he could, then leaned out his door and hollered: 'Will somebody *please* give that man a drink.'"

Patrick Hughes had to wipe the tears from his eyes. Even Mrs. Hughes turned pink with pleasure. Temperance people loved to hear stories about drunks. Lillian glowed at her success.

Will looked at her with approval, making her heart beat faster. He could do that to her with those eyes, looking at her as if she were a jewel he'd found.

In the car after lunch, Will said, "They liked you."

Inside, Lillian gloated. On the outside, she merely smiled. "I hope so."

"You should be flattered. Mother doesn't like many girls."

"Have there been lots of them?"

"Hundreds."

"Then I *am* flattered."

He gave her a teasing smile. "That's a joke. The way my father works me, I'm practically a hermit."

"He doesn't seem like a tyrant. I think he's sweet." Lillian smoothed her gray skirt. It was the mother she worried about.

Will turned left on Fortification. "You don't have to work for him. Nothing I do ever quite meets my father's expectations."

This was the most personal thing Will Hughes had ever told her. Lillian felt the same way around Ernestine. She longed to put a sympathetic hand on Will's arm, but he didn't seem like a man who would welcome sympathy. "I'll bet you're a super lawyer."

"I'm trying."

"And very lucky."

"How's that?"

"You still have both your parents." Her voice quivered.

"Did I make you cry? I'm terrible with tears."

Lillian straightened and smiled. "Nothing so pitiful as self-pity is there?" Another rule to remember: don't cry.

"We'll stop by Hilda's and get your stuff," Will said. "I'll drive you home."

"You don't need to. It's such a long way."

"More time to talk. You okay with that?"

"You're a saint." Lillian glowed with satisfaction. In Will's eyes, she was not crazy about him, which was how she felt—off-balance and nervous, worried that one mistake might spoil everything. They stopped in front of Hilda and Troy's apartment.

Lillian said, "I'll go grab my bag."

Inside, she threw things into her suitcase. Hilda said, "Will's driving you all the way back to the hotel?" Shaking her head in admiration.

"I hope this means he's serious," Lillian said.

"Don't go counting your chickens. He's broken hearts before."

A chill crept up the back of Lillian's neck. "Has he?"

"I know of at least two girls who thought they had him bagged."

Lillian snapped the suitcase shut. "I'm not counting on a thing." Hilda's words brought her down from the triumph of lunch.

On the way to the hotel, she kept the conversation light. Will told her about his grandfather, a circuit-riding Methodist minister. She told him how the five of them used to catch the train back and forth to school in Canton, and how her brother Leland missed it one afternoon. Nobody could find him and the whole family grew frantic. Their father realized the little boy might be trying to make his way home along the railroad tracks, the only way he knew. Hours later, that's where they found him. Leland hated wearing shoes. He had taken them off and walked barefoot the whole eleven miles."

At the hotel, Will came round and opened her door. "I'd like to stay, but I need to get back and catch up on the hours I missed at the office. Will you be down next weekend?"

Lillian shook her head. "I promised Ernestine I'd fill in for her here."

Another kiss, in broad daylight this time. *Another amazing kiss.* He held her at arm's length. "I wish you didn't live so far away."

She could hardly speak. "So do I."

Lillian was smack-dab in love. Will Hughes acted as if he felt the same, but he hadn't said the words and she'd heard Hilda's warning.

7

Straightening the office on a Sunday afternoon in late October, Lillian emptied the stationery cabinets according to Ernestine's instructions. She dusted the interior and made a list of what remained from last summer, and what they needed to order for the next. Her mind refused to stay focused. She stopped counting letterhead and counted on her fingers. She and Will Hughes had known each other for seven months and gone out nine times. Surely that counted as a relationship. He never mentioned taking any other girls out and, not wanting to seem jealous, Lillian didn't ask.

When the phone on the wall rang, she jumped. Hearing Will's voice gave her goose bumps.

"How about I come pick you up next Saturday? You can spend the night at Hilda's and I'll drive you back Sunday."

"That sounds wonderful. It's dead around here. I'll write and tell Hilda I'm coming."

"See you around two."

Fizzing with happiness, Lillian hung up the phone. She'd totally lost count of the letterhead. This would make ten dates, eleven if you counted Saturday and Sunday.

Saturday turned out glorious, crisp under a late October sun. Perfect for putting the top down on the roadster. Lillian added a jacket and scarf to her ensemble. When she and Will walked out to the gravel parking area, she looked around for the little blue roadster. Her first thought was that it had been stolen and this would somehow be her fault.

"Where's your car?"

Will walked toward a Chevrolet sedan, tobacco brown with a black top and fenders. He opened the passenger door and bowed. "My new carriage, Madam. Not brand new, but new enough."

She felt squashed, as if he'd told her that from now on there'd be no dancing, only church. "What happened to the other one?"

"I sold it. Thought it might be nice to have a car I could trust to make it up here."

That sounded reassuring. At least he planned to keep coming. They pulled out of the drive and headed toward Highway 51. The car smelled of leather and machine oil, masculine and unfriendly.

Will drove with both hands on the wheel. "You haven't told me what you think of her."

And it was female. "I'm surprised. You never said a word."

Will Hughes sat upright. He looked like a different person behind the wheel of this sober sedan. "You know what this means, don't you?" Looking at the road, not at her.

She shook her head, feeling a twinge of dread. If this meant something new, it was probably going to be bad.

He pulled to the side of the country road, turned off the engine, and looked at her, his blue eyes serious. "This means enough playing around. I need to settle down."

Ice grew around Lillian's heart. This was it. Their little fling was over and he had come to break the bad news. Being a gentleman, he wanted to do it in person. It was time to stop playing around. He needed a real girlfriend, a college graduate, a young woman his family would approve of. But why drive her all the way to Jackson? Her thoughts were a tangle.

"What do you think about that?" Will said.

She gave the smallest possible shrug, looking out her window at the last of the blackberries, shriveled on their bare brambles. "It is a very grownup car."

"I mean, what do you think about settling down?"

"If that's what you want." She would not cry. She refused to show any sign of weakness.

"As in getting married?" he said.

She looked at him. Her face felt stiff. "Marriage is a private decision. You shouldn't have to ask another person's opinion." She sounded like Ernestine.

"What kind of answer is that?"

Her ears rang. She tried to parse his words. "What was the question?"

He looked miffed. "About settling down."

"I don't wish to give you advice about how to live your life."

"You're acting dense," Will said. "I meant with me."

For a moment Lillian was sure she'd misheard. "Are you asking me to marry you?"

"If I were, would you?" His eyes laughed into hers.

If I were? Was this some kind of lawyer trick, trying to make her answer a question he hadn't asked? If it was a trick, she would murder him and then kill herself.

"I've never noticed that mark before—on your forehead," Will said.

The stupid blazing birthmark, advertising her fury. "Well, it's there." She tried once more to sort through Will's words. "If you were, what if I said yes?"

He sobered. "Are you?"

She couldn't take anymore. "What if I am?"

"We couldn't do anything big, not with the economy the way it is."

Lillian let the words penetrate, then burst into tears and flung her arms around Will's neck.

He looked horrified. "What's wrong?"

She peppered his face with wet kisses. "Do you really mean it? Us—getting married?"

She felt a slight withdrawal. "I try not to say things I don't mean."

"Then the answer is yes." She couldn't restrain herself, bouncing on the seat with joy. "Yes, yes, yes, yes, yes."

"All right then." Will took a deep breath as if he were about to dive into cold water. "Stop jumping and give me a proper kiss."

She gave him the most thorough kiss she could manage without actually crawling inside his suit.

Face flushed, Will started the car. Lillian took out a handkerchief, wiped off her smeared lipstick, and applied more. "Does this mean you love me?" He had never actually said it.

"Of course."

"That's so swell because I love you, too." She took his arm. "This is so amazing. Turn the car around. We have to go back and tell Maude and Ernestine." She shook the way you did with a fever, but it was a good kind of shaking. Mrs. Will Hughes. Mrs. Will Hughes of Jackson, Mississippi. Mrs. Will Hughes of Hughes & Blair, Attorneys at Law.

At the ancient age of twenty-five, she was *engaged*. Twenty-three, she corrected herself. Will hadn't said any of the things she'd fantasized about. He didn't say he adored her or couldn't live without her. He hadn't fallen to his knees (which would have been difficult in the car) or wept with happiness when she accepted. He hadn't offered undying love, or any love at all until she asked. This was a different kind of man, one who did not gush, but meant what he said. A practical man. The kind who bought a chocolate brown, plush upholstered, almost-new Chevrolet instead of a ring.

One thing was for sure: she adored him. Will Hughes was everything she'd ever hoped for. She couldn't believe her good fortune and kept pinching her arm through the tweed wool to make sure she wasn't dreaming. If trading a convertible for this sober ride indicated how Will saw marriage, she vowed to transform herself into exactly what he wanted. She would be the best lawyer's wife in the country. She knew how to run an entire hotel; pleasing one man should be easy.

8

At the engagement dinner in December, held at the Hughes' home on North State Street, Lillian found herself seated on Patrick Hughes' right. At the far end of the table, Will sat on his mother's right. Peculiar for the betrothed couple not to sit together. The Creeekmores were lined up along Lillian's side: James and Faye, Ernestine and Knox, Leland and Maude. Across the table, Will's lawyer sister Mag, the professor sister Frances and her silent husband Bill; Emmy, the pretty sister and her cute husband who owned a drugstore; Will's older brother, Patrick Junior. Lillian found them a formidable lot.

The large table she remembered from Sunday dinner had been extended. There were silver sconces filled with roses and ivy, and white candles in silver candelabras. The damask napkins stood up like starched tents and unfolded into enormous lap-enveloping squares. Polished silver flatware flanked the dinner service. Lillian didn't recognize the pattern, but she'd bet Ernestine did. Even *she* looked impressed with the surroundings, and Lillian prayed she wouldn't turn over a plate to look at the mark. Maude, as if unaware of the splendor, behaved in her usual relaxed way.

Patrick Hughes made a stirring speech about how delighted he and his wife were to receive Lillian into the family. A young woman, he said, with the ability to manage an entire hotel should be able to keep his youngest in line. Lillian watched Will's face. He didn't enjoy being joked about.

She kept her eye on Mrs. Hughes, trying to decipher her expression. Her future mother-in-law did not appear quite as delighted as her husband. No mother liked losing a son, and these two were particularly close. Will was her baby. When he was little, he'd confessed, his mother crocheted tatting around the hems of all his underwear.

"Smart to pick a man who loves his mother," Maude told Lillian. "That's an indication of the way he'll treat you."

Ernestine, being the eloquent one, made a speech for the Creekmores. Neither of Lillian's brothers had been willing. Lillian looked at them, so flushed in their starched collars they looked boiled. She watched Will's face as Ernestine began talking about the Creekmore family history: "Our late Father," she said, pronouncing it in her fake way, making it sound as if he'd founded the Illinois Central Railroad instead of engineering one stretch of it. *God, please don't let her say we're kin to Charlemagne.*

She didn't. Actually, it was a lovely speech. Even Mrs. Hughes looked impressed. Ernestine had a way with words, and she ended by quoting Tennyson: "For this is the golden morning of love/ And you are his morning star."

That was nice. Lillian liked being the morning star, and Will flashed her a particularly sweet smile.

Patrick Junior, the oldest Hughes sibling, told a story about Will wrecking his first car, which, it turned out, he'd been given at age *fourteen.* Lillian watched her husband-to-be smiling at something said by his mother. The gap between their upbringings yawned wider.

With Faye's nudging encouragement, James got up his nerve and rose to speak. He said what a grand shot Lillian was, and if Will ever needed to put meat on the table, he could send his sister out hunting. Everyone laughed, Will winked from the other end of the table, and Lillian glowed. Things were going well. Her brothers weren't going to embarrass her, and she liked being known as a crack shot. Made her sound dangerous.

Crowded into the car for the drive back to the hotel, she asked Ernestine about the seating arrangements.

"At formal dinners," Ernestine said, "it is customary for the female guest of honor to be seated on the right of the host, and the male guest of honor on the right of the hostess. If you had paid the slightest attention to what I've tried to teach you, you would have felt flattered rather than insulted."

Lillian said, "Thank you." This was why people hated going to Ernestine for advice.

9

Maude pinned the hem of what had once been Ernestine's wedding-dress. Lillian stood in front of the dresser mirror, eyeing her reflection critically.

"I think it came out well." Maude put another pin through the skirt marker. "Turn."

"Were we right to cut it shorter in front?" Lillian said.

"It's what the fashion magazines are showing. To the knee in front with a bit of train in back."

Lillian twisted to look at her backside. "You could hardly call this a train."

"Stop moving." Maude spoke through the pins in her mouth. "It's a demi-train, and let's hear a little gratitude for me here crawling around your feet."

Lillian gave her sister's dark head a pat. "I am very grateful. The satin feels heavenly, and cutting it on the bias made all the difference. It drapes beautifully."

"That was strictly *your* doing," Maude said. "I wouldn't have the nerve to cut up Ernestine's wedding dress."

Lillian giggled. "She did give it to me."

"To wear, not to turn into something else entirely."

Lillian quit admiring herself. "Do you think she'll be angry?"

Maude got up. "Let's make sure she doesn't see it until you come down those stairs on your wedding day. Ernestine would never throw a fit in front of our newest and most august relatives." She placed a lace cap and veil on Lillian's short brown hair. "Step back and let me see the whole effect."

Lillian circled in front of the mirror, squinting to see herself as others might. "I love it with the veil. And the short front shows off my legs?"

Maude snorted. "We do love our legs."

"Don't tease. Do you think Will's family will approve?"

Maude removed the cap and began undoing the row of tiny satin buttons down Lillian's back. "You shouldn't worry about what the Hughes family thinks. You're marrying Will and he loves you."

Lillian slid the dress off, letting it puddle around her feet. She imagined Will's face when she did this on her wedding night. "I *hope* he loves me."

"He chose you and I see the look in his eyes."

"I'm not sure he knows the real me."

"No one knows the real anyone," Maude said, "but if you mean College Lillian, the girl who ran around the Delta to a different dance every weekend, breaking hearts and throwing up cheap gin, he probably doesn't need to know her. She had a good go before we ran out of money. Just remember, you're marrying a lawyer, not your brother James."

"Am I never supposed to have fun again?" Lillian pouted at herself in the mirror, admiring the way her body looked in the camisole and lace-trimmed knickers.

"Sober, lawyerly fun." Maude sounded as if she were only half-teasing.

"That sounds dull."

"Which may be why you don't see me racing to get married."

"But I *want* to be married." Lillian pulled her day dress over her head. "I want to keep house and give wonderful dinner parties and have Will's beautiful children."

"As I said, a nice sober life."

"I'll make it fun." Lillian leaned toward the mirror and put on more lipstick. "I can make anything fun."

10

On February 22, 1935, her wedding day, Lillian came down the stairs into the hotel's entrance hall as Knox played Lohengrin's bridal march on the big piano. The stairs were tucked into a corner, and Lillian felt her entrance wasn't as dramatic as it might have been. There were white candles on the piano and swags of greenery over the fireplace in the big parlor. She carried a bouquet of waxy fragrant orange blossoms Leland had ordered from a florist in New Orleans.

Ernestine looked startled when she saw what remained of her dress, but she straightened her shoulders and retrieved her hostess smile.

Will Hughes waited, tall and gorgeous in front of the fireplace. Seeing him took Lillian's breath away. His smile when he saw her told her everything he never said in words.

Leland met her at the bottom step, offering an arm, looking handsome and quite frighteningly sober in his navy suit.

He spoke in a hoarse whisper. "Let me know if this guy doesn't treat you right."

Lillian gave him a peck on the cheek. They had all spoiled her, ruined her, Ernestine claimed. Her eyes filled with tears. If only Mama were here to see how well she'd done. Will's parents looked stern and proud. She wondered if they were gratified by their son's choice or with themselves for producing him.

Only the family had been invited, but the hall and parlor felt crowded, for which Lillian felt thankful. The crush of people hid the frayed rug and the faded wallpaper. No one would look up and notice the water stains on the ceiling from last winter's leak.

Lillian smiled and the people she loved smiled back. Her heart expanded enough to hold everyone, even Will's professor sister, who scared her into stuttering. None of that mattered. This was her day and she was the luckiest girl ever born. When the minister pronounced them man and wife, Will Hughes gave her the sweetest kiss. Lillian shivered with joy. She was Mrs. Will Hughes, sealed by love and by law.

They celebrated the union with a dinner around the banquet table in the hotel dining room. The main course was roast chicken. Chicken, Ernestine said, gave value for the money, and no one turned out a bird as crisp-skinned, tender and moist as Creekmore's cook Lena. Lillian kept an eye on Will's parents. With Ernestine on one side and Maude on the other, her new in-laws appeared to be enjoying themselves.

Leland and James kept slipping out to the side porch for a swig of the whiskey James had stashed there. She didn't blame them. Will's older brother Patrick slipped out with them. Frances, who, Will said, was more Temperance than even their mother, kept sniffing like a hound after the liquor. She had Will's nose, which was not nearly so attractive on a woman. But nobody could scare Lillian today. With Will by her side, she felt giddy with happiness.

After a night in the corner bedroom upstairs, they planned to drive the brown Chevrolet to New Orleans for a two-day honeymoon. Will needed to be back in the office on Monday. Lillian didn't mind. She was eager to get on with the work of being Mrs. Hughes in their small rented house: sewing curtains, planning dinner every night. Imagine making dinner for only two people? It was going to be such a treat. She studied Will's profile, picturing them sitting down together. He'd be surprised by what a good cook she was.

There was dessert—rich, airy Charlotte Russe in parfait glasses with a slice of wedding cake. There were speeches. Lillian hardly listened, except when she heard her name. She beamed at everyone and held Will's hand.

Finally, it was over. Lillian kissed everyone goodnight and went upstairs. Her first night outfit, a gift from James and Faye, was a heavy cream-colored satin gown with a matching chiffon and lace peignoir. It had arrived from Maison Blanche in New Orleans in a white box filled with silver tissue. Lillian didn't want to think what it must have cost. James brokered cotton full-time in Canton now, and made a lot more money than he had running the hotel.

Faye came up to help Lillian out of the wedding dress, so she didn't get to drop it to the floor in front of Will, who said to call him in from the hall when she was decent.

She sat propped in bed when Will came out of the bathroom wearing striped pajamas, his hair damp from combing. He looked more nervous than she'd ever seen him.

He climbed into bed and settled beside her under the covers. "I don't think I can perform any husbandly duties tonight. Not surrounded by your family."

Lillian felt surprised. They had done some pretty intense hugging and kissing in both of Will's automobiles. His unease made her feel tender. She wriggled out of the peignoir, dropping it on the floor as if it hadn't cost more than the rest of her wardrobe put together.

A fire crackled in the hearth, making shadows on the wall. "Come here." She snuggled closer to Will. "I bet I know a way to help you relax." She disappeared underneath the covers.

Lillian felt him start and try to push her head away. When she took him into her mouth, he let out a staggered breath and quit resisting. It didn't take long. He groaned, shuddered, and smothered a cry.

She swallowed, wiped her mouth on the sheet, and came out from under the comforter smiling.

Will Hughes frowned. "Who taught you that?"

Lillian's heart stumbled with fear. The dark-haired Italian at Ole Miss who'd showed her, said men loved it. She'd never met one who didn't, but Will Hughes wasn't like other men. Maude had tried to warn her, and here she was, showing off on the first night, and maybe ruining everything. Her thoughts skittered, trying to land on an excuse that sounded plausible.

When she spoke, Lillian let herself sound anxious. "Hilda said Troy loves it. He told her every man does. She explained how it was done. I thought you'd be pleased." Her voice quivered. She nestled nearer, seeking reassurance. "This is what happens when a girl doesn't have a mother to talk to. Tell me you're not mad."

Will wrapped a warm arm around her. "Shocked maybe, but not angry. Hope nobody heard me." Hugging her against his chest, he looked into her eyes. "I'm surprised Hilda would speak that way to an unmarried woman."

Lillian breathed again, weak with relief. "I'm so glad everything is okay. You scared me."

Will slept. She settled beside him, pretending to. Who would have thought he was such a prude? He would never mention anything this intimate to Hilda or Troy. She was safe as long as she kept her lies straight. Not lies, really. It wasn't a lie if you needed it to survive.

11

A month after the honeymoon, with Will off at work, Lillian cleared the breakfast table and made a fresh pot of coffee. Maude was coming down for supplies and would stop by, bringing copies of the out-of-town newspapers with reports of Lillian and Will's wedding. She'd reported that both papers printed the photograph in a good spot on the page. Lillian couldn't wait to see with her own eyes.

She wiped the table clean, looking critically around the small yellow kitchen. The house on Monroe Street felt tiny after living at the hotel, but she'd tried to make it presentable with furniture scrounged from their siblings.

Maude arrived carrying the thick Sunday papers. She pulled the society sections from the Memphis *Commercial Appeal* and the New Orleans *Times Picayune*.

"There, satisfied?"

Lillian admired her smiling image: front page of the Society section, two columns, top left in both newspapers. "Nobody would guess from these that I came down a corner staircase in Ernestine's old dress."

"You look decidedly posh," Maude said.

Lillian poured her sister a cup of coffee and cut her a slice of the chocolate meringue pie she'd made for last night's dinner.

"This looks delicious," Maude said.

"Will enjoyed it."

Maude ate her pie while Lillian read the wedding stories twice. She put the newspapers back together to show Will. "Everyone in the South must know I'm married."

"How is life with the handsome lawyer?"

"This last month it dawned on me that someone else has been cooking my meals and cleaning up after me my whole life."

Maude laughed out loud.

Lillian leaned closer. "You'd call the Hughes family rich, wouldn't you?"

"I guess."

"I've never met a man as careful with money as Will. When we eat at restaurants, which is not often, he checks every item on the bill, then counts his change." He keeps the folding money in his wallet by denomination with the bills all facing the same way."

Maude started laughing again.

"It's not funny."

"You're getting to know each other."

"It's the opposite of James and Leland. They'd happily spend their last dollar having fun."

Maude scraped the last crumbs onto her fork. "Tell me five things you like about being married."

Lillian thought. "Seeing Will come in the door after work. The look on his face when he eats my cooking." She felt embarrassed, but went on. "The bedroom stuff counts for about three."

Maude gave her an encouraging smile. "Well, then."

"I get nervous. He's book smart and I'm not. If I'd been able to finish college—"

Maude shook her index finger like a metronome. "I don't want to hear about you being dumb. You can run an entire hotel."

"Which doesn't mean I know the defendant from the plaintiff or the appellant from the appellee."

"Does that come up a lot around your dinner table?"

"You'd be surprised. When Will talks to me about one of his cases, I smile and look entranced, hoping I'll understand before—" She put her head in her hands.

"Before what?"

"If I ask him something twice, he gets this disgusted look."

"Listen to me." Maude took Lillian's hand. "You are not stupid and you must never think of yourself that way. You sew well enough to be a professional. You can cook like a chef. Did he faint when he tasted this pie?" She indicated her empty plate. "You and Will have different skills."

"He says he doesn't enjoy having to repeat himself."

"Then stop asking him to. Wait until he leaves and look it up. You have a dictionary. Or go to his lawyer sister, what's-her-name."

"Mag."

"She seems nice enough. Get her alone and ask her to explain. And when you get the answer, write it down." Maude tried to scrape more chocolate from her empty plate.

"I can give you another piece."

Maude looked tempted. "Better get back. Ernestine and Knox go to Chattanooga next week. They're leaving Leland and me to run the place alone. It's not as much fun without you."

Lillian stood on the front walk, waving as her sister pulled away. It wasn't as much fun living anywhere without Maude.

Lillian realized that by marrying Will Hughes, she had acquired something valuable: a last name recognized by almost everyone in the city of Jackson. She loved telephoning the grocery store: "This is Mrs. Will Hughes," and hearing the manager's voice drop with respect. "Shall we put this on your account?" he said. She couldn't get over the thrill of that, though she had learned to treat the privilege with caution. Last month, when the grocery bill arrived in the mail, Will turned pale and gave her a stern money lecture. She listened, humiliated to be talked to like a child, and hating herself for disappointing him. Marriage should come with a rule book.

Being the wife of a new lawyer meant spending weeknights at home on the sofa, reading novels from the library with the radio turned off. Will worked on briefs at a card table in the corner, bent over his yellow legal pad, scribbling away. The man practically vibrated with the desire to excel. She could plug a lamp into him, but she refrained from sharing this amusing idea. As Will's wife, she was expected to sit quietly until he was done, showing that she took his work as seriously as he did.

She made up for the long evenings of silence by challenging him to gin rummy games when he was through. They played for back-tickling, which frequently turned into front-tickling, and further delights.

Whenever Lillian felt the slightest glimmer of resentment at being stuck at home while Will worked, she recalled the long winters marooned at Creekmore. Summer was here now, though, and guests must be piling in. On every visit to Jackson, Maude told stories: how she had to sweet-talk a drunk into bed; trying to convince one of the old ladies that, no, the rocking chairs on the veranda could not be reserved. Lillian listened with a pang. She missed the excitement, the bridge and poker games, the dancing and drinking (with nobody saying, "That's enough, Lillian.") She reminded herself of the enormous labor required to create that fun: feeding a hundred people three meals a day, dealing with piles of dirty linens, the help that doesn't show up. Not to mention those winters.

She was happy for now to play house with her new husband here on Monroe Street. She was a good cook and, after her scolding over the grocery bill, she mastered the art of making much out of little. Will adored her food.

Tonight, she'd cooked chicken, purchased for twenty cents a pound, cut into pieces, baked, and smothered in brown gravy. She'd mashed the potatoes (eighteen cents for ten pounds), and flavored them with butter and the cream off the top of the milk. In Lillian's opinion, which she kept rigorously to herself, Will's mother did not know how to properly season food. She prided herself on making up for that lack. She'd bought spinach for a nickel a pound and planned to sauté it in butter and serve it topped with chopped hard-boiled egg. Bananas cost nineteen cents for four pounds. For dessert, she'd baked a banana pudding with a Vanilla Wafer crust and waves of toasty meringue.

Will pushed back from the dinner table with a groan of pleasure. "I swear, I sit in the office all afternoon thinking about supper. I can hardly wait to get home." The smile he gave Lillian made their silent evenings, and even the scolding, worthwhile.

There was enough money in the budget to cover a junior membership at the Jackson Country Club. Being seen there was good for Will's practice. On Saturday nights they dressed up for the club dance. Will brought along a fifth of bourbon and warned Lillian not to order more than one set up, which consisted of a pitcher of plain water, a bottle of soda water, and a bucket of ice.

Lillian adored dancing. Will didn't care for it as much as she did, but there were plenty of spare men.

"Love to," she said, when Buford Laird came over to their table to ask for a dance. "Absolutely," she told Ted Gainey. She especially relished the fast numbers, when her feet and skirt flew as if she were eighteen again.

She came back to the table after one of those, giddy with twirling. "I am perishing for a drink." She mixed one. "I get cut in on almost as much as when I was single."

"You could sit out one or two, you know," Will said.

"Are you *jealous*?" Lillian felt delighted.

A wall came down behind the blue eyes, shutting her out.

Lillian sat beside him, feeling chilled. Another mistake. Another unwritten rule broken. Will refused to look at her. Love felt like a thing that could be snatched away in a moment. She refused two offers to dance. When Will said he was ready to leave, she picked up her purse and followed him without complaint.

As always, he drove carefully, going just under the speed limit. "In answer to your question, I am not a jealous man, and I did not appreciate being asked that in public."

His voice sounded cold. In the passenger seat, Lillian made herself smaller.

"What I am trying to say is, you are my wife now, and you don't need to be out on the dance floor every minute flinging yourself around."

Flinging herself — was that how he saw it? Maybe Vaughn or Carter had held her a little close on the slow numbers. They were only fooling around. Everyone did it. She'd noticed a warning look from Will when she told the story about the cat in the outhouse, and a frown when she'd mixed herself a third drink.

"I am so sorry." A quaver in her voice.

His warm hand covered her cold one, and when she looked at him, Will smiled. The sun was in its heaven again.

She formed a silent resolve to be more careful.

12

At the hotel, Lillian hadn't thought about class. She treated all guests the same and left the distinctions to Ernestine. Now that she was married, she came to understand, without anyone saying the words, that the Hughes considered themselves in a higher class than the hotel-owning Creekmores. She'd become a Hughes by marriage, so she was accepted, but she warned James and Leland to stay sober in front of Will's parents, and to keep their voices down. No loud talking about cockfights or bootleg whiskey. She'd made the point so often that whenever the two families got together, which wasn't often, thank God, her brothers stood like wooden soldiers, looking starched and miserable, keeping resolutely silent.

Two Sundays a month they went to Will's parents' house for dinner after church. Patrick and Margaret Hughes could not have been more gracious, but Lillian still felt uneasy around her mother-in-law, as if she were always on the verge of being caught in an error she hadn't been aware of committing.

On this Sunday, the Hughes had invited the Creekmores to join them. Both families, minus Ernestine, who was in Chattanooga, and Maude who'd stayed behind to run the hotel, were seated in the dark, formal dining room on North State Street.

Patrick Junior, Will's older brother, spoke to his father. "Germany and Italy have signed a pact. I reckon we're headed for another fool war." He was a big man with a hearty voice and pink skin that smelled of Florida Water. He had already grown a belly.

Will's mother frowned over the word "fool."

Patrick Junior looked around the table for confirmation.

Will joined in, and Lillian tried to follow. Politics bored her, especially foreign politics. Law did too, if she could be honest. Whenever Will explained his cases, she listened with rapt attentiveness, and ten minutes later couldn't remember a thing.

She watched Patrick's mouth move. He had no wife or children. He was—in this house the word was whispered—*divorced*. Will's turn to talk. Patrick Junior tried to interrupt and was cut off in mid-sentence by his father. His face grew redder. He might be older, but Lillian noticed he was not the favorite. From his flushed face, she suspected the man was a drinker. She'd seen the type often enough. Being ignored at his father's table probably didn't help.

Patrick Junior turned to Leland. "What is it you two do again?"

Leland, who had begun buying and selling oil leases, tried to explain, using words like "an eighth of a quarter of a section of a range." Lillian let her brother's talk go right through her while she watched Patrick Junior, who continued cutting his pork roast, forking pieces into his mouth, saying "I see" while he chewed.

He was goading her brothers, condescending to men who might not have law degrees, but were making more money in oil and cotton than Patrick Junior would ever see. When asked, James' description of cotton brokering was, if anything, worse. He talked about Good Middling and Low Middling and pronounced them "middlin'." Lillian swallowed her resentment and wiped her mouth. This was her new family. She might not be as educated as they were, but she had charm. She would make them love her.

Frances, scary, long-nosed Frances, made an "ahem" noise. "Why don't you help yourself to a roll."

In southern-speak this meant, quit hogging the bread basket and pass it along. Lillian obeyed. Frances was the one who enjoyed catching people in grammar errors. Lillian did not wish to be caught. "I'm so impressed that you teach at the college," she said.

Frances pointed her nose in Lillian's direction. "I assure you I am only at Millsaps because the public schools would not allow a married woman to teach."

So, she hadn't wanted to be college professor? Lillian nodded politely, cut a bite of meat, and glanced at Frances' husband Ted Reed, who worked for the First National Bank. He was a tidy, graying man who smiled often and spoke rarely. Lillian wouldn't talk either if she were married to Frances.

She craved a cigarette. When the meal was done, Mag invited her outside. Emmy, the youngest sister, came, too. The three of them puffed away at the top of the backyard, behind a row of crape myrtles.

"Your sister Frances scares me to death," Lillian said.

Mag nodded. "She's a terror. When Mama turned religious, Frances had to become twice as devout. When Mama joined the Temperance Union, Frances decided alcohol was the devil. Being around her makes you long for strong drink"

Emmy said, "Sunday dinner at this house makes me want to be drunk."

Emmy's pharmacist husband owned the drugstore next to the Jitney Jungle where Lillian shopped for groceries. In his white jacket, Price Cain looked almost like a doctor, but Lillian sensed that the Hughes family did not hold pharmacy in high esteem, nor banking at the level Ted Reed did it. In this family, law and the ministry reigned. The military was acceptable. All other occupations, though they were too polite to say so, were considered common.

Lillian watched Emmy, admiring her height and slender build. Definitely the prettiest Hughes daughter and the rebel. She loved a good time and didn't care who knew it. Lillian liked Mag, too. When she and Will went to her house, Mag treated Lillian to more alcohol than she ever got in her own home. Margaret Laughlin kept a bar in one corner of the living room. She poured good, stiff drinks and couldn't stand to see an empty glass. On her coffee table, she had a brass bowl filled with unopened packages of Chesterfields. She liked to put her heavy legs up, lean back on the couch with a drink, and squint through the smoke while Lillian told stories. Mag's superior education, college plus law school, made Lillian nervous at first, but Will's sister seemed to get a kick out of her, laughing heartily at her tales of the hotel. She had one of those low smoker laughs that ended in a cough.

Behind the crape myrtles, Mag passed around Sen-Sen to hide the smell of tobacco, and the women returned to the house.

Sunday dinner over, Lillian and Will Hughes were free to go home. She thanked her in-laws, perhaps too profusely, because when she hugged Will's mother, she sensed a stiffness. What Lillian thought of as charm, Margaret Hughes seemed to find excessive.

They needed a nap after one of these meals. This was the only day Will didn't work, and Sunday afternoon naps frequently led to late afternoon sex. Will seemed to be as hungry for Lillian's body as she was for his, and she resolved never to become one of those wives who got headaches or were too tired to bother.

On the Sundays they didn't eat with the Hughes, they drove up to the hotel. Lillian loved sitting with her brothers and Will, laughing and playing bridge after lunch. Nobody at Creekmore thought card-playing on Sunday was sinful, and if they stayed until five, nobody minded a drink either.

They hadn't stayed until five today. Will said he needed to get back to work on a brief. In the car, he seemed out of humor.

"Did you have a good time?" Lillian said.

"It was fine." His voice formal.

"I know it's a long way to drive, but it's only fair to divide Sundays between our families."

"I said it was fine."

"You didn't look like you were enjoying yourself today."

"Your brothers are good company. I like Maude."

"So, it's Ernestine?"

Will grimaced. "They're all fine. I'd be happier if your sister stopped touching me."

"Ernestine *touches* you?"

"Every three or four words, she gives me a little pat." Will demonstrated on Lillian's wrist. "Like I should pay closer attention."

Lillian laughed. "You're right. I'm so used to her I don't notice anymore."

"And your brothers drink too much."

He was right about that, too, but Lillian felt a need to come to their defense. "So does yours. What harm does it do?"

"If you don't know, I can't tell you."

Here she was, being lectured again. Lillian straightened in her seat. She'd learned when Will got in one of his moods, silence was the wisest course.

James and Leland were getting rich, James in Canton brokering cotton, and Leland buying and selling oil leases over at Tinsley Field in Yazoo City. They loved making good money and didn't mind sharing it.

As if he'd read her mind, Will said, "Did your brothers try and slip you cash again?"

"No." Lillian felt herself flush at the lie. When they said goodbye, Leland had pressed a tightly folded fifty-dollar bill into her hand.

Will Hughes, like his father, believed in "law for the law's sake" Which, as far as Lillian could tell, meant don't make too much money. No one in his family approved of vulgar displays of wealth, Will told her. He particularly disapproved of "the boys," as Lillian called them, giving money to his wife.

"I'm glad to hear it," Will said. "I consider it my job to support you."

He had made Lillian return a cardinal-colored winter coat she admitted buying with the money Leland gave her the month before. After that argument, playful on her side and increasingly stern on Will's, Lillian decided that from now on, she would accept money from her brothers secretly, and claim that her thrift stretched Will's small salary.

She did not consider what she was doing scheming. Will was brilliant at the law and almost oblivious to the world around him. If she bought a yard of red wool, and sat over the sewing machine in the evenings for a week, she could take the fifty dollars Leland gave her today and retrieve the red coat. With the label cut out, she would try it on for Will Hughes and tell him how much money her thrifty sewing had saved them. He would have her pirouette, and say how proud he was of those clever fingers. This was not lying. This was making the best of what life provided, a thing Lillian had always done. Will admired thrift, so she would be thrifty, without turning down Leland's gifts or going around dressed like an orphan.

13

They had been married for almost a year and Lillian was pregnant. Nobody uttered the actual word. People said she was expecting, or in a family way, or averted their eyes and pretended to notice nothing. Everyone waited for the glorious arrival of Will Junior, bringing with him the perpetuation of the Hughes name. Patrick Junior had no son; it was all up to Lillian. Will's family was so solicitous, with pillows and chairs and offers of special food, she started to feel like the Virgin Mary.

"Let me get that." Will leapt from the kitchen table in the second week of her eighth month, taking a soup tureen from Lillian's hands.

"I'm carrying an entire baby. I can carry a pot of soup." She watched his face redden. The physical changes of pregnancy seemed to mortify him. He hadn't made love to her for four months—claiming he didn't want to hurt the baby. She noticed the way his eyes hastened over her swelling body. She didn't blame him. Who would want to climb on top of a watermelon to make love? But Will's withdrawal felt more like disgust than embarrassment. She saw the look he gave her swollen, vein-marked stomach when she pulled off a top. The same look he'd given the bloody sanitary pad she once accidentally left in the bathroom. The private parts of women revolted him.

Before the pregnancy, they made enthusiastic love, but it was always mouth-on-mouth and private part to private part. When Lillian had tried a repeat of her wedding night surprise, Will pushed her away saying, while he appreciated the thought, he preferred she didn't. Except to help himself inside her, he never touched her down there. Maybe in the Hughes family, all private parts were revolting.

Lillian reassured herself: It didn't matter how she looked right now. After she presented Will Hughes with a son, she would shrink back into being darling, and their love life would resume, maybe better.

Bent over the sewing machine, she ran up two brightly colored maternity tops. If she couldn't be desirable, she would at least look cheerful. She bit off a thread. There was nothing wrong with being treated like a fragile and precious object (as long as she remembered to keep her body covered). She was the egg that must not break before producing the precious chick, the heir to the name of Hughes.

When the time came, Lillian produced neither Jesus nor Will Junior: on January 12, 1936, she gave birth to a baby girl. Lying alone in the small white hospital room, tears ran unwiped. She had failed at her most crucial job. No matter how many curtains she sewed or how delicious her meals were, she had not given Will the one thing he wanted.

She saw it in his face when he appeared at the door, hiding disappointment behind a bunch of yellow roses. "We could name her Willie," he said.

Yellow roses were his favorite, not hers. Lillian tried to smile back, but her lips trembled.

"Hey." He leaned over the bed and kissed her forehead. "Never mind. There's always next time."

Which made Lillian want to cry more, but not until after he left. If Will knew how much her bottom hurt, he'd thank her for this baby and keep his mouth shut about the next one.

The door opened again and it was Maude. Lillian wailed.

"What's this?" Maude bent over the bed, kissing a wet cheek.

Lillian inhaled the crisp smell of winter air. "I am so happy to see you, and you brought violets."

Maude handed her the small bouquet, tied with a pink satin ribbon. "Your favorites. What's wrong?"

"Will hates me for not having a boy."

"Of course he doesn't hate you."

Lillian nodded, pressing her wet face into the flowers' heavy scent. "I promise you, he does. He's already talking about the son we'll have next time."

"Men." Maude said the word as if it explained everything. She put the violets in Lillian's water glass. "They don't know what they want. You wait and see. He will worship this little girl. For the male ego, the only thing better than one adoring female is two."

Lillian wiped her eyes on a tissue.

Maude plumped the pillows. "Comb your hair and put on lipstick."

Lillian took the comb and mirror Maude offered. "Will's mother and father haven't come yet. I dread seeing them."

"Don't be a goose. Here, let me comb the back. They'll put on a brave face and you put on a braver one. Stand them down. We aren't descended from Charlemagne for nothing."

They snickered.

Lillian quoted her most proper sister. "We may be poor as church mice, but we know who we are."

"Damn right," Maude said. "Let me see the look you will give Will's folks."

"Lillian pulled herself up in the bed, tied the bow of her bed jacket, and gave her sister a queenly smile."

"That's the ticket. They'll be on their knees."

An aide popped her head in the door. "Shall I bring the baby in to nurse?"

"I won't be nursing," Lillian said.

Maude waited for the door to close. "Why ever not?"

"It ruins your breasts, and an article I read said formula is more sterile."

Maude looked dubious. "I stopped by the nursery and saw the baby. She's an angel."

Lillian smiled. "Well, look who made her."

When the senior Hughes arrived, Lillian sat up straighter and gave them the smile she'd practiced.

"The Lord giveth and the Lord taketh away," Margaret Hughes said, "and the Lord has given you a beautiful little girl."

"She is an angel," Lillian said.

Patrick Hughes said, "You'll have all kinds. Look at our brood."

Lillian was pretty sure he meant she'd do better next time.

"We've already told Will," Margaret Hughes said. "We want to give you the gift of a nurse for the baby. To make things easier at home."

"My goodness." Lillian felt genuinely happy for the first time since the birth. "What a generous thing to do."

"No rush," Margaret said, "but I did get a good recommendation. Do you feel up to interviewing?"

"Absolutely." If there was one thing Lillian knew how to do after years at Creekmore, it was manage servants.

"Excellent. The girl I have my eye on can be at the house when you get out of the hospital next week."

Doreen Austin was perfect: a small, light-skinned young woman in a starched uniform, with a sweet smile and a quiet voice.

"I think we'll get along just fine," Lillian said.

"I'm good with babies," Doreen said, "but I don't cook."

"That's okay because I do."

With a nurse, she wouldn't be tied down. She could play bridge with her friends and go get her hair done. The only thing she lacked now was a car. When she needed to use one, she drove Will to work. Maybe, when she produced the son, his parents would give them a car.

They named the baby for Lillian's mother: Helen Creekmore Hughes. Filling out the birth certificate, Lillian remembered to make herself two years younger. She'd done the same thing on the marriage license. Seeing it on paper, she almost believed the lie.

She made an effort to love this baby daughter as much as the son Will wanted. She did love Helen's sweet smell after a bath, and how Doreen wet the scant brown hair into a curl over the baby's forehead. She loved seeing her daughter wearing the tiny garments she had hand-smocked. Helen smiled toothlessly and Lillian felt a tug at her heart.

The first try had simply been a misstep, and no one could hold one mistake against her. Next time, as Will said, next time she'd produce Will Junior. A child's sex was a fifty-fifty proposition and she'd already used up the female half.

Once he got over the shock, Will appeared to genuinely love his girl, and became the most solicitous of fathers. "Hush little baby, don't you cry." He sang in an off-key tenor, bending over the crib.

Lillian heard him cooing from the kitchen.

When Helen's neck grew strong enough to support her head, Will came home at night, took off his hat and, before kissing Lillian, lifted the baby high over his head, making her giggle. "Who's the best baby? Who's my good girl?"

Watching the breaded chicken bubble gently in Crisco, the heat Lillian felt did not come entirely from the stove. All cooing should be directed at her. Will wasn't around when Helen screamed her lungs out and spit up on Lillian's clean dress. He wasn't there when Helen chose to fill a nasty diaper after Doreen left for the day, a diaper which Lillian, not Will, had to dump out in the toilet and scrub.

Lillian had been the baby of her family as Will had in his. Married, they'd been babies together, playing house. All of that was somehow marred by the addition of this third being.

14

Two and half years later, pregnant again, Lillian explained the situation to Maude. They sat in Lillian's kitchen with cups of coffee, Maude bouncing Helen on her lap.

"Three of the Hughes' children are girls." Lillian counted on her fingers. "Frances and Emmy both have sons, but they don't count."

"What do you mean, 'don't count?'" Maude said. "Do you have any pie?"

Lillian cut her a slice of last night's lemon meringue and took the baby so Maude could eat. "No matter how many males the Hughes girls produce, none of them carry the family name, so they don't count. Mag has two daughters. Patrick Junior adopted a son with his second wife and named him Patrick Hughes III, but that doesn't count either."

Maude took a bite of the pie and closed her eyes in ecstasy.

"Will explained it to me. An adopted child doesn't have Hughes blood."

"*God.* Pardon my French." Maude put down her fork. "What do they think they're building over there in that white house, a dynasty?"

"If this one's a girl—" Lillian left the sentence unfinished.

"We'll smother her with love the way we do Helen. And if Will doesn't like it, he can sleep in the car."

Lillian laughed, but she did not feel as confident this time, and Maude's joking failed to ease the dread.

On March 16, 1939, Lillian gave birth to a second daughter. She named her April for the month when she'd been expected.

"Do you like that name?" She waited on Will's approval before signing the birth certificate.

"I honestly don't care," Will said.

Lillian looked at his closed face. He meant it. A second girl was worth so little, her very name didn't matter. She would not cry; he hated crying women. "April has a pretty sound and we can't name a baby March."

There were no yellow roses this time and no kiss. Will stood a foot away from the hospital bed. Lillian saw how badly he itched to get away to his Saturday bridge game.

"Is your family mad at me?" She sounded like a child.

"They've managed to swallow their disappointment."

"Are you being sarcastic?"

Will's eyes darkened, a wall of disapproval dropping behind the blue. "Mother sends her regards and hopes you and baby are well."

"That's very kind of her."

"I have to go," Will said.

"May I at least have a kiss?"

"Of course." He approached the bed and gave Lillian a peck on the forehead.

The child was tiny, and tests found Lillian to be anemic. The doctor said she and the baby must stay in the hospital, not for the usual seven days, but for ten. So, there was that: the added burden of being an extra expense.

At home, Doreen took care of the house and little Helen.

Will complained on his second visit. "She only knows how to cook carrots."

"We're lucky to have her. I wrote your parents thanking them for April's silver baby cup, and I told them again how much we appreciate Doreen."

"Mother said you write delightful notes."

At least she did something right. Lillian turned her face to the wall after Will left. He talked to his mother more than he did to her.

Maude visited, bringing Lillian two fat novels from the Canton library. "How is the Hughes family taking the treasonous appearance of another female child?"

"It's not a joke," Lillian said.

"Listen, you're not a racehorse. They can't put you down for not giving them an heir."

Lillian wasn't so sure. She wasn't sure of anything anymore.

15

Will waited three months after the second birth before making love to her again, and even now, in August, Lillian had to coax him into bed. Not ask him to make love—he hated being asked directly. She was forced to mount a campaign: a good supper, laughing at the right moments during his stories, keeping the girls quiet while he worked, low light and the satin nightgown when he came to bed. Tickling his back.

After a day of housework and cooking, even with Doreen's help, Lillian frequently felt too tired to go to the trouble. And there were nights like tonight: smothered steak and mashed potatoes for dinner, the children down, the house quiet for Will, the satin nightgown, cologne. When he came to bed, she offered to tickle his back. He groaned with appreciation under her caressing fingers, but when Lillian moved closer and began kissing him, she heard him snore. She sat back, disappointed. She might as well be a nun. Nuns probably didn't have to work this hard.

When Maude called the next day, inviting Lillian to bring the girls and come take her place at the hotel for a few days, it felt like a reprieve. Ernestine now lived in Chattanooga, where Knox had a job in advertising for a pharmaceutical company. Maude and Leland ran Creekmore alone, and half the time Leland was off buying oil leases. Maude planned to travel north to visit Ernestine, who'd given birth to a second son. *A second son.* Lillian couldn't produce one and Ernestine had made two.

Maude planned to drive to the christening in Chattanooga with a friend, a *gentleman* friend who might turn into a fiancé, according to excited family rumor. Lillian had been invited to the christening, but she made the baby a darling jacket and sent her regrets. She had no desire to go and watch her older sister gloat.

A visit to the hotel might be nice. Fall now. Two of the hotel's wings were closed for the season and only a few guests remained in the Warm Part. There wouldn't be much work. When she told Will she wanted to do it, he minded less than she would have liked.

"With the quiet," he said, "I can get more work done."

She took Helen, baby April, and Doreen. Leland now had a romantic interest, a tall, pale Texan. Olive Rentwell stayed at the hotel while she bought and sold oil leases for her boss. She apparently knew more about the business than Leland. He followed her around like a puppy and Lillian couldn't tell which he liked better, her looks or her skill at negotiation.

When Lillian arrived, the three of them ate, drank, and played cards every night.

"I so envy you." Lillian spoke to Olive over a hand of Hearts. "How did you ever learn about the oil business?"

"I picked it up from my boss," Olive said. "He's buying leases so fast in Texas, he didn't have time to come to Mississippi, so he sent me."

Olive spoke softly and Lillian had to practically quit breathing to hear her.

Leland laughed. "People are dumbfounded to see a woman out there. Olive outfoxes them before they can get their mouths shut."

"Well, I think it's just wonderful." In her head, Lillian mentally tried on Olive's life: the freedom to travel, make money, and not be corrected for mistakes you didn't realize you'd made. But then she'd be with someone like Leland and, love him as she did, her brother was no Will Hughes.

Tonight, after three drinks (which no one complained about) and dinner, Lillian snuggled into the corner bedroom upstairs, the same room where she'd slept in as a child, and the room where she'd spent her wedding night. With Ernestine away and Will home with his law briefs, she felt unrestricted, as free as she'd been before she married.

The phone downstairs in the front hall rang and rang. Lillian woke to hear Leland cussing as he banged down the stairs to answer it. Then nothing. She might have drifted back to sleep, but the silence felt odd. Her brother hadn't stomped back up as he usually did, swearing at guests who didn't know the meaning of the word "Closed", waking a man in the middle of the night to ask a stupid question.

She put on her robe and went down. Leland sat on the bottom step next to the wall phone, head in his hands, shoulders shaking.

"Leland?"

He looked at her, his face wet. She had never, not once in her life, seen her brother cry.

He couldn't get the words out.

She held her breath. Whatever it was must be awful.

"It's Maude."

Lillian covered her mouth to muffle a scream. She slid down beside him. "Has something happened?"

"An accident." He couldn't go on.

"Is it—is she going to be all right?"

He gave a choking groan.

"Maude's not *dead*?"

He nodded, face buried in his hands.

Knees to chest, Lillian rocked and howled—over being left behind, the fear and pain Maude must have suffered, the horror of never seeing her sister again.

How would they go on? Ernestine liked to play the mother, bossing everyone around, setting standards no one met, but Maude was their heart. Generous and funny, with that glorious laugh. Lillian would never hear that voice again, never feel those arms around her, or hear Maude telling her, no matter how bad Lillian felt, that things would get better. It was Maude who claimed, when Lillian raged over Ernestine's sons, that daughters stuck by you in the end. "Look at us." Maude said, "We're sisters and we'll always have each other." And now they didn't.

A week later, on a windy day in late September, the sky heavy with clouds, Lillian watched as they lowered Maude's casket into a grave next to their parents. She sobbed so audibly Ernestine jabbed her in the ribs with a wool-coated elbow. People crowded around them. Maude was beloved, and half of Canton had come.

Leland didn't want to invite anyone to the hotel after. "Can't stand the sympathy," he said. "Don't want to hear people speak her name." But Ernestine insisted, claiming it was customary and obligatory. Leland went to his room, took off his funeral suit, grabbed his gun, and went hunting. He didn't return until far past dark, when everyone had left and the place had been shut down for the night. Lying next to a snoring Will, who had been unusually tender since her sister's death, Lillian heard her brother's heavy tread on the stairs, the whisper of Olive's voice, a door closing.

Lillian stayed for a week after the funeral. The hardest part, aside from the ache of a vanished Maude, was Leland refusing to let anyone mention her name.

Olive tried to explain. "It hurts too much."

But it hurt more not to be able to remember out loud how wonderful Maude had been or repeat the funny things she said. Her death was a wound that wouldn't heal. The silence made it worse.

Lillian whispered to Will in bed when she was back in Jackson. "We're like a body that's lost a limb."

Will stared at the ceiling. "Germany invaded Poland while you were gone. France and Great Britain declared war today."

"What?"

"Our country may be at war soon." He switched off his light and turned on his side.

Lillian lay in the dark, stewing. Her sister was dead; she couldn't worry about Poland. How could anybody snore that loud and not wake himself up?

On visits back to the hotel, Lillian watched as Olive Rentwell led her brother out of grief. Lillian thanked the Lord for the young woman's quiet kindness. She never drank more than a small glass of sherry; she was brilliant at the oil business, but in company said little, satisfied to smile and agree with Leland. Her constancy kept him afloat.

Six months after Maude's death, Leland and Olive quietly married at the hotel. Following the wedding, they moved to Yazoo City to be closer to Tinsley field. James and Faye still lived in Canton. Back for the wedding, Ernestine announced she would move from Chattanooga and take up the burden of running Creekmore. No one else spoke up asking for the job. Leland had papers drawn up giving his older sister sole ownership. She had finally gotten her wish to be the boss of everything. And why should that make Lillian feel aggrieved? She certainly didn't want to run Creekmore. They should be grateful. For now, Knox would keep his job in Tennessee; Knox III was away at prep school. Ernestine packed their house on Lookout Mountain and drove to Mississippi, accompanied by the baby, little Leland, and the family silver.

16

There was no avoiding the alarming headlines: Germany invaded Norway, then Denmark, France, Belgium, and the Netherlands. Italy took Greece. London suffered massive bombings. At home, the government froze enemy assets, but America remained neutral.

That's all Lillian asked of God: please let the troubles stay on the other side of the Atlantic.

On December 7, 1941, the Japanese bombed Pearl Harbor and the war came home. All around them, people quit their jobs and joined up. Mag's oldest daughter became a WAVE. Frances' son Owen went into the Army, and Ernestine's Knox III into the Navy. James was too old to enlist, but Leland volunteered. He possessed a needed skill: he knew how to run a hotel. The Navy put him in charge of the officer's club in Key West.

In public, Lillian talked like a patriot, but, privately, she remained an isolationist. Will Hughes was the country she fought for, and she did not want him anywhere near this war.

Her immediate job was to keep the family fed. In April of 1942, sugar was rationed—half a pound a week per person. In November, coffee followed: a pound every five weeks. By the end of the year, much of what she bought at the Jitney Jungle required a ration coupon: meat, cheese, butter, margarine, canned foods. She was in charge of the family's ration books, doling out the stamps, saving the blue and red pressed-wood tokens she received as change.

She prided herself on her ability to make delicious meals under the new restrictions: a moist, well-seasoned meatloaf; macaroni and cheese enriched with chicken left over from Sunday dinner; chili con carne on top of her homemade cornbread. When jams and jellies were rationed, she made use of skills learned at the hotel, producing batches of strawberry preserves and plum jelly during the summer. She made a decent cake using half corn syrup instead of sugar.

By 1943, she felt she'd held the war at bay by the sheer force of her will. She'd kept her family fed and, in her spare time, volunteered for the Red Cross, knitting enough mufflers, socks, and fingerless mitts, she hoped, to prevent anyone from taking Will.

This was a secret strategy, not to be shared with her husband. Since Pearl Harbor, Will kept up with the war in two daily newspapers and a nightly radio broadcast. Each time someone they knew left for the service, Will told Lillian he, too, longed to go. Lillian reminded him of his age — thirty-three. He was the father of two children. She said how thankful she was that he was too old to make the sacrifice. As the need for men increased, the age barrier was raised: you had to be over forty-five or have three children to be safe from the draft. She hadn't gotten pregnant again, so knitting and praying had to be enough.

In a corner of the back yard, she had a coop built, and they raised chickens for the eggs. Will Hughes liked to tell people *he* raised chickens, but his duties were limited to collecting eggs and making encouraging chicken-like noises. Lillian had been around poultry her entire life. It was she who fed them, cleaned the pen, and when a hen turned out to be a rooster, wrung its neck and cooked it. Will claimed the smell of chicken droppings made him sick, and was horrified to discover that hens shat upon their own eggs. He also claimed to be too tenderhearted to ever kill one.

But he'd happily go halfway around the world to murder Japs? Lillian did not speak this thought aloud.

In the spring of that year, on one of those unexpectedly gray days that made the yellow kitchen look especially cheerful, Lillian checked the seasoning in her soup, a hearty vegetable mixture containing the remnants of a chuck roast. She had been a married woman for eight years now, and still got an electric thrill when she heard Will's car pull into the garage.

He came in the back door, gave her a kiss, picked up Helen, who was seven, then April, four, and whirled them around. "How are my girls?" He pretended to look down April's throat. "Are you still eating worms?"

The child squealed in delight.

Lillian said, "Go to your room, girls. Give your father a chance to relax."

"Will you read to us later?" Helen said.

"You can read to yourself now." Will Hughes kissed the top of her head. "You don't need me."

"We want you to read," April said. "Helen cheats. She reads without saying the words."

"After supper," he promised.

Lillian shooed them out. If she didn't intervene, Will would spend every minute before supper playing with the children, and go straight to his law briefs after. Her better self admitted to feeling jealous. She *did* have a better self. Mixing them bourbon and waters, she put Will's on the breakfast room table and sipped hers while finishing dinner.

His fingers drummed the yellow Formica. "Spoke to a guy in New Orleans today."

Lillian tasted the thick soup and added salt.

"He said I may be called up at any time."

Shock caused her to drop the wooden spoon.

Will stooped to pick it up.

Lillian tried to keep her voice even. "You have a wife and family. Your father depends on you."

"Here's the thing. Instead of waiting to be drafted into the Army, I could volunteer now for the Navy. The guy said I can probably get a commission.

"But they may not call you up."

"Or they might, and I would be stuck in the infantry. If I have to serve, I'll be a lot safer in the Navy."

"What does your father think?"

"I haven't told him."

"You know how he feels about the war."

Will's shoulders drooped. "Only fools volunteer."

In Lillian's opinion, Patrick Hughes underpaid and over-criticized his younger son. Mentioning his name had been underhanded, but she was willing to use whatever ammunition she had.

"But you know how *I* feel about the war." Will persisted.

She did: stars and stripes forever.

"Sit down for a minute." He covered one of her hands with both of his. "I love you and the girls. Nothing is more important than keeping you safe. But nobody will be safe if we don't win this war. It's bigger than our family. The existence of the free world is at stake."

Lillian didn't want to hear about the free world. Nothing was more important than this man, her house, the small, happy life she had worked to achieve. "I could not bear it if anything happened to you."

Will gave her a steady look. "For two years I've made excuses: I'm married, I'm too old, I have children. But the war grinds on and the time has come to do my part."

"If they thought you had a part, they would have drafted you already."

His blue eyes stared into hers. "A patriotic wife would not argue."

Lillian felt as if she'd been slapped. *A patriotic wife?* She'd done everything a wife could — months of volunteer work; thousands of delicious meals made from scraps; sewing every stitch she and the girls wore — she'd done everything except hand over Will Hughes. "What about us?" She tried not to cry.

Will's voice turned gentle. "Let's wait and see what the Navy says, okay? They might reject me, but at least I will have tried."

Lillian wiped her eyes. *They might reject him.* There was that shred to hold onto. "If anything happened to you —"

"Honey, to the Navy I'm an old man. I won't be sent to any battlefields."

"They're bombing ships, too."

"I'm probably too old for a ship. They'll stick me in some office job — if they take me at all."

Lillian tried to turn her dread into something positive. An office job sounded okay. Maybe he'd get assigned to a base where she and the girls could join him. "If you enlisted, what rank would you be?"

"The guy said, with a law degree, I'd probably go in as a Lieutenant Junior Grade."

An officer. Lillian pictured Will in a white uniform and saw herself wearing something bare-shouldered and gauzy, dancing in an officers' club in some distant place with palm trees and tropical air. There would be other wives to play bridge with. If the worst happened, if he were accepted, this might turn into an adventure, like *Casablanca,* but with a better ending. And maybe the Navy would reject him. She got up to check on the cornbread. "We'll work it out."

"I knew I could count on you." Will pulled her into a kiss that made her knees go weak.

The next morning, he left to take the Navy physical, and Lillian spent the day in nervous misery. She took it out on the girls, who received two switchings by late afternoon. When Will came in the door at five-thirty, his downcast face told the story.

"What happened?"

"I failed the physical."

Lillian matched her expression to his disappointment, but inside she exulted. He wasn't going to leave her. "But you're so healthy."

He shrugged out of his suit coat and bent to pick Helen up for a hug. "They say I don't weigh enough."

He will not leave. She wanted to sing it. She wouldn't have to go live on some tacky base, or sacrifice one thing she loved about their lives. She could stay in the Junior League, to which she'd recently been invited, and play tennis twice a week at the country club. She could keep enjoying bridge luncheons with her girlfriends, and Saturday night dances. Not to mention sex. Will had forgotten childbirth and enjoyed making love to her once more. Except for the crushing disappointment of not producing a son, this marriage, this man, this yellow kitchen, represented everything she'd ever wanted.

No need to let the pleasure show in her voice. "Well, don't feel bad. You tried, and you do a lot of good right here."

"I'm not giving up," Will said. "I looked at the photograph in my office today and got more determined."

"The boy in the Confederate uniform?" Lillian did not let her voice reflect the weariness she felt at hearing about this ancestor again. She put the rooster she'd stewed into tenderness on the table, along with rice, gravy, and butterbeans. Will liked his dinner at straight up six o'clock.

"My great-great-grandfather, the first Will Hughes, barely seventeen when he enlisted as a private." He paused to say the blessing. "Service is in my blood. I went to a military school for six years." He took a bite and closed his eyes in appreciation. "I'm more prepared for this war than most of the people they're signing up. I refuse to give up."

"But you failed the physical."

"They say I can try again in two weeks. I need to gain ten pounds." Will Hughes took Lillian's hand and gave her one of those intense blue looks that could persuade her to sell the children. "Do you have any ideas?"

Lillian wanted to say no. She wanted him safe in this house—well, in a better house someday—away from war until they both grew as old as his parents. But she adored being asked for help, especially from this man who rarely needed anything from her outside of food and sex. She could try to help him, fail, and still get credit for trying.

"Bananas and cream," she said.

Will Hughes looked perplexed.

"The hotel has an account with a wholesale produce company. I'll get you a stalk of bananas tomorrow. If you eat bananas and cream three times a day, we can fatten you up like a pig for the slaughter." *Terrible comparison.*

"Can't it be cake and ice cream?"

"You can have whatever you like after your bananas and cream."

By the next evening, a stalk of bananas hung from the ceiling next to the back door, ripening from the bottom up. Before Will left for work each day, she gave him a bowl of sliced bananas, covered in cream from the top of the milk bottle. He carried bananas in his suit pockets. He had another bowlful with cream when he walked in the house after work, and yet another before bed. By the fifth day, he groaned in protest. "I can't stand looking at a banana."

"Get on the bathroom scale." Lillian had no idea whether a person could gain ten pounds in two weeks, or whether that was healthy, but she intended to receive full glory for her efforts.

He had gained four pounds.

Hurray. He won't make it. "See? We can do this."

"If I last two weeks, I promise never to eat another banana for the rest of my life."

"If it works, you won't have to." *What a two-faced bitch she'd become.*

The girls were entranced by the endeavor. They had never seen a stalk of bananas, which bent like a green arm as Will ate his way up and around. They made disgusted noises over the thick cream.

On the day before his next physical, Lillian was frightened to see that he'd gained nine pounds. *A pound was a pound. There was still hope.* She straightened Will's tie before he left. "Maybe you could keep your suit coat on when they weigh you. And don't take off your shoes. Keep eating bananas until you get on the scale."

"They make us strip," Will said.

Good. "Before you step on the scale, take a deep breath. Air has weight."

After he left, Lillian prayed. If he passed, making her a hero, maybe God would let him fail something else. All that snoring had to mean something. His sinuses might keep him out of the war. She knew what she didn't want—to be left behind in Jackson, Mississippi, folding bandages and knitting for the Red Cross. If Will left her, he might never return.

He came straight home to give her the news, not even stopping at the office. She knew the result by the exuberant way he slammed the back door.

"I passed," he yelled. "Where are you?"

When she came into the kitchen, he picked her up and swung her around the room, practically crowing with success. Lillian didn't know you could feel two such opposing emotions: glad for his happiness and choked with disappointment. She tried to hide the latter, keeping the possibility of an officers' club and palm trees firmly in mind.

"I was so nervous," Will said. "The guy moved the big weight to 150 and the little indicator kind of bounced up and down, and then I remembered what you said—I took a big breath and tried to think myself heavier."

She should have kept her mouth shut.

He swung her around again. "I *passed*. Can you believe it? I could never have done it without you."

Lillian let herself be whirled. Was there anything a wife loved hearing better: "I could never have done it without you." She shouldn't have been so persistent with the bananas, but no use crying over it now. She would turn into another one of those women at the Red Cross: husband gone, talking about duty and sacrifice. Pretending to be patriotic made Will love her more. She could handle whatever came.

Will came home the next week with a page of figures. They sat together at the dining table to go over them. "Dad says he can't pay me if I'm not here working. This is my Navy salary, including the allotment for family." He showed her an astonishingly small number, and then pointed to a list he'd made down the other side of the page. "Here's the rent on the house and the cost of utilities." He underlined the total, a figure considerably larger than his Navy salary.

Lillian looked at him. "I think it's awful your father won't keep paying you. It's unpatriotic."

Will shrugged. "You only get paid if you bring in money. He thinks I'm a fool for volunteering."

Lillian agreed with her father-in-law. "What will we do?"

Will shook his head. "We have to give up the house. I don't see any other way."

"And I'll go with you?" *Officers' club; palm trees.*

"Families aren't allowed during basic training. After that, we'll need to see where I'm stationed."

"Where are we supposed to live?" Lillian heard the wail in her voice.

"You could move in with my parents."

She pictured the three of them tiptoeing around that big, dark house on North State Street, with Margaret Hughes as boss. Not that Will's mother hadn't been kind, but Lillian couldn't abide the thought of living under her watchful eye. The girls would make too much noise. Lillian would always be apologizing. No drinking on the premises. Anything was better than that.

"I can go back to the hotel."

Will looked surprised. "You always said how glad you were to get away."

"I was. I am. But I can work there. We'll be able to live for free and Ernestine will pay me. They always need help and we could use the extra money." Ten minutes before, the idea of moving back to Creekmore would have made Lillian sick to her stomach, but compared to living with Patrick and Margaret Hughes, it seemed like summer camp.

"Where will the children go to school?"

"We'll figure it out. I grew up at the hotel and managed to get an education. Oh, God." She put a hand to her forehead. "You'll have to break the news to Helen. She just got the good third grade teacher."

Will left to change out of his suit and Lillian allowed herself to cry, wiping her tears on the kitchen towel. Everything lost: the country club, Junior League, friends. Condemned to return to where she started and work under Ernestine.

Mrs. Culley up on Pinehurst received word last week that her only son had been killed at Guadalcanal. She had a gold star in the window. Lillian couldn't survive that. If Will died, it was her fault. He would never have thought of bananas.

17

On a golden September day in 1943, Lillian drove the girls to the station to see Will off. He'd gone to the house on North State Street the day before to say goodbye to his parents. His father told him volunteering was a boyish indulgence and he was no longer a boy. Lillian agreed, but she'd learned her lesson: a patriotic wife did not argue.

She wore the red silk dress Will liked. She wanted to be the last, best thing he saw. The conductor shouted "All aboard." Lillian gave Will a fierce hug and a desperate kiss. He stood in the door as the train pulled out. The girls wept and Lillian bit her lip trying not to. Lieutenant Junior Grade William Hughes rode away from Jackson, Mississippi, waving and smiling. He looked happy to be leaving.

Lillian herded the children back to the car. War was an adventure and she had not been invited.

Back at home, she folded the red dress into a suitcase, put on an old housedress, and got back to packing. She'd been left with the job of emptying the house. Will Hughes might be a skilled lawyer, but he was useless at anything practical. She swiped at a tear with a dirty hand, not sure if the choking tightness in her chest was anger or sorrow.

The van would arrive tomorrow to take their furniture to storage. Clothes, toys, and the four of them, counting Doreen, would then stuff themselves into the Chevrolet and head north to the hotel. Including chickens — Will had made Lillian promise to take the girls' two favorite chickens along.

What to do about sheets? They would need to sleep on them tonight and store them dirty. Lillian stared at the mess still to be packed. She lugged another box to the trunk of the Chevrolet. Straightening to ease the pain in her lower back, she waved to Mrs. McNair next door. Her doctor husband didn't have to go. Linda McNair wasn't packing her family up like a bunch of gypsies. Lillian went inside for another box. *No complaining allowed; complaining was unpatriotic.*

Helen watched as her mother filled a box with toys. "I need this." She pulled out an ancient Raggedy Ann doll.

"We don't have another inch of room in that car." Lillian took the doll back. "She'll be waiting for you in storage when the war is over."

"I don't care about the war." Voice like fingernails on a blackboard. "I already lost Daddy." Helen grabbed at the doll.

"You did not lose your father. He volunteered to go help our side win."

Helen stamped her foot, clutching the doll she hadn't played with in a year. "I won't go. You can't make me. I don't want to live in a hotel." Voice rising to a wail. "I won't have my friends. I won't have Miss Pierce for third grade."

Lillian felt the headache coming. She sat back on her heels. "I'll tell you what you will have — a whipping — if you don't stop that howling."

Helen stomped her way up the hall. "You can't make me get in the car. I won't live there, and I won't drink the stinky water."

Lillian felt exactly the same way. She wiped away tears. Leaving wouldn't be as hard if Maude were waiting at the hotel. Passing a mirror, she caught sight of herself: dirt-smeared face and filthy dress. Good thing Will hadn't waved goodbye to this.

18

At The Creekmore Hotel and Spa, with Helen settled in third grade, Lillian told herself she could manage this. She'd made it through Christmas without murdering either Ernestine or her children. But now came frozen January, with gray-lidded February right behind. Lillian hated winters at the hotel. Except for Alan, who cared for the animals and kept the furnace going, and Lena, who was too crippled with arthritis to move, the servants had been sent home. There was no money to pay them in the off-season. Even Doreen returned to Jackson.

With Alan's help, Lillian and Ernestine struggled to stay warm, keeping a fire going in the front parlor and the wood stove lighted in the kitchen. They hurried through the frigid rooms from one pocket of heat to the next. The skies were leaden. It grew dark by five in the afternoon. Ernestine wouldn't take a drink before five, and then only one. If she drank quickly, Lillian could squeeze in two. They ate supper in the small parlor on a table pulled close to the fire. In the mornings, everyone dressed under the covers to keep from freezing.

Ernestine took the train to Chattanooga to be with Knox for a few weeks. Lillian felt stifled by her sister's company, but she was at least another adult. On one late afternoon, walking around the front parlor with a dust cloth, she thought about her friends in Jackson, the fun they must be having without her: bridge luncheons, tea dances at the club—not that there were many men left to dance with. She remembered a long-ago train trip to New Orleans, sitting in the bar car, smoking and laughing, bourbon sloshing in her glass when they rounded a curve. When was the last time she'd laughed?

She touched her lips, thinking of Will's mouth on hers and how safe she felt in his arms. He was somewhere in the Pacific. The War Department wouldn't allow him to say where, but he'd been assigned to an office, exactly as he promised. His office was a tent in the sand, and she had no chance of joining him because families were not allowed in a war zone. A letter arrived once every ten days. For Christmas, he'd sent Lillian pearls and the girls cowrie shell necklaces.

She wrote him on the almost transparent blue airmail stationery, scribbling the details of their days: Helen hated third grade at her country school and kept threatening to quit; April was teaching herself the alphabet, smart little thing. Lillian put a lipstick kiss at the bottom and folded the letter into an envelope. On every missive, she wanted to write across the back: "I hate this boring life," but that would not sound patriotic.

No letter expected from Will for at least a week. She stared out the French doors of the living room at the winter murk. Four o'clock. With Ernestine away, maybe she'd start early and allow herself three drinks tonight.

The crunch of a car on the gravel drive. A dusty black sedan pulled up. Lillian's heart stuttered. She wasn't expecting anyone, but didn't they send a man with a telegram to tell you if your husband had been...? She refused to think the word, and watched, shivering, as a man got out, a tall man, not in uniform. She waited on the porch.

He waved and smiled. "Don't you recognize an old friend?"

Lillian went weak with relief. "Bob Bradshaw." Laughing to cover her fear. Bob was a friend of Will's from the club. They had played tennis together; she'd had him to dinner once—spaghetti with French bread. So good to see a familiar face. It was all she could do not to fling herself on him in gratitude for not being the military coming to report Will dead.

In the small parlor, she helped him out of his heavy wool coat and made them drinks. "Sit, sit."

He sat on the sofa and she pulled a chair closer. Taking a pack of Camels from his shirt pocket, he offered her one, lit them both, and watched her over the flame. "You look as good as ever."

"Nice to hear. I feel like I'm fading into the wallpaper." *God, it had been a hundred years since she flirted.* "Why aren't you off at war?"

"I am, in a way. Purchasing for the military. Got anything you want to sell?" He gave her a crooked grin. She didn't remember him being this attractive.

"And you just happened to be passing by?" Giving him a sideways look.

"Driving from Jackson to Memphis. Saw your friend Hilda at the club last week and she told me you were here."

Lillian crossed her knees, showing off her legs. "Castaways, I'm afraid, until this unpleasantness ends."

"What do you hear from Will?"

"In the Pacific somewhere. Working for the Judge Advocate General's Corps. Not fighting, thank God."

Helen ran in and stopped short.

Bob Bradshaw held out his arms. "Here's my girl." He picked her up for a hug. "You grew up on me. You've gotten so pretty."

Helen nodded. "I'm eight now."

"I bet I know where you got that cute face." He gave Lillian a wink over Helen's head. "Here." He fished in his jacket pocket and brought out a Hershey's bar. "If you were a little older, we could get married. How would you like that?"

Helen took the candy and looked at him thoughtfully. "I would like it."

"Don't eat that before supper," Lillian said.

"I tell you what," Bob said. "If you promise to grow up fast, I promise to wait. Do we have a deal?"

Helen gave him a wide gap-toothed grin. "I promise."

"It's a deal now. Don't forget," Bob said.

Helen looked bedazzled. "I won't."

"Run on now," Lillian said. "Let the grownups talk."

Helen backed out of the room, staring at Bob Bradshaw.

"Misses her daddy," Lillian said. "Drink up." She mixed them another drink and sat on the couch next to him. It was so nice to smell a man, wet wool and tobacco, to have someone light your cigarette, clink glasses, and look at you as if you were darling.

She fed the girls and put them to bed. She and Bob returned to the kitchen and she fixed the two of them plates—rewarmed roast chicken, rice, a can of the good peas. So much more fun to cook with a man standing by, chatting, telling jokes, offering to help and making a mess of it. She was having such a good time she hardly noticed when he refilled her glass. She'd forgotten how sexy Bob Bradshaw could be, or maybe it was the queer things loneliness did to a person. After dinner, she poured them tiny glasses of Ernestine's precious brandy. When he leaned down to kiss her, she turned her face up and kissed him right back. Desire and brandy floated her. She heard Ernestine's voice in her head, *You are drunk, Lillian,* and turned her off. For one night she wanted not to care. She locked the doors and stumbled up the stairs to her room, Bob Bradshaw close behind. She lit a fire in the corner fireplace and remembered to turn the latch on the bedroom door. She laughed as he undressed her.

A gray dawn. Lillian woke, stupefied, and sat up with a lurch of fear. Bob Bradshaw was in her bed with the children asleep next door. *What the hell had she been thinking?* She squinted at her watch. Six o'clock. "Up, up." She poked him awake. "You have to get dressed and out of here before the girls wake up."

He rubbed his eyes, grinned, and grabbed for her. Lillian moved out of reach. "I mean it. This never happened."

Bob made his way into the bathroom. She heard him pee. The girls probably heard it, too. He came out rubbing his teeth with a wet finger. "Do I at least get coffee?"

Lillian was sober now, a headache drumming at her temples. Her only thought was to get this man out of the hotel without anyone knowing he'd been there overnight. "You can get coffee in Pickens." She marched him down to his car. He tried to pull her in for a final squeeze. She backed away. "Never happened."

"Yes, ma'am." He gave her a salute and drove away.

She watched the car disappear, went upstairs, woke the girls, and got them dressed. In the kitchen, Alan fed them breakfast and walked Helen out to catch the school bus. Lillian carried April upstairs. The child stood watching her put clean sheets on the bed, sucking her fingers and asking no questions.

She tried to remember the sex. It had been fun, a new man and an explosion of feeling through a haze of alcohol. It all felt disgusting now: an accident of war, caused by a lack of affection and too many drinks. Maybe a little residual anger at Will for leaving. She would put it out of her mind. If Ernestine had been at the hotel, it would never have happened. As far as Lillian was concerned, from this moment on, it hadn't happened.

A week later, when Lillian tucked Helen in, the child brought up the forbidden evening. "I can't remember his name."

"Whose name, sweetie?"

"The man who wants to marry me when I grow up."

Good grief. "Me neither."

"You *have* to remember." Helen looked as if she were about to cry.

And you have to forget. "I'll try."

Lillian's period arrived on schedule. Nothing had come of that night, thank God. Ernestine returned, and Lillian was so glad to see her sister she almost wept. From now on, she promised to count her blessings and never complain.

A month later, while she and Ernestine were having their nightly drink, Helen spoke up. "Did you remember the man?"

Ernestine gave Lillian a look. "What man was this?"

Lillian shook her head. "I can't imagine." Heart pounding so hard it hurt.

Helen insisted. "You know, the one who promised to marry me."

Lillian gave her daughter a little push, harder than she meant to. "I don't know what you're talking about, honey. Run on and let the grownups have some peace."

"But how can I marry him if I can't remember his name?" Helen whined her way out the door.

Lillian rolled her eyes at Ernestine. "The child reads fairy tales and invents a prince." She asked her sister about Knox and Knox III, and young Leland. The moment passed, and she hoped the incident had been forgotten.

In front of the mirror that night Lillian rubbed cleanser onto her face. Odd the way Helen clung to Bob Bradshaw's visit. The child was like a bad conscience.

19

On the last Sunday in May, 1943, Velma Vernon sat alone at the Church of the Redeemer picnic. Rough wooden tables were scattered across the patchy lawn, a few in the shade of oak trees, most, like Velma's, baking in the afternoon sun. Her friends Annette and Shirley had gone for dessert, but Velma had more on her mind than sweets. Freshly graduated from high school, with hazel eyes and light brown hair, she was almost pretty. That's what Papa said when she got dressed up. Almost a compliment.

She felt a damp hand on her shoulder. Glancing up, she managed a smile. "Hey, Chalmers."

Chalmers Root leaned close to Velma's ear, his breath a souvenir of the hot dog he'd eaten. "How about it, Velma?"

She tried to shrug out from under the hand without seeming to. She disliked his touch, his limp, and the black hairs sprouting above his knuckles. Silently, she asked God to forgive her lack of charity. Like Annette said, a man couldn't help the way he'd been born. "How about what, Chalmers?"

"You know—me and you—hitching up?"

Exactly what she had feared. She waited a long moment, as if considering the request. "I don't think so."

Chalmers sat down heavily on the bench beside her. "Why not?"

"I'm not ready is all." Not looking at him. Velma didn't want to marry Chalmers Root, but she hated disappointing people.

"When you think you will be ready?"

She stared at the plate in front of her, empty except for a puddle of mayonnaise. Looking at it made her feel slightly ill. Chalmers, with his hot breath, represented the future. One movie, a date to the senior prom, and now they were supposed to get married. People probably thought she was lucky to get him, being tall, and shy on top of it. Velma tried to be a good girl. Until this moment, she had never knowingly entertained a rebellious thought.

Speaking to the paper plate. "I may have plans."

"What kind of plans?" Chalmers's voice swelled with annoyance.

Velma imagined a lifetime listening to this voice demand meals, a fresh shirt, or the stuff married people did in bed. The thought of spending a night with Chalmers Root sent a fingernail down her spine.

"Plans for my future." Velma's voice cracked on "future" the way a lie would. Miss Buford, her shorthand teacher, had mentioned that Velma ought to go to business school. She would find a way into town tomorrow and ask Miss Buford how long that took and how much it cost.

The wooden bench rose as Chalmers stood. Velma experienced his going as an easing in her chest.

He spoke from behind her. "Your Pap won't like it. He's counting on me for the driving."

Chalmers meant driving the farm's produce down to the air base on the gulf coast. She'd seen her father talking to him at graduation. Papa needed a hand. That's why he wanted to marry her off. A son-in-law counted as free help.

America was deep in the war. Allied forces had cornered the Germans in Tunis. Forty-four U-boats had been sunk that month. In south Mississippi, every able-bodied man under forty was off fighting.

"Shouldn't take things for granted." The words came unbidden out of Velma's mouth.

"What'd you say?" Chalmers still stood behind her.

"I said, 'Thank you for the offer.'" Two lies in as many minutes. Velma looked across the church grounds, tables filled with fanning women and sweating, shirt-sleeved men. She spotted her parents under an oak tree, sitting with the preacher. Papa grinned at her from under his fedora.

Chalmers stumped away, leaning into the shorter leg that kept him out of the war. Velma felt bad for him, but pity was not enough reason to marry somebody you did not love.

20

At supper the next evening, Velma could hardly eat for worrying what to say to Mama after Papa left to close up the animals. She studied the scrubbed wooden table, bare except for their plates. "Remember how Uncle Drew used to bring flowers in from the field, Mama, and you'd make a vase for the table?"

Her mother smiled. "Drew was a thoughtful man."

"Not so thoughtful he didn't get himself killed," Papa said.

"He used to say my cornbread melted in his mouth," Mama said.

"Foolishness," Papa said.

Velma saw how it pleased Mama to recall the sweet words. She studied her mother's hands, raw and swollen at the joints, and Papa's face, creased into a permanent frown. Soft things were foolishness and hard things were farming.

At the sink after supper, Velma dried the dishes while her mother washed. Her hands shook and she almost dropped a platter.

"You're as jumpy as a cat tonight," Mama said.

Velma felt choked by the words she needed to say and dreaded what she might hear back. Pleading unfinished school business, she'd caught a ride into town that morning with the man who delivered feed, and back home with the postman. Lying to her parents made her feverish.

"My shorthand teacher Miss Buford thinks I could be a secretary." She waited for a response, the air thick with apprehension.

"Does she now?" Her mother scrubbed a skillet.

"I'd like to try." The words rushed out. "I'd need to go to Jackson and get a certificate from a business school first, but Miss Buford says secretaries make good money in the capitol, and I'm already fast with shorthand and typing." Velma paused for a breath. "She claims there are plenty of jobs for a trained girl."

"Let's sit." Her mother finished the last dish and dried her hands on an apron Velma remembered from childhood, its pattern of daffodils faded to gray shadows.

They sat at the table they'd just cleared and Velma stared at her hands. "I don't know why everybody thinks I'm supposed to marry Chalmers Root."

"Who said you're supposed to marry anyone?"

"Papa already told Chalmers he could drive the produce to the coast after we're married."

Her mother waved a hand, brushing away expectation like a fly. "This secretary business. What are we talking about in the way of money?"

Velma felt a tingle of hope. She pictured herself moving out into an unknown but infinitely better future. "Miss Buford says there's tuition. The course at the business college takes six weeks. I'd have to pay room and board while I went to school, but Miss Buford knows a widow lady who doesn't charge much." Velma stopped, gathering her nerve to say the number. "She thinks a hundred and fifty dollars would cover it." She dared a glance at her mother, who looked back with an unreadable expression. "I've got seventy-six dollars saved from selling books at the School Depository. If Papa paid me to work the fields this summer, I could earn the rest." Her voice trailed away. A hundred and fifty dollars might as well be a thousand. Her mother said nothing and Velma let the spark of hope fade. "That is, if you don't mind me leaving and not marrying Chalmers."

"Sounds like you and Miss Buford had a lot to say to each other."

Velma felt her face heat up. "It was just talk until Chalmers asked me to marry him yesterday. I didn't mean to go behind your back."

"What'd you tell poor Chalmers?"

"I told him I had plans."

Her mother snorted. For one moment, she looked like the engagement picture in the parlor, when she'd been Flora Dinkens and as pretty as her name.

Velma said, "I think I hurt his feelings."

Her mother left the table and went into the big bedroom. She returned carrying a black change purse with a brass snap.

Velma watched as she eased herself into the chair. "You hurting?"

"Just rheumatism." Her mother's tone declined sympathy. "You are book-smart, Sister, the first person in this family to earn a high school diploma." She held the change purse in both hands. "Your Papa and me were proud seeing you walk across that stage at graduation. You have plenty of time to get married. Plenty of time to *be* married."

Hope rose again. This seesawing between possibility and disappointment made Velma feel giddy. She reached out and gave her mother's hand a squeeze. "Papa listens to you. Will you ask him if I can work for pay this summer?"

Her mother said nothing. From the purse she removed a roll of bills and began counting them out, fives in one stack, ones in another.

Velma's mouth opened and closed. "Where you get that?"

"I put it aside for your wedding."

"But I'm not getting married."

"If you get yourself one of those fancy jobs in the city, maybe you'll be able to pay for your own wedding."

Velma watched the money move through her mother's hands. "How'd you get so much? I thought Papa knew every nickel that walked through the door."

"A dozen eggs here, a pint of cream there. It adds up. You'll find out when you're married. No need to tell them every little thing."

"You hid it from him?"

Her mother gave her a flat look. "I worked hard for this money. Every woman needs a bit to call her own. How much did you say you have?"

Velma couldn't take her eyes off the wrinkled bills. "Seventy-six dollars."

"And how much do you need?"

"Miss Buford says a hundred and fifty."

"Four ones makes eighty, plus four fives is a hundred." Florence reached to the bottom of the roll and pulled out two twenties. "Two more fives should do it." She snapped the few bills left back inside the black purse and counted Velma's share again, licking her finger like a bank teller.

"Velma swallowed. "Where do I tell Papa I got the money?"

"You tell him nothing. You say you've been saving and you think you've got enough."

Velma swallowed. "Will you ask him about me going?" Papa did not welcome change. "Will you talk to him first?"

Mama pushed the bills toward Velma. "Put that money somewhere safe. Tomorrow we'll make your daddy a batch of molasses gingerbread. I'll show you how to soften a hard man's heart."

21

At Sunday dinner two weeks later, Uncle Drew's widow Aunt Orrie, joined them, passing along gossip with the biscuits: "People say Velma's forgotten who she is, bless her heart. Say she'll be running home before the first frost."

Mama said, "That'll be enough, Orrie." Which closed her sister-in-law's mouth.

Papa made a grunting noise, which might have been agreement, but for which side Velma couldn't tell. She swallowed her aunt's criticism, more determined than ever to get out of south Mississippi, away from people telling you who you were, and what you ought to do if you knew what was good for you.

She had been raised strict Southern Baptist. The decision to leave for the city instead of marrying Chalmers Root had been seen by church members as a sign of willfulness. No one said this to Velma's face, but she knew from the sideways glances she caught. Her friend Annette, who planned to be a teacher, would be going to Mississippi State College for Women. She said Velma would be a fool not to grab the opportunity. Shirley planned to marry her long-time boyfriend Eddie, kept out of the war due to flat feet. She acted peeved at both of them. "We promised to get houses next to each other and raise our babies together."

On the Sunday before Velma left, Preacher Clement took his text from Ephesians 6:11: *"Put on the whole armor of God, that ye may be able to stand against the wiles of the devil."*

Was he talking about her? Velma looked across the aisle at Miss Buford, who sent back an encouraging nod. Leaving church, Reverend Clement pressed a small Bible into Velma's hands. "A pocket edition of the New Testament with Jesus' words printed in red." He put a hand on her shoulder. "To protect you from sin out there among strangers."

The sermon *had* been about her.

Velma hugged Miss Buford goodbye. "You could do with the company of strangers after growing up around here." Miss Buford squeezed her arm.

"You have qualities," Mama told her. They sat on Velma's bed the night before she left. "People around here may not see it, but I do, and those folks up in the city will, too."

Velma nodded, throat aching with apprehension. Her infinitely better future suddenly felt more like being pitched into the unknown. She wanted to believe there was more to her than showed on the outside. If she could take Mama with her, nothing in Jackson would scare her.

22

Papa drove Velma up to Jackson in the wheezing truck. After getting lost and cursing cities, he located Pinehurst Street where Velma had rented a room, sight unseen. This was a nice neighborhood, Miss Buford said, a safe place for a young, single woman. Velma studied the houses while they searched for the address: small and one-story, close to one another, shaded by old trees.

Silent for most of the drive, Papa pulled the truck to a stop and looked at her. "Hope this is not a mistake on your part, Sister." He gave her a peck on the cheek and set her suitcase out on the sidewalk. "Catch the bus home if you don't like it." He drove away.

Velma watched until the truck disappeared. Taking a deep breath, she steered her bag between pots of sweet-smelling petunias to the front door. The house was painted tan with white trim under a steep, red-shingled roof. The curtains were closed. She knocked on the front door. Maybe she knocked too timidly because nobody came. The landlady might not be home, though Miss Buford had written to say when Velma might be expected. If nobody answered, she'd be standing here until dark, not knowing one soul in this entire city, and with nowhere to go. She'd about worked up a good cry when the door opened.

"Lord, child, you're early. Wasn't expecting you until suppertime." Mrs. Moseley was small and what Velma thought of as middle aged, with powdered white cheeks, red lipstick, and very black hair. She peered behind Velma. "Didn't your pa stay long enough to see you in?"

"He needed to get back."

"Never mind, though I do like to see the kind of folks a person comes from. Otherwise, it's like picking a puppy without seeing the mother." Mrs. Moseley tittered. "Not that you're a puppy." She looked Velma up and down. "Too big to be a puppy, aren't you? Hard on a girl being tall, but don't slouch, never slouch, that's what I say. Stand straight and make people look up to you. Bring that suitcase along."

Velma decided she wouldn't have to worry about being shy around Mrs. Moseley, who seemed perfectly capable of talking for both of them. She led Velma through the dim crowded parlor, every flat surface crowded with China figurines.

"Small, but cozy," Mrs. Moseley said. "That's my late husband, Frank, bless his soul." She indicated a silver-framed photograph. "This is the dining room, where we'll have our evening meals. Here's the kitchen. Nothing fancy. Always wanted a bigger kitchen, but, alas, Frank perished before he got around to it."

Perished. Such a romantic word for a plain looking man.

"This is my bedroom."

Velma caught a glimpse of pink through a half-closed door.

"You're down the hall. The bath is at the back. You are my sole tenant, Miss Vernon. One nice girl at a time and no gentleman callers." She gave Velma a sharp look.

"No, Ma'am." Velma was startled by the idea of a gentleman caller, or that Mrs. Moseley considered her the kind of girl who might have one. She pictured Chalmers Root ringing the bell in his greasy overalls, and the expression on her landlady's face at the sight of him. Which wasn't fair because for senior prom he'd worn a perfectly decent suit.

"Are you listening, dear?"

"Yes, Ma'am."

Mrs. Moseley stared at her with bright animal eyes. "Good. Delilah Buford gave you a very high recommendation."

Miss Buford's first name was *Delilah*? Delilah, the biblical temptress? A day filled with surprises. Maybe that's what the preacher meant. Miss Buford had tempted Velma.

The tour complete, Mrs. Moseley left Velma in her room. "Dinner at six. Make yourself at home."

Velma looked around: a bed with a white cotton spread and a painted table beside it; a straight chair, three-drawer dresser, and double-sided blackout curtains to pull over the double windows. Unlike the crowded living room, the only ornament here was a gold-framed picture of Jesus over the bed, blond and blue-eyed, gazing heavenward.

Velma opened her suitcase and hung her good suit in the small closet, along with two blouses and a pair of slacks for weekends. Everything else went into the drawers. She placed a small photograph of her parents on the dresser: Papa frowning, Mama squinting into the sun. Seeing their faces and the way Mama clutched the apron she'd removed to have her picture taken, made Velma's throat close.

She slid the empty suitcase under the bed. For the first time in her life, she was on her own. It had taken all the courage she possessed to get herself out of Picayune and, now that she was here, she felt wrung out. The future stretched in front of her like one of those maps of unexplored lands.

She wouldn't be feeling hollow and alone if she'd said yes to Chalmers Root. She could have stayed home where everyone knew her. Had a nice church wedding. Except she couldn't stand the feel of Chalmers's big hands on her skin, and the one time he'd kissed her, she hadn't liked that either.

My big, smart girl, Mama called her. Velma could have done without the big, but she was book smart, and she had come north to discover her "qualities." She wouldn't run back to Picayune, no matter how scary things got.

From the living room, she heard the faint sound of a radio and Edward R. Murrow's voice. Comforting familiarity in this strange house.

Mrs. Moseley called her to supper, which was Campbell's Chicken with Rice soup with soda crackers. Next to the soup bowl, a side plate held a slice of Dole's pineapple on a piece of iceberg lettuce, topped with a dab of mayonnaise. Mrs. Moseley called this her Welcome salad. Not much like Mama's farewell supper the night before: a flaky-crusted pie filled with beef, potatoes, carrots, and a thick, peppery gravy.

"You'll find I am a plain person, Velma. Most nights it'll just be the soup."

"Yes, Ma'am." Velma planned on causing this small woman no trouble.

The dining room felt airless. Mrs. Moseley said, "I like things closed in the daytime to keep out the heat. At night, of course, we observe the blackout. Once it's dark, I'll switch on the attic fan. When you turn your light out, open a window and leave your door cracked. You'll get a nice breeze."

She said grace. Velma swallowed a spoonful of soup, making what sounded to her like an enormous sound in the silent room. She couldn't think of a subject to talk about and kept her eyes on her food. Mrs. Moseley had no problem with words. She explained the bathroom. They would each take two baths a week. She took hers in the mornings, so Velma should plan on Monday and Thursday evenings. Sponge baths in between. "Not too much hot water, there's a good girl."

Mrs. Moseley was not an early riser, so breakfast was each to her own. She would leave the teakettle on the stove and a bottle of Postum on the counter. All Velma needed to do was light the gas. Matches on the wall to the right of the stove. Plenty of bread for toast, but no butter unless Velma had her own ration coupons. If she wanted an egg, she should leave a dime on the counter.

Velma carried her bowl and plate into the kitchen and offered to wash dishes. Mrs. Moseley said, "What a good girl," and returned to the radio in the living room.

Back in her room, Velma peered through a crack in the curtains at the almost dark sky. She put on the white cotton nightgown she'd ordered from Sears, and brushed her teeth in the hall bathroom. Back in bed, she allowed herself to cry, but not much. Her first night away from home. She took out her new Bible and opened it to Revelations: "*...he that overcometh, and keepeth my works unto the end, to him will I give power over the nations.*" She didn't need power over nations; she'd settle for finding her way to school tomorrow.

She knelt and asked God to bless her parents, Aunt Orrie, and Uncle Drew in heaven. For herself, she asked not to be afraid.

Dark enough now to open the curtains. She turned out the light and pulled them back. From the hall, she heard the attic fan start up. She raised both windows and opened the door. Mrs. Moseley was right: a cool breeze moved over the bed. Lying there, looking out at the dark shapes of unfamiliar trees, Velma practiced the names of streets she'd take on the way to school: Pinehurst, Fortification, North State, Pearl. She considered it a good sign for one to be called Fortification.

She woke with her heart trying to pound out of her chest. The dream again—Uncle Drew under the tractor, the pink froth. She hadn't had it in years. Sitting up, she took deep breaths. The radium hands on her travel clock pointed to five.

Mama said a bad choice could kill you. Was leaving home one of those? Papa believed kin was all you could count on, and nobody should take themselves more than a holler away. Velma heard Mama's voice in her head: Pay him no mind.

The sky turned from black to gray. That was Pinehurst Street out the window. She was in Jackson, Mississippi, and today was the first day of business school. The thought made her jump out of bed.

She wasn't sure what people wore in the city, so she put on her best, the gray gabardine suit with a pink nylon blouse. She set the flat black straw hat on her head and frowned at herself in the mirror. Hats did nothing for her, but a lady didn't go downtown without one. Because of the distance and the heat, she wore flats. She carried the suit coat folded over her arm and put her good white cotton gloves in her purse. For an extra dime, Mrs. Moseley said she was welcome to make herself a sandwich with two pieces of light bread and a slice of Velveeta. Velma wrapped it in waxed paper and put it inside Mama's good black purse.

This was not much of a lunch, but Mrs. Moseley had not offered mayonnaise. On the farm, they'd been plain people, and that meant buying only what you couldn't grow, but they grew plenty. For Mrs. Moseley, it must mean taking in a tenant, and making do with war rations. Velma decided that was fine. She'd expected things to be different here in the city.

August, and the morning sun already heating up the sidewalks. North State Street was lined with crape myrtle trees in their last bloom. Looking up at the ruffled pink flowers, Velma thought this also might be a sign: her in a pink blouse and the pink trees. After being surrounded for nineteen years by plowed fields, Jackson looked green and lush. Around the big houses, thick shrubs had been trimmed into shapes, and the mown grass looked smooth as velvet. Everything smelled fresh and nothing smelled like manure. Papa said he didn't give a spit for grass—you couldn't eat it—but Papa was not here. Mama always said the Bible got it wrong: it was gumption that was next to godliness, not cleanliness. Velma felt like Dorothy entering the Emerald City of Oz. Anything could happen.

23

Baldwin Business School did not look like Oz. The two-story red brick building gave away no more than its name, printed in steel letters over the double doors. Inside, the ceilings were low, the lights fluorescent. Along the front, heavy blackout curtains had been pulled open to let a weak light through pebbled glass.

Velma had registered by mail and the lady behind a counter checked her name off a list. Velma counted out Mama's wrinkled bills and got a receipt stamped "Paid." Other girls arrived, dressed in sandals and flowered cotton, chattering as if they already knew each other. Velma felt damp from her walk and flushed with anxiety. "Where do I go?" she asked the lady. The woman pointed up the stairs.

Velma checked her schedule. She was signed up for Advanced Shorthand and Office Procedures in the morning, Advanced Typing and something called Decorum in the afternoon.

No one else had on a hat. Velma took hers off. She found the door marked Shorthand, but when the roll was called, her name was not on it.

The teacher motioned her forward. "Let me see your schedule."

Getting up from the desk, Velma tripped over her own feet. Being in front of people was her worst thing.

"This is Beginning Shorthand," the teacher said. "You're in Advanced, downstairs and to the right."

By the time she located the room, class had started. Everyone turned to stare and the teacher frowned. "I prefer to begin," she said, "as we end: promptly."

"Yes. Ma'am." Velma found an empty desk and fumbled a pencil and tablet out of her bag. Embarrassed at being late, she couldn't make her ears work and missed part of the first dictation.

The teacher stood over her. "You were not here for my introduction. My name is Miss Higgett. And you are?"

"Velma Vernon," she whispered.

"Are you sure you belong in Advanced Shorthand, Miss Vernon?"

"Yes, Ma'am."

"Speak up, girl."

Velma's skin burned. "I'm pretty sure." Around her, she heard a murmur of laughter.

"Ladies, please," Miss Higgett said. "Let us continue."

"The second dictation," she announced, "is a passage from Shakespeare,

Henry IV, Part 2."

Velma readied her pencil.

The gaudy, blabbing and remorseful day — line break
Is crept into the bosom of the sea — line break
And now loud-howling wolves arouse the jades — line break
That drag the tragic melancholy night — line break

There was more, sentences filled with "foul contagious darkness" and blood on a discolored shore. Everything was about war these days. Velma's high school wasn't so country they didn't have Shakespeare. She'd read *Romeo and Juliet* in eleventh grade, and *Macbeth* in twelfth, but she'd never heard of this Henry. She guessed at the spelling and got it down as best she could.

Miss Higgett came around checking their transcriptions. At Velma's desk, she said, "Downs is a place and should be capitalized and you didn't catch all the line breaks, but not bad, not bad at all. Perhaps you do belong with us, Miss Vernon."

Blood rushed to Velma's face. The hated blush.

More Shakespeare for the third dictation. Miss Higgett had one of those deep, throaty voices, and seemed to enjoy listening to herself. Looking around, Velma realized they were all women. It was called a business school, but no male students were in attendance, only women learning to be secretaries. Men must learn business somewhere else. Of course, most men were off at war.

One of the students (chewing gum—an infraction that would have gotten you thrown out of Miss Buford's class) raised her hand. "We would *never* have to do Shakespeare in a real job."

"Aha." Miss Higgett pounced as if she'd caught a mouse. "I hoped one of you would object. There is method behind what may seem like madness, ladies. Out in the real world, you will run into all manner of unfamiliar terms. You must be prepared for the unexpected. Forewarned is forearmed."

Velma decided to always be forearmed.

Office Procedures was taught by the head of the school, Miss Webb, a short, round woman in extremely high heels. They practiced filing. They practiced phone technique. In future classes, Miss Webb said, they would master the basics of bookkeeping.

Many of the girls went out for lunch. Velma would never waste Mama's money on restaurant food. The few that remained gathered in a room on the ground floor. They seemed to already know one another, so Velma ate her sandwich alone.

In the afternoon, by the time she got done with Typing, Velma let herself relax. Typing had been her best course in high school, and she was the fastest in the room here.

The last class, Decorum, was required for all students. Taking her seat, Velma heard one girl say "decorum" in a sarcastic voice. A friend rolled her eyes in agreement.

"I saw that." Miss Webb again. She stood at the blackboard and pointed her chalk at the offenders. "You who mock would do well to pay special attention. What we cover in this class will make or break you in the working world." They would, she said, learn how to dress properly for an office, how and how not to wear their hair, and how much makeup was appropriate. Velma was thrilled and mortified to be singled out as the only person in the room dressed the way a proper secretary should be. Everyone turned to stare while Velma studied her hands, feeling heat creep up her neck.

A girl behind her whispered audibly: "If you don't mind looking like your mother."

The gray suit was the best thing Velma owned. She sat up straighter. Let them make fun of her; Miss Webb approved.

Over Cream of Mushroom soup that night, she answered Mrs. Moseley's questions about her first day. Mrs. Moseley had rented to other girls attending Baldwin. "I particularly approve of Decorum." She opened her mouth and, avoiding the lipstick, dabbed each corner with her napkin. "'De-*cor*-um.' I admire a word that sounds like what it means."

That night, Velma spoke to the mirror on the medicine cabinet as she brushed her teeth. "Be prepared for the unexpected."

On the second day, Velma sat closer to a group of girls in the lunchroom. The one with a blonde perm said, "I'm Henrietta. Where you from anyway?"

"Out from Picayune," Velma said.

Henrietta almost choked with amusement. "Reeely?" Her friends joined in the hilarity. Velma couldn't figure out what was funny.

As the weeks moved from August to hotter September, she quit trying to make friends. City girls didn't seem to want to know anyone new. Velma tried to comfort herself. She already had friends, friends who wrote letters that were almost as good as a visit. At school, she kept her mouth shut and listened.

Baldwin Business School served as a refresher for her skills and Velma excelled. Watching her classmates gossip over their machines, snickering in that secret way, making her feel left out, she figured out the difference. They were waiting for real life to begin when the war ended and the men came home. This *was* her life, her main chance.

Graduation wasn't fancy. No rented robes or procession. At the end of a brief ceremony, Velma was called up front to receive the Medal of Excellence. Miss Webb told the audience Velma Vernon typed ninety words a minute without error and took dictation at one hundred and sixty words per minute.

After the ceremony, Miss Webb asked Velma to step into her office. "You have been an exemplary student, Velma."

Velma nodded, cheeks blazing.

"I gather you do not have a surfeit of connections here in the city." Miss Webb waited, her bright eyes fixed on Velma.

Surfeit — an excess amount. Velma shook her head. No connections.

"Never mind. Aware of your situation, I have taken the liberty of setting up an appointment for you with a local law firm." She handed Velma a slip of paper with a name and address. "Monday morning, ten o'clock. This is one of the finest firms in the city, my dear, and the man who heads it is a friend. Do not disappoint me."

Velma took the paper and found her voice. "Thank you so much. I've enjoyed my time here." They had learned to talk like this in Decorum. These were called Polite Responses. Velma realized the words were true: she'd grown comfortable with her morning walk, the school day, a cheese sandwich in waxed paper, and soup with crackers at supper. Graduation meant being pushed out of the familiar — again.

"A little parting advice," Miss Webb said. "Watch what the other secretaries do, and if there is anything you don't understand, fake it. If you run into trouble, give me a call." She gave Velma's arm a pat. "You'll do fine."

Velma bobbed her head. "Thank you for everything." In one day, she'd been called excellent and told to fake it. Faking it seemed like the kind of thing an excellent person would never do, but she knew nothing about the business world. Miss Webb said to call if she got into trouble. How kind. She packed her pens, the shorthand tablets and typing workbooks, the Graduation Certificate, her Medal of Excellence, and walked home. It occurred to her that two women, neither of them kin to her, had done her favors that might change her life: Miss Buford down in Picayune and now Miss Webb.

"Oh." Mrs. Moseley looked startled when Velma appeared at three in the afternoon instead of the usual five-thirty. *Oh*, like maybe she'd gotten thrown out of school instead of graduated.

Shyly, Velma held out the medal.

Mrs. Moseley peered nearsightedly at the raised letters. "Aren't you the good girl? Excellence is another very good word." She smiled up at Velma. "You are my first girl to get a medal. This calls for a celebration. I'll make my special salad." She headed to the kitchen, speaking to Velma over her shoulder. "Just because you've graduated, no need to move out. I wrote Delilah to say what a good tenant you've been. Stay as long as you like."

Move out? Did the other girls leave after they finished school? Where would she go? Velma slowed the wheel of worry long enough to take in Mrs. Moseley's final words.

On Saturdays, she washed her blouses and underwear and hung them to dry on the line in Mrs. Moseley's small back yard. She shampooed and rolled her hair for church on Sunday and ironed the blouses after they dried.

But on the Saturday after graduation, she celebrated by taking a walk downtown. Capitol Street bustled with cars. Buses threw off clouds of exhaust. She strolled from the Old Capital at the top of the street all the way to the train station at the bottom. As she watched, a silver train pulled in, whistle blowing, people staring out the windows while Velma stared in. "All aboard the City of New Orleans," a conductor shouted.

The City of New Orleans. She would love to ride a train named that. Walking back up Capitol Street, she examined store windows for things she might buy if she got the job: a reading lamp, a portable radio, though the sign in the window said, due to wartime shortages, the radios had a waiting list.

Back in her room, Velma counted off the weeks on her calendar. She'd been gone from Picayune for six weeks and two days. In each square, she'd written a word. Mondays through Fridays, were mostly "good." Saturdays were "okay," and Sundays were all "hard."

God's day shouldn't be the worst, but that was the truth. At home on Sundays, the Church of the Redeemer throbbed with singing and praying. A big home-cooked meal after, with Mama frying chicken and Papa slicing the ham. Here in Jackson, she went to First Baptist over on North State. The church was enormous. Velma felt like a pea in a bucket. So far, she'd tried the nine o'clock Adult Sunday School and the eleven o'clock service.

At Sunday School, she sat in silence, dreading the prayer circle at the end, when each person was supposed to contribute a line. She couldn't listen to the others for trying to keep her own words ready. She squeaked out the same thing every week: "May the Lord walk with us along the way." Some Sundays, she said "beside us" to change it up. Speaking in front of people brought the blood rushing to her face, and when she was done, she sat breathing hard, waiting for the embarrassment to subside, hoping everyone kept their eyes closed the way they were supposed to.

The preacher was a big man with a citified voice and a lot of wavy hair. At the front door after the service each week, he gave Velma a meaty handshake while looking past her to see who was next.

On Sundays, Mrs. Moseley served a hot meal after church : a sliver of meat, boiled rice, canned green beans or peas. Mrs. Moseley's idea of a hot meal made Velma want to weep.

Her landlady was a Methodist, so Velma didn't see her in church, but while they ate, Mrs. Moseley shared the sermon she'd heard at Galloway Memorial, word for word as near as Velma could tell, nodding in agreement with herself.

On the Sunday after graduation, Velma made a cheese sandwich for supper, ate it alone in her room, and tried to ready herself for Monday's interview. She could not have dreaded the coming event more if the word interview meant a beating.

She remembered Shakespeare's *King Henry*. The gray suit was her armor and this interview a battle: forewarned was forearmed. The suit and pink blouse were pressed and hanging from the curtain rod. She would wear her black heels, even though they made her taller than most men. She'd wear the hat and gloves and carry Mama's good purse.

On her knees that night, her prayer was fervent: *Please.* She tried to find words for what she feared. *Don't let me shame myself.*

24

The appointment was for ten. By nine-thirty, Velma sat in the outer office of Hughes & Blair Attorneys at Law on the tenth floor of the Plaza building, the highest she'd ever been in an elevator.

She kept her knees pressed together and, in her lap, clutched her mother's purse and a manila folder containing the Baldwin Graduation Certificate. She'd brought the medal in her purse in case anyone wanted to see it.

At school, they had practiced writing resumes, what Miss Webb called their *Curriculum Vitae*. Velma loved the way that sounded, but she had little to put in hers. Except for the farm, the only place she'd worked was the Depository, packaging and selling school supplies. She entertained herself by imagining the letter of recommendation Papa might write for her: strong back, good at stoop labor, talented with a hoe.

Nervous perspiration came through the pink blouse and Velma feared it might make its way through the suit coat and show in dark circles. She squeezed her arms against her sides and held on tighter to the purse. She studied her fingernails, which she had painted the night before in a color from the drugstore called Vanilla Blush. A lot of girls at business school painted their nails, mostly red. None of the women at Church of the Redeemer wore nail polish, but Velma didn't think the Baptists had a rule against it like the one against dancing. Ladies at the Baptist church on North State Street had manicures. Not that she liked to stare, which she was trying not to do now, observing the other secretaries without seeming to.

They looked sophisticated in their starched blouses and dark skirts, except for the lady at the front desk, who wore a navy suit. A suit like hers, except probably not from the Sears catalog. The secretary nearest Velma had blonde hair, rolled up in front with curls behind her ears, and crimson lipstick. She read off her shorthand tablet and tapped at a big Underwood typewriter, looking confident and employed. Which was why she was here, Velma reminded herself. She put her shoulders back and sat up straighter.

Miss Webb had said there was a vacancy. Velma wondered if one of these women was leaving. Three were young. The woman in the suit, who'd greeted Velma in what she considered a not friendly way, looked old, more than fifty.

Dread of the approaching interview made her sweat more. They had practiced doing job interviews in Office Procedures. The two questions most commonly asked were: Why do you want this job and why do you think you'd be good at it? Velma went over her answers: she wanted this job because—Miss Webb said to say, "Because I am ready to be someone's very good secretary." She would never get that many words out of her mouth at one go. Velma planned to say, "Because I'm ready." When asked why she would be good at the job, she would answer: "I can type ninety words a minute." Should she include her shorthand speed, or would that sound like bragging? She didn't think men cared how fast you wrote things down as long as you got every word they said.

Her heart beat uncomfortably. She took deep breaths and focused on the metal stands holding the secretaries' shorthand tablets. Exactly like the ones they used at Baldwin Business School, which raised Velma's spirits. This was the real world and the skills she had perfected would be put to use.

She hadn't realized she was smiling until the older lady at the front desk asked if there was anything she needed. Velma shook her head, ashamed to have attracted attention in this important place with its dark red carpeting, polished desks, the neat, busy women watched from above by gold-framed portraits of stern old men.

A door on the left opened and a white-haired man appeared. He looked at her and at the paper in his hand. "Velma Vernon?"

She stood and nodded, tongue thick in her mouth, heart hammering like a cottonseed press.

He held the door. Taller than she was, even in heels, and old, older than Papa — grandfather old. Dressed like a preacher in a dark suit and tie, a white shirt gleaming with starch. He indicated a chair and Velma sat, eyes on her knees. Her damp slip stuck to the backs of her legs.

He sat on the other side of the desk and stared at her. "My name is Patrick Hughes. I'm in charge of this place."

Velma's face got hotter. She tried one of her Polite Responses: "I am pleased to meet you."

"Why don't you tell me about yourself, Miss Vernon?"

That was not one of the questions she'd rehearsed. Her mouth opened and closed. Wordlessly, she handed him the folder and watched as he opened it.

He studied the Baldwin Graduation Certificate and looked up. Light reflected off his glasses. "An Award of Excellence…with an impressive gold seal."

That was funny, him noticing the seal. Velma laughed. She hadn't meant to open her mouth this wide because she hated the way her pink gums showed above her teeth. She put a hand up to cover it.

"I hear from your teacher that you're pretty good," Mr. Hughes said.

"Yes sir." A whisper.

"Not fibbing, is she?"

"No, sir."

He handed the folder back. "Then why don't we give you a try? You can show up tomorrow morning." He stood.

Was that it? Velma got to her feet, clutching purse and folder.

"You'll be working for me, Miss Vernon, and when my son returns from his adventures in the Pacific, you'll work for him, too." Patrick Hughes indicated a photograph on the windowsill behind his desk.

Velma saw a serious-faced young man in a white navy uniform.

"Think you can handle that?"

"Yes sir." She smiled, careful this time to keep her mouth closed.

He held open the door. "Mrs. Evans here will show you around." He spoke loud enough for the older lady to hear. "Mrs. Evans is leaving me, retiring to the Gulf Coast with her husband. Been here thirty-two years and quitting on me already. If you work out, Miss Vernon, I hope you won't run off after thirty-two years."

"No sir."

Mrs. Evans did not smile. She pursed her lips in a way that indicated she was accustomed to this foolishness. "Eight o'clock tomorrow morning," she said to Velma and showed her out the door.

Velma walked to the elevator feeling numb. No mention of a salary or what her hours would be or vacation time. Just show up tomorrow at eight. Her throat ached with relief. She had a job. She had twenty-one dollars of Mama's money left and *a job*.

She was going to be the *boss's* secretary. Wait until they heard about that at home. Mama had been the only person besides Miss Betts with faith in her. Papa thought people should stay where they were planted.

Walking a block over to Capitol Street, she looked into the windows of the big department stores: The Emporium on the near corner and Kennington's facing it across the street. After her first paycheck, maybe she'd get up the nerve to enter one of those fancy stores. She wanted a black skirt and a nice white blouse like the girls at the law firm wore.

Her new boss's secretary had looked Velma up and down in a way that made her feel she hadn't met expectations. Scary. She would pray about that tonight. For now, she let herself be happy.

She walked down Capitol Street, head high, an employed person. The Episcopal Church rose on her left, gray stone with a steeple, bells counting out the hours. Eleven o'clock and warm for October. Velma took off her suit coat and folded it carefully over her purse. The carved wooden doors of the church stood open. She went up the marble steps and peeked inside. Darkness, rich wood, stained glass, and a smell she didn't recognize. She couldn't imagine going in to sit or pray the way the sign outside invited you to. Papa said Catholics were bad enough, and Episcopalians were nothing but Catholics with divorces.

On the other side of the street, the Governor's mansion sat in the middle of a tree-shaded lawn. She recognized it from a field trip her Civics class had taken to Jackson. They'd toured the Old Capitol, built with bricks made by slaves, and the New Capitol, which contained a genuine Egyptian mummy. No one explained how a mummy fit into state government, but it had been a sight. They'd walked around the Governor's Mansion and over to City Hall, one of the few structures not burned during the Civil War. Built by Masons, they were told, and spared because General Sherman was a Mason.

She wasn't positive about this last part, which was the trouble with school learning. You only held on to dribs. In Decorum, Miss Webb told them a good secretary should always be ready to make Polite Conversation. Velma thought the Mason business might be a good topic, if it came up naturally. Better than the mummy.

Thinking about Miss Webb, Velma vowed to do better tomorrow. She would not stand around mute as a mule. If Mr. Hughes spoke to her, she'd think of something sensible to say back. Good thing Miss Webb had put in a word for her. She would never have gotten that job on her own.

Be happy, she reminded herself. Two months ago, she'd been in Picayune with nothing to look forward to but marrying Chalmers Root. She passed the Rexall drugstore, went inside, and sat at the counter. She would treat her newly employed self to a cherry coke. The soda jerk smiled and Velma smiled back, gums and all.

25

On her first official day of work, Mrs. Evans introduced Velma to the three other secretaries, who nodded and smiled, barely pausing in their typing. She sat Velma at her desk with a sample brief and had her type the first two pages as a test of her speed and accuracy. Looking at the results, Mrs. Evans gave a little cluck of approval. She showed Velma the law library and explained the filing system. She paused outside each office and whispered the name of the lawyer working inside: Mr. Saunders, Mr. Gainey, and Mr. Hughes' partner Mr. Blair. Halfway down the hall the office was occupied by a woman half hidden behind a stack of large books, smoking with one hand and writing furiously with the other.

"Mr. Hughes' daughter Margaret." Mrs. Evans corrected herself. "Mrs. Laughlin to you."

Velma whispered. "Is she a lawyer?"

"In a manner of speaking."

Velma had not realized women could be lawyers. Mrs. Evans did not respond to her look of wonder.

Velma found Mrs. Evans intimidating on the first day, and she remained so. The older woman arrived each morning before eight, and Velma walked double time from Pinehurst, trying to get to the office first. Together, they opened Mr. Hughes' mail, and Velma watched as Mrs. Evans arranged it on his desk in order of importance. "Never open an envelope marked Personal." She gave Velma a sharp look, as if she might be the kind of girl who would do that.

Velma nodded. The rule about personal mail had been drilled into them at Baldwin.

Mrs. Evans moved in a quick, tidy way that made Velma feel like a plodding cow. Each morning, her small, plump body arrived encased in a different jewel-toned suit. She wore black pumps with a sensible heel, sheer stockings with pencil-straight seams, and a single strand of pearls. Her gray perm looked ironed into place. When Velma bent closer to observe the correct way to paginate a legal brief, she spied an almost invisible gray hairnet.

She took mental notes. A perfect secretary kept her hair immobile and her body encased in what appeared to be a one-piece girdle. Heels, but not too high, a light coating of face powder, and almost no rouge. Discreet button earrings, which, like the pearl necklace, looked genuine. A gold watch on her left wrist and a plain gold band on her left hand. Velma had no need of the latter, marriage being the condition she had escaped.

During the week of training, Velma marveled at the quiet efficiency of the office. Phones rang, typewriters clacked, people spoke to one another, but voices were never raised and sound seemed to be absorbed by the thick wool carpet.

She sat beside Mrs. Evans at the front desk and practiced answering the telephone in a calm but confident voice. "Hughes & Blair." "Hughes & Blair." A higher note on "Blair."

On the fourth try, Mrs. Evans said, "What *is* that accent?"

Velma's face got hot. "I beg your pardon?"

"The way you speak, dear. It sounds a bit flat. Never mind. I don't suppose you do it on purpose."

Everyone in Picayune talked like Velma. There was no time for self-pity. "Hughes & Blair", "Hughes & Blair," she repeated, trying not to sound flat.

"This is a small law office," Mrs. Evans said. "Smaller now with several of our young associates off at war. But do not be misled by the size. We are perhaps the most respected firm in the state. You sit at the front desk. You are the first person that visitors will see." She gave Velma a severe look. "You are the face of the firm."

Velma wondered if the look referred to the gray suit, which she had now worn for a fourth day, alternating the pink and white blouses. She arranged her face in an expression she hoped conveyed dignity. She might never be as perfectly put together as Mrs. Evans, but she would not let this firm down.

The secretaries took turns having lunch. Doris, the blonde, bustled out at eleven, with a fresh coat of red lipstick and a secretive smile. Pauline, who was married, ate in the mailroom. The small one, Garnett, left when Doris returned. Mrs. Evans told Velma to take her lunch from one to two. Every day that first week, Velma carried her cheese sandwich to a small park across from the office building and sat on a bench. Overhead, the tree branches met, the sky a clear blue between. A breeze sent yellow and orange leaves flying. She liked sitting here alone, seeing without being seen. City people walked faster than people in Picayune.

On her last day, Mrs. Evens took Velma to the drugstore on the building's ground floor and treated her to lunch. Outside the confines of Hughes & Blair, over a steaming bowl of tomato soup and a cellophane-wrapped package of Saltines, the older woman grew more confiding. "You may wonder how a newcomer like yourself got the job of secretary to the head of the firm?"

Velma hadn't known enough to wonder, but she swallowed a bite of her tuna fish sandwich and nodded.

"Each of the partners has his own secretary and the other lawyers share Doris and Pauline. No one at Hughes & Blair would dream of taking another person's girl. There is no rising through the ranks. You start in an important position and, unless you fail…" She paused for another piercing look. "you remain where you were placed. We get to know the habits of the person for whom we work. These men may be lawyers and we mere secretaries, but we become their eyes and ears." Mrs. Evans nibbled the corner of a cracker. "I might go so far as to say we are their hands and minds."

Velma nodded her head to indicate that she understood the seriousness of her position. "I'm afraid no one will be able to replace you."

Mrs. Evans smiled with the assurance of a woman who knew this to be true. "Mr. Hughes is a patient man, and he will adjust."

"Are you sad to be leaving?" A personal question. Was it appropriate to ask personal questions?

Mrs. Evans sat straighter if that were possible. "After thirty-two years?" The look this time was testing and inquisitive. "Mr. Evans and I were never blessed with children and I enjoy using my brain, so if it were up to me, they would carry me out of here on a stretcher. But my husband retired and wants to move to Pascagoula and fish." She said the word "fish" as if she smelled one. Mrs. Evans' eyes blinked in a way that made Velma think she might cry. The moment passed and there was silence.

This was the most formidable person Velma had ever met, and even she gave in to a husband's wishes. Another reason to forego marriage. "Mr. Hughes said I would be working for his son, too."

The stern face softened. "Will Hughes is a lovely boy. I shouldn't say boy, he's married with children now, but he's Mr. Pat's baby.

Velma stopped her. "Mr. Pat?"

Mrs. Evans leaned closer. "That's what we call Mr. Hughes when clients aren't present. He doesn't mind, in fact he prefers it."

She leaned back. "Will Hughes will always be a boy to me. I've known him since he was small enough to hide in the well of my desk. You'll enjoy working for him. He's not a bit of trouble. His father gives him a hard time, but that's just Mr. Pat's way. They're a pair." Mrs. Evans exhaled what Velma interpreted as nostalgia. "I'll miss the jokes."

Jokes? Velma hadn't realized there would be jokes. She was terrible at jokes.

26

On Friday afternoon, the office held a goodbye party for Mrs. Evans, with fruit punch and an iced cake from the grocery called Jitney Jungle. Velma couldn't believe the name the first time she heard it, but no one else seemed to find it odd. The Jitney was around the corner from Mrs. Moseley's on Fortification. She told Velma all the Belhaven ladies shopped there.

Mrs. Evans was given a little gold clock with feet, engraved with her name and the dates she'd worked for Hughes & Blair. Mr. Hughes made a speech and Velma saw tears in his eyes. Mrs. Evans allowed a peck on the cheek that appeared to make them both uncomfortable. Party over, everyone went back to work. Mrs. Evans cleaned out the top drawer of her desk and, dry-eyed, departed.

Mr. Hughes went back to his office and shut the door. The other secretaries bent over their typewriters. Velma sat at the front desk and told herself to stop shaking.

Over the weekend she had worried about what she might be expected to do on Monday, but mostly she worried about her appearance. For four days, she'd worn the gray suit with either the white blouse or the pink. On Friday, she'd worn the blue shirtwaist she'd traveled in from Picayune. The dress had been good enough for church at home but looked shabby in the brighter light of Jackson. There was nothing to do about clothes until she got paid. She told herself men did not notice such things. Papa certainly didn't.

That night, she repainted her fingernails. She looked in the mirror and hated her hair, which tended to bunch and curl, but not in a stylish way. She tried pinning it up, stared at herself, and took it down again. Nothing she did transformed her into Mrs. Evans.

On Monday, alone behind the front desk, Velma's lips ached from her efforts to smile without opening her mouth. The small secretary, the one called Garnett, (With an emphasis on the *"nett,"* she told Velma), stopped at the desk and whispered. "If you need anything, come find me."

The gesture was so unexpected and kind, Velma had to swallow to keep from crying. She thanked Garnett and told herself not to be a ninny. She knew how to do this.

She settled in, growing confident under the eyes of Mr. Pat, which she finally got up the nerve to call him.

"Excellent," he said, glancing over a freshly typed brief. "Good work, young lady."

Mama and Papa had always told Velma she was a good girl. She tried to live up to the advertising, as Papa would say, and felt proud of her work. Pages and pages of heavy legal-size bond, the typing fresh and black, properly spaced, indented, and error free. A finished brief could be eighty of these pages or even a hundred. She looked upon her output with satisfaction. She had created something real and important, and in doing so, she had pleased Mr. Pat.

When she wasn't typing or taking dictation, Velma felt awkward. She tried to act easy around the other girls, but she hadn't learned to make small talk with city people, and everyone went their separate ways at lunchtime. Pauline gave her a friendly, "Good morning" each day. She noticed the one named Doris eyeing the gray suit on its eighth appearance in two weeks.

At quitting time on the second Friday, Garnett stopped by Velma's desk. "Pay day. I usually go shopping on the Saturday after if you want to come."

Velma nodded, tongue-tied. Garnett said to meet her outside the Emporium the next morning at ten. When she walked away, Velma sat very still, exulting. She had an invitation, which was so sweet. With Garnett leading the way, she would not fear entering that store.

27

On Saturday morning, Velma arrived a few minutes late, perspiring.

"You came on foot?" Garnett looked astonished. "Where do you live?"

"Pinehurst and Jefferson."

"And you *walked*?"

"I walk to work every day," Velma said. "I got a late start. My landlady decided to tell me how she lost her husband."

Garnett laughed. "Don't you love it when people say they've 'lost' someone, like they misplaced them?"

Velma had never thought about it, but now that she did, it *was* funny.

Garnett Coleman was a full head shorter than Velma, with a pointed face and a dimple in her left cheek. She wore her black hair pulled up on the sides and fastened with tortoise-shell combs. She was single, she told Velma, and lived at home with her folks. She talked as easily as a fountain bubbled.

"Remind me when we're done, and I'll teach you how to catch the bus." Garnett pulled open one of the Emporium's big double doors. "Ready?"

Velma followed, as if she too belonged in this cool, perfumed air.

Her salary, it turned out, was thirty dollars a week. She had two weeks' pay in the good black pocketbook borrowed from Mama.

"What are you looking for?" Garnett said.

Velma hesitated. "Something to wear to work?"

"That's easy." Garnett took her up a floor and they walked along racks of skirts and blouses. "Something like this?" Garnett held up a white blouse with a bow at the neck.

Velma nodded.

Garnett fingered the skirts. "What size are you?" She studied Velma. "Probably a ten, maybe a twelve to get the length. You're lucky being so tall. You get to see over people's heads, and men respect tall women."

Velma stood straighter. She followed along, holding hangers as Garnett picked things out for her to try, worried about the cost. Garnett sent her into a dressing room and waited outside.

"Good," she said, as Velma showed herself. Or, "Too frou-frou." Garnett recommended a black gabardine skirt with a pleat down the front and two blouses, the white one and a pale yellow with a jewel neckline.

At the cash register, Velma opened her purse and watched a week's pay disappear. Clutching her shopping bag, she kept up as Garnett searched unsuccessfully for a belt. They stopped at the jewelry counter. "You could get these." Garnett held up a strand of pearls.

Velma said, "Not really. Maybe in two weeks." Garnett might not invite her on another shopping trip. She hadn't bought herself a thing. The shopping had all been for Velma. Maybe the girls at the office talked about her country clothes and Garnett took pity.

They walked down the street to Woolworth's, where Garnett purchased a Tangee lipstick. Velma bought a comb for the top drawer of her desk and three white handkerchiefs. In Decorum, Miss Webb said a good secretary should never be without a clean handkerchief. They had lunch at the Rexall down from the Episcopal Church. Velma listened as Garnett chattered.

She had been at the law firm for three years, and knew things Mrs. Evans didn't, or hadn't chosen to share. Garnett said Mr. Pat and his wife were teetotalers, but their daughter Margaret—definitely not. At the law firm, people called her Miss Margaret or Mrs. Laughlin, but the family called her Mag. Mag sneaked and went to law school at night, against her father's wishes. Passed the bar exam and then told him. Being a woman, the firm didn't let her try many cases, but she did most of the research. It was her work that made the men look good in court. "She used to be married to a Colonel." Garnett said, "but now she's divorced, and she chain smokes."

Mrs. Laughlin, Miss Margaret, Mag—Velma found the names confusing, but then the idea of a woman lawyer was pretty confounding.

Mr. Blair, Garnett's boss, was a go-getter, she said. Unlike Patrick Hughes, who was more a pure lawyer, Mr. Blair wanted in on the deal. He wasn't satisfied with a legal fee. If he represented a company, he liked to own a piece of it. Mr. Pat and he argued about this.

Pauline and Doris, secretaries to the younger lawyers, were nice. Especially Pauline, who was married to a policeman. Doris tended to get a little above herself, Garnett said, if Velma took her meaning.

Velma didn't.

"She'd like to grab herself a young lawyer," Garnett said. "Thinks she might just marry her way into the firm."

"Can you do that?"

Garnett giggled and shook her head. "Doris fluffs up that blonde pompadour and wears her belts so tight she can't take a breath, but it will never happen. All the eligible men are off at war anyway, but hope keeps her going." She glanced up at Velma. "Did you leave some boy broken-hearted back home?"

Velma laughed. "No, I'm heart free." She decided not to mention Chalmers.

"I have a boyfriend," Garnett said. "Bobby's off with the army in Europe."

Velma nodded, but Garnett did not offer more.

She gave Velma an appraising look. "You have a pretty face. Have you ever had your hair styled?"

"People at home go to Sadie's Salon for special occasions, but nothing that happens there could properly be called styling."

Garnett lowered her voice. "Week after next, when we get paid again, maybe we'll go to the beauty parlor."

Velma turned warm with happiness. There *would* be another time. "That sounds good."

Garnett walked her to the bus stop and showed her which bus to take to Belhaven. "Tell the driver where you're going and he'll show you where to get off."

Velma waved from her seat and Garnett waved back. Riding home with the fall air blowing through the open window, Velma decided she'd never had a better day. She'd write Mama tonight and put five dollars in the envelope. She planned on sending five dollars every two weeks until she'd repaid everything she owed.

28

Two weeks later, Velma found herself sitting with Garnett in the waiting area of The Beauty Barn. Fancier than Sadie's, six chairs faced six large mirrors down a long narrow room. In each chair, a woman sat being cut or curled by another woman. Six dryers roared. In the back, over black porcelain sinks, young women bent, hands white with lather. The air smelled of shampoo and peroxide. Velma waited, stiff with nervousness. She would never enter such a place without Garnett.

"You have nice hair, but too much of it," Garnett said.

Velma said, "I know. You have great hair."

"I really don't," Garnett said, "but I've figured out what to do with it. You need a look." She handed Velma a hairstyle magazine. "Go through and find one you like."

Velma flipped through the pages: hair up and down, parted in the middle and rolled; sultry waves covering one eye; pompadours shaped like ocean waves. She asked Garnett what she liked and chose the style Garnett preferred—not quite shoulder length with soft waves around the face.

Her beautician was an older woman with bright yellow hair and dark lipstick. Velma showed her the picture. She pushed and poked at Velma's hair, looking at her in the mirror. "We can do something with this."

Alongside Garnett, Velma got shampooed, cut, curled, dried and combed out. She spent almost the entire experience staring into her lap to keep from facing her own reflection.

The bill was five dollars and Garnett whispered that Velma should add a fifty-cent tip for the beautician and a dime for the hair wash girl. Mama would be scandalized at the amount Velma had just spent on hair, but she had to admit, she looked better. She looked like someone who'd been styled.

When they were back on the sidewalk, Garnett said, "You only need to get a cut every few months. I can show you how to roll it up."

In bed that night, Velma thought about the day. She wasn't sure why Garnett had singled her out, but she felt chosen. The weekends were no longer empty and she had interesting things to say to Mrs. Moseley over their nightly soup.

On the Saturdays between paydays, Garnett took Velma to a movie at the Paramount, and for ice cream sodas afterward at the Seale-Lily. They walked through the cosmetic departments of Kenningtons and the Emporium, trying out the sample lipsticks, spraying their wrists with perfume.

They should each pick a signature scent, Garnett said. Hers was Chanel's Gardenia. Velma couldn't decide between Miss Dior and something named *L'Air Du Temps*. Neither of them could afford perfume, but Garnett said it was the kind of thing a man should buy for you anyway, once you knew what you liked.

Once you *had* a man. Velma doubted Chalmers Root had ever been near a perfume counter.

29

The next Saturday, walking down Capitol Street, Velma made Garnett laugh by naming the soups Mrs. Moseley had served that week for dinner: Campbell's Cream of Tomato, Campbell's Vegetable Beef, Campbell's Green Pea, Campbell's Chicken Noodle, and Tomato again.

Garnett said her mother still came to her bedroom every night and tucked her in.

Velma felt a stitch of pain. "That's so sweet."

"Sweet? I'm twenty-three years old."

They walked on in silence. Velma decided not to mention how much she missed her mother.

"You know what we should do?" Garnett lowered her voice as if the other pedestrians might be eavesdropping. "We should get an apartment together."

Velma stared at her friend, unmoored by the idea of such an enormous change. "Could we afford an apartment?"

"Think of it this way. Whatever it costs gets divided by two, so everything's only half as expensive."

There was something wrong with this logic, but Velma let herself be pulled along by Garnett's enthusiasm. She wondered at this new and surprising friendship. Garnett was her opposite: short to her tall, funny and talkative instead of quiet, cute to—whatever she was. Mr. Pat had complimented Velma's new hairdo, and Velma knew she looked better than when she'd started at the firm. But studying her image in the mirror at night, the face looking back at her wavered, as if it hadn't decided who to be.

She got up the courage to ask Garnett the next Saturday over after-movie sodas. "Why did you pick me? As a friend, I mean."

Garnett looked surprised. "You're a good person. Anyone can see that. Plus, you're smart, and you don't go tattling everything we say."

Velma shook her head. "Never." She sipped her drink in silence. "Remember I said I was raised on a farm?"

Garnett nodded.

"Our place is out from town, so I mostly saw my friends at school." Her face grew warm from the struggle to say what she meant. "I'm really glad—I mean, you've been so nice to me."

"Who wouldn't be nice to you? You're a terrific person and a great listener."

Same as with Annette and Shirley down in Picayune: If you didn't have a lot to say, you could be a great listener. In a world of talkers, there was a need for people like Velma.

30

Garnett found an apartment bordering the railroad track on the outskirts of Belhaven. Three rooms: living/dining, bedroom, and kitchen, upstairs over the landlady, for thirty-five dollars a month.

Mrs. Moseley's eyes got glassy when Velma confessed she was moving.

"I'm floored, Velma, just floored. Still waters run deep." She followed Velma down the hall. "Don't let me read in the newspaper that you've been murdered."

The new place was so close to the tracks, the midnight freight felt as if it might be coming up the hall. The whole house trembled; the windows rattled in their frames. For the first few nights, the train's plaintive wail almost lifted Velma out of bed. By the end of the month, it became an echo in her dreams.

She and Garnett managed fine with the bits and pieces Garnett's parents lent them. It was like playing house. For supper, they made tuna surprise or baked potatoes. They painted each other's toenails and hung underwear to dry all over the bathroom. "No men around to mind," Garnett said. Neither of them had a beau, though Garnett did have Bobby-away-at-war. His photograph, in a gold frame, stood on their borrowed bureau: blond hair cut Army short, brown eyes. He looked nice. Garnett wrote him a letter every night.

When Velma thought about her escape from Chalmers Root, she felt grateful not to have a boyfriend. Garnett kept threatening to introduce her to somebody nice, but between work and the lack of available men, nothing came of it.

The country was engulfed by war. Mr. Pat's son and grandson were in the service. Miss Margaret's daughter was in the WAVES. Garnett and Velma saved tin foil and rubber bands. They bought war bond stamps and learned how to feed themselves on their ration cards.

Garnett taught Velma to do cross-stitch. At night, she did the border around a tablecloth while Velma cross-stitched daisies on pillowcases. "For our hope chests," Garnett said. Velma did not contradict her, but she doubted she'd ever need such a thing. The pillowcases were nice, though, and would make a fine Christmas gift. In the backyard, Velma planted a small Victory Garden: carrots, onions, and collards thrived in a sunny patch.

When she said her prayers at night, Velma asked for the war to end, but inside her own small world, she felt content. She had a job she was good at, a kind boss, and a friend. She wrote telling Mama she must be the luckiest girl in the world. She put the three-cent stamp on upside down, meaning, "Sent with a kiss." If there were a whisper of longing for anything more, Velma did not hear it.

31

Once she relaxed into her work, Velma had more time to observe her boss. She had never met anyone like Patrick Hughes, and had not realized such people existed. He had never learned to drive, preferring, he told her, to be driven. His wife, who was known inside the family as Big Margaret, came from Missouri, a distant and unknown state. Velma could not imagine how they'd managed to find one another. Big Margaret drove Mr. Pat to work in the morning, brought him home for a hot lunch, back in the afternoon, and fetched him at five. Four trips, every single weekday.

He had never learned to shave himself either. He began his mornings downstairs in the building's barbershop, swathed in white, while Sal the barber bent tenderly over him with a straight razor. Hurrying to work, Velma spotted them through the glass window, Mr. Pat tilted back in the chair, his long legs crossed, the polished black shoes on the footrest, a glimpse of clocked socks, his eyes closed in perfect ease. After a quick peek, she looked away, embarrassed. He appeared in the office ten minutes later, pink-cheeked and smelling of bay rum.

Mr. Pat was a formal man. He stood with a little bow when a woman entered a room. He pulled back chairs for women and held open doors. Every day, he wore a blue suit so dark it looked almost black, with a white handkerchief folded into a point in the breast pocket, a perfectly starched and ironed white shirt, topped by a dark tie. In season, he wore a fresh rosebud from his wife's garden pinned to his lapel.

He loved his grown children, surely he must, but he did not show physical affection. Daughter Mag got a nod each morning; he accepted a dry peck on the cheek from the professor daughter Frances when she dropped by.

Velma noticed that Mr. Pat appeared to have forgiven Mag for sneaking off to law school, and was proud of her accomplishments, but he could not abide the cigarettes. He told her smoking was a nasty habit and said she stank of nicotine. He refused to enter her office. Mag had to come to him, which she did with good humor, making a face at Velma as she passed, a face that conveyed how provoking men could be. Velma smiled back as if she agreed, although she worshipped Mr. Pat, and if he complained about any habit of hers, she would have gotten rid of it instantly.

She laughed about him with Garnett over supper. "If he told me he'd rather look at a redhead, I'd come home and dye my hair."

Garnett said it was good to respect Mr. Pat, who was certainly admirable, but Velma shouldn't give any man that kind of power.

Velma nodded in agreement, but privately decided Garnett was wrong. If you truly admired someone—not *loved*, she wasn't talking about romance, which except for Chalmers Root, she did not know a thing about and most likely never would. But if you admired someone, it was normal to want to please them.

32

In mid-December, after Velma had been working at Hughes & Blair for three months, Mr. Pat called her in, not to take dictation, he said, but for "a talk." In spite of being fairly sure she was doing okay ("Super," Garnett claimed), Velma's stomach lurched at the summons. She sat opposite Mr. Pat, hands clasped in her lap, resisting the urge to press them against her chest and calm the thudding heart she feared he could hear. Her breath sounded as loud as a winded horse. No wonder she was being fired.

Mr. Pat looked up from the paper in his hand, his eyes serious behind dark- rimmed glasses. "I've got your report card here."

She *was* being fired.

His mouth twisted into a smile. "Don't sit there looking like a scared rabbit, Velma. Makes a man want to tease you." He looked back at the paper. "I'm here to report that your period of probation is over, Miss Vernon. You do not nag me as well as Evans did, and that may have caused a slippage in my upright habits, but—" His eyes squinted with laughter. "—you'll do. How does five dollars more a week sound?"

Velma's face crumpled and she put her hands up to hide the shameful tears. Miss Webb had warned them in Decorum: *Never* cry. If they felt like crying, they should go shut themselves in the Ladies Room. Plus, Velma had forgotten to bring her handkerchief.

Mr. Pat whipped out his white pocket square. "I thought you'd be pleased."

Velma nodded, face still covered.

"Well, you don't appear pleased."

She nodded more vehemently.

"You have a very strange way of showing pleasure, Miss Vernon."

Velma wiped her face and his lovely handkerchief grew damp. "I'm very grateful."

"You'd better go back out there and do something that doesn't make you cry."

She pushed the handkerchief across his desk.

He looked at it with distaste. "The next time I decide to do you a favor, Miss Vernon, remind me to put it in a letter."

"Yes sir." Velma exited and did a quickstep back to Garnett's desk.

"I told you," Garnett said. "Nobody is as fast as you."

Compliments. A raise. Too much for one day. Velma retreated to the place where she felt safest—behind the Underwood.

33

On Christmas Eve, the Hughes family hosted a party for the firm. This was an annual event, but Velma's first invitation. Walking up the front steps behind Garnett, wearing a new red wool dress with a pleated skirt, she tried not to appear as nervous as she felt.

Mr. Pat and his wife lived in a white-columned house on North State Street, one of the places Velma had gazed upon in wonder on those mornings walking to Baldwin Business School. She'd seen the movie *Gone with the Wind* twice; the Hughes' house looked like Tara.

In the front hall, Mrs. Pat stood next to her husband in a long gown of some heavy, silvery fabric. Her hair was up and fastened with silver combs. Looking at her made Velma question her own outfit. She'd had it made by a dressmaker Garnett recommended, using a pattern Garnett and the dressmaker liked, but next to Mr. Pat's wife, the color looked garish and the pleats — Velma did not own a full-length mirror, but she hated to think what these pleats might be doing to her hips.

Margaret Hughes greeted her with apparent delight. "Velma. I've heard *such* good things about you." She clasped one of Velma's cold hands between her warm ones.

Velma had to resist a curtsey. She managed a Polite Response: "I'm pleased to meet you."

This was high class, the way Margaret Hughes had of talking with strangers and making them feel known.

Mr. Pat teased. "Velma doesn't say much, but she types like a machine gun." He teased Mrs. Hughes, too, telling Velma and Garnett that she was a good wife, but a terrible cook, and the two young women probably shouldn't eat or drink anything.

Mrs. Hughes gave him a rap on the hand. "Pay the silly man no mind. Go and enjoy yourselves."

Velma stared in awe.

Garnett pulled her away. "Let's find somewhere to put these coats."

Mr. Pat and his wife had such an easy way with each other, nothing like her own parents. Working as hard as Mama and Papa did, most of their talking sounded like crop reports. When you had money, there was room for teasing. If she ever married, Velma decided, she wanted it to be like Margaret and Patrick Hughes.

They added their coats to a pile in a dark bedroom. They drank thick, rich, non-alcoholic eggnog out of cut crystal cups. There were cookies on a silver platter with a blob of jam in the center. Garnett said they were called Raspberry Thumbprints.

Velma whispered. "I cannot imagine Mrs. Hughes putting her thumb into a cookie." She picked one up and took a bite.

"They have help in the kitchen to make these cookies," Garnett said. "And, if not, remember what Mr. Pat said about his wife's cooking."

Velma laughed. The raspberry thumbprint broke, landing a glob of seedy red jelly on the white tablecloth.

An elderly Negro man appeared at Velma's side. "Never mind, Miss. I'll see to it."

She felt herself firing up a blush. "I am so sorry."

Garnett led her away. "I don't think you're supposed to apologize to a servant."

Velma had never heard of that rule. "Lucky I didn't break the cup. You go ahead. I'm going to stand back where I can't get into trouble."

A pretty young woman sat down at the piano and began playing. "That's Emmy, Mr. Pat's youngest daughter," Garnett whispered.

Everyone joined in the singing. The familiar words made Velma long for Christmas Eve at Church of the Redeemer.

Emmy played, "I'll Be Home for Christmas," and it was as if the lights in the room had dimmed. Mr. Pat's wife dabbed at her eyes and Velma found herself weeping—for Garnett's Bobby and Mr. Pat's son, for the boys she known in high school, for men everywhere who couldn't be home for Christmas and might never come home again.

The tune switched to "I'm a Boogie-Woogie Bugle Boy from Company B." Everyone's mood lightened. Velma watched, amazed at the ease Garnett talked to the other guests. She could not think of a thing to say to these people she saw every day. There was Doris, blinking her blue eyes at an older lawyer.

Circling the crowd, Velma passed a large gilded mirror.

"Having fun?" Mag-Margaret-Mrs. Laughlin said. "You look very festive." She gave Velma a friendly thump on the back.

Velma wanted to say how nice Mag looked in her green silk, but by the time she got the words lined up, the older woman had moved on. Twisting, Velma tried to see her backside in the mirror. Red wool pleats were what happened when you had no taste of your own.

She looked up, admiring the high ceiling and the wide staircase with its curved balustrade, leading to unknown splendors on a second floor. She passed a small parlor with brocade couches and a potted tree. A *tree* growing inside. A larger room was lined with floor to ceiling shelves, every shelf filled with books. Had Mr. Pat read all of these? At the far end, two easy chairs sat in front of a fireplace. If she lived in this house, this is where she would come. She spotted Frances, Mr. Pat's professor daughter. The woman looked up from her book and smiled. Velma did a little dip in response. *Why did she keep curtseying?* She picked up her pace. Garnett said Frances enjoyed looking down her long nose for errors in other people's grammar. A person to avoid.

After what felt like hours of stretching her mouth into smiles and nodding to anyone who spoke to her, Garnett said they could go. Velma got her coat and they thanked Mr. and Mrs. Pat.

"Don't let all this frivolity go to your head," Mr. Pat said. "I want to see you raring to go on Monday morning."

"Yes, sir," Velma said. *Raring.* Even he thought she looked like a horse.

The heavy front door closed and Velma walked gratefully into the cold night air, taking what felt like her first easy breath since they arrived.

"Wasn't that fun?" Garnett said. They headed home, moving fast, arms linked to keep warm.

"I guess so." Velma didn't know if anything that uncomfortable could be called fun. "I'm a failure at parties."

"You just need practice." Garnett gave her arm an encouraging squeeze.

Velma knew better. She was good at being a secretary. That was her chief quality. If Garnett hadn't befriended her, she'd still be at Mrs. Moseley's eating soup.

Now that she was safely outside, Velma remembered with pleasure the large, glowing house, the rich oriental rugs and glittering chandeliers, the smell of Christmas greens, and the way the light caught Mrs. Hughes' dress and her silver combs. She wished there were a way to show it all to the folks down in Picayune.

34

Velma was given five days off between Christmas and New Year's. She took the Trailways bus to Picayune where Papa picked her up. Inside the little farmhouse, she tried to describe the Hughes' house.

"Sounds mighty pretty," Mama said.

Pretty? Pretty didn't begin to describe it. At dinner, she told them about Mr. Pat at the barbershop and being driven back and forth by his wife.

Aunt Orrie, visiting from Poplarville for the holidays, made a disbelieving noise. "I never heard of a man who couldn't *shave* himself."

Velma saw from their faces that she had failed: they could not visualize the house or understand Mr. Pat any more than they could see her in an office taking dictation.

Over the remains of apple pie, Papa said, "I hear Chalmers is dating a girl from over in Wiggins." He gave Velma a grin. "Guess he got over his grief."

She refused to respond.

"I hear the girl's daddy owns a grocery store." He nodded sagely.

Like what? If she'd played her cards better, Velma could somehow have ended up with Chalmers and a grocery store?

She and Annette went to visit the newly married Shirley. They admired the tiny house, the matching furniture, the new dishes. Shirley was already three months pregnant. She talked about how

Eddie liked his bacon cooked and how hunger made him ornery. Annette described her professors at M.S.C.W. and the horrors of Freshman Algebra. Velma listened, exclaimed, and wondered what happened to the ease she once felt being with them.

Scrunched against the wall in the narrow bed on her final night, Velma tried to make room for Aunt Orrie. She loved Mama and Papa and she still cared about her friends, but life here felt small, especially people's minds.

Aunt Orrie let out a snore that made Velma long for the apartment by the railroad tracks. She tried to give shape to the disappointment of this visit. Living in Jackson robbed the farm of its magic, and being here shrank the wonders of Jackson.

35

In the early fall of 1944, Mr. Pat called Velma into his office for another talk. She sat opposite, less afraid this time, able to look up from her clenched hands and breathe almost normally.

"You're a smart girl, Velma."

She blinked. Compliments felt like blows. She had to close her eyes to take them.

"Too smart not to advance your education. I've been speaking about you to my daughter Frances, the one who teaches at Millsaps College."

Velma knew. The idea of her name being mentioned to this formidable woman made the blood rise to her face.

Mr. Pat waited for a response.

Velma swallowed. "Yes, sir."

"Frances agrees with me. You should go back to school."

"*School?*" Velma's voice squeaked in surprise. Hadn't she finished high school and gotten a business certificate besides?

"College. We think you should go back and earn your degree."

"I'm not sure—"

"If it's money you're worried about, put it out of your mind. The firm wants to cover your tuition."

Mr. Pat always said the firm wanted something when what he meant was, *he* wanted it.

"Well?"

"That's very kind of you, but I don't think I'm—"

"No buts. We will consider it settled. Get yourself over to the campus and sign up for a class or two. The firm can spare you for a few hours." He made harrumphing noises, his way of expressing emotion, and waved her out.

36

At the age of twenty, Velma found herself enrolled in a Tuesday-Thursday English class, surrounded by loud, confident freshmen. She'd been careful when choosing a course *not* to get in one taught by Mr. Pat's daughter Frances.

The first afternoon, she sat petrified in the back row, taking down in shorthand every word the professor uttered. He gave them an assignment to write a personal essay about a point when their lives had changed. He said it could be an event or something intangible like a choice.

Velma went home, re-read her notes, and looked up both "personal" and "essay" in her newly purchased Collegiate Dictionary. Once she was clear that "personal" meant a story about the writer, she thought about her decision not to marry Chalmers Root, to leave Picayune instead and come to Jackson. She wrote a few tortured paragraphs, scratched through most of it, and tried again. By the time she got a clean draft typed, she was sick of the whole business. Words didn't go down on the page the way they went in your mind. Writing essays made taking dictation and typing briefs feel like play. She handed the paper in, got it back with an A, and a scribbled note that said, "Thanks for typing."

Their second assignment was a comparison-contrast paper. Velma figured out what that meant (Who knew there were so many kinds of writing?) She decided to compare her life in a law office with raising vegetables down in Picayune. Clean versus dirty, sitting versus stooping, a steady salary versus depending on the weather. This one got an A, too, with a note that said, "Funny." She read it over. Why was it funny? She hadn't meant to be funny. Worse than not understanding jokes was not knowing when you'd made one.

Velma made it through twelve weeks, grinding out essay after essay, not uttering a word in class or speaking to another student. She continued to get A's on her papers and wrote Mama that college might not be as bad as she'd feared. When Mr. Pat asked about her progress, she said, "Good."

He looked pleased. "I knew you could do it."

Velma's heart swelled. She was a college student. Her life was changing again, and in a way she'd never imagined. She sat straighter at her typewriter and dared to look ahead through the semesters all the way to graduation, to the black robe and gold tassel. The future grew dim after that. What did a secretary do with a college degree?

Mr. Pat's daughter Mag bent over Velma's desk one afternoon, whispering in her smoke-raddled voice. "We're rooting for you, V. Sky's the limit, right? Maybe law school after this."

Law School? The world went bright then dark.

"You okay?" Mag said.

Velma remembered to breathe. "Yes, ma'am."

"Sky's the limit." She gave Velma's shoulder a solid squeeze.

On the thirteenth week, Professor Whitehead assigned the final essay. This one was to be presented orally and counted as thirty percent of their grade. He handed around a sheet to sign up for the presentation.

At her desk in the back, Velma turned to stone. She knew without looking anything up what oral meant: by mouth. She was supposed to get up and talk out loud *in front of the class.* Notions of graduation fled; she would never make it out of this room.

Her presentation was two weeks away. She wrote a paper about Baldwin Business School and listened as the other students read theirs. She thought about asking Professor Whitehead if she could hand hers in instead of reading it aloud, but a braver student asked and was refused.

At home she practiced, whispering in front of the bathroom mirror so Garnett couldn't hear. Speaking to her reflection, fear rose from her gut and closed her throat. The spit dried in her mouth. She stopped, drank water out of her toothbrush glass, and tried again.

Every night, the torturous pattern repeated itself. She started in an almost normal voice, but by the end of the first paragraph, her mouth grew too dry to speak. It wasn't thirst; it was terror and, with practice, it got worse instead of better. By the tenth night, she couldn't get through two sentences. She stared at her face in the bathroom mirror. "In August of 1943, I left our family's small farm to attend…" No use. Her tongue stuck to the roof of her mouth and the words refused to form. Frustration made her weep and the crying made her angry. Why was it her eyes could spout water, but her mouth turned dry as a creek bed in August? She gave up and came out of the bathroom.

Garnett looked up from her letter to Bobby. "Are you okay? It's that school, isn't it? I think they're pushing you too hard, expecting you to go to college and work full time. You ought to speak to Mr. Pat."

It's not being in school, Velma wanted to say, but her mouth did not cooperate.

Failure, or the fear of failure, began to affect her work. Twice in the past week, Mr. Pat interrupted his dictation to ask if she was all right. Being reminded of why she felt upset turned words to sand. Velma nodded mutely.

She could only imagine what would happen when she actually stood in front of the class. She would cry or throw up, maybe faint. The one thing she would not be able to do—and she knew this as certainly as she knew her name—was speak.

On the day she was scheduled to present, Velma Vernon skipped class, went to the Registrar's office, and dropped out of school.

37

She couldn't sleep that night for worrying about what Mr. Pat would say. The next morning, she sat in his office, staring at her knees, unable to meet his eyes. "It's not that I'm not grateful." She took a breath. "I just don't think I'm college material." The tears began. "But I want you to know how happy I am here in this office and working for you." He did not offer his handkerchief, but she had remembered to bring hers this time and wiped her eyes. "I'm truly sorry, but they told me I dropped out too late to get the firm's money back." She cleared her throat and looked up.

His dark eyes watched her. "Never mind. We will go on as before."

The gleam of approval was gone. She saw that she had disappointed him and went home that afternoon feeling forlorn.

She prayed about it. The answer she received was she didn't need to go to college. She'd grown up on a farm in Picayune, Mississippi, a girl whose only prospect had been to marry Chalmers Root. She'd found her way to the capital and become secretary to the founding partner of Hughes & Blair, the best law firm in the city, or maybe in the whole State of Mississippi. She had a new friend and was able to afford rent on half an apartment. This was her place and this was her talent. To some, it might not seem like enough, but she was satisfied being good at one small thing.

Praying calmed her enough to fall asleep, but she woke the next morning with the same nagging feeling of failure.

She wrote Mama, telling her what happened. Three days later, an answer arrived. "Best not to get ahead of ourselves in this world. College wasn't what you wanted. It was what others wanted for you, people who don't know us or our ways."

Velma never went against Mama, but she wasn't sure she agreed. If she hadn't stepped ahead of expectations, she'd still be on the farm, married to Chalmers, and probably pregnant by now.

Every day, she had to swallow the distress of failing the person she most admired. She watched Mr. Pat closely, trying to see if his opinion of her had changed. He was kind, always, but he seemed more remote. The air in the office felt chillier, as if potential had been sucked away along with college. She stayed later and typed faster to compensate for letting him down.

38

Bobby's letters quit coming. Velma noticed the worry on Garnett's face under the smile her friend put on each morning like makeup.

"I knew from his letters something big was coming." Garnett stood at the stove, frying them each an egg. "Between the censored parts I could tell."

"Do you know where he is?"

"He can't tell me. It's strictly forbidden, but I keep up with the news. The Fifth Army is headed for battle somewhere in Europe." She plopped an egg on Velma's plate and one on her own. "Every time we go to the movies and that music comes up for the news reel, I think I'm going to see him. Isn't that silly? Hundreds of men marching by the camera, and I'm going to spot Bobby's face."

"I don't think it's silly. I don't know how you stay so calm."

Garnett dragged her egg onto a piece of toast and cut it into squares. "That's our job, isn't it? Write letters, knit scarves, and act happy." She looked miserable.

"Bobby is very careful. You've always said so."

Garnett's face came alive. "His letters are actually numbered. That's how precise the man is. The last one I got was number forty-three."

On a Monday morning, halfway through the month, a worried looking woman came into the office. "I need to see Garnett Davis."

Velma went to the back to get her. When Garnett saw who it was, she started crying.

"Bobby's mother," Pauline whispered. The woman steered Garnett out into the corridor.

The door closed behind them and Velma waited, not even trying to type.

Minutes passed.

Garnett came back, smiling through her tears. "He's not dead. His parents got a telegram. Bobby's wounded, but he's not dead."

Velma threw her arms around her friend. Mag came out of her office and Mr. Pat out of his.

"Bobby's not dead," Garnett kept saying, wiping her eyes on Velma's handkerchief. "He's here in the States. He's in a hospital somewhere."

Mr. Pat took off his glasses and dabbed at his eyes. "What happy news."

Pauline hugged Garnett. "The very best news."

It felt like a celebration.

A week later, Garnett came flying into the apartment waving an envelope. "Letter number forty-five."

Velma quit mixing the potted meat for their next day's sandwiches. "What happened to forty-four?"

"Must have gotten lost." She ran a knife under the flap.

Velma watched as she pulled out a single sheet.

"This doesn't look like Bobby's handwriting." Dropping into a chair at the kitchen table, she read silently.

"Oh." Tears in her voice.

Velma felt her own eyes sting. "What?"

"Bobby lost an arm." Garnett's head dropped onto her arms and she sobbed.

Stricken, Velma got up and tried to hug her friend over the back of the chair. "I'm so sorry."

Garnett sat up. "I'm crying, okay, but only in front of you." She wiped her face with the dishtowel. "He's alive, isn't he? He's going to recover." She checked the postmark. "This came from Sam Houston,

Texas. He's out of the war, that's the good part. He won't come home in a box."

"I'm glad he's safe from the fighting," Velma said, "but I'm sorry for the reason."

Garnett's next words emerged muffled by the dishtowel. "He had such beautiful hands."

Velma recalled hating the look of Chalmers' hands. She felt small and selfish next to her friend.

Garnett went smiling into work the next day. "Bobby may have lost an arm, but he says he's still got one to put around me."

Bobby returned from Texas in late November and took up a lot of Garnett's free time. Velma tried not to mind. It was only right that her friend wanted to be with her beloved on Saturdays and Sundays and most nights. She was still there at bedtime and in the morning, wasn't she? They rode the bus together and worked in the same office.

Garnett gave Velma regular reports. Bobby had gotten much of the strength back in what remained of that arm. He was being fitted with a prosthetic. His old boss at the hardware store had kept his job for him. Wasn't that sweet? Velma tried to be a good listener, but she missed the days when she and Garnett rolled each other's hair and wandered through department stores.

Life is nothing but change. Might as well get used to it. That's what Mama said. On weekends, Velma walked through Kennington's and the Emporium by herself. She joined a knitting group that met at the church on Sunday afternoons. Comfortably-shaped ladies gently gossiped while their clicking needles turned out yards of scratchy, army-green scarves for the fighting men.

39

Velma was asleep on the Saturday night when Garnett turned on the overhead light and plopped onto her twin bed. "Guess what? We're getting married. Bobby proposed tonight."

Velma sat up. "That's … wonderful."

"He was so sweet, down on one knee in the parking lot outside the Rotisserie. Said he didn't want to do it inside the restaurant and cause a fuss." Garnett held out her left hand so Velma could see the tiny diamond set in gold. "We'll have a small church wedding, nothing fancy, but you'll be a bridesmaid, won't you? Say yes."

"It's beautiful, Garnett. I'm so happy for you."

"You haven't said yes."

Velma wrapped her arms around her knees. "Could I maybe serve punch instead?" The thought of walking down an aisle with people gawking was nearly as frightening as speaking in public.

Garnett said, "Don't be silly. My sister will be maid of honor and you and my cousin Marybeth will be bridesmaids. All you need to do is walk behind them."

"And try not to stumble." Velma pulled a foot out from under the covers. "Have you seen the size of my feet?"

"You won't stumble, and you're my best friend. You have to be in my wedding."

My best friend. The pleasure of those words almost banished dread.

In February of 1945, Velma marched down the aisle of Capitol Street Methodist church carrying a tight little bouquet of pink roses. She stared fixedly at the brunette curls of Garnett's cousin Marybeth, and kept her lips pressed into a smile small enough to hide her gums. In her private opinion, the purple taffeta dress ("Deep lilac," Garnett called it.) transformed her into an enormous grape, made worse by the dyed-to-match satin shoes in size ten. The store had to order a special pair to fit her. Her body had stopped its upward climb but, horrifyingly, her feet must still be growing.

Turning at the front of the church, Velma spotted Garnett waiting at the top of the aisle on her father's arm—a dark-haired princess in white satin and a gauzy veil. Velma had never seen anyone so beautiful or so blazingly happy. At the altar, Bobby looked thunderstruck.

During the reception in the church hall, the bridesmaids stood with the bride and groom and their parents, smiling and speaking to everyone who came through. Garnett's mother called it a "Receiving Line," and Bobby and Garnett seemed to enjoy themselves. Velma put on her gum-hiding smile, nodded, agreed how lovely the ceremony had been, and yes, weren't the bridesmaids' dresses pretty. Personally, she decided there must be a special room in hell where people were forced to stand in receiving lines.

"You're next," Garnett whispered. She stood on a chair and tossed her bouquet in Velma's direction, but Marybeth made a flying leap and grabbed it out of the air. Velma would not be next, but then she hadn't expected to be, and the only thing she minded was Garnett thinking she had.

Back in the empty apartment, stepping out of the lilac taffeta, Velma felt as alone as she had on her first night at Mrs. Moseley's. From the kitchen, the refrigerator came on with a grinding sound. Praying about solitude, the answer Velma received as she crawled under the covers was to cast aside self-pity the same way she'd stepped out of that purple dress. Garnett had not vanished from the earth. She'd married Bobby, her high school sweetheart. Velma would still see her every day. Was she jealous? Did she long for a white dress and her own Bobby? The only face she saw when she asked that question was Chalmers Root, and the answer was *No*.

She turned on her side. A sickle moon hung low in the sky outside the dark window. She was Mr. Pat's secretary, the face of Hughes & Blair, and perfectly capable of taking care of herself. Plenty of things to do on her own: get her hair done, the laundry, buy groceries. One of the Sunday knitting ladies had taught her how to crochet. During her lunch break on Monday, she would pick out yarn and start a set of place mats.

Everyone but Garnett seemed to think it odd that Velma chose to continue living alone. Mama wrote wondering if she planned to move back in with Mrs. Moseley. At the office, Doris, who lived with her parents, snickered that it must be nice to be able to invite a man home anytime you liked. Velma didn't know any men. She gave Doris the tight smile she'd learned from Mrs. Evans and did not respond.

Other women lived alone. Mr. Pat's daughter Mag did. Of course, she was older and divorced. The truth was, Velma had no intention of going back to Mrs. Moseley and her soup, and she didn't know any other girls well enough to be roommates. She could advertise and choose a stranger, but what if that stranger turned out like Doris, gumsnapping and yakking like a blue jay? She'd never get up the nerve to ask an unpleasant person to leave. Mr. Pat had raised her salary again. She could afford to pay rent on the entire apartment, an accomplishment that filled her with pride. When she identified this feeling, Velma felt ashamed. A good Christian should strive for humility.

Men were coming home from the war and Garnett said one of them had Velma's name on him. They just needed to figure out which one. That tickled Velma, thinking her name might be fastened to some man like a sales tag.

At night, in the apartment without her friend, she spoke sternly to herself. While she waited for this hypothetical man, she would learn to live alone, which she'd never done in her life, come to think of it. She'd gone from the farm to Mrs. Moseley's to rooming with Garnett. The magazines said you weren't ready to love someone else until you learned to love yourself. Velma set that as a goal.

Garnett and her new husband needed most of the apartment's furniture for their place. On Saturday, two weeks after the wedding, they arrived with a borrowed truck. Between the three of them, even with Bobby and his one arm, they managed to get the furniture down the outside stairs and into the truck bed.

Garnett looked around when they were done. "You don't have a table to eat on or a bed to sleep in."

"I've bought a mattress.

"You should get a roommate," Garnett said. "I worry about you rattling around here."

One thing that hadn't ended with marriage. Garnett still gave advice.

"Bobby worries, too," Garnett said. "Don't you, Bobby?"

Bobby nodded. He didn't look worried.

Another change Velma noticed in her friend. Bobby didn't talk much and Garnett spoke for him.

She helped them tie the furniture down. "I'll think about it," Velma said. "For now, I plan on furnishing this place." The word "furnish" made her feel very grown up.

40

At Batte's Furniture the next Saturday, Velma realized how little she knew about equipping a home. Mrs. Miller, the lady clerk, asked if she'd decided on a palette, and Velma didn't know what the word meant. She stared at the woman's daisy brooch instead of answering.

"Never mind," Mrs. Miller said. "Let's page through the catalog and you tell me what you like."

"I need a bed first," Velma said.

Mrs. Miller showed her a maple bedroom suite. They called it a suite, Velma learned, when the pieces matched. The bed had a headboard with turned posts, and there was a side table with a drawer and a cubby for magazines. It came with a four-drawer bureau for what Mrs. Miller called, "your undies." Because she'd always wanted one, Velma added a matching rocking chair. Everything had to be ordered from pictures because of the war shortages. Velma didn't mind. She had her mattress. This gave her something to look forward to. From another picture, she selected an oval dining table with four chairs. Mrs. Miller said the set was made of solid mahogany.

"I'll need to pay for the bedroom suite before we can order the table and chairs," Velma said. Mrs. Miller told her not to worry; she could set everything up on a monthly payment plan. She mentioned a figure that made Velma swallow hard, but she told Mrs. Miller to go ahead and order the dining room set. Without a table, she'd been eating her meals at the kitchen counter, sitting on a step-stool Garnett left behind, and listening to the radio for company.

Two months later, the maple bedroom set arrived. Velma made up the bed with a newly purchased white chenille spread, carefully centering the tufted medallion. She stood back admiring the effect. She practiced sitting on the bed and then lying on it. She went out of the room and came back in to surprise herself. She wished Garnett were here to see. She wished she had someone, anyone, to admire her first room.

She had chosen a china ballerina with a ruffled shade for her bedside lamp. Mrs. Miller said it was meant for a teenager, but Velma loved it and she'd never gotten to pick out anything so pretty when she'd been a teenager. Each time she turned the lamp on or off, it made her smile. The best part of living alone was suiting your own tastes.

A month after that, the dining room furniture arrived and Velma stared in awe at its formality. She ate her tuna surprise on the dark shining wood, using a place mat she'd crocheted. Seated at one end of the gleaming table, she felt as if she'd accidentally stumbled into someone else's house.

With Mrs. Miller's help, Velma next chose a sofa upholstered in a dusty rose and gray checked silk. She ordered a mahogany coffee table that rolled on little wheels. She bought herself a set of flowered china and a set of silver-plated flatware from Sears. The payments felt frightening, but walking from the bedroom to the dining room, and on into the living area, made Velma feel almost sinfully house-proud. A dozen more payments and it would all be hers. Time to show off.

Garnett had stopped by to admire things as they arrived, but now that the place was complete, Velma invited Bobby and her for dinner. She pulled one of the dining room chairs into the living area, so the three of them wouldn't be forced to sit lined up on the sofa like birds on a wire. After she'd paid for everything, she planned on adding an armchair. Dressing for work, Velma put on the blouse she'd worn to her job interview and realized she matched the couch. Dusty rose must be part of her palette.

At the library, Velma found a book on dinner parties: *Miss Love's Guide to Southern Feasts*. Miss Love said, "At a proper dinner party, you serve the guests at least three courses." They'd never had courses at the farm. They had dinner and, if Mama had time to make one, a dessert. Velma worried about a first course until she found an easy recipe for baked grapefruit. Her main course would be roasted chicken with baked potatoes and canned peas. For dessert, she tried Floating Island, described in *The Joy of Cooking* as an elegant and easy dessert. That turned out to be a lie. The result (poached egg whites in a vanilla sauce) hadn't been one bit easy, and the result did not look particularly appetizing.

Both Garnett and Bobby carried on over what Velma had done to the place. It was nice having three people at her new table, eating off her crocheted mats.

Velma asked Bobby to say the blessing. The halves of baked grapefruit looked festive, each one topped with a maraschino cherry.

"Very tasty." With one arm and his prosthetic, Bobby had trouble keeping the grapefruit in place while digging out the sections.

Velma watched, mortified. She should have remembered. In the kitchen, she cut up the roast chicken before bringing the platter out.

"It is the duty of the hostess to keep conversation flowing," the book on dinner parties said. Velma realized she should have made a list of topics. "Do you have trouble getting inventory for the hardware store with the shortages?" she asked Bobby.

"During the early years the boss says it was hard," Bobby said. "But since I've been back, the supply chain seems to be working better."

"Delicious chicken," Garnett said.

"Everything I know I learned from *The Joy of Cooking*," Velma said. She'd meant it as a joke, but the two of them nodded seriously.

"I got a copy as a wedding present," Garnett said.

Velma had bought hers.

"Every night, she's bent over that cookbook like it's the bible." Bobby looked at his wife fondly.

It was a comment Aunt Orrie would have found blasphemous, but Orrie, thankfully lived far, far away.

Garnett got Bobby to tell the story of acquiring their second-hand Ford.

"He is such a shrewd bargainer," Garnett said. "Stands his ground."

Bobby told the story, looking pleased.

Velma made a mental note. This was how it worked when you were married. You encouraged the other person to talk and then complimented what they said.

She brought out bowls of Floating Island. "I'm not sure about this dessert."

Garnett took a spoonful. "Tastes delicious."

"Frothy," Bobby said.

"He means light," Garnett said. "And it is, almost like eating a cloud." They scraped their bowls, claiming everything Velma fed them had been perfect.

When they were gone, Velma washed the dishes and left them to drain. She felt almost too tired to undress and sat on the edge of the bed rubbing her feet. This had been her first attempt at a dinner party, and she recognized the problem. When entertaining, you were supposed to cook *and* talk, either one of which took her entire attention. But the dinner had not been a failure and, if she gave more of them, things would probably get easier.

41

Garnett invited Velma on an outing. "Not a date," she said. Just Bobby bringing along a friend. The man's name was Harold Meeks and he worked as a printer for the morning newspaper.

"Why isn't he off in the service?" Velma said. They were having their lunchtime sandwiches in the mailroom.

"Asthma." Garnett spoke through a mouthful of ham salad.

"Where are we going?" Velma wondered why she'd said yes. She dreaded the evening already.

"We'll let the men decide." Garnett licked mayonnaise off her upper lip. "Won't be anything fancy. Don't dress up."

It was definitely a date and Velma hadn't been on one since Chalmers Root took her to the senior prom. She kept trying on clothes, finally settling on a dress she'd bought for church—navy blue and white plaid with a black collar and a narrow belt. The "Fit and Flare" look, according to the salesclerk at Kenningtons. Velma tilted the mirror above the bureau to see the bottom half. The flared skirt did make her waist look smaller.

Harold was a little shorter. She shouldn't have worn heels. He had thinning brown hair and a nice smile. When he held open the car door, Velma spotted a rind of black under every fingernail. Nothing wrong with honest labor, but she would have scrubbed harder.

Now came the difficult part: conversation. Sitting in the backseat of Bobby's car, Velma asked what a printer did. Harold explained. The work sounded hard, and dirty enough to explain the fingernails.

He asked if she enjoyed being a secretary. Garnett chimed in from the front seat: "Velma is a *terrific* secretary." Harold asked what church she went to, and told her he was a Presbyterian.

Velma asked if he'd always lived in Jackson (Yes). Where was she from? After she said "Out from Picayune," Velma couldn't think of any more questions and the backseat went quiet.

They went to a bowling alley. Velma had never bowled and turned out to be terrible at it. When they handed out shoes, she had to be fitted with a pair from the men's side. Everyone got a kick out of that. Velma felt her face doing its tomato imitation.

Bobby was a good bowler. With only one arm, he knocked down more pins than the rest of them. Everyone was better than Velma. She suffered through their chuckles at her awkwardness and tried to pay attention to the lessons Harold gave: how to hold the ball, how to walk forward, the proper way to bend a knee, swing her arm, and keep her eye on the pins. No matter. Her balls rumbled weakly down the lane before limping into an alley. "Harder," Garnett said. The next one leapt across their lane and into the next. Groans all around.

Finally, thank heaven, bowling was finished. They went to the Toddle House for pie and coffee. Offered a choice between chocolate and butterscotch cream, Velma decided butterscotch counted as a new experience. She kept mental track of these, the good ones like butterscotch pie, and the bad like bowling.

"Did you enjoy yourself?" Harold said.

"Yes, thank you," Velma lied. She wanted him to stop talking. She had never tasted anything so delicious as butterscotch cream pie, and took tiny bites to make it last.

"She hated bowling." Garnett poked Velma and laughed. "Try not to hold it against her."

Velma wished Garnett wouldn't speak for her. "I wasn't very good at it."

"I won't hold it against you." Harold Meeks smiled his nice smile.

He and Bobby started talking about the Senators, which turned out to be Jackson's baseball team. Velma knew as little about baseball as she did about bowling, but tried to look interested and laugh in the right places.

They took her home and Harold walked her to the bottom of the stairs.

"I had a very nice time," Velma said. "Thank you for inviting me." Polite Responses, it turned out, worked for dates, too.

Harold said he had a nice time, also, and made a move like he might want to take her hand. Velma kept hold of her purse. They nodded at one another and Harold left.

She met Garnett in the mailroom the next morning. "That was a failure."

"Don't be silly. Harold thought you were cute."

Cute? No one had ever called Velma cute. If she were a betting person and, being Baptist, she wasn't, she would put money on never hearing from Harold Meeks again. Which was fine with her. He was a step up from Chalmers Root, but he didn't make her heart beat the way magazines said love should, and dating took as much out of her as a dinner party.

42

At Garnett's urging, Velma joined the Mississippi Secretaries Association. It was a good way to meet people. All the other secretaries belonged. Velma attended the monthly meetings and in June, Garnett, Pauline, and Doris decided to go to Biloxi for the annual convention. Velma must come. Garnett and Pauline would leave their husbands at home. They could share two rooms. It would be such fun—just the four of them in Pauline's car.

Velma was too excited to sleep the night before they left. She kept packing and re-packing her suitcase. Should she bring her bathing suit, a modest navy one piece? She couldn't picture showing that much skin in front of a bunch of strangers, but she put it in. Her new beige suit for meetings. She settled on the Fit-and-Flare plaid for evenings.

This was her first vacation. No one in her family took them. The notion of paying good money to go to another town and sleep in a strange bed, possibly not as comfortable as your own, and then pay more money to eat unfamiliar food, surrounded by folks you'd never see again, was so foreign that Papa found it, if not criminal, highly suspicious. Other people took vacations. President Roosevelt went down to Warm Springs for his health. Papa said he felt sorry for him having to go so far when a decent wife could have kept him happy at home, but Papa had never approved of Mrs. Roosevelt. Mama said presidents were in a special class and the man wasn't well.

A camp meeting, now, that was different. A good camp meeting with a hellfire and damnation preacher could set a person up for a year. Papa said it was as good as a tonic. Velma had been to plenty of camp meetings: sitting under a tent, in a hard chair on bumpy ground, sweltering through a hot summer night, slapping mosquitoes and flapping away moths with a funeral parlor fan. Sweat running down her legs while she looked around without seeming to for cute boys. At the front of the tent on a wooden stage, the visiting preacher would threaten the audience with eternal fire if they didn't rise in full view of everybody and testify, if they didn't march up to the stage and be saved or get born again outside in the muddy river. Some people got into it, had themselves saved and reborn every year, testifying to stuff nobody wanted to hear. Velma followed the saved people down to the lake after the meeting and watched them get dunked. She and Mama did not participate. Mama said she'd been saved at her first baptism and there was no need to show off by doing it again. Besides, there might be moccasins in that water.

Velma struggled briefly over taking the trip to Biloxi, spending money she could be saving, but decided it didn't count as a vacation, being secretarial, and it happened on a weekend so she wouldn't miss work. She might pick up tips on how to do her job better, and, this was a secret she had not shared, she'd seen a notice in the program for a typing contest and signed herself up.

Signing up was the easy part, although watching the application disappear down the brass mail chute outside the firm's tenth floor office made her slightly ill. Being good at something like typing was part of her job, but entering a contest came close to what Mama might call showing off. Velma went over the reasons she'd done it: she could only know how good she was by being measured against others. She'd been the best at Baldwin Business College and she was the fastest secretary at Hughes & Blair, but what did that mean in the larger world? This was a way of testing herself. If she did well, Mr. Pat would see that, although she might not be college material, she wasn't a failure.

On Saturday morning in Biloxi, Velma woke with her heart pounding as if she'd been chased through sleep. Not the dream about

Uncle Drew again—but something. She sat up in the strange room, Garnett still asleep in the other bed. *The contest.* Her stomach lurched. *What had she been thinking?* When Garnett woke, Velma confessed to what she'd done.

"You're competing?" Garnett screamed. "I'm so proud of you." She gave Velma a breath-squeezing hug. "You'll be fantastic."

"I'm scared to death."

"Wait until I tell the others. We'll all come watch you in the finals."

"I don't think I'll make it to the finals."

"If you do, we'll be there."

After breakfast, which Velma couldn't eat for the snake fastened around her throat and the cats galloping through her stomach, the contestants gathered in one of the big meeting rooms. Rows of typewriters, each with a number. She got her name checked off and found her machine. A stack of paper had been placed next to each. Velma settled into her chair with her purse at her feet and smiled at the lady to her left. The lady nodded back. Most of the women looked older and more experienced. Winning didn't matter. She was only here to measure her skill and see where there might be room for improvement.

A large woman with short gray hair stood and cleared her throat. She wore what Velma called old lady shoes, the kind with sensible heels and laces. They were given five minutes of practice to limber their fingers. Velma rolled a piece of bond paper into her machine. Her nervousness showed itself as an odd tremble, which seemed to begin in the keys she struck, vibrate up through her elbows, shoulders and down to her knees, which jerked uncontrollably. She quit typing, flexed her hands, and tried again. If she focused on the words, the shaking subsided. They were typing a piece her class had used in high school, used so often that Velma had memorized it.

When the Proctor, which was what the gray-haired woman called herself, said "Time," Velma quit typing and looked around. The woman to her left, the one who'd nodded, had three whole pages. No way of knowing how many errors, which were deducted from your speed on the real test. Only the accurate words counted. The Proctor announced the rules. They would begin with a three-minute exercise.

Scores would be tabulated, and the top twenty typists would remain for the second session. Everyone eliminated was free to leave.

Velma relaxed. If she got knocked out in the first round, she'd have time to join Garnett, who was down the hall in a session called, "How to Deal with a Difficult Boss." A text was handed out and they were warned to keep it face down until the Proctor told them to start. She checked the stopwatch she carried on a leather strap and said, "Begin."

Velma turned her paper over and started typing. She felt easy in her body, as if the nervousness had used itself up during the practice test. She let the words flow from the page through her fingers without bothering her mind with their meaning. At the word "Stop," she took her fingers off the keys. The Proctor's assistants made their way around the room collecting results. A buzz of voices while they were tallied.

Velma's mind wandered, for no reason, back to Chalmers Root. If she had married him, she'd have a child by now, maybe two. She'd be at a Camp Meeting instead of here in Biloxi, sitting next to Papa and Mama with a family of her own. She tried to imagine what a child of Chalmers would look like and saw a large boy, red-faced from the sun, freckled the way Velma got in summer, with Chalmers' big hands. He'd be grabbing her around the neck, giving sticky kisses.

Names were called and Velma heard her own. "The rest of you may leave," the Proctor said. People rustled papers and gathered their things. The woman on Velma's left was gone. Twenty of them remained scattered around the room, glancing self-consciously at each other.

The next test lasted five minutes and, after that one, ten typists were left. Velma started getting nervous again and reminded herself not to be foolish. Mr. Pat would be proud as Punch if she went home as one of the ten fastest typists in the State of Mississippi. He'd forget all about the college business. Hadn't the lady said all ten finalists would receive a Certificate? Personal items weren't allowed in the office, but she could hang it next to her bed. Pauline kept pictures of her children taped to the desk's pullout writing surface. Garnett kept Bobby's photo in her top drawer. When Mr. Blair got mean because he'd had a bad day or gotten a bad judge, Garnett waited until he closed his office door, opened the drawer, and spoke to her husband. "See what I mean, Bobby?" Mr. Blair's temper was why she chose that session down the hall.

The next round was the semi-final. Ten minutes and only three people would be left. Velma couldn't believe her ears when her name was called. She was a *state finalist*. She didn't care how she did after this. Glory enough.

The three finalists were moved to a table at the front of the room facing the audience. People filed in to watch. Velma felt self-conscious about her legs until she peeked under the table and saw that the cloth came all the way to the floor.

She watched Garnett, Pauline, and Doris take seats. This contest was scary, but it didn't hold a candle to giving a speech in front of a class. This was only typing and Velma typed every day of her life. Typing was what she did best. She made a bridge with her fingers and flexed her hands. Garnett gave her two thumbs up. Velma grinned, and covered her mouth to hide her gums.

She sat in the middle. The lady on her left was small and round with plaited hair wrapped around her head like Heidi. She possessed a formidable bosom, discreetly displayed under a belted, black dress. She looked fiercely efficient. On Velma's right, the finalist was older than her, but still young. The woman hunched over the machine as if getting ready to wrestle. She wore a pink suit over an aqua blouse. An unfortunate combination, Miss Webb might say, but clothes did not affect typing speed.

The Proctor introduced them, "Our three finalists," giving their names, home towns, and where they each worked. There would be three, three-minute speed trials. Scores would be averaged. The material had never been seen by the contestants.

Velma focused on her machine and on her fingers with their fresh coat of Vanilla Blush. She decided not to look at the audience until this was over. Up went the stopwatch, and she heard the word "Begin." Turning over the first page, her fingers flew over the keys. Her mind traveled to a place where no one watched; there were no other contestants, no timekeeper, only the words and her fingers flashing them onto the page.

Three times they did this and finally it was over. The finalists sat back and smiled at each other in relief. Velma felt odd, almost dizzy, as if she'd been carried off to some kind of typing wonderland, but was now returned to her own awkward body.

The judges conferred. Papers were marked. Nods exchanged. The Proctor came to the front. "Our third-place winner at ninety words per minute is…" Velma didn't hear the name, but watched as the girl in the pink suit stood to applause and accepted her medal.

"Our second-place winner at ninety-six words per minute is…" All Velma sensed in the confusion—It wasn't her.

The lady in black stood and then there was only Velma, standing in her new beige suit, ears ringing with embarrassment. She smiled at the applause that arrived in waves, burning against her skin. Feeling very tall, she gave the audience a little bow of appreciation and walked to the Proctor. No, she wouldn't say anything, no thank you, not into the microphone.

"This is such an honor." She whispered to the Proctor, bending her head so the gold medal on its red ribbon could be placed around her neck.

To celebrate, the girls took her out to Mary Mahoney's for dinner. Pauline said the place was famous for seafood, and Velma ordered flounder stuffed with crabmeat. The girls insisted on buying champagne. Mississippi was a dry state, but the Gulf Coast operated like a foreign country. Anything was possible down here at the edge, including alcohol passing Velma's Baptist lips for the first time in her life.

Velma Vernon, the fastest typist in the entire State of Mississippi, with champagne bubbling through her like liquid silver, lighting her up, making her giggle and not care if her gums showed. Mr. Pat was going to be so proud.

43

April and warm at last at Creekmore Inn. Reservations poured in for the summer. The hotel had prospered during the war. People didn't have enough gas coupons to take distant vacations and were happy to come to a country resort.

Brushing her teeth, Lillian smiled at her image in the mirror. She'd gotten a telegram. After a year away, Will had a leave. She wasn't sure where the ship was returning from, but it would dock in Long Beach, California, seven days from now. The thought of seeing him brought such happiness, she thought she might burst.

First, she needed to get to the west coast. Ernestine agreed to watch the girls. Jimbo, James and Faye's son, was stationed a hundred miles south in San Diego, and his wife Kitty agreed to accompany Lillian across country. James offered to lend them his Cadillac and managed to scrounge enough gas coupons to get them there and back. In the big car, taking turns driving, they could arrive before Will's ship docked.

Lillian felt almost drunk with excitement. She loved a road trip and this was her first real adventure since Will left. Kitty, a dozen years younger, was nothing but fun. If you said you craved a beer at eleven in the morning, she didn't frown and shake her head like Ernestine. She said, "Good idea."

Another telegram arrived. Will's ship would arrive Saturday, a day earlier than expected. He had seventy-two hours leave, and now they only had five days to get themselves there. James bribed a travel agent and found them hotel rooms in Anaheim.

Lillian pulled clothes from her closet, folding them roughly. California was warm, people said, but got cool at night. She packed the red silk dress she'd waved goodbye in, along with a flowered sundress and matching jacket she'd copied from a picture in Vogue. She'd never been to California and didn't want to look like a hick.

Helen walked in and spotted the suitcase. "Where are you going?"

"To see Daddy."

"Take me with you."

"I can't, sweetie."

"Don't leave me." Helen's voice quivered. "Please."

The whining irritated Lillian. "Not now. Mama needs to think."

"You can't leave me." The child sounded panicked.

"Daddy only has three days. I have to hurry." Lillian considered the brown and white striped sundress and decided it looked drab.

"I won't let you go without me."

"Sweetie, this is a grownup trip. Aunt Ernestine will be here with you and your sister."

"Aunt Ernestine makes us pray." Helen was screeching. "She doesn't let us talk while we're eating."

The piercing sound produced an instant headache. Lillian squeezed her temples. "Stop it this minute."

Helen stomped the floor, shrieking. "I won't let you go without me."

Lillian slapped her daughter across the face. Hard.

The sound echoed in a suddenly silent room. Helen's eyes went wide with shock.

Penitent, Lillian said, "Look what you made me do." She had spanked Helen's bottom plenty of times, but she'd never slapped her face. Helen's stunned expression and the ugly red handprint on the child's cheek, made Lillian ashamed. "Go wash your face and let me finish packing." She folded the best of her underwear, replaying the slap. She'd been forced into it. Helen would drive a saint to violence. She must never admit to doing it.

Never mind. She threw her suitcase into the back of the hotel Woody. Ernestine drove her to Canton. *Helen would forget.* Nothing mattered now but reaching Long Beach before Saturday.

At James's house, she and Kitty put their bags in the trunk of the big white Cadillac. Lillian got into the driver's seat, ready for the first shift. James handed her a wad of folded bills through the driver's window. "In case you need a little extra."

"Best brother ever." She blew him a kiss and set her face west, putting her daughters and the hotel further from her mind with every mile.

She and Kitty swapped drivers every four hours, one of them sleeping in the back seat while the other drove. They stopped only for gas, coffee, and greasy hamburgers. The Cadillac's powerful engine took them up and across Arkansas, into and out of a corner of Oklahoma, and through interminable Texas. In the fresh March air, they rolled the windows down, and during the times both were awake, played the radio loud and sang along to "Paper Doll" and "Pistol-Packing Mama."

Lillian searched the static for a new station. "You've got a good voice."

"Yours is good, too," Kitty said.

Lillian shook her head. "None of us Creekmores can sing."

When they crossed the line into New Mexico, Lillian said, "We're almost there."

Kitty unfolded the map. "Not yet." She poked at it and Lillian glanced. "Oh, shoot, I forgot Arizona." Kitty crawled into the back seat and Lillian turned the radio low. Bing Crosby crooned "Moonlight Becomes You." She had never felt so dirty, parched, and windblown in her entire life. She tilted the rearview mirror and studied her image. The desert air must be terrible for her looks, or maybe it was the worrying; something had aged her. Her face looked thinner and there were fine lines at the corners of her eyes that hadn't been there when Will left.

What if he didn't love her anymore? Her heart gave a painful skip. She kept her foot on the gas and told herself not to jinx the reunion. All women probably had these doubts. Will wrote almost every week, the letters filled with talk of how much he missed her and the girls. She got teary thinking about those letters, and wiped her eyes on her hem of her skirt. She would see him in, she glanced at the tiny gold Bulova watch he'd given her, fifteen hours.

They didn't have time to drive into Anaheim and find their hotel before the ship docked. At a restaurant on the outskirts of Long Beach, they carried their square makeup cases inside and sat at the counter, one ordering coffee while the other cleaned up and changed in the rest room. Lillian put on the red dress, washed her face, and re-creamed it, but nothing made the lines disappear. She'd bought a new lipstick: Jungle Red. Will liked red. She dabbed Blue Grass cologne behind her ears and on her wrists.

Kitty came out in a yellow sundress that made the men at the counter turn and stare. She held out a bottle of perfume called Shocking. "Want to try it?"

Lillian sniffed and shook her head. "Will likes Blue Grass. At least he used to." She gave herself a last critical look in the mirror of her compact. Who knew what he liked now?

Soldiers and sailors crowded the area around the dock. Pretty girls carried flowers. She should have gotten flowers; she hadn't thought to bring him anything except herself. Children whined, pulled along by harried mothers. Lillian smiled, happy not to have Helen and April in tow. The warm air shimmered with a circus smell of popcorn and roasting peanuts. An enormous gray ship rose above them like a steel building.

She couldn't find Will in the sea of men waving from the rail. Then she did. At almost the same moment, his eyes found hers. It felt like an electric shock the way he smiled and waved, a validation. The crowd and noise disappeared. She waved back with one hand and wiped tears with the other.

In his white dress uniform, he was as blazingly beautiful as she remembered, and when he finally made it down the gangplank and fought his way through the crowd, he grabbed her in a rib-crushing hug, lifting her off her feet. Lillian closed her eyes and held on, as happy as she ever had been in her life. This was her man and he had come back still loving her.

In bed that night, in their small hotel in Anaheim, Lillian lay in Will's arms. "Let's just stay here for three days and only get up to brush our teeth," she said.

Will pushed her hair back with one hand and searched her face. "Do you know how much I've missed you?"

Lillian gave his shoulder a mock bite. "Show me again."

He looked thinner and more muscular than she remembered, and so tan. She couldn't get over it, and kept running her hands over his chest and arms. There was a confidence to him now, a swagger she didn't remember.

They interrupted lovemaking only to eat giggling meals with Kitty and Jimbo and to take the Cadillac on brief explorations along the California coast. Jimbo offered Will a turn driving, but Will refused, saying the twisting roads made him dizzy.

More often than she wished, that February night with Bob Bradshaw rose into Lillian's mind, not comparing, but in shame. She pushed the images out as soon as they arrived. Will never needed to know.

"Too long gone and too soon over." Lillian stood on her toes at the dock, her head pressed against Will's chest.

"It's harder leaving this time," he said. He couldn't tell her where the ship had come from or where they were headed.

Lillian wanted to wail the way her daughter had. "You can't go. I won't let you." But she was a patriotic wife and strong women did not wail. She held Will's face in her hands. "Stay safe, you hear me?"

He hugged her tighter.

"I love you, Will Hughes."

"I love you, too, Lillian Hughes. Take care of the girls. Won't be long now."

After he went aboard, Lillian let herself cry.

"Oh, honey." Kitty put an arm around her. "He'll be back before you know it. You saw the newspapers. The Chinese have invaded Burma and our boys took back New Guinea. We've about whipped those Japs."

Kitty didn't need to worry about Jimbo. As an enlisted man, he worked in Navy stores in San Diego, handing out uniforms and other gear. She missed him, but he wouldn't get killed.

On the trip back east, they took their time, spending James' money on cheap motels, eating chicken-fried steaks in roadside restaurants, and drinking in dark bars. Inside the car, they drove in silence until Lillian would start. "Didn't Will look amazing?" Or Kitty. "Wasn't Jimbo skinny? I hardly recognized him." Jimbo had lost a lot of weight in basic training and looked, for him, almost svelte. They picked apart those three magic days thread by thread.

Kitty was a pretty girl, with long legs, a voluptuous body, and dark hair that curled around her face. At every stop, men tried to pick her up. In a diner outside nowhere Texas, a grizzly man leaned between them with beery breath. "You're the cutest thing east of Albuquerque."

Kitty gave the guy a steely smile. "Why don't I turn around so you can butter the other side?"

Watching this, Lillian realized men no longer looked at her in this way. She might be cute, but she was no longer young like Kitty. The bloom had faded.

She drove with her skirt hiked up, letting the wind from the open windows cool her legs. On the road, they talked about how neither one of them would ever, *ever* cheat on their husbands. If there was any person in the world Lillian might confide in about that night with Bob Bradshaw, it was easy-going Kitty. But she did not. Her mouth was closed forever on that mistake. Better to lie and swear never, ever. She would keep the whole mess in the back of her mind, where it would grow tinier and tinier until it became a mere pinprick in her memory.

44

Throughout the summer of 1944, Lillian followed the war news on Knox's crackling shortwave radio. The Germans attacked London with V-1 rockets, terrorizing the population. In the Pacific, Navy fighter pilots downed 220 Japanese planes, losing only twenty of their own. She wouldn't be gloating over that "only" if Will were one of those pilots. Three months and twelve letters since she'd seen him in California. From hints between the words blacked out by the censors, she guessed he was somewhere near Hawaii. Lillian stored the letters in a cigar box next to her bed, and reread them almost superstitiously. Her eyes on his words kept him safe. She wrote back once a week, making Helen sit still long enough to add a page of words and pictures.

At the hotel, in spite of rationing and shortages, guests filled every room. Wartime meant fewer men, and more of them in uniform, but older couples still came for the cure. Ernestine was off again to Chattanooga. Left in charge, Lillian felt unaccountably tired. She didn't resent her sister's going, and God knows the hotel needed Knox's salary. "Doing his part for the war effort in pharmaceuticals," as Ernestine like to say.

She started her day in the kitchen with Lena, checking the menus for lunch and dinner to make sure nothing needed to be ordered from the wholesaler in Canton. In the dark, low-ceilinged room, the big wood stove pumped heat.

"Sliced ham for lunch today," Lillian said to Lena. She felt sweat roll between her breasts. The room was already hot as the inside of a bake oven. She mopped her forehead with a damp handkerchief.

Lena sat on her stool, elbow-deep in dough. "Can't be bothering with you until I get my rolls set." Lena Fletcher reigned over the kitchen. During the season, she oversaw three meals a day, seven days a week, and had done so for four decades. Bent by arthritis, her thunderous voice still caused the other servants to jump. The job had not improved her disposition.

"Roast chicken for dinner." Lillian checked the big refrigerator on the side porch. "Looks like we have plenty of birds."

"*Wood.*" Lena hollered at two little boys, who galloped down the steep back stairs to the woodlot.

In the dank washroom off the far side of the kitchen, Bobby Lee sang while he scrubbed the breakfast dishes. Lillian stuck her head in the dining room. The tables were being reset. Everything looked in order.

"Parthenia?" She walked down the porch of the one-story family wing and peered into the windowless linen room. "Has Savannah finished with the rooms in the Annex?"

The head housekeeper stepped into the light with an armload of fresh sheets. "Believe she has."

"Check on her, will you? Yesterday she forgot to change the towels." Savannah was a lanky, long-legged woman, scatter-brained as a chicken.

"Soon as I get done with the Cold Part," Parthenia said.

The Hotel had grown with its clientele. The original house was called the Warm Part; the Cold Part, built parallel to the first building, had been named for its lack of heat. The newest wing, parallel to that, was the Annex. The Cold Part and the Annex were closed from Labor to Memorial Day, but now, in summer, every room was occupied: three wings, two stories, sixty-six rooms, everything, upstairs and down, connected by covered verandas.

Lillian walked out to the office to get a lunch count from Jimmy Ray. On weekends, people made reservations to come for a meal, not to stay overnight, driving up from Canton or Jackson. This meant two, sometimes three seatings.

Back in the kitchen, Lillian gave Lena a final number and made sure the waiters' white coats were clean and starched. A quick trip around the dining room to check on the flowers Flora May had arranged. The tablecloths and napkins were spotless; the silverware sparkled. Lillian gave Ellis a nod to ring the big bell out front announcing lunch.

Once people were seated, she did a quick run by the children's porch to make sure Helen and April were eating with the other under-twelves and behaving themselves. Back to the kitchen to help with the service. The place hummed with a kind of controlled frenzy.

On the side porch next to the family wing, she joined Flora May in peeling and dicing peaches for the first course of fruit compote. She checked that the lettuce had been washed, dried, and torn for the green salads. She tasted the dressing and added salt. On a long table inside the steaming kitchen, Lena and her son Johnny filled plates with sliced ham, parsley potatoes, and butterbeans. The corn bread, baked into crisp sticks, would be passed around the tables by Ellis and Preston. The waiters went smoothly through the two doors to the dining room, carrying round trays laden with food through the right door, and bringing empty dishes to the washroom through the left. Bobby Lee, wrapped in an enormous, filthy apron, scraped leftovers into the slop barrel for the pigs, before soaping and scalding plates, cups, glasses, and cutlery. By the time dessert was served, blackberry cobbler with hard sauce today, the worst was over.

Lillian made sure the girls went down for their naps and gave Jimmy Ray a break in the office to have lunch. This was Friday, which meant payday. She totaled the hours next to each servant's name, got cash from the safe, counted wages into envelopes, and labeled them. In the late afternoon, the help would gather outside the back door of the office, a trailing line of tired, cheerful people collecting their week's pay.

Between lunch and dinner, she made sure the dining room was re-set, and saw the children up from their naps.

"Mama, Mama, Mama." For Helen, saying something once was never enough. "Can we go swimming, can we, can we?"

"Do you have a grownup to watch you?"

"We can ask Flora May."

"I meant a grownup who can swim. See if you can find Ernest." Ernest, Jimmy Ray's nephew had lifeguard training.

"Ernest tries to drown us. Every day he drowns us."

If only. Helen's shrill voice brought on another headache. "You heard me."

The child ran off, shrieking. "Ernest, Ernest, Ernest. Mama says you have to watch us swim."

Lillian craved a cigarette. She needed to put her swollen ankles up and have a cold beer. Instead, she chatted with guests rocking on the verandas and invited three or four of them to come for drinks in the Retreat before dinner. She went to the Fishes' Club to make sure BeeBee had everything he needed for the late afternoon crowd: ice, soft drinks, soda water and tonic for set ups, plenty of cold beer and packaged snacks.

She stuck her head in the door of the women's bathhouse next to the Fishes' Club. Parthenia was giving a sweet oil massage to a woman in the sulfur-smelling room. Two other ladies waited their turn, neck-deep in iron-stained tubs filled with hot mineral water, heads wrapped in towels, steam rising around them. Lillian smiled, greeted everyone, and reminded herself to make sure these "extras" got put on the tab.

Flora May took the wet children back to clean up for dinner. Lillian supervised the payroll. She reminded Ellis to bring ice and set-ups down to the Retreat, checked on dinner with Lena, and went to change.

At five, she unlocked the liquor cabinet and received her guests in the cool, screened room Knox had built for Ernestine beneath the Family Wing. From five to six, Lillian could almost relax. Talking, smoking, sipping bourbon and water, she asked where the new people were from and where they were headed. Almost as good as traveling.

The dinner bell rang and she tactfully parted the guests from their silver mint julep cups and sent them to the dining room. She poured

Lena a jigger of bourbon, took a slug herself, and locked the liquor cabinet. Stopping first by the kitchen to leave Lena her liquor, she went out to the office. Jimmy Ray confirmed the hotel was full; he'd been turning people away all afternoon. In addition to the massages Lillian saw in the women's side of the bathhouse, Preston had given two in the men's section. At six, Jimmy Ray left for the day, and Lillian was in charge of the office until it closed at nine.

Her feet hurt. Behind the desk, she slipped her heels off and rubbed her arches. Forcing the tight shoes back on, she made change for the jukebox, sold candy bars and cigarettes, checked in late arrivals, rang up money for dinners, and took reservations over the telephone. At nine, she locked the office and said goodnight to the guests still rocking on the veranda or dancing and playing pool in the Pavilion.

On her way to her room, she picked up the plate Lena had left warming for her on the shelf over the kitchen stove. Setting it on the small table by her bed, she went through to the screened sleeping porch and checked on her slumbering daughters.

Back in her room, Lillian slipped her feet out of the heels she'd put on for dinner, peeled off her damp clothes, and put on her nightgown. She climbed into bed to eat, almost too tired to chew. She must have walked eight miles today. She re-read Will's last letter and looked at the small snapshot he'd sent. In it, he leaned against a thatched hut, sand underfoot, palm trees in the background. He wore his khaki officer's hat and trousers, but no shirt. Still the handsomest man she'd ever seen. She rubbed an aching foot. Hawaii, or wherever he was, looked like fun.

Stretched out on the bed, Lillian examined her ankles, as swollen as Lena's. She needed to get off her feet more.

When Ernestine was here, they divided the tasks and work didn't seem as hard. Her older sister refused to get frazzled. Everything got done, but Ernestine never appeared to hurry or raise her voice. She strolled through the rose garden early in the morning with a basket and shears, cutting a few flowers for the tables before the dew dried. During the weeks Knox was home, they ate breakfast out there in a little gazebo. Ellis had to bring their food on a tray all the way from the kitchen. At night, no matter how exhausting the day had been,

Ernestine and Knox ate together after the dining room cleared, using candles and the good silver.

Part of Lillian found this admirable, even enviable, but another part thought it a pity they never noticed how late the help had to stay to serve them. At midnight, when the guests were asleep, or ought to be, Ernestine and Knox went down to the pool, took off their clothes, and swam naked. This sounded romantic, except Lillian knew the frigid temperature of that dark green water. The two of them got caught one night by late-arriving guests. Ernestine told Lillian how hilarious it had been trying to pull clothes on over their wet skin.

Was she jealous of her sister? Lillian was jealous of anyone who had a husband around these days, even a husband as short and balding as Knox. It was Maude she missed, Maude she thought of when something funny happened, or when she longed to complain about Ernestine, with her "a lady never" rules and her more-religious-than-thou reminders. "Everything in moderation," Ernestine liked to say when Lillian poured a second drink. Her sister had never once, to Lillian's knowledge, let loose and gotten drunk. She never shouted, or burst into laughter either.

Lillian massaged her other foot. In spite of the killing work and not having Maude to talk to, with Ernestine gone, she got to enjoy her drinks in the Retreat without being frowned at like a drunk.

She put Will's letter away and closed the cigar box. Sleepily, she thought how proud he would be to see her running this entire hotel. Not as easy now as it had been before marriage and the children. She never remembered being this tired.

45

In August, Lillian discovered a reason for the exhaustion and swollen ankles—she was pregnant. Three months along the doctor in Canton said. Things had been so hectic she'd hardly noticed the missed periods. Thank whatever goodness existed because counting back, three months ago Will Hughes had been stateside, instead of— She shivered at the thought of the one night she forgot who she was and gave in to lust, too drunk and lonely to care. This baby must be God's way of showing forgiveness.

Kitty nicknamed it Mister Anaheim because that's where he'd been conceived. Another chance, and this one had better be a Mister. She wrote Will the thrilling news. He wrote back, saying how happy he was, and how much he hated being far away (A lie, though appreciated. He had never liked seeing her pregnant.). Will wrote that he counted the days until his return. A package arrived with a little seaman's cap for Will Junior.

The doctor in Canton sent Lillian to another in Jackson. "You have a dickey ticker," this doctor said.

"My heart?" Lillian felt it beat harder with apprehension.

"Nothing you need to worry about," he said, "but pregnancy puts an extra burden on it."

Ernestine, back from Chattanooga, had driven down with her.

"He said I would need a Caesarean," Lillian told her sister. "And not to plan on another baby."

"Three is plenty," Ernestine said.

Lillian looked at her sister's prim mouth. Ernestine probably thought two was enough, but then she'd managed to produce two sons. A Caesarean meant a scar, but at least she'd be knocked out, which was how she preferred experiencing childbirth. She'd been unconscious for the first two. People carried on about the glories of natural childbirth. *No, thank you.* She would wake to the news of her son.

46

On January 2, 1945, Lillian came out of the anesthetic into gut-wrenching pain. She turned her head to see a strange woman in the other bed holding a tiny blue bundle. Her heart jumped. This must be the room for the mothers of sons.

A nurse came by. "Mrs. Hughes, you're awake. Congratulations. You have a beautiful baby girl."

Lillian closed her eyes and groaned.

"I'll get you something for that pain."

The nurse left. Tears trickled into Lillian's ears. She had failed again. No Will Junior. Through a fog of pain, she tried to think her way back: They were in Jackson. The baby was due. Ernestine was there. They had given her a pill to help her relax before the anesthetist put her to sleep. She couldn't remember anything after that.

The door opened. Ernestine stuck her head around. "The nurse said you were awake. How do you feel?"

"Horrible. It's a girl."

Ernestine stood by the bed patting Lillian's hand. "I know you're disappointed, but you have a healthy baby. Let's be thankful for that."

"Feels like I've been cut in two."

"The operation took longer than Dr. O'Ferrell expected."

"No wonder I hurt so bad. They had to cut the baby out."

"And then the hysterectomy."

Lillian screamed and Ernestine jumped

"Control yourself. There are other people present." Ernestine pulled the curtain between the two beds.

"Tell me you didn't let them give me a hysterectomy."

"Stop yelling." Ernestine whispered. "The doctor told you your heart couldn't take another pregnancy. You agreed. I was there."

"I meant if this one was a boy," Lillian wailed.

"Here's a tissue. Stop crying."

Lillian blew her nose. Crying made her stomach hurt worse. "You shouldn't have let them do it. I wasn't in my right mind."

"You made a joke about it. When the doctor said you shouldn't have another baby, you said, 'I couldn't agree more.' We laughed."

"No woman nine months pregnant wants another baby. You should have stopped him."

There was a tap on the door. "I wasn't going to let you die." Ernestine hissed.

She opened the door and her voice rose an octave. "Mr. and Mrs. Hughes. How nice. Will's parents are here, Lillian."

Lillian tried to hitch herself higher on the pillows.

"My dear." Will's mother gave her a cool, dry peck on the cheek. "You look terribly pale. Perhaps we've come too soon."

"Did you see the baby?" Ernestine spoke with a forced cheerfulness, the voice she used with guests at the hotel when the plumbing gave out.

"We did," Will's mother said, "and she is darling. Have you decided on a name?"

"Not yet." Not for a girl, Lillian meant. She felt the leak of tears.

"Never mind." Margaret Hughes clasped Lillian's hand in her gloved ones. "God has his ways."

"Maude." Lillian took her hand back and propped up straighter, gritting her teeth at the pain. "We will name her for my sister Maude."

Throughout her recovery, through visits from her Jackson friends, breezing in and out with flowers and magazines, Lillian tried to figure out a way to tell Will. Not about his third daughter: Ernestine sent a telegram and Lillian had written to him, enclosing a photograph of tiny Maude. About the other thing.

She asked Ernestine to write and tell Will about the operation and that she could have died. She read her sister's first draft. "Don't say I 'might have died.' Tell him I *would* have died. Tell him it was the doctor's decision and I was unconscious when it happened."

Ten days and no reply. Lillian wrote her weekly letter, sending more photographs, telling Will she'd decided on Margaret, after his mother, for the baby's middle name. She did not tell him that she lay in the bed staring at this daughter, knowing what she ought to feel and not feeling it. She wrote that little Maude Margaret was beautiful, with a blonde fuzz that promised to become curls and enormous eyes, as blue as her daddy's. What Will thought after receiving these letters, Lillian did not know, for no word came back from the Pacific. Blond curls on a boy would have melted his heart. He would have sent yellow roses.

When word did come, Will's letters were bland. "Love to you and the baby. Kiss the girls for me. Glad you are all doing well." He never called Maude by her name.

Lillian tried to bury her apprehension. This was 1945, and the Allies were winning. Ernestine fired up the furnace, keeping things warm for Little Miss Anaheim. A fire kept the corner bedroom toasty. Everyone felt optimistic. The war would soon end. Wood could be spared.

The world was coming around right again. Surely, she and Will would, too. But to Lillian, his silence about the operation felt ominous. She tried to provide excuses.

Germany might have surrendered, but the Japanese were still at war. Will had bigger things to worry about than home and a baby. She had done the best she could. None of this was her fault.

She wrote Will that they needed to find a house before all the men got home and there were no houses to be had. In another of his bland letters, Will agreed. Lillian drove to Jackson and chose a white shingled bungalow in a newer part of northeast Jackson. Helen was going into fifth grade and April into first. The house had three bedrooms for their expanded family and was within walking distance of Duling Elementary, the girls' new school. Lillian negotiated a price and signed the papers. Leland co-signed for Will. By law, a married woman was not allowed to purchase property without her husband's permission. Still, Lillian looked at the deed and felt clever. She could run a hotel *and* buy a house. There was nothing here not to love.

47

Lillian's oldest daughter did her best to drive her mad. "Where is our new house?" Helen, face twisted in suspicion, leaned over the bed where Lillian lay in her slip, trying to rest her eyes for a few minutes.

"I told you, it's in North Jackson. A newer neighborhood." Trying to paint a happy picture.

"I'd rather go back to our old house."

Lillian closed her eyes. "Another family lives in our old house, sweetie."

"I need to live near Cornelia."

"That's not possible, darling. There were no houses for sale in Belhaven."

"Will I still be at Power school?"

"You'll have a new school."

"I don't *want* a new school." Shouting now. "I want to be with my *friends*."

Lillian surrendered and pulled herself upright. Her daughter's high-pitched caterwauling set her teeth on edge. "Try and calm down. War changes things and we have to do our part by not complaining." She hoped the changed things didn't include Will.

"It's not fair." Helen shrieked. "You're a terrible mother."

Lillian resisted slapping her daughter. Her hand longed to. "You are not allowed to speak to me that way. Go to your room."

"I don't have a room. I have a screened porch." Helen looked pleased with this comeback.

Lillian took a breath, trying to find patience before speaking. "Go to your screened porch or I will give you something to cry about."

She thought of Leland and Olive's blissful, child-free life. Breakfast in bed, where Leland claimed Olive buttered, not just the front and back of his toast, but the edges. Olive got to spend the entire war in Key West, sleeping next to her husband in a big hotel the Navy had requisitioned.

The days passed and no one's disposition improved. "When is Daddy is coming home?" Helen said. "When, when, when?" Standing over Lillian in the office. She asked the same thing every day.

The first fifty times, Lillian said, "When the war is over." In August, America dropped two huge bombs on Hiroshima and Nagasaki. On September 2, 1945, Ernestine opened a precious bottle of champagne to celebrate Japan's surrender.

Lillian changed her response. "Your daddy will be home as soon as he can."

She began to wonder herself. Will was in San Diego; he was waiting to be de-commissioned; he had traveled with a buddy named Truman. Now he was waiting for Truman to be de-commissioned; they were trying to get on a train. It was almost as if he didn't want to come home. She pushed that thought out of her head. At least she had a job; she could earn money while they waited.

September 10, and no Will. Lillian rented the new house to a couple on a month-to-month basis. September 15, and still nothing. She started the girls in school in Canton.

"This is so unfair." Helen stomped and whined around her mother's bedroom. "I don't think he's ever coming."

"You're going to make me do something I'll regret," Lillian said. The map of South America must be glowing on her forehead because her daughter, for once, shut her mouth.

Doreen came in with an armful of clean diapers. Thank God and the senior Hughes. The girls' nurse had returned after Maude's birth to help with the baby.

"When you're done folding those, Doreen, I'll get you to take the baby. I need a break."

Maude tried to eat Lillian's watch. Lillian pushed the wet little mouth away, keeping her cigarette safely distant from the blonde hair. Did she love this child? Of course, she did, but the love was mixed with such terrible disappointment. Sometimes Lillian forgot that none of it was Maude's fault.

48

September continued hot. Ernestine kept the hotel open for returning soldiers and their families, and Lillian carried on working herself into a gray exhaustion. On September 20, the call finally came. Will Hughes would arrive in Jackson on the next Monday. Could she drive down and meet the train?

Staring into the dressing table's mirror Lillian decided she didn't look well, and hadn't since Maude was born. She tired easily and the heat drained her. On Monday morning early, she dressed with care, disguising her pallor with a dusting of rouge. She wore a red and white striped dress Will had once admired, along with the pearls he'd sent from Hawaii. She put on the lipstick she'd worn in California. Staring at her reflection in the dresser mirror, her shoulders drooped. She'd done the best she could.

Before she left for school, Helen nagged. "Take me, take me, please take me."

"This is a private time for your daddy and me." Lillian tried not to sound as impatient as she felt.

Helen changed to: "When will you be back? When? When? Will I be home from school? Tell me exactly what time?"

On the way to Jackson, Lillian's mind traveled between dread and exhilaration. How could she not be excited, remembering Anaheim, the feel of Will's arms, and all those delicious hours together in bed?

Countered by apprehension: Will never asked about baby Maude. He'd not yet mentioned the operation. She tried to reassure herself. No sensible man blamed his wife for something she couldn't help, and Will was nothing if not sensible.

She spotted him the instant he got off the train. "Will," she called.

He must not have heard her. He turned to help someone down the steps. A black high heel and a long, tan leg appeared. A red suit, black hair, with what looked like a red hibiscus tucked behind one ear. The woman stared around as if she couldn't believe where she'd landed. Will leaned close to say something and she laughed. He still held her hand. *Who in the hell was this?* Behind her, a large boy dragged an equally large suitcase.

"Will." Lillian's voice rose.

He turned and waved. "There you are."

Lillian tried to throw herself into his arms the way she'd done in California, but he had a suitcase in one hand.

He gave her a one-armed hug and a peck on the cheek. "This is my friend Truman's wife Sylvia. Sylvia, this is Lillian. And this big guy is their son Peter."

A son—everyone but Lillian produced a son. Will beamed at the boy, all cheer and busyness, hefting suitcases, herding them along.

"My, what a surprise." Lillian gave the taller woman a sideways glance, hating her for spoiling this homecoming.

"I tried to wire you from the train, but the lines must be down," Will said.

Sylvia grabbed Lillian's hand. "Very kind of you. Don't know where we would have landed otherwise. No quarters available, I mean nothing. My husband is on his way."

She was tall, big-bosomed, and wearing some heavy flowery perfume. Lillian took a breath and found her manners. "Luckily, we have a hotel. Always room for one or two more." Staring at the long legs, the tight skirt, the hair like black satin. Feeling like a hick in her homemade cotton sundress.

Will Hughes put the suitcases in the trunk of the Chevrolet. "Do you mind driving?" He climbed in the passenger seat and turned so he could point the sights out to Sylvia in the backseat. "This is Capitol Street. That's the Governor's Mansion. Turn left on Congress, would you, Lillian? That's my office building. And straight ahead, our state capitol. You can just see the gold dome through the trees."

And here's the wife I haven't seen in over a year and am totally ignoring.

49

"There's a parking place in front of the building," Will said. "Pull in for a minute. I'll run upstairs and say hi to Dad."

"Now?" Lillian said.

"Back in a second."

Lillian turned off the engine and rolled down the window. She lit a cigarette and tilted the rearview mirror so she could see big-hipped Miss Hawaii in the backseat. *What kind of person rides a train with a flower in her hair?*

"Doesn't look like much of a town," Sylvia said.

"It's small, but New Orleans is right down the road."

"That's where I'm meeting Truman."

"When?" This whine emerged from the son.

"Yes, when do you expect he'll arrive?" Lillian tried not to sound eager.

Sylvia straightened the red skirt over her nylons. "Who knows? The Navy takes forever with paperwork." She opened the car door and got out to look in the drugstore window.

Every passing man stared at her. Watching, Lillian tried to take even breaths. What was Will thinking bringing a third person home, plus her unpleasant son? She twisted around to look at Peter, slumped in a corner of the back seat blowing spit bubbles.

"You're a big boy," Lillian said. "Your mother must have been very young when she had you."

He didn't raise his head. The heavy shoulders lifted and fell.

She'd never met a more unattractive child.

Sylvia got back in the car. "Is it always this hot?" She fanned her legs with her skirt, Lillian's trick, but Sylvia possessed a lot more leg.

"She wants to know how old you are," Peter said.

I will wring his fat neck. Lillian laughed to cover her embarrassment. "That is not what I asked." *God, I sound like a jealous wife.*

"I'm twenty-nine."

Lillian was now thirty-six, pretending to be thirty-four. "You look young to have a boy as big as Peter."

"Old enough to know better." Sylvia let out a musical trill of laughter.

What was that supposed to mean? Lillian got out of the car before she said something rude and stomped her cigarette out on the curb. "I'll just run in the drugstore." She fiddled around the perfume counter, anxiously watching through the front window for Will's return. He hadn't even given her a real kiss. He hadn't said he missed her or asked about the children. She didn't trust the cavalier way Sylvia acted around him, not to mention the pig-faced son. They had ruined her special day, and there was not one damned thing she could do about it.

50

On a Monday in late September, 1945, the best-looking man Velma Vernon had ever seen walked through the doors of Hughes & Blair. Dressed in Navy whites, brasses gleaming, an officer's cap tucked under one arm.

She blinked. "May I help you?"

Will stared down at her with a slight frown, which made Velma go warm and study her typewriter keys.

"Where's Evans?" As if Velma had done something with the firm's former secretary.

She looked up and quickly down again. His face was like the sun. Gaze too long and be blinded. "Mrs. Evans retired. To the Gulf Coast. Her husband fishes." She couldn't seem to speak a sentence with more than four words.

"Is Dad in?"

Velma squinted once more into that blazing brilliance. "I beg your pardon?"

The young man pointed to the closed door behind Velma and raised his voice as if she were deaf. "Is my father in his office?"

This was *the son*, the one off in the Navy, and she'd just made an utter fool of herself by not recognizing him. The hateful blood rushed to her face. "Mr. Pat? Yes, he's in his office." Velma knew how she looked. Embarrassment colored her, not pink and pretty, but a dull brick red. She stood as if to show him the way.

The beautiful stranger said, "Thanks." and vanished into the corner office.

Velma dropped back into her chair. She should have recognized him from the photograph on the windowsill. Still, he could have said his name. That would have been the courteous thing to do. But she hadn't said hers either. This was her introduction to Will Hughes, a man soon to be her boss, and she'd made a complete mess of it. She took swallows of air until her face cooled. She heard their voices behind the closed office door, one deeper than the other. Laughter. When the door opened, Velma made sure to be typing, fingers flying over the keys, face turned toward her shorthand pad.

Mr. Pat said, "You met my son Will?"

Velma paused, but left her fingers on the keys. Going red again, she smiled and nodded, a small smile, not enough to show her gums.

"This is Velma Vernon," Mr. Pat said. "Been with us for two years now. She's a shy little thing but a crackerjack secretary, aren't you, Velma?"

What was she supposed to say to that? Velma nodded again. Will Hughes must think she was addled, head bobbing like a chicken.

The son, the beautiful son, smiled down upon her. His blue eyes twinkled. He held out a hand and Velma took it, a warm and solid hand. The contact sent a jolt through her. It was like that painting of God and Adam. His touch gave her life. She tried to hear Mr. Pat's words through the ringing in her ears.

"He'll be with us soon. Worthless, I'm sure, until we whip him into shape. You'll have to help me with that, Velma. You've learned more law than Will here remembers."

She kept nodding, smiling her closed-mouth smile. Will Hughes released her hand and she felt abandoned.

"I'll be back in a week or two. I look forward to working with you."

Velma heard the words as if from underwater. Her head bobbed again. The door closed behind him, and it was as if the lights had gone off.

At lunch in the drugstore downstairs, over tomato soup and crackers, she grilled Garnett about Will Hughes.

"Isn't he handsome?" Garnett shook her head as if waving away those good looks. "But not nearly so easy to work for as Mr. Pat. You'll see. He gets sharp with the secretaries, probably because he's young and not sure of himself." She took a spoonful of soup. "Personally, I think Mr. Pat is way too hard on him. Might be why he volunteered and went off to war." Garnett bit the corner off a cracker.

Velma waited. She didn't care about eating. She wanted to hear more about Will Hughes.

"Mr. Pat treats him like a boy. Pays him like one too, from what I hear." Garnett scraped her bowl "Maybe things will change now that he's been off at war."

Lifting her spoon, Velma's hand shook.

Garnett studied her. "We all had a crush on Will Hughes before he left, but he's married. He has a darling wife named Lillian, and three daughters." She lowered her voice. "*Very* married."

Velma did not need to be warned. She wasn't about to jeopardize her new life with a crush, especially on a married man, which would not only be useless but a sin. It was the shock of that first meeting that made her tremble. She would be able to look at him the next time. She wiped her mouth and gave Garnett a prim look. "I wouldn't dream of having feelings for a married man."

Back in the office, she went to the ladies' room and stared into the mirror. Instead of her own flushed face, she pictured his: the long nose and fine lips, the way the skin creased around his eyes when he smiled. Velma had never believed in love at first sight, but no one on God's earth ever made her feel this way before. She closed her eyes and prayed for good sense. A man like Will Hughes wouldn't look at a person like her. If those blue eyes appeared to be smiling especially for her, she needed to keep in mind what Garnett said. Concentrate on what she'd been hired to do. She would be Will's very good secretary. And, next time, she would not let the sight of him turn her into a stuttering ninny.

On her knees that night, Velma prayed for Mama and Papa, her aunt and cousins, for Mr. Pat, and for world peace. She asked for tranquility at work and for God to please stop her blushing. Her mind fluttered at the thought of Will Hughes, but she slammed the door on that. "Remove us from temptation," she said aloud. The words echoed in the empty apartment.

Velma laid her pin-curled head on the pillow feeling better. A loving God would surely hear and take pity.

51

From inside the drugstore, Lillian spotted Will heading for the car and darted out. She didn't want him alone with Sylvia for one second. "How's your dad?" she said.

Will stood in the open car door, coughing into his fist. "It's as if I never left. No questions about where I was or what I did. All he wants to know is when am I coming back to work."

"I hope you told him not until you get a few weeks of vacation."

Will made a noncommittal noise and got in the car. He coughed again.

"I don't like the sound of that." Lillian started the engine.

"It's nothing. A sinus infection the doc said turned into bronchitis."

"You need a good rest." *Without the company of those two in the back seat.*

At the top of Capitol and North State Street, Will resumed his tour. "That's our *Old* Capitol Building." Pointing. "The bricks were handmade by slaves." No comment from the back seat. They drove north on State Street. "There's my parents' house," Will said.

Lillian glanced in the rearview mirror.

Sylvia leaned forward. "You didn't tell me you were rich." Her voice low and teasing.

Lillian looked sideways at Will. *What had he told her?*

Will pointed out a large white Art Deco building. "That's Bailey Junior High."

"Did you go there?" Sylvia said.

"No, my parents sent me away to military school."

Making himself sound like a complete snot.

"Rich *and* snooty." Sylvia's laugh rose from deep in her throat.

Lillian wanted to strangle her. In the mirror, she studied the two of them. Were they very tan or might that be some racial mixture? The son was not just large, he was fat.

Will spoke over his shoulder. "You'll like it up at the hotel. Lillian's a wonderful hostess, aren't you?"

Lillian nodded. "Born to please." She *was* a good hostess and at least Will remembered that much. Making people feel comfortable was one of her talents, and she would try it on these two. "What grade are you in, Peter?"

The boy unwrapped a piece of candy and stared out the window. The car filled with the smell of cinnamon.

Sylvia said, "Don't be rude, Peter." She gave the child a playful slap on the knee. "He's twelve and in sixth grade. Will says you have two little girls. They'll have such fun together."

Peter made a derisive sound.

"Three," Lillian said. "We have three girls. The new baby is called Maude." Will had not asked about her.

"How is she?" he said now.

"Darling." Lillian stared straight ahead. What had Sylvia meant by having fun together? She glanced back with a smile. "How long will you be able to stay?" (Southern for: When will we see the back of you?) Will knew it. His head turned abruptly toward her. She felt him giving her the stern look and pretended not to notice.

"How long do you think, Will, before they let Truman go?" Sylvia leaned over the front seat, breathing down Will's neck.

"Shouldn't be more than two or three weeks."

Weeks. "And you'll be joining us for the whole time?" Lillian kept her voice light.

Will answered. "Of course. I promised Truman I'd take care of his family."

"I wish I'd known," Lillian said. "I could have set aside a couple of rooms. The hotel is completely filled." She would move Helen and April back onto the screen porch and give Sylvia and Peter the small bedroom next to hers. In celebration of Will's homecoming, Ernestine and Knox had offered to sleep downstairs in the Retreat, leaving the nicest and most private bedroom in the family wing for Lillian and Will.

"Just stick us in any old corner." Sylvia ruffled her son's dark wiry hair. "We don't mind, do we, Peter Pumpkin?"

He pulled his head away from the caress. Watching in the rearview mirror, Lillian thought how nicely behaved her girls were in comparison.

All the way to the hotel, Will and Sylvia shared stories about Hawaii, reminding each other of details. The stories included white beaches, warm blue water, drinks made with gin, staying up all night, and wearing coconut shells as apparel. "Ha, ha, ha," they said. "Ha, ha, ha, ha, ha."

Lillian listened, growing increasingly hostile. "Will, I thought you told me dependents weren't allowed."

"I was born in Hawaii," Sylvia said, "and Truman is a genius at getting around the bureaucracy."

Did that mean Will could have brought his family if he'd tried? A sour taste filled Lillian's mouth. She glanced in the mirror, watching Sylvia open her purse and check herself in a gold compact. What the hell had been going on out there in the Pacific, and what was going on now? She didn't like the way they laughed together, or the way Sylvia sat on the edge of her seat and Will twisted around, closer than she was to her own husband. Most of the drive back, Will kept his back against the window looking at Sylvia.

"I thought you were out there fighting a war," Lillian said. Frustrated by how bitter she sounded.

"It's the fun in between that makes war bearable," Will said. His job with the Judge Advocate's Office had been to write letters to families of the men who died, which did not sound like fun. Lillian felt ashamed of herself, but she had run out of polite. For the last few miles, they rode in silence.

"Here we are." Lillian drove between the brick posts and over the cattle guard at the entrance to Creekmore. They rode past the rose garden and Annex into the parking area.

"This is it?" Sylvia sounded dismayed.

"It isn't a fancy place," Will said. "Our house in Jackson wasn't available."

Listen to him, apologizing for his wife's home, the place that supported them while he was off gallivanting in coconut shells. Talking about the new house like he'd had anything to do with buying it, or with finding a tenant until they moved in. "This is my family's hotel," Lillian said. "It's pretty well known here in the South."

"You sure put it in the middle of nowhere." Sylvia stood outside the car in her flame red suit, hands on her hips, staring at the row of older ladies rocking on the Pavilion's front porch.

Helen came running across the lawn with April close behind. "Daddy, Daddy, Daddy." She took a flying leap into her father's arms.

"Whoa, look who's grown up on me." Will's knees bent under her weight.

"I'm nine years old. Who is *that*?" Helen pointed at Sylvia.

Lillian wanted to kiss her daughter.

"That is Sylvia and this is her son, Peter," Will said. "They're Daddy's friends."

"Why are they here?" Helen said.

Will set her down and picked up April, who wet his face with kisses. "Don't be rude," he said to Helen. "They're our guests."

But Lillian's oldest daughter seemed determined to show how disappointed she was at this intrusion, acting out in all the ways Lillian longed to: sulking, pointedly refusing to shake hands with Peter, stomping off.

Doreen stepped forward with Maude in her arms. The baby dimpled winningly and Will touched her on the nose. "Who have we here?"

"Isn't she darling?" Lillian said.

"She is." Will picked up the suitcases and indicated the hotel's entrance to Sylvia.

"Tomorrow I'll try and find you two a room in the Annex." Lillian pointed right. She didn't want this woman anywhere near the family wing.

That night, she put on her trousseau nightgown and robe, combed her hair, and daubed Blue Grass behind her ears. Will did not appear to notice. He climbed into his side of bed and turned off the light. "I'm whipped."

On her side, Lillian took off the chiffon robe, feeling like one of Cinderella's stepsisters. He had not taken her into his arms or said he loved her. This was the opposite of Anaheim, and not one bit how she'd pictured the first night of their restored life. She must look as bad as she feared. She lay there in the scratchy lace nightgown, wanting to cry with frustration.

Will spoke into the dark. "Dad hired a new secretary."

At least he still talked to her. "What happened to the other one?"

"Retired."

"What's the new one like?"

"Shy." He pulled the sheet over his shoulders. "Tall. Young. Turns bright red when you speak to her. From down in the country somewhere. Dad hired her right out of high school."

"Doesn't sound much like Mrs. Evans."

"He claims she's a wonder. Twice as fast as the other girls. Apparently has no life outside the office."

"The young ones tend to get married and quit."

Will gave a grunt of agreement.

Lillian listened to Will cough and dismissed the new secretary from her list of worries. A tall, uneducated country girl would not be Will's cup of tea. The man was too much of a snob. "Did you mention needing a raise?"

She felt him stiffen. "You can't walk in after two years away and ask for more money. I'm lucky to have a job. A lot of men don't."

"We talked about this in Anaheim. Your dad has never given you the credit you deserve."

"You let me worry about that." Will turned his back on her, taking most of the sheet with him.

Lillian tried cuddling up behind him. He did not respond. There would be no sex tonight. This was nothing like a year ago, with Will wanting to make love every chance they had. She lay in the dark feeling squashed and frustrated. "Can I at least have a kiss?"

"Sorry." Will turned his head. Lillian pressed her lips to his. He did not rebuff her. He allowed himself to be kissed. She wished she hadn't tried.

In the dark, she seethed while Will coughed and snored. He snored louder than she remembered, maybe because of the sinus trouble. Definitely not the homecoming she'd dreamed of, and it was the Hawaiian woman's fault. Helen had picked up on it right away, the clever child. The thought of Sylvia made Lillian feel murderous. Will had come home with the Whore of Babylon. Lillian wasn't a Bible reader like Ernestine, and didn't know where that particular whore appeared in the holy scriptures, but the words fit and she enjoyed the way they felt in her head. Whatever her husband and Truman's wife were up to, she would put a stop to it. No tramp from across the Pacific was going to slink into her world and steal Will Hughes. Not while she had a breath left to fight.

52

Will brought Helen and April little grass skirts from Hawaii. Sylvia offered to teach nine-year-old Helen to hula. Wearing the skirt over her two-piece bathing suit, Helen learned to sway her hips and make movements with her hands while singing the Hawaiian words to "Three Blind Mice." Lillian watched with growing dismay as her sole ally wriggled over to the enemy's side.

At James and Faye's fishing camp during the second week of the intruder's stay, Sylvia tried to make Helen perform her hula in the little grass skirt without the bathing suit top.

"In Hawaii, it's traditional for children to go bare chested," Sylvia said.

Helen said, "No. People could see me."

"For God's sake," Sylvia said, "you don't have anything to see."

Helen wept.

Lillian intervened. "We don't usually make the children perform naked." She did not try to keep the sarcasm from her voice.

"Fine, but it won't be authentic."

Helen danced the hula in her bathing suit and grass skirt, her face wet with tears She ignored the applause and twisted away from Sylvia's attempts to hug her after. She came and sat beside her mother. Lillian put an arm around her daughter, pulling her close, glad to have at least one person back on her side.

The children were put to bed in the big pine-paneled bedroom upstairs, Helen and April in one bed, Little Leland and Peter in the other. A half hour later, the grownups heard screaming. Lillian and James ran up to check. Helen pointed at Peter, who looked more sullen than usual. Crying, Helen refused to sleep in the same room with the boy. That broke the party up.

Helen fell asleep driving back to the hotel, but the next day, Lillian sat her down on the sofa in Knox and Ernestine's sitting room. "Tell me what happened last night."

Helen ducked her head. "I can't."

"Why can't you?"

"It's too nasty."

"Did that boy touch you?" Lillian prayed for it to be so, not in any harmful way, of course, but damaging enough to demand that Sylvia and her son leave immediately.

Helen shook her head so hard her straight brown hair whipped her face. "Worse."

"Tell Mama."

Helen took a big breath. "Peter said my daddy—" She stopped.

"Go on."

Another breath. "He says my daddy sucks his mother's titties. He said hers are bigger than yours." The words came out in gulps. "He said Daddy puts his thing between that lady Sylvia's legs and makes her holler."

Lillian sat stunned, stomach roiling in disbelief. She stared at her daughter, wanting to slap the hateful words out of the girl's head, except they weren't Helen's words. What should she do? The boy must have made it up. No, a twelve-year-old boy could never invent anything so horrible. She must confront Will. Or was it better to pretend it never happened? She felt crazed.

Helen sat, still and silent, her eyes on the floor. "Are you mad at me?"

"Of course not, darling. Mama's just thinking. You run and play."

Helen headed out the door looking relieved.

Lillian called after her. "Stay away from that Peter. He's a terrible boy and you shouldn't believe a word he says."

At dinner, Lillian watched Will and Sylvia. They weren't seated next to one another, she'd seen to that, but she caught the way Will glanced at Sylvia for a reaction after one of his stories. Her own feelings were a churn of resentment and hatred. *That bitch. That whore.* Whatever was happening, whatever had happened, she planned to put a stop to it.

After supper, Lillian confronted Will in their bedroom. She didn't wait for him to get into his pajamas. "We need to talk," she said. She felt the disadvantage of having to look up at him.

She didn't know what to expect: denial, perhaps shame and an apology. She had already made up her mind to forgive him. She loved Will Hughes and if, in the heat of war, he'd made a mistake — who was she to throw stones?

What she got instead was rage, anger like she'd never seen from Will before. Fists clenched, eyes blazing, a tone so harsh she backed away.

"I cannot believe you would speak such filth to me."

Lillian's voice trembled. "I didn't say it and I'm not the one who did it." Frightened by the look on Will's face.

"You should have washed that child's mouth out with soap."

"Helen did not make that up. She doesn't know words like that."

"This is my fault," Will said, "for leaving you in a place like this with every kind of person coming and going. You should have stayed with my parents the way I asked you to." He looked around in distaste. "I've never liked it here."

"This is my home." Lillian felt the point of this argument slipping from her grasp. "What I'm trying to say is, did you — ?"

He actually raised a hand to hit her. She flinched.

He stopped himself, shaking his head. "I cannot believe it — I won't even entertain an accusation so disgusting."

"Will you at least speak to Sylvia about her son's behavior?"

"I will not." Will glared at her with what felt like hatred. "Neither will you. And you are never to speak to me of this again." He walked out, slamming the screen door behind him.

Lillian sat sobbing at the dressing table, hating her face in the mirror. Never speak of it. That's how Will put an end to unpleasantness. This was supposed to be her special time with him, a second honeymoon, and everything had been spoiled. Will acted as if he didn't even like her. She couldn't compete with a Hawaiian lady with cleavage and a flower behind her ear, a woman who knew how to hula. Wiggling all over the place while she taught Helen that dance. Lillian had seen the way Will watched and the hunger in his eyes. If what the boy said was true—she could not allow herself to believe it. Will had certainly been angry enough to make it a lie. She didn't know what to think or what to do. This wasn't the same man who'd left her two years ago, or the man she'd met in Long Beach.

He'd been home two weeks and had only tried to make love to her once. Couldn't manage it then, and from the way he'd acted, that too had somehow been Lillian's fault. The way Helen's story had become the hotel's fault.

The government advised wives to be patient. Returning servicemen needed time to make the transition. Adjustment to civilian life was difficult and families shouldn't make it harder on them—the way she'd just done.

Helen came in to say goodnight. "What's wrong?"

"Nothing, darling. Mama's just tired."

"Where's Daddy?" She sounded suspicious.

"Gone out for some air."

"When will Peter and his mother leave?"

Lillian put her arms around her daughter and kissed the top of her head. "I don't know, sugar. We have to be nice until they do. They're our guests."

"I hate them both."

Helen squeezed her. "It'll be over soon."

"And we'll move into our new house?"

"We will."

"And be a real family again?"

"Yes." Lillian held her daughter tighter. Pray God this was true.

Two more weeks of patience were required. The tenants would move out on Friday, October 1. Lillian needed to get her own family moved in over the weekend, so Helen and April could begin their new school the following Monday. Truman had not shown up, so that meant they would have to bring Sylvia and that terrible boy along. Lillian had not again brought up what Helen told her, and Will acted as if he never heard it.

Gathered in the Retreat for drinks in the late afternoon, Sylvia gave a throaty laugh in response to something Will said. Lillian stretched her lips into a smile and mixed a bourbon and water. Will would sit next to her at dinner and respond when she spoke, but nothing felt the same. He treated Lillian as if she were someone he'd asked out by mistake and must now treat politely until he could get her home. It was like living with a stranger.

Yesterday, she'd found herself sniffing his shirts for the lingering smell of Sylvia's heavy perfume. She had nothing specific to accuse him of, and no one to blame for his coldness but Sylvia. Lillian put on a mask of friendship, waiting the woman out.

Before they moved, Truman showed up in New Orleans. Sylvia and Peter would take the train to meet him. Will drove them to the station in Jackson and Lillian sent Helen along to make sure he came back.

To celebrate the witch's departure, Lillian locked herself in the bathroom with a small glass of brandy pilfered from Ernestine's liquor cabinet. She filled the claw-footed tub with hot water and lowered herself with a satisfied groan. Her sister's bathroom was much nicer than the dark, damp one she shared with the girls. Ernestine collected old perfume bottles in a glass-fronted cabinet next to the sink. Lovely bottles with woven silk atomizer bulbs and tassels; cut crystal bottles with tops like ornate jewels. Outside the locked door, she heard her sister calling her name. The lunch bell had sounded and she was needed. Lillian ignored her. Sipping the brandy, she felt like a princess released from a spell. Finally, she had Will to herself.

She stood in front of Ernestine's mirror with her stomach sucked in and her small chest thrust out, smiling at the reflection. The bath had improved her looks. Her face had some color. She put on the red and white striped dress and Jungle Red lipstick. It was not too late to be darling.

Late in the afternoon, when Will and Helen returned from the station, Will looked subdued and Helen had a story for her mother at bedtime. "Sylvia wanted Daddy to ride the train with her to New Orleans. She said I could come, too. I wanted to, but Daddy said no. He said we'd go on the train another time."

The bitch had tried to keep him longer and had not succeeded. Lillian felt triumphant and reminded herself to be patient. She had won Will's heart once and she could do it again. It might take time, but she now had all the time she needed. So much good in her life: three healthy children, a new house, a husband home safe from the war. Not the old husband, perhaps, but time healed all wounds, or so people claimed. Be thankful for small blessings: Will had not once brought up the operation.

On the Saturday morning after Sylvia left, Lillian sat at the dresser brushing Helen's hair.

"Ow, ow, ow." Helen wriggled under her hand.

Will sat on the bed pulling on his socks. "I'll head back to work on Monday."

Lillian put the brush down. "I assumed you were going to wait until we moved into the new house." Had she? Will hated assumptions.

"Dad needs me now. I spoke to the people renting our house. They're willing to let me use the front bedroom and bath."

Lillian felt the birthmark light up. He'd made these plans behind her back. "We'll go with you." Her voice eager, almost desperate.

Will waved the idea away. "Ernestine needs you here and we can use the money. It's only a couple of weeks and I'll come back on the weekends."

She felt abandoned.

Helen came to the rescue. "Don't leave, Daddy. Please." Grabbing him around the waist.

He hugged her. "Don't you worry, Pumpkin. Maybe you'll come down and visit, keep house for your old dad."

Helen clutched at this. "Can I, Mama, can I?"

Lillian nodded without speaking. Will had called Helen *Pumpkin*. He never called the girls that. Pumpkin had been Sylvia's pet name for her son. Hearing Will use it made her want to retch. But Sylvia was back with her husband. Out of their lives. Lillian swallowed hard and said nothing, the way she'd done with every bad thing since Will Hughes got off that train. Swallowed her medicine like a good girl.

53

On Sunday night before Will Hughes left for the city, they had what Lillian thought of afterwards as "The Talk." They had moved into her old room, returning the nicer one to Ernestine and Knox. The children were in bed a room away on the screened porch and the servants gone for the night. Lillian sat at her dresser in the trousseau nightgown, dotting perfume on her collarbones, hoping they might make love.

Will sat on the edge of the bed untying his shoes. "I've been meaning to speak to you about what happened while I was gone."

A tightness in his voice. She'd waited in dread for him to bring this up, and when he didn't, hoped silence meant forgiveness.

"You mean the operation." She kept her voice light "I was so drugged I had no idea what was going on."

"You must have given the doctor permission."

She felt herself stuttering. "I'm sure I told him only if the baby was a boy."

He stood. "If you'd said that, it wouldn't have happened."

Lillian felt as if she'd been slapped. She blinked trying not to cry. "You saw what the doctor said in Ernestine's letter." Watching him in the mirror. "I'm not strong enough to have another child."

Will's mouth twisted. "You could have waited and spoken to me."

He went into the bathroom and shut the door. Lillian shouted through it. "You were thousands of miles away. It was an *emergency*." Her voice shook. Had it been an emergency? Did the doctor say she *"should"* have a hysterectomy or *"must"* have one? Everything about that night was a blur.

He came out in his striped pajamas. "You could have waited for me to get home."

"The doctor said my heart couldn't stand another pregnancy."

"I assume you weren't doing anything to get pregnant while I was away. We could have talked it over, gotten a second opinion.

"You would have wanted to try again." She picked up her silver-backed brush and pulled it through her hair, pretending a calmness she did not feel.

"You don't know what I wanted because you didn't wait to find out." He folded back the spread and turned down his side of the bed. "There are two adults in this marriage, and you made the most important decision of our lives without consulting me." His voice turned bitter. "I get to hear about it halfway around the world—in a letter from your sister, no less, a letter telling me you'd had yourself *spayed*." The last word practically spat.

Lillian threw down the brush. "I am not a dog."

"I'm sorry. I shouldn't have said that." Will climbed into bed. He didn't sound sorry. "I'm just disappointed you didn't care enough about what I wanted to wait and discuss it with me."

Lillian felt trapped and infuriated by the circle of his logic. He always won arguments. "It wouldn't matter to you if I died, would it, as long as you got your son?" She felt the birthmark on her forehead raging.

He pulled the covers up to his chest. "We'll never know now, will we?"

It was then that she recognized the looks he'd given her since he got off the train. She was spoiled goods; she was his barren wife, as hollow and scooped out as a melon. And he was stuck with her. She started out of the room.

"Where are you going?"

"To unlock the whiskey cabinet."

"That's your answer to everything, isn't it? Have another drink."

She cried then, knowing how much he hated tears. "You have a wife who loves you, you have three beautiful children. You have work you care about. Why isn't that enough?"

"Go get your drink."

She was the one shouting now. "You'd rather have me dead, though, wouldn't you? If I died, you could marry someone else and get your precious son."

"Close the door, and for God's sake, keep your voice down."

When she returned to bed, her mouth on fire from drinking straight from the bottle, he had fallen asleep. She felt wrecked. His words had smashed her, and whiskey did nothing to ease the pain. She stared at the ceiling until the alcohol did its work. When she woke, he was gone.

The Talk, the horrid talk. Worse than she had ever imagined. She must go on as if it had never happened. Lock the hateful words in the compartment where she kept every bad thing: the money she took from her brothers, the night with Bob Bradshaw, lying about her age. The words could be shut away, but their meaning was harder to erase. She recognized what had been wrong since Will Hughes stepped off that train: he no longer loved her.

54

On Thursday afternoon, a week later, with Will in the city working, Lillian relaxed on Faye's back porch in Canton. Feet up on the couch, seven-month-old Maude in her lap, she took a deep swallow of her first gin and tonic. Faye sat in her back-support lounger with a matching drink. Since Maude's death, Faye had become Lillian's favorite confidante, more like a sister than a sister-in-law. Faye's only child was grown and gone; James spent the day at his office on the town square. This left Faye free to indulge in an indolence Lillian envied. She took a drag off her cigarette and wriggled her bare toes. Here in this house with a tall drink in her hand, she let herself relax. The worries about Will retreated.

"Helen had an adventure this week," she told Faye. "On Tuesday, Ernestine took her down to Jackson to spend the night with her daddy in his rented room. She had begged to go and he finally agreed. When she got home yesterday, I couldn't wait to find out what it looked like. All Helen said was 'Messy.'"

Faye took a sip of her drink. "Children can be disappointingly unforthcoming."

"I said, 'Messy, how?' and Helen said, 'You know, a mess.' She claims she spent the whole day cleaning, which would be a miracle because she can't be bothered to pick up a wet towel in her own room. If my oldest daughter found it necessary to clean, the place must truly be a sty, which is fine with me. I don't want him too comfortable living alone." Lillian bounced little Maude on her stomach.

Faye nodded sympathetically. She wore black silk slacks with a black and white checked blouse. Lillian coveted her long, lean body and pale skin. Faye painted her lips a deep red. Her dark hair curled loosely around her face. James treated her exactly the way she looked—like she was made of porcelain.

Lillian went on. "You'd think two years off in the Navy would be enough of being alone for Will, but maybe that's the problem. The man is so used to being on his own, he doesn't know how to be married anymore." This was not close to the whole truth, but Lillian wasn't ready to talk about Sylvia or Will's coldness. He'd returned to the hotel last weekend acting friendly and distracted, as if their talk had never happened. Lillian spent the two days longing to probe his feelings and not daring to utter a word. It had been exhausting.

Faye sipped her drink. "Will never seems to enjoy the hotel."

"He claims he never gets enough to eat. Says the portions Ernestine serves are too small."

"I think it's more likely Ernestine, don't you?'

Lillian laughed. "She does drive him crazy."

Faye held out her arms. "Honey, you look bone tired. Let me hold that baby."

Lillian passed Maude over.

Faye kissed little Maude's nose. "Ernestine would drive a saint crazy." The baby gurgled happily.

Lillian settled back on the couch with a fresh cigarette and her drink. "Being here with you makes me realize how much I need this. Summers at the hotel are hell and September's been no easier. It's a relief to get away."

"You are always welcome in this house, you know that."

Lillian watched Faye cuddling Maude. "I swear, that child will never learn to walk. Somebody carries her every minute of the day."

Faye nuzzled the baby's yellow curls. "There's no such thing as too much love."

Was there such a thing as too little? Could you die from not being loved? Lillian shook her head. No bad thoughts today. "Helen says

Will took her to the drugstore for dinner. The *drugstore*, can you imagine? They had hamburgers and milkshakes. She said the man sitting next to her at the counter ordered squash."

Faye giggled. "At a drugstore?"

"It was a joke. The man asked for a cup of coffee and a side order of squash. When the waitress told him they didn't serve squash, he said, 'What kind of drugstore is this?'"

Lillian held out her empty glass. "I'll hold the baby and you mix us another drink. Helen has repeated that story about thirty times. It's her first joke."

Lillian propped Maude on one shoulder and took a puff of her cigarette. Faye mixed them another gin and tonic. Lillian exhaled contentment. Unlike Ernestine, Faye enjoyed drinking in the afternoon. On this couch, on Faye and James's cool back porch, she felt easy in her skin. Every person in this house loved her. She crossed her legs and let Maude play with her pearl necklace. "Do you think I could spend the night?"

"James would love that," Faye said.

With Lillian carrying Maude, they went and checked the guest room "You and the baby will have to sleep in the same bed," Faye said, "but we can put pillows down the side so she won't fall out."

Lillian kissed Maude's head. "This one sleeps like an angel. Let me call Ernestine. I picked up a load of dry goods at the wholesalers, but nothing that will spoil before tomorrow. I need time with my favorite sister-in-law."

"We girls have to stick together," Faye said.

On the wall phone in the hall, Lillian took a deep breath before dialing. Ernestine did not sound pleased, but Lillian closed her ears to the disapproval and made her excuses. That settled, she returned to the sofa with her gin and tonic. Faye held little Maude, talking nonsense.

Lillian let their voices fade. The alcohol's buzz made her feel blessedly carefree. Will and his hateful words seemed far, far way. James would soon be home from the cotton brokerage. They would switch to Scotch. He would make little open-faced cream cheese and olive sandwiches to snack on while he broiled steaks for dinner. She drained her glass, ice clicking against her teeth.

Faye said. "Mix us another."

Lillian took Faye's empty glass. "You look awfully cute with a baby in your lap."

Faye raised her eyebrows. "I hope that's not a hint."

"Certainly not." Lillian poured the gin. "We have both closed down the baby farm."

"Thank God."

Faye sympathized with Lillian's troubles and laughed at her jokes. What more could you ask of a friend? She was the one person who might understand the pain of what Will said, but Lillian could not bear to confide. Some things were too terrible to admit.

55

In late September, on Will Hughes' first day in the office, Velma Vernon solved the problem of blushing by never looking directly at him. She brought him a fresh supply of yellow legal pads and made sure he had a row of sharpened pencils. She asked if he wanted coffee and discovered he liked it with three spoons of sugar and a lot of milk.

She did not look up from her typewriter when he disappeared into his father's office and emerged with a stack of files. He stopped by her desk. "If I don't come out by closing time, please check on me, Miss Vernon. I may have passed away under a pile of ancient lawsuits."

She gave a small smile, acknowledging the joke. "Is there anything else I can get for you, Mr. Hughes?"

"Will, please. You make me feel like an old man."

"Yes, sir."

"And no sirs."

The dimpled glass door to his office closed and Velma took a breath. That hadn't gone too bad. Not looking at him helped.

Working for two men gave her more to do, but no more than Velma could handle. As the days passed, she found herself growing easier around Will Hughes, gradually able to look him in the eye without her face burning. She kept her smiles small to hide the hated gums, but otherwise felt almost comfortable. She took his dictation fluidly, and thanked him like a normal person when he complimented her typing.

After three weeks, she found herself laughing openly at his jokes. One morning, when both Mr. Pat and Will Hughes stood at her desk, she got up the courage to tell a joke of her own. She'd read it in *Reader's Digest.*

"What's the difference between a good lawyer and a great lawyer?

Mr. Pat said, "What?"

The punchline kept trying to fly out of her head and Velma almost lost her nerve. "A good lawyer knows the law. A great lawyer knows the judge." She stared at her typewriter keys, fearing she'd been too bold.

Mr. Pat shook with glee and Will Hughes threw his head back and laughed out loud. "A great lawyer knows the judge." He said it was almost too true to be funny.

Too true to be funny or too funny to be true? Jokes were confusing, but they had laughed.

As the weeks and months went by, Velma decided God had heard her prayer and granted her a peaceful heart. She worked with Will Hughes like a good secretary, without stammering or staring—or at least without getting caught staring.

Doris, the third secretary, kept flirting with him, batting her eyes and standing too close. Velma watched Will Hughes, listening to her politely while taking small steps backwards.

One day in December, a small, pretty woman came flying into the office followed by a child. She bent over Velma's desk in a confidential way. "I'm Lillian Hughes and you must be Velma."

Velma tried not to look startled. "Pleased to meet you, Mrs. Hughes."

"I've heard just the *best things* about you."

Velma tried to think of a clever response and settled on "Thank you."

Lillian pushed the child forward. "This is our oldest, who is in dire need of shoes. Helen, say hello to Velma."

Will's wife was as cute as Garnett had said, with the smallest feet Velma had ever seen on a grown woman. She flitted around the office like a hummingbird, smiling, saying hello to everyone, knocking on Will's door and disappearing behind it.

The little girl stood watching Velma with serious brown eyes, "You type fast."

"As fast as I can."

There was a silence and Velma glanced up. The girl was still staring.

"Do you get paid more for typing fast?" she said.

That was impertinent, but this was the boss's daughter. "I get raises."

Helen twisted the wheel and made the cards in Velma's Rolodex go round. "What's a raise?"

"More money for typing fast."

The child honked with laughter, which made Velma giggle.

Lillian reappeared and apologized for interrupting. "I hope Helen has not been bothering you, Velma." Not waiting for an answer, she put a hand on the child's back and ushered her out. "Bye-bye" Waving to everyone. The door closed and a silence descended. It felt as if a storm had blown through.

Next to Lillian Hughes, Velma felt like a cow, plodding through life on size ten hooves.

Throughout the days, while never slacking on her job, Velma kept an eye on her new boss. Will Hughes stayed as fixed in her mind as the first star of evening, and just as unreachable.

He was not lazy. From the first day he arrived, he worked like a man who had already wasted too much time. Mr. Pat kept reminding his son how long he'd been away and how much he'd forgotten, treating him like a junior associate instead of a man with ten years of legal experience, a man who'd spent two years defending his country. Velma saw the younger man's face crease with distress when Mr. Pat told him it had been a fine thing to serve, but the firm couldn't afford to let patriotism get in the way of progress.

Velma privately disagreed.

"Everybody's got to pull his weight around here," Mr. Pat said. As if his son had run off to the Pacific to have fun.

If she had been the correcting kind, Velma might have spoken to Mr. Pat. Secretaries noticed what was going on. Will Hughes worked harder than any other lawyer at the firm, and carried briefs home to work on at night. But she wasn't a correcting kind of person, and Will Hughes never said a word in his own defense. He put his head down like a mule, and seemed determined to prove his father wrong. She loved the way a lock of his blond hair fell over his forehead when he concentrated on a file.

Will joined the Veterans of Foreign Wars and attended Post meetings. After a few months, they elected him president. He got a hat with gold braid.

Once a week, he went to a Rotary luncheon. "There's another hour I'll never get back," he said to Velma when he returned. He told her he met men at those luncheons who might bring business into the firm.

Gradually, he acquired his own clients. A gas company put the firm on retainer. "It's not a big company like Mississippi Valley Gas," Will told her between dictations. "Our friends over at Brunini represent them, but Mississippi Gas is growing."

Velma knew. She had typed the letters and the contract, but Will's excitement made her feel part of the achievement.

An insurance company hired him to pursue fraudulent claims. Typing the briefs, Velma almost pitied the defendants, most of them criminally stupid before they became actual criminals. One nightclub owner actually moved the club's furniture out to the parking lot before setting his building on fire.

She noticed that Will Hughes, like his father, enjoyed regular habits. He arrived at eight every morning and left at five-fifteen. He brought a single rose from his wife's garden, which Velma put in a vase on his desk. Except on Rotary day, he ordered the same lunch in the drugstore downstairs: tomato soup with saltine crackers. She knew his suits—light gray, dark gray, navy blue, and had never seen a man wear a suit better. She admired the white handkerchief, its jaunty points peeping out of his jacket's breast pocket, a handkerchief which was never removed for a sneeze. He carried another clean handkerchief in his pants pocket for that. She knew his hats, a dark gray fedora for winter, cream-colored straw for summer.

She watched the way he pinched the bridge of his nose when concentrating. He did not like to be interrupted, and she learned to move silently in and out of his office.

She loved taking dictation from him. He often paused, staring into space thinking. Velma took these opportunities to observe him. When he needed a section read back, he looked straight at her while she read, his blue eyes so intense she flushed.

He liked to explain difficult legal points, hands chopping the air as if directing her understanding. When Velma nodded that she did indeed apprehend, she received a coveted smile of approval. For all his seriousness, Will Hughes loved making other people laugh, and when he heard a funny story, he threw back his head, as if laughter knocked him off balance.

Velma never showed, by look or gesture, how she felt. She would never become a Doris, but she couldn't help watching his hands when he marked her work: slender fingers, the nails short and scrupulously clean, hands that looked as if they'd never done manual labor. When he leaned over her shoulder to check her typing, she breathed him in: Old Spice and Listerine, with something toasty underneath.

When she wasn't watching Will Hughes, Velma found herself thinking about him. According to her Baptist beliefs, even this was a sin. Two sins actually: coveting and adultery. Not exactly adultery since she hadn't done anything, but thoughts about a married man came close. The Baptists believed a sinful thought made room for a sinful deed. She prayed every night for pure thoughts, and hoped God was listening; but if He wasn't, surely time would do the trick. She was twenty-five now, practically an old maid.

56

The new house became Lillian's focus, giving her a place to put her energies and a way to ignore Will's coolness. She planned renovations, but knew better than to ask for change directly. Every move had to be thought out and acted upon with caution. Her husband was like a forest animal, happy in his routines, but easily startled by new ideas, especially if they meant spending money. As a first move, she walked around with him, pointing out the faded wallpaper in the dining room and the chipped paint around the living room windows.

"The house is fine," Will said.

"You will be bringing important people home to dinner. We can't afford to appear shabby."

That got his attention. She made suggestions, nothing big, nothing that would upset his routine or interfere with his work.

She began by having the living room re-papered in dark green and the trim painted a fresh white. The couch got a new beige linen slipcover. Two wing chairs were reupholstered. For the dining room, she chose a Chinese-red wallpaper with a motif of pagodas and coolies carrying paper umbrellas.

She waited a year before bringing up the front porch. She wanted to remove the screens and turn the space into a glassed-in sunroom like Faye's in Canton. When that was done (She confided this idea only to Leland and Olive.), she hoped to replace the garage with a master bedroom and bath. For projects requiring more than paint and wallpaper, Leland said, Lillian needed real money.

He gave her the paperwork to apply for a home improvement loan. In a savings account, co-signed by James while Will was away in the Pacific, Lillian had placed her earnings from working at the hotel, along with her brothers' cash donations. She had not yet mentioned this account to Will.

With her plans readied, Lillian cooked Will his favorite meal: fried oysters, creamed corn, boiled okra, with a custard pie for dessert. She persuaded him to try a second piece of pie and excused the children from the table.

"Leland thinks we can double the value of the house by closing in the screen porch and adding another bedroom."

She saw his frown and talked fast. "Sleeping on the far side of the kitchen would keep you from being bothered by the children." The night before, Helen and April had waked him with their arguing.

She hurried on. "You know how good Leland is with money. He says we can get a home improvement loan to cover the cost and it will only slightly increase our monthly mortgage." All big ideas must seem to come from men. "Here are his figures."

Will took the home improvement application and Lillian's budget. "I'll think about it."

She left the table feeling deflated. Thinking about things was how Will got rid of matters he didn't wish to think about. Lillian followed him into the living room. "And I still have my earnings from the hotel." She retrieved her savings book from the secretary and handed it to him.

Will looked at her suspiciously. "How did you open a savings account without my signature?"

"You were overseas, so the bank accepted James as co-signer."

Will flipped to the last entry. "*Twelve thousand dollars.*" He stared at her in disbelief. "Where did you get this kind of money?"

Lillian tried not to look smug. "I worked at the hotel for two years. I've been saving it for a project like this." Will loved the word "save."

The budget and loan papers disappeared. Lillian tried to be patient. A month went by before Will cleared his throat one night at dinner. "I went over the figures with Leland and spoke to Ben Maury at the bank. The project may be doable."

With promises that construction would not interrupt either his sleep or his work, and that Lillian would not nag him with details, Will signed the loan papers.

Once the loan was approved, Lillian found herself in possession of a construction account, giddy at the idea of controlling this much money. Will made sure her savings went into the building fund, but Lillian held $100 back to keep the account open. You never knew.

She began with the front porch. The wire screens disappeared, and waist-to-ceiling windows took their place. Lillian stood in the street to admire the difference. The house already looked more solid. She would plant pink azaleas across the front.

Will loved telling people about Hawaii: the flowers, the water, the white sand beaches and perfect climate. Lillian had no desire to remind him of Sylvia, but she did long to make him happy. In furnishing the new sunroom, she gave him a reminder of that tropical paradise: heavy bamboo porch furniture, with cushions covered in a nubby cotton printed with hibiscus and banana leaves. She had the concrete floor painted red and covered it with a sisal rug. For their new stereo, she bought an album of the musical *South Pacific*. "We've got mangos and bananas we can pick right off the trees." Lillian sang along in off-key snatches as she traveled up and down the hall checking on the workmen.

If Will didn't love her for who she was, maybe he could love her for what she accomplished. That was the hope anyway and she wasn't ready to give it up. She showed him around the finished room.

"Nice." Will said, and took the afternoon paper to his usual chair in the living room.

Nice? Lillian wanted to hit him over the head with one of her bamboo bridge chairs.

Thirteen-year-old Helen adored the sunroom. When she wasn't in school, she could be found propped against a hibiscus-covered cushion with her bare feet dangling over a bamboo arm. She liked to read on the porch while listening to *South Pacific*. Her favorite song was "You've Got to be Carefully Taught." She played it repeatedly, singing along. "You've got to be taught before it's too late/To hate all the people your relatives hate." When Lillian asked her to please lower her voice, Helen said she wanted to make sure her parents got the message. She'd grown from whining into sarcasm, a stage Lillian thought she might not make it through.

The biggest project Lillian saved for last. The one-car garage came down and a bedroom and bath rose in its place. Will Hughes complained about having to park on the street, but Lillian made sure the workmen were gone by the time he got home. She did everything she could to minimize the mess. Plywood hid the new construction from the kitchen, and they sat down to dinner promptly at six in the Chinese red dining room. Each week, as she paid the construction bills, she worried that the money might not last.

Three months later, aside from furniture, the new bedroom was completed. She chose pale green wall-to-wall carpeting and had the room painted the same shade with cream-colored trim. Moving their dark bedroom furniture into this pristine space felt wrong, but when she mentioned new furniture, Will said: "Are you trying to send me to the poor house?"

The man who arrived in Lillian's life driving a sporty convertible had turned out to be extraordinarily frugal. When he decided to get married, Will got rid of the car and, as far as Lillian knew, hadn't spent a spontaneous dollar since. He worked incessantly and no longer merely to please his father. He would deny this if asked, but Lillian sensed the scope of Will's ambition. Her role was to be the presentable wife, raise polite children, and provide him with a comfortable house and a good dinner every evening precisely at six.

He had always been strange about money. Not just careful— secretive. He gave her an allowance to pay Doreen, buy food, and cover the household expenses. Beyond that, what he earned and how much he was worth became his business alone. Growing up at the hotel, managing expenses had been a family affair. Everyone knew how much the hotel earned and what they needed to cover expenses, the former usually smaller than the latter.

As a married woman, when Lillian asked for extra money, Will's almost automatic answer became: "We can't afford it." She had no idea if this was true because she wasn't allowed to know how much he made. When he did decide to spend money, he did it without consulting her. Cars, for instance. Every four years, before the new models came out, Will brought home a leftover from the previous year. Always a Chevrolet. She would have enjoyed walking around the dealership, deciding on color and interior details, but she was never invited. Will Hughes' wife should be waiting at the back door, hands raised in surprise and pleasure.

Lillian was not supposed to accept cash gifts from her brothers. Used cars were an exception. Whenever Leland bought a new Buick, he offered Will the old one for Lillian, and Will did not object.

She had married a man regular in his habits and cautious with his money. She hadn't expected that, but had learned to work carefully, even secretively, around it. She loved Will and also feared him. Worse, she feared that he no longer loved her. She could no more ask about that than she could ask twice for new bedroom furniture.

Olive came to the rescue. She and Leland now lived in a large house in a wealthy subdivision called Woodland Hills. Olive had redone her ground floor guest suite, and was getting rid of two blonde chests with a matching mirror and two side tables. Lillian could have it all if she wanted. She did. Everything Olive owned had been bought new, and everything Lillian owned, including most of the furniture in the house, had been handed down from someone. She was thrilled. All she needed now was a new bed.

Will said no. Their old bed would do just fine. Olive added a headboard to the offer, a padded, tufted, caramel-colored, leather headboard. *Perfect.* Lillian now only needed to purchase a bed frame and mattress. Two models fit under the gift headboard: a new thing called a king, or two twins. She was terrified Will would say no to both, and she filled him up with chocolate meringue pie before broaching the subject. When he heard the words "twin beds," he admitted that he'd grown accustomed to sleeping alone in the Navy. He'd read somewhere that a double bed (like the one they'd slept on since the day they married) gave each person the space of a baby's crib.

Lillian got the message. He no longer wished to sleep next to her and was willing to spend money not to. She consoled herself. They would still be side by side under the tufted headboard, practically in the same bed, and the vision of caramel leather against the pale green walls cheered her.

Helen would get their old room, along with its furniture. Lillian made the mistake of letting the two older girls choose wallpaper for their newly separate bedrooms. April agreed to Lillian's choice, a cheerful pattern of yellow roses on a white background. Helen insisted on an almost black-green paper with dogwood blossoms. Her room looked as dark as a cellar.

In the newly-built addition, the leather headboard looked more impressive than Lillian had hoped. She made up the twin beds with pristine white sheets and beige bedspreads (purchases she would need to justify when the bill arrived). She put their clothes in the drawers of the new chests and in the freshly painted closets. The wall-mounted brass lamps beside each bed had also been gifts from Olive. They had weighted pulleys that raised and lowered the reading light at a touch. Lillian adored them.

She stood back and admired the results. The bedside lamps hung at identical heights over the blond wood side tables. The two beds pushed together under the leather headboard looked like one. She placed the newest copy of *Time* magazine on Will's bedside table and a *Ladies Home Journal* on hers. A glass ashtray for each of them. From the old bedroom, she'd brought a small armchair and slip-covered it in a deeper green linen. That went beside her bed. A Windsor chair, a gift from Will's mother, stood in the opposite corner. He could use it to put on his shoes. Lillian squinted: The completed room looked like a picture in a magazine.

She played bridge three times a week now with Dimple, Hilda, and Frances. They had been crazy about the Hawaiian sunroom. Wait until they saw this.

When Will came in from work that afternoon, Lillian opened the freshly painted door off the kitchen and led him down a step into the new space. She pointed out its features, unable to keep the excitement out of her voice.

"I didn't realize we'd have to step down," Will said.

"The new room is built on a slab," Lillian said. "It's only one step."

Will looked around in silence.

Lillian spoke for him. "Isn't it splendid?"

"Fine. Fine." He sniffed. "Is that paint?"

"The smell will go away. Are you pleased?"

"Nice to be able to park in my own driveway again." He hung his jacket and tie on the brass caddy she'd put next to his closet and went to find the afternoon paper.

Lillian felt squashed. But she kept the disappointment to herself. Will had never been a decorating kind of man.

That night, as they lay side by side with their magazines, she stretched out an arm and could not reach him. The new beds were wider than she expected. She looked past her new bed jacket, the pink satin ribbons tied over her small breasts, to her legs stretched alone beneath the covers. Over there, Will's legs, longer and under entirely separate covers.

All her efforts, from the dining room wallpaper to the flowered cushions on the sun porch, had been aimed at creating a home so warm and lovely, Will might forgive her for not producing a son. This would be the place where they rediscovered the lost intimacy. She had failed. Will resented the money she'd spent and neither noticed nor appreciated the results.

She took a breath to lift the weight of disappointment, opened her magazine, and pretended to read. The man she married had never welcomed change, but wait until the first important lawyer came to dinner and Will got complimented on his home. Her efforts had not been wasted; the reward was simply delayed.

Breathe. Some days you needed to be your own cheerleader.

Snores rose and fell beside her. In their old double bed, once Will fell asleep, Lillian liked to slide close to his back, curling herself to fit his warmth. The twin beds rendered him untouchable.

57

Lillian loved seeing the newly refurbished house filled with people. She encouraged Will to bring colleagues home for dinner. Once a week, she hosted the bridge luncheon. Helen brought friends over after school and to spend the night on weekends.

Under her breath, Doreen muttered about this increased traffic. "Can't get my work done. Soon as I get things right, here come more folks, messing up my clean house."

When Lillian interrupted and asked straight out what was wrong, Doreen claimed innocence, but the low growl of discontent continued and dampened everyone's enjoyment. Helen complained that her friends didn't feel welcome.

Lillian brought the subject up at bedtime, making the mistake of starting with Doreen's bad mood.

Will put down his *Time* magazine. "You're in charge of the household. Take care of it."

"Now that the girls are getting older, I thought maybe we should cut Doreen's days and get a cook."

"As long as that doesn't cost more." A pause. "Would Doreen still do my shirts?"

Will was particular about his white dress shirts. The collars and cuffs, along with the placket, should be starched as stiff as a priest's collar. He liked the body lightly starched. This took a lot of skill with a box of Argo and a hot iron.

"It may cost a little more to have the two of them."

His mouth turned down, forehead creasing in disapproval.

"But without Doreen we'd have to send your shirts to the cleaner's and you know what they do to them."

Will Hughes exhaled, shaking his head to indicate that Lillian would drive him into penury. "Do what you have to."

Had there ever been a man who so hated spending money? You'd think he'd ridden freight trains through the Depression instead of getting his own car at fourteen.

The next morning, Lillian asked Doreen to sit with her at the kitchen table. "Mr. Hughes wants to entertain more, so we've decided to hire a cook."

Doreen gazed at her without expression. "Yes ma'am."

Lillian had known a lot of colored people at the hotel. Most didn't enjoy looking white people in the eye, but Doreen stared straight at her, which was disconcerting. She found saying the words harder than when she practiced in front of the bathroom mirror. "Which means, I'm afraid, cutting back on your days." She hurried on, counting on her fingers instead of looking at Doreen. "Starting next week, I'll get you to come on Monday, Wednesday and Friday."

"Yes ma'am."

Four-year-old Maude, sucking her thumb, leaned into Doreen.

Doreen put an arm around the child.

Lillian shook her head. "Honestly, you'd think she was two the way she holds onto you." She found the clinging irritating, as if the child thought Doreen was her mother. "I've told my friends how wonderful you are, Doreen, and I expect they'll be fighting over your free days."

"Yes ma'am."

Colored people appeared to listen, but you never knew what they were thinking.

When Doreen left for the day, Lillian told Helen and April.

"You can't do that." Helen's voice so biting it made Lillian flinch. "She's been with us our whole lives."

"Don't use that tone with me, young lady. And don't you start crying, April. Look, now you've upset your baby sister." The kitchen sounded like a mad house. Lillian stirred the vegetable soup. Will hated vegetable soup night and she was in a foul mood over Doreen, who'd kept quiet as a monk after their talk. She answered if Lillian asked a question, but was mute otherwise. It felt like a rebuke.

Lillian turned on Helen. "You made me do it, complaining about her bad mood, so don't start with 'How could you.'" Enjoying the crushed look on her daughter's face. "Besides, I did not 'let Doreen go.' She will still be here three days a week." At dinner, she pretended not to hear when Will looked up from the soup and said, "Where's the meat?"

She hired a tall, heavy, very dark-skinned woman, with a booming laugh and a mouth filled with white teeth. Her name was Bessie Johnson. She told Lillian she knew how to cook fine, as long as it was nothing fancy. From the size of her she certainly enjoyed her food. Whatever skills she lacked Lillian could teach her.

Two weeks later, Helen stood frowning in Lillian's doorway.

"What now?"

"Bessie lurks."

"I beg your pardon?"

"She comes down the hall and stands in my door when I'm reading. Doesn't say a word. Just stands there."

"She's trying not to interrupt you. She's waiting for you to acknowledge her."

"Feels like she's waiting to murder me."

"Don't be absurd."

Bessie was large, maybe 250 pounds, and she did have a heavy tread. It had been like adding a bear to the house, a large bear in a white uniform. Bessie replaced small, tidy Doreen's muttering with loud good cheer. Lillian watched Will wince each time she hollered, "Morning' Mr. Will." But her fried chicken was divine and her creamed corn better than Lillian's.

Three days a week, Doreen cleaned and ironed as only she could, and without much muttering. She and Bessie chatted pleasantly. For three days, Lillian didn't have Maude following along behind her whimpering. "Where's D'reen?"

One Thursday, Lillian turned and shouted. "Doreen is not your mother. I'm your mother." Which, of course, caused a fit. "Want D'reen," Maude sobbed as Lillian wiped her snotty nose. It was all she could do not to slap the child.

58

In January of 1950, Mr. Pat retired. He'd been a member of the Mississippi Bar since 1898, and declared fifty-two years of practice enough. His eyes were going bad; he wanted to stay home in the mornings and enjoy the newspaper with Margaret.

The office threw a huge party with non-alcoholic punch (Mr. Pat being a non-drinker). People came from all over the state: lawyers, judges, and politicians. Mr. Pat gave a talk about what the law had meant to him. Other people made speeches about what Patrick Hughes had meant to the law.

Standing behind the punch bowl in the carpeted lobby, Velma filled cups, smiled, and observed the men in dark suits with their important voices, the secretaries in bright dresses like decorative birds.

Mr. Pat stood the midst of it all, still straight and handsome with his shock of white hair. She'd never met a nobler man. He had believed in her when she was a raw eighteen-year-old from Picayune. With skill and principle, he had built Hughes & Blair into one of the finest law firms in the state and brought her along as it grew. He demanded the best, but he was always kind, and ready with a quip to lift people's spirits. She wept thinking how much she would miss him. Once again, life was changing.

Will held out his cup. "A cup of punch, please, without tears."

Velma wiped her face with the back of her hand, embarrassed.

"Just you and me now," Will said. "Think we can handle it?"

She smiled but did not trust herself to speak. *Just you and me.* Heart bumping at the words. She told herself not to be ridiculous. She had asked to serve punch today because she felt more comfortable behind this table than in front of it. If she knew anything, she knew her place. She and Will Hughes had worked together for five years now and were comfortable enough to tease each other. She had been around his wife Lillian a dozen times. From a distance, she had watched his children grow. She had no illusions.

On Monday, Will would move into the big corner office and she would become his secretary. *Just you and me.* She could never be his wife, but she would be the person closest to him for most of their waking hours. In a strange and pure way, she could be his office wife.

Standing with the ladle in her hand, Velma listened to Mr. Pat speak. Will stood beside her, sipping his punch, laughing at his father's jokes, content to wait his turn.

Velma took a silent vow of celibacy: she would never marry. She hadn't been able to stand Chalmers Root, and hadn't taken to Harold Meeks (who never called her back). This man standing beside her owned her heart. Mr. Right had come along, exactly the way Garnett predicted, but he was taken. She would devote herself to the job and to Will Hughes. He need never know.

She had never slept with a man, but hundreds, no thousands of women gave up men for God. Mostly they were nuns, not Baptists. Velma made a vow to forsake marriage for God and Will Hughes. She would be a secret order of one.

59

Will moved his things into his father's office. He handed Velma a framed tintype. "My great-great-grandfather." Velma studied the faded face of a scared looking boy wearing a Confederate uniform. Will pointed to where he wanted it hung. "I'm afraid I'm no good at this."

"That's all right." Velma found a hammer, a small nail, pounded it in, and leveled the frame.

Will stood back admiring. "He's my hero, you know. Enlisted at sixteen when he was just a boy, willing to go and die for the South. I was named for him." He nodded with satisfaction and that was the end of his decorating.

The briefs, thick inside their legal-size manila folders, began piling up. Velma suggested filing them and offered to, but Will said a brief should not be put away until the case was closed, either settled or tried, appealed or not, but finished, done. Which meant the stacks of briefs on Will's desk multiplied; older briefs accumulated on the floor; piles of briefs leaned against the ends of the leather couch; heaps grew on the wide marble window ledges.

Velma worried about the dust. She heard Will sneezing in the mornings and mentioned tidying. Will said not to bother. He knew where everything was and didn't want anything disturbed. She worried aloud about the sneezing and he gave her what she came to think of as the blue freeze, a look that let her know she'd crossed a line. She should take a step back and stay out of his business.

Velma never mentioned the state of his office again. She made her way around the stacks to take dictation and to leave completed work on Will's desk. She returned to her own pristine desk, kept as Mrs. Evans recommended when Velma arrived at the firm seven years before: nothing visible but her shorthand notebook or the brief she corrected. "You are the face of this office," Mrs. Evans had said. Velma never forgot.

60

In March, Hughes & Blair got the biggest case ever to come into the office. The company owning Jackson's morning newspaper, *The Clarion Ledger*, tried a hostile take-over of the afternoon paper, *The Jackson Daily News*. The afternoon paper resisted, choosing Will Hughes as their lawyer. Velma swelled with reflected pride.

Will sat her down in his office, his face alive with excitement "I have an idea. It may sound crazy, but I want you to go to court with me during the trial."

Velma nodded. She had never been invited to watch him argue.

"Do you think you can get down everything both sides say?"

"I believe so." Six to eight hours of dictation. That meant a half dozen shorthand pads.

"After court each day, if you were able to type up a transcript, I could go over the testimony before we begin the next morning. Think you can do it?"

"I'll certainly try."

"This will give me an advantage over the other side. Those guys will have no access to a transcript." He grinned like a boy. "It's a lot to ask, but it may give us a winning edge."

The thrill of battle was contagious. Velma sat up straighter. They were in this war together.

She had never felt so vital and necessary as those days spent in court. She worked eighteen hours. Eight hours in court, writing furiously, going through one shorthand tablet after another. During their lunch break, over soup and crackers, Will asked her to read portions aloud, amazed he claimed, at her ability to translate those squiggles into English. At night, he brought sandwiches and coffee to the office while she typed furiously. He read over the pages as they came out of her machine.

"See this?" He got so excited reading, he forgot to eat his ham and cheese. "Caught the bastard." He meant Mr. H, President of the company, trying to illegally take advantage of the afternoon newspaper. Velma looked up from the typewriter, proud of his quick mind and happy to be a part of this important endeavor.

Together, they fought the evils of monopoly. The country was in the middle of a war in Korea—General McArthur and his troops had just recaptured Seoul and were pushing toward the 38th Parallel. No town of Jackson's size and prominence should have to depend on a single source for news.

They shared a smile over his cleverness, *their* cleverness. She smiled openly at him now, long over any self-consciousness about her gums.

Will insisted on driving Velma home when they were done. Said it wasn't safe for a woman to be out after 10:00 at night. She accepted the ride and his concern because they came from him, not out of any fear for her safety. She was twenty-six years old and had been on her own for eight years. She'd taken plenty of bus rides at night. No one ever bothered her. She was accustomed to being the type of person others did not notice. Invisibility turned out to be a good place from which to observe.

This was a new feeling, being taken care of, told to go straight to bed because they had another long day tomorrow. It was almost like marriage, she imagined, except for the bed part, which she did her best not to think about. She had prayed her way into neutrality, asking God to remove the temptation without taking away the man, and God had granted her wish.

At home, after the third long day, soaking her aching hands in Epson salts, Velma thought about her celibate life, the chaste bed where she slept alone, and probably always would. She waited for a stab of regret, but none arrived. Drying her hands, she rubbed on

Jergens lotion, breathing in the almond scent, and flexed her fingers. Good and faithful servants, these hands. They earned her keep and the respect of the man she— She switched the word in her head to "most admired."

On her knees, Velma prayed for her family down in Picayune, for Will and his wife and their three girls, and for a peaceful end to the war. Her hands and the small of her back ached, but with a few hours of sleep she would awake renewed.

Will had taken that day's transcript home to read. He would pick her up at 6:30 in the morning. Breakfast would be coffee and toast in the downstairs drugstore while Will plotted the day's strategy. With no typewriter to distract her, Velma watched him, admiring the way his ears fit close to his head, the noble shape of his nose. She found these breakfasts more difficult than their sandwiches at night, or even the soup at midday. Maybe because she came to him fresh from her bed—and there she went, thinking things she shouldn't. She went through her bag, counting the shorthand pads and sharpened pencils.

Will looked up from her typed pages. "Eat."

She took tiny bites of toast so as not to look like a horse chewing, and watched his long fingers moving through her white pages, the nails cut close and very clean. Papa would laugh at a man who never got his hands dirty, but Velma liked the look of Will fingers, now curled around the thick china cup. She loved seeing the light spring into his blue eyes when he conjured up a new trick against the opposition. Each time she caught herself staring, she felt her face go hot. Will never noticed, too caught up in thickets of legal logic to see her. As he should be.

That night, on her knees, thinking about Will instead of praying, Velma apologized to God for the lapse and got into bed, reciting the twenty-third Psalm to clear her mind: "Yea, though I walk through the Valley of the Shadow of Death, I will fear no evil, for Thou art with me." She reached over to turn off the ballerina light. She wanted this trial to go on forever.

Every good thing must end. Will's side won. The two papers would not be joined. The afternoon paper carried huge black headlines heralding this victory for freedom of the press. The story mentioned

Will Hughes and his brilliant courtroom tactics. People stopped by the office to offer congratulations. Velma felt fully part of this celebration, though no one knew the part she'd played. Will gave her a week's pay as a bonus and told her to take a few days off. Go and see her folks.

"I appreciate the offer," Velma said. "Maybe later." For now, she wanted to be here, basking in the glow of their shared victory.

The very next month, the owner of *The Jackson Daily News* called to tell Will he'd decided to sell the paper after all. Mr. H, owner of the morning paper, had made an offer too sweet to refuse. He wasn't being forced, so he was ready to sell. The firm should draw up the papers.

Typing the sales contract, Velma felt confused and disillusioned. Wasn't principle what the whole case had been about? She asked Will. Hadn't they fought for diversity against monopoly, only to have their client choose monopoly? Will said the only principle she needed to worry about was an error-free contract. The client came first and this was what the client wanted.

Feeling squelched, Velma returned to her typewriter. She hadn't minded the long hours of shorthand and typing because they were for a higher cause. For the first time, the law felt slippery and mean. If Mr. Pat were still here, he would tell the afternoon paper to go find themselves another lawyer. If they wanted to trade principle for forty pieces of silver, they could do it with another firm. Not that she was criticizing Will. This was the way business operated. This was how the world worked. Besides, she would never criticize Will.

61

Lillian and Will had met Alice and Avery Staples at the country club before the war. They were a colorful addition to Jackson—Alice large and blonde, Avery small and dark. They were generous with their hospitality and became Lillian's new favorite people. When she and Will moved back to Jackson, she got in touch.

With the money Avery made staying out of the war (Oil, Lillian heard; the black market, Will hinted), he and Alice built themselves a large two-story house out on Old Canton Road. Invitations followed. The Staples seemed to find Lillian charming and Will clever.

This past winter, they had taken the two of them to New Orleans for the Sugar Bowl, put them up in a suite, and treated them to dinners at Antoine's and Commander's Palace, and to breakfast at Brennan's with milk punch. Alice and Avery liked having them around and money did not appear to be an issue; they had enough to share. This was exactly the life Lillian had dreamed of when she was stuck at the hotel. Plus, she got to do it with the man she loved, who did not appear as thrilled.

Getting dressed to go to yet another Staples party, Will said, "It offends me to accept favors I can't repay, especially from a man I don't respect."

Lillian leaned into the mirror putting on lipstick. "Avery and Alice are very generous people. Why can't you just enjoy them?"

"I'll let you enjoy them for both of us."

Lillian found this ridiculous. Maybe Avery hadn't finished college, but neither had Lillian or her brothers, and a lot of other people who had come through the Depression. With Will, it was always about the war: a man who chose making money over serving his country could never be admired.

Avery got loud and maybe a little coarse when he drank, but Lillian had grown up with Leland and James. Avery reminded her of Frank Sinatra with his big head of shiny dark hair and his skinny little body. Their parties were filled with drink and laughter. Lillian adored her husband in spite of his 6:00 dinners and 9:00 bedtime, but she missed having fun.

Will could be the wittiest person Lillian had ever known when he chose to be. When he brought visiting attorneys home for dinner, he told stories that made the room echo with laughter. Around Avery Staples, he turned silent: No, thank you, he didn't believe he cared for a martini or a gin fizz, or anything except perhaps a glass of water, if that wouldn't be too much trouble. With that little edge in his voice Lillian hated. Avery didn't seem to hear it. He kept trying to find something Will liked: "Try this sausage. I have it shipped down from Chicago. You won't believe this rye bread. Alice, bring out that caviar pie you made. I'll bet old Will here never tasted anything like it." Will stared at Alice's pie, the caviar layered with hard-boiled eggs and sour cream, and said thank you, but he'd never cared for fish eggs.

Lillian convinced him to swallow his distaste and at least attend the parties. Plenty of oilmen were moving to Jackson. Any one of them could be a new client for the firm.

The Friday night gatherings had turned into an almost weekly event. Lillian had never attended a cocktail party until she met the Staples, but cocktails had become her favorite kind of get-together. No quick drink—two if you were lucky—followed by a long, tedious dinner, course after course where you could only talk to the person on either side of you or across the table, and hearing laughter at the other end, you knew you were missing the best stuff. At cocktail parties, drinking was the point. You drank standing up and ate little bits of this and that. You got to mingle. If you heard a burst of laughter from across the room, you walked right over.

On this Saturday in May, Lillian felt especially attractive. She'd made herself a dress of white silk with red polka dots, the waist cinched by a big red belt. She wore new red heels. She'd sipped her way through two martinis and felt exhilarated. Avery told her she had the tiniest feet he'd ever seen on a woman.

From the couch in the Staples' den, half-reclined, a third martini in hand, Lillian lifted a leg toward him. "Really?" She made it sound funny, saying "Reeeely?" Grinning at Will across the room to show him it was all a joke.

Avery grabbed her foot. "Whoa, whoa, whoa, whoa," he said. Moving both hands up one silky stocking to her garter. Lillian giggled and pushed him away. Will leapt, his face white, and punched Avery in the nose.

Their host fell sideways, dripping blood onto his lovely blue silk tie. Lillian whipped a small, lace-trimmed handkerchief from her purse. "I am so sorry." Other people in the room went quiet and stared.

Holding Lillian's now bloody handkerchief to his nose, Avery stood. He put a hand on Will's arm. "Think nothing of it, old man. Meant no harm. What's a little blood between friends?"

Will peeled Avery's hand off him. To Lillian he said, "I'll be in the car."

Leaving her to apologize for the mess, for his atrocious behavior, and with no choice but to pick up her purse and go.

Cold silence on the drive home. Lillian finally said, "I don't know why you're so mad. He was only kidding around."

Will drove without looking at her. "If you don't know why I'm angry, then you're not the woman I married."

"For God's sake, Will, where's your sense of humor?"

"Must have lost it watching you pour down those martinis."

"That's what you're really mad about, isn't it? That I know how to have a good time?"

"There's a good time and there's pickled. You embarrass yourself."

"I can hold my liquor, thank you."

"That's why you like these parties—nobody's counting your drinks."

Which was exactly why she liked them, and had believed herself unwatched. All this time Will had been counting. Lillian kept quiet.

"You drink too much. You're always squeezing in an extra one before dinner, or suggesting everybody have a nightcap after. Your brothers drink too much. It's a family problem."

"Your problem is you don't drink enough." Lillian hiccupped, which spoiled the effect.

"None of you Creekmores can drink without getting drunk," Will said. "You need to think about that."

"Ernestine doesn't drink too much."

"Ernestine has other problems."

Will disliked being around her older sister, which tickled Lillian.

They went to their separate beds. Lillian felt dizzy and knew she would have a headache tomorrow, but it was nothing two cups of coffee and a couple of Bufferin couldn't fix. She thought about the party: Avery hadn't put his hands above her garter, so what had been so terrible? She smiled. He must like her. She didn't care for him in that way, but the attention was invigorating. Will never commented on how she looked anymore. Tonight, he'd gotten insanely jealous. Jealousy was good. Jealousy meant he still had feelings for her.

The evening had gone swimmingly until Will lost his temper. He probably wouldn't want to go to the Staples again, even though Avery had been so forgiving and generous about being punched. Plus, Will got to preach his little sermon in the car coming home. She'd held her own though.

She remembered Avery's hands on her leg, small and too soft. She wouldn't trade Will for six Avery Staples, not even to get the money. Tomorrow she'd make that chess pie Will loved. He'd forget all about this.

62

The summer after the newspaper case, Will seemed out of sorts. Velma responded by trying to make herself even more unobtrusive. On a Thursday in early September, he asked if she would mind staying late to finish a motion due the next day.

"Not at all."

When she was done and had put the cover over her typewriter, Will offered to take her to dinner. "Not sandwiches in the office," he said. "Let's have a real dinner."

She excused herself and went to the Ladies Room to check how she looked. No better or worse than usual. She combed her hair and put on more lipstick. What did a dinner invitation mean? Nothing, her sensible mind answered.

Will drove to a place called The Rotisserie on the other side of town. Velma recognized the name from Garnett's engagement. During the drive, he kept silent.

Velma tried to think of something to say. "Is this one of your favorite places?"

"They make a good Chicken Cacciatore." He guided her through the door and, at the table, pulled out her chair. He ordered chicken for the two of them and beer to drink.

On her date with Harold Meeks, they'd only eaten pie, but Velma had been allowed to choose her flavor. Maybe this was how professional men behaved: pulling out your chair and deciding what you ate. Plus, she needed to remember, this wasn't a date; this was her boss.

Their chicken arrived along with the beers. Velma eyed the tall glass of brown liquid. "I don't drink." Not the entire truth. She'd had champagne after the typing contest.

Will smiled. "Mississippi beer is only 3.2 per cent alcohol, so it almost doesn't count."

Velma took a swallow. Bitter and horrid-tasting.

He laughed at the face she made.

She tried again. It felt rude not to. A small sip with each bite of chicken made the beer a little less terrible. She was nervous eating in front of Will and had to stop herself from holding the napkin in front of her mouth while she chewed. He was right about the chicken, though; it was delicious,

"Trust me." Will nodded at the beer. "You won't need to ask forgiveness from your Baptist God."

She was being made fun of. Velma had never thought of God as having a denomination, and she never discussed religion at the office. How did Will Hughes know she was a Baptist? Not that it was a secret. In Mississippi, practically the first thing a new acquaintance got asked was where she went to church. But Will had never asked. Maybe she'd mentioned it and forgotten.

"Hey." Will's voice brought her back. "I was only kidding."

When she glanced up from her plate, she saw him looking at her in a different way, as if for the first time he actually saw her. She couldn't hold his gaze. In her lap, she rolled her napkin into a tube.

"Now I've embarrassed you," he said. "I like watching you enjoy your food."

Instead of being mature and saying she wasn't embarrassed, Velma giggled and covered her mouth.

"Why do you do that?"

"What?" She knew what.

"Cover your mouth when you laugh."

"Your father once said the same thing."

Will Hughes' eyebrows went up in mock horror: "My father said he liked watching you?"

She felt her face growing hotter. "He said I shouldn't cover my mouth."

"He was right. You have a very nice smile." Will cleared his throat, looked for the waitress, and got their check.

He drove her home, asked if she could manage the stairs on her own (as if she didn't manage the stairs every night of her life), and said he'd see her tomorrow.

Velma climbed, feeling giddy. Must be the beer. Brushing her teeth, she practiced smiling with a mouthful of froth. "You have a very nice smile," she said to the woman in the mirror.

On her knees, she thanked God for giving her such an amazing person to work for. She hadn't done one thing tonight that required forgiveness. Well, maybe the beer. She lay in bed, unable to sleep. Every time she began to drift off, she saw Will's intense blue eyes watching—and actually seeing her.

63

Lillian climbed into bed with *Redbook*. She'd finished making back-to-school outfits for the girls and felt tired but satisfied. When Will called and said not to wait supper, she celebrated by feeding the children in the kitchen, calling Bessie a cab, and having three drinks.

At eight o'clock, Will walked into the bedroom and put his suit coat on the brass caddy the way he did every other night. Except tonight he said, "I don't want to be married anymore."

Lillian thought she must have heard wrong. "I beg your pardon." It couldn't be the drinks. She had brushed her teeth twice.

"I'm sorry, but that's the truth of it." He shook his head as if to clear it.

Lillian sat up straighter in bed and took her reading glasses off. Her heart pounded and her skin felt clammy.

I've been thinking about this for a long time," he said. "When I got that letter telling me what you'd done, something drained away."

Drained away? Like love was a leaking tub? Anger made Lillian's head pound. "That was six years ago. You're telling me you don't want to be married because I refused to die giving you a son?"

The fury she felt, along with a gut panic, made her want to do something rash: scream or fire a gun, except they didn't own a gun. Humiliating to be told such a thing while sitting in bed in a blue nylon nightgown with her make-up off. "The doctor wasn't willing to let me die." Her voice shook.

Will's voice sounded flat. "We've already had this discussion."

"Is there someone else?"

He shook his head. "I just want to be free."

"Well, you're not free. You have a wife and three daughters." She tried to light a cigarette, but shook so hard she had to hold the lighter with both hands. She saw Will's eyes squint the way they did when he saw something he didn't like. He'd never said it, but she suspected he didn't approve of a woman smoking. His precious mother hadn't smoked. She got the cigarette lit and took a deep drag. Nicotine fed the anger. "Serve you right if I killed myself."

"Don't be dramatic."

"Why not? If you leave, my life is over."

"A lot of people get divorced." He took off his tie and began unbuttoning his shirt.

"Not in my family." Which was true. In his—that snotty bunch of religious hypocrites—everyone had been divorced except for his parents and Frances, the English professor. And, until tonight, them.

"What about our vows?" She squashed the cigarette and tried reason. If only her hands would stop shaking. "I blame the war." Talking fast so he couldn't interrupt. "You haven't been the same since you came home. Working nights, Saturdays and Sundays. You've run yourself down." She took a breath. "We've been married for sixteen years. You can't just walk in here on a Friday night and tell me it's over."

Nothing in his face changed. She tried the final weapon. "What about the children? This will kill them."

She saw him wince. In this house, he got to be the good daddy, the one who told funny stories at the dinner table and handed out allowances. She had become, by necessity, the disciplinarian, the parent who shouted and spanked, and sent them to their rooms.

"I'm not staying." Will's shoulders were as stiff as his mouth.

"Then you'll have to tell them." Her face crumpled. "You can't do this to us." She watched him turn his back on her tears. Her face turned ugly when she cried. No man liked that. Women think crying will prick a man's conscience, but tears only make them want to run. She wiped her face and blew her nose on a tissue. "And I promise you one thing—I'm not giving you a divorce."

"We'll tell the children we're separating." Will paused. "*I will tell them.*

She started crying again, she couldn't help it.

He looked at her with what appeared to be dislike. "You can cry all night, Lillian. It won't change my mind. I'll find somewhere to live tomorrow."

"*Tomorrow?* You're leaving *tomorrow?*" Her voice rose.

"Could you keep it down, please? We're not going to talk about this anymore." He disappeared into the bathroom and came out in his pajamas. "I'm going to sleep now."

He crawled into his bed as if this were any other night and turned his back on her. Lillian listened as his breathing slowed. He had always been able to fall asleep in seconds while she lay next to him with her legs twitching. Lillian stood it as long as she could and threw the covers off. A shot of bourbon would calm her nerves.

Will spoke from the depths of his pillow. "I hope you're not getting up to drink."

She tied her robe and picked up her cigarettes. "Not your problem anymore, is it?"

Will grunted as she shut the bedroom door. She took the bottle of bourbon out of the sideboard, along with the silver shot glass, and went into the dark living room. The operation had made him stop loving her? A thing she'd agreed to when she was doped up and crazy with fear, about to get a baby cut out of her stomach? Had she even agreed to a hysterectomy? She certainly hadn't signed anything. Surely, she'd told them to do it only if she had a son. Ernestine had written Will a letter explaining, she remembered that much, the letter he claimed drained his love.

Looking back felt like finding her way through a tangle of lies. Taking two years off her age that day of their drive; pretending to be the kind of girl he wanted, one who didn't talk too much or cry. Or drink. Pretending she cared about the law. Sneaking money from her brothers. Not to mention the big lie—that night with Bob Bradshaw, which was *nothing,* compared with him and Sylvia.

On the day Will asked her to marry him, he said: "I don't say things I don't mean." Now he meant to leave. She took another sip of bourbon. Her stomach burned. Pacing the living room, she wiped her eyes and nose with the tail of her nightgown. She was helpless. If a man said he wanted to go, there was not a damned thing a woman could do about it.

She dropped onto the couch, wrapping her arms around her shoulders. This was pitiful, sitting here the dark hugging herself, but she might never have anyone else to hug. The hopelessness of that thought brought on sobbing, ugly animal sounds. When she'd worn those out, she blew her nose on her nightgown.

Outside, the night was quiet. Everyone else snug in their houses, lying in their beds two by two, living their lives, dreaming their dreams. Everyone but her. She took a final swallow of bourbon and changed her nightgown before crawling into bed.

The next morning, Will's face remained hard. He went into the bathroom without speaking. Lillian addressed the closed door. "You'll have to tell the girls. It will break their hearts."

Water running; toilet flushing; silence.

Will came out in his underwear and a fresh shirt. "I said I would, didn't I?" He didn't look at her. He pulled on his pants, threaded a belt through the loops, turned his back, and chose a tie.

"You can tell them tonight." She hesitated. "Before you move out." Maybe Will would say there was no reason to do anything so quickly. He didn't. Here she was, in the dregs of her life, talking to a man who refused to look at her.

Will ate breakfast with his usual appetite, kissed the girls, and left.

Lillian needed to speak to somebody with more sense than she possessed at this moment. Who? Faye up in Canton, Dimple, Frances, Hilda? The only thing worse than being left was being pitied. Pity would finish her off. No one must know.

Will came home at five-thirty, took the suitcase from his closet shelf, and opened it on the bed. Lillian watched, hollowed by dread. He was actually going to do this. He put in underwear, pajamas, the newest *Time* magazine and his shaving kit.

She hoped her watching made it harder. She thought of everything she'd done to win him, and all the effort she'd made to keep him. None of it worth a damn tonight. He hadn't taken many clothes. Maybe he planned on coming home for refills.

From the kitchen, Bessie spied the suitcase. "Where you headed with me about to put dinner on the table?"

Neither of them answered.

Lillian asked the children to come out into the hall between Helen and April's rooms. "Your father has something he'd like to say." Fourteen-year-old Helen had to be pulled away from her book. She appeared looking grumpy. Lillian waited. This was what Will wanted, let him do it. April looked apprehensive. Lillian held Maude, who was five and heavy, but liked to be high enough to see what was going on. Lillian's face was puffy from crying and no sleep, but she had powdered under her eyes to try and cover the worst of it. Children never noticed how their parents looked anyway, not until they got to Helen's age, when they noticed nothing but flaws.

Awful, standing in a hall smelling of roast beef, waiting for her life to end.

Will squatted to April's height. Looking down on him, Lillian loved the silly pompadour he was so proud of and the shape of his ears. She shifted Maude and sniffed, trying not to cry.

Will gave her a look over his shoulder, a warning not to make this harder. "Girls, first, I want you to know that none of it is your fault. I love you more than anything, but—" His voice cracked. "Your mother and I—" His voice broke again. "—are separating."

At eleven, April was nothing but feelings. She began sobbing. Maude joined in. Helen frowned, staring at her father. Will was crying too now, tears running down his face. Lillian had never seen him cry. "I will be living somewhere else—"

April flung her arms around him, almost knocking him backwards. "Don't leave, Daddy. Please don't leave us."

The noise brought Bessie out of the kitchen. She stood at the other end of the hall glowering. "My dinner's getting cold."

"In a minute, Bessie." Lillian shifted Maude's weight. The child blubbered.

Will hugged April. "I won't be far away, sugar."

"Why?" Helen said.

He let go of April and stood. "It's something your mother and I have to work out." His eyes pleading with her to understand.

"Why can't you work it out here with us?"

Helen, ever practical. Silently, Lillian cheered her on.

"Because it's a grownup thing, and it doesn't involve you children." Lillian heard Will's voice turn testy. He didn't like being questioned. "We'll still see each other. I'll just be sleeping somewhere else." He stopped. "While your mother and I figure things out."

Helen said, "How long is that going to take?"

Will shook his head. He had no answer.

"We never see you now," she said.

"I know, baby, but this will be different. I'll make time, I promise. We'll do things together on the weekends, like go to baseball games."

Lillian watched as her oldest daughter perked up.

Will gave them each a kiss, walked through the kitchen, and picked up his suitcase. They followed him up the hall and stood watching.

To Bessie, he said, "I'm counting on you to care of things around here." The back door closed behind him.

No one spoke except Maude, who said, "Bye, Daddy."

Lillian kept swallowing, trying not to cry in front of the children.

"I don't know," Bessie said. "I just don't know."

"We're hungry though, aren't we, girls?" Lillian looked at the dining room table, set for the five of them, with the lace place mats, the good silver, a vase of roses she'd picked yesterday before any of this happened. "You know what? Let's eat in the kitchen tonight, just the four of us." She pulled the red Formica table away from the wall and moved a chair around. "Won't that be fun?"

Helen speared pieces of her pot roast and chewed. "Where's he going?"

"Don't talk with your mouth full and he didn't tell me." Lillian couldn't eat a bite. She cut her slice of roast and moved the pieces around her plate. She shaped her rice into a square.

April started crying again and pushed her plate away. "Will Daddy have to sleep in the street?"

"Of course not," Lillian said. "Don't be silly." She quit pretending to eat and mixed herself a drink, ignoring Helen's watchful look. Where *was* Will going with that suitcase? She had no idea and no way to get in touch except by calling the office. He would be back. He had to come back. He didn't mean it when he said he didn't love her. She was a loveable person. Besides, he hadn't said that. He said his feelings had drained away. Well, she would refill them. She sat in front of her cold dinner, reminding herself to breathe. When Will calmed down, he would come to his senses. This was a temporary craziness.

Bessie stood at the stove, her broad back a reproach.

64

Will looked different to Velma, as if he'd forgotten to check himself in the mirror. His collar wasn't folded properly over his tie, and the shirt, though perfectly clean, was wrinkled. He had on the same suit he'd worn yesterday, which was not his habit. She knew his clothes. What else, outside of her daily tasks, did she have to give attention to?

By Wednesday, he'd worn the blue suit for three days. Where was the dark gray and the lighter gray? That was the shirt from yesterday, too, and the same tie. Will Hughes was usually impeccable, as Mr. Pat had been. They dressed the way lawyers should, unlike Mr. Blair, the other senior partner, who was older and should know better, but came to the office wearing a canary yellow vest and ties that looked like paintings. On non-court days, Mr. Blair wore suspenders embroidered with flowers and *colored* shirts. But according to Garnett, Mr. Blair did not need to follow the rules of decorum. He could afford to dress any way he chose, being more businessman than lawyer. Instead of fighting people in court, he put together deals.

Velma preferred Will's formality, along with his way of practicing law. She took her stenography pad into his office and sat in the chair facing his desk. The difference this week was not only in his clothes; his eyes looked tired, as if he hadn't slept well. Not her place to ask. Velma crossed her knees, lifted her pad, and waited for the morning's dictation to begin.

Will cleared his throat. She raised her pen. "Tell me something about yourself, Miss Vernon."

Not Velma. The words took her back to that first job interview with Mr. Pat. She opened her mouth, hoping something more sensible might emerge this time. "What would you like to know?"

Will Hughes made a steeple with his hands. "Tell me about your family."

Velma stared past him out the window toward the dome of the new capitol. Easier than looking him in the eye. She described the small house set among large and mostly flat green fields, the barn and their animals, the corn, onions, peppers and tomatoes they grew and trucked to the airbase on the coast. She told him about Papa and Mama and the uncle who died. This was the most words she had ever spoken to Will Hughes, and she kept waiting for him to interrupt. Talking about home made a picture in her mind. She tried to describe how the mist hung over the lower fields in the cool early mornings, and the way the sun turned it gold.

"Sounds wonderful," Will said.

She glanced at him and down at her tablet. "It's only a farm. Not nearly as wonderful when you're hoeing weeds."

"I'd love to see it one day."

Velma could not imagine introducing Will Hughes to her father with his overalls and sour outlook. Maybe if Papa put on that rusty black suit he wore to funerals. No, even dressed up, it wouldn't work.

Instead of answering, Velma smiled. Will seemed pleased by this response because he smiled back. What an odd day.

He cleared his throat and began to dictate.

65

On the morning after Will left, Lillian's anger propelled her into action. She had worked too hard to win this man to give him up without a fight. She'd given him children, a nice house, and thousands of meals. She'd done everything required of a good wife. Besides, she loved him. Hurtful to admit loving someone who didn't want to be in the same room with you, but Will Hughes was everything she'd ever wanted and she would not let him walk away.

With the older children off to school and Maude shut up in the kitchen with Bessie, she telephoned James. Leland was closer, but James felt more approachable. She got him at his office in Canton. "Will has left me."

Silence. She heard her brother's cigarette lighter click. "Are you sure, Angie? When?"

"Moved out last night. Said he didn't want to be married anymore. Packed a few clothes and left."

"That damned fool. How are you doing?"

"I didn't lie down in front of a train if that's what you mean." She would cry if they kept talking about it.

"You sit tight. Let me talk to Leland. You got enough money?"

Money hadn't crossed Lillian's mind, but hearing the word, she did start crying. "We didn't even talk about money."

"Now, now." James reacted like most men confronted with tears. "You hang on. I'll call you back."

Faye called instead. "Honey, I cannot believe it. What a snake."

Lillian blew her nose. "I am mowed flat, Faye. I don't know where to turn."

"Don't you worry, sweetheart. Prop yourself in bed with a big drink and let the boys take care of it."

Leland called back. "Family council," he said. "Tomorrow at your place. Two o'clock."

"Just you and James, okay?" Lillian said. "Please don't tell Ernestine." If there was one person she could not bear pity from right now, it was her sister.

The next day, they sat in her living room. James and Leland weren't huggers and didn't like talking about feelings, but Lillian felt bolstered by their presence. Seeing them made her want to cry again, but she swallowed hard instead.

The men had dressed for the occasion. Settling down to business, they shed their coats and loosened their ties. Their bellies strained the buttons of their white dress shirts. Lillian offered iced tea. Her brothers looked big and awkward on the beige sofa, thighs spread, pants legs riding up, skinny white shins showing above their socks. Nothing truly bad could happen with James and Leland by her side. Well, something bad *had* happened, but they would make it right.

Beads of perspiration appeared at the edges of their slicked-back hair.

"What's the best way to go?" James said.

"Straight to the horse's mouth." Leland took a pack of Camels out of his pocket and offered them around. "Go to Will, man to man. Tell him, 'You can't do this. Nothing right about it. You got kids to think of.'"

"He's a lawyer," James said. "He'll have all kind of fancy arguments."

"We could send Ernestine after him," Leland said. "Scare him home."

"Absolutely not," Lillian said. "I don't want Ernestine to know if we can help it." She pictured the sanctimonious look her sister would give from the security of her own marriage. She looked from one brother to the other. "Promise?"

"I'll go see him." Leland said. "I'm the one who plays bridge with the man every Saturday. I'll go to his office and put it to him straight." He stirred more sugar into his tea, looking stricken by the task ahead. "I'll say, 'Will, you got to go back home. Whatever's wrong between you and my sister, I know you can fix it.'"

His eyes kept skipping over Lillian like she might actually tell him what had gone wrong. She stood and gave them kisses on their damp cheeks. "I knew I could count on you."

James slipped her five hundred dollars on the way out. "Faye says you should come live with us."

Sweet, but not exactly practical. Lillian mixed herself a strong drink, feeling hopeful and scared. Whatever it took, she would get Will Hughes back in that twin bed.

66

Will had been gone for two weeks. He'd come by for most of his clothes while Lillian was out playing bridge. She hated not being here to confront him with her misery.

Nights without him made her jittery. James said he would get her a pistol, but for now, she had to depend on a tennis racquet to beat off intruders. Something had awakened her. A thump and the sound of voices. There it was again. She put on her robe and got the racquet out of the closet.

Switching on lights as she went, Lillian tiptoed through the empty kitchen and down the hall. Helen's door was closed. Her friend Gail had spent the night. Lillian glanced at her watch: 4:30 in the morning. She heard another thump and giggling. Opening Helen's bedroom door, she flipped on the light.

The screen was out of one of the windows. Helen was trying to pull Gail inside. Both faces turned to Lillian, looking scared.

"What the hell is going on?

"Mama." Helen's voice cracked. "Did we wake you up?"

Gail managed to crawl over the sill.

Relief at seeing the girls instead of a burglar made Lillian's legs weak. She sat down hard on Helen's bed, letting the tennis racquet dangle between her knees. "What were you two doing?"

Helen blinked. "Going out?"

"Looked more like coming in to me. What's that in your hand?"

Helen held an open bottle of chocolate milk. She stared at it as if surprised. "Milk."

They were dressed in shorts, their bare feet wet and covered in bits of grass. Lillian's anger grew. She felt the birthmark burning on her forehead. "I better start hearing the truth."

"We only went out for a little while," Helen said.

Lillian raised her eyebrows. "In the middle of the night?"

Helen studied the floor. "Just to walk around."

Lillian kept her voice level. "And this was such a good idea you needed to go through the window?"

"We didn't want to wake you up."

"Because if you did wake me, I'd say what?"

Helen muttered. "No."

"Look at me, young lady. Where did you go?" Lillian banged the racquet against the wooden floor.

Helen jumped. "Around."

Lillian gave the floor another bang.

Helen said, "Up to North State and back down to Council Circle."

"How long were you out?"

The girls looked at each other. Helen said, "Awhile."

"What about that?" Lillian pointed to the half-full bottle of chocolate milk.

"We didn't steal it," Helen said.

Gail spoke. "The milkman gave it to us when we got out—" Helen poked her and Gail's voice dropped to a whisper "—of his truck."

Lillian thought she might explode. "And what were you doing in a milkman's truck?"

Thoroughly cowed, Gail said, "Hitchhiking?"

Lillian stood. "You went out in the middle of the night and *hitchhiked*?" She raised the tennis racquet as if to strike them.

The girls' arms went up to protect their heads.

"It was just for fun." Helen pleaded. "We stuck out our thumbs and the milk truck stopped. He brought us back home and told us never to do it again."

Lillian lowered the racquet, suddenly exhausted, and sat on the bed. "We can't go on like this, Helen. You are too much for me."

"I'm sorry, Mama."

"Do you girls have any idea what might have happened? The kind of people who are out at this hour? You're fifteen years old. You could have been raped and murdered, dismembered, and thrown into that ravine." She pointed across to where the street dropped behind Mrs. Polk's house. "As soon as it's daylight, I'm taking you home, Gail."

Gail whispered. "I can walk."

"No, you may not walk. I'm taking you to your door and I'm telling your mother what you did. And you, young lady — " she turned on Helen. " — I'm telling your father."

Helen opened her mouth to protest.

"Don't even start. You can forget any weekend outings with him. No sense wrinkling up your face to cry. You should have thought about that before you pulled this stunt. For the next month you leave home only to go to school." She started out of the room. "And keep this door open."

"A *month*?" Helen's rising voice followed her.

"No phone calls, no movies, no spend-the-night parties, nothing. You go to school, you come straight home. Is that clear?"

"Yes, Ma'am."

"Put that screen back in the window, get into your pajamas, and go to bed, both of you. I don't want to hear one peep."

Back in her own room, Lillian raised the tennis racquet and slammed it onto Will's bed, wishing it were his head. The blow felt good. She did it again. This is what he deserved for leaving her, and what she would have done to Helen if Gail hadn't been there. She beat the bed until her arms got tired. Drained, she took off her robe, kicked off her slippers, and crawled under the covers.

She was too wrecked to sleep. Lying in the dark, she went over every mean word Will had ever said to her. She pressed a hand against her forehead to push back the headache. She should get up and take an aspirin, but she was too beat to move. The man had almost killed her by leaving, and now Helen would finish her off.

67

By October, Will looked himself again, rotating through his suits, shirts spotless, but he still acted odd. Taking dictation, Velma glanced up and caught him watching her. A shock ran through her, like touching a metal doorknob on a cold day, but nicer. She lost her place in the transcription and had to ask him to repeat the last part.

At 5:00, when the office emptied, Will remained. Velma took out her pocketbook and put the folded brown paper bag from today's sandwich inside.

Will stood in the door of his office. "Could you come in, please?"

She put down her purse and got out her shorthand pad.

"You won't need that."

She sat in her usual chair, but he did not return to his desk. Instead, he paced in front of the black leather sofa, staring at the carpet. When he did look up, he said, "Do you think you could have supper with me? I hate eating alone." He sounded almost angry.

"Of course." This must be what the novels meant by a thrill—this feeling coursing through her. Velma told herself not to be an idiot. His family must be out of town. The only other man she'd known up close was Papa. If Mama left town (not that she ever had), Papa would starve.

Early evening and hot for September. They rolled the windows down in the car and a breeze cooled Velma's face. He said nothing until they were seated in the same distant restaurant with glasses of iced tea. Velma felt relieved not to see beer, but, once again, she hadn't been asked.

"Lillian and I have separated."

Another shock, a cold one this time.

He stared into his tea. "I'm living in an apartment."

Velma took shallow breaths to quiet the pounding in her chest. This had nothing to do with her. "I am so sorry."

"Don't be. It's no one's fault."

Their meals arrived—Chicken Cacciatore again. She kept her eyes down while cutting the meat, taking small bites, washing them down with tea. Did this separation mean—she wasn't sure what it meant. Her underarms prickled with sweat.

"Actually, it probably *is* my fault." Will continued as if they hadn't been silent for ten minutes.

Velma shook her head. "I'm sure it's not."

"I can be hard to live with."

"You're not hard to work with—I mean *for*." She felt her face reddening. What was she thinking, saying "with" as if she were his partner instead of his secretary?

"No, 'with' is all right. With is fine."

She looked up and his blue eyes held hers.

"We work well together. We're a good team."

She broke away from his gaze, staring at her plate, too confused to reply. It means nothing, she told herself. He is talking about work.

"You are a calming influence."

Velma almost choked and had to cover her mouth with her napkin. *She was a calming influence?* Sitting here prickly with sweat, her heart thudding, and that's what Will Hughes thought?

"You really are." He looked down again, and she watched him struggle for words.

"You can't imagine how—" He stopped. "—emotional things get at home."

"Is everyone okay?" Which she should have asked first thing.

"In shock, I guess." He called the waitress over and asked for the check.

Will drove her back to the apartment without speaking, his profile stern. He insisted on getting out and ushering her up the walk, holding onto an elbow as if she were an old woman. He accompanied her up the outside stairs and waited while she unlocked the door. Was she supposed to invite him in? Surely not.

He said, "Thank you for keeping me company."

"You're welcome."

She closed the door and leaned against it, listening to his retreating footsteps.

Washing her face for bed, Velma wanted to weep into the washcloth: a calming influence. That's how he saw her. She'd sat there at dinner, perspiring and palpitating, and he found her calming.

The man had separated from his wife. He needed to talk to someone and she was the closest person available. She had no idea what went on in his home and it was none of her business. She was his secretary, a person to share a meal with when he didn't want to eat alone. Nothing more. Garnett had been right to warn her. The Bible was right, too. Bad intentions pulled a person as deeply into sin as bad deeds. All those half-smothered thoughts about Will and his blue-eyed glances, the fervent prayers. Well, she had learned her lesson. Velma tried to smile at the scrubbed face in the mirror.

She went to bed feeling cleansed. A calming influence indeed — at least now she knew her role.

68

Leland called Lillian on a Wednesday afternoon. "I went by Will's office this morning."

"And?" She held her breath.

"He said he appreciated my concern, but James and I shouldn't worry about your welfare. Told me he would provide for you and the children, but he wasn't coming back."

Lillian digested this failure in silence, trying to inhale against the weight of disappointment. "Thank you for trying." She heard the quaver in her voice. "What do we do next?"

"You know I'll do anything I can," Leland said.

"I don't guess it would help to send James up there with a gun."

Leland didn't laugh. "Nope." After another silence, he said, "You've always got us."

"I know, sweetie, and I appreciate it, but I've been Mrs. Will Hughes for sixteen years and I like it. I'm used to it. Plus, the man has children. He can't walk away just because he changed his mind."

"We could talk to his people," Leland said.

Lillian pictured them gathering in the dim parlor on North State Street with Mr. Pat and Margaret, Mag, and stern Frances. If Will's father agreed to confront his son, what would Will Hughes tell them about her? That he'd married a drunk? Whatever it might be, she didn't want them hearing it.

"Let me speak to Will's sister, Mag." She dreaded any of that formidable family thinking less of her, but they would find out he'd left eventually, and she'd rather confess to Mag than the others. "I'll call you back," she told Leland.

She telephoned Mag at the office and invited her over for a drink after work.

At five-thirty, they sat on the tropical sun porch, the room designed to make Will happy thinking of Hawaii. Lillian mixed them drinks and they both lit cigarettes, ice clinking in their Scotch and waters.

"Will's always gotten what he wanted," Mag said. "Being the youngest, we spoiled him to death."

"Me, too," Lillian said. "I am the youngest and I got spoiled."

"Two youngest children married to each other." Mag shook her head over the folly of it. "But that's not the point, is it? He chose you, and he can't decide he wants strawberry after he's ordered vanilla."

Lillian's heart did a nosedive. Had Will found someone? "What does that mean?"

"I'm divorced." Mag said. "So are Patrick Junior and Emmy" (Emmy had left the cute pharmacist for a tall, dark opera singer.).

"I love him, Mag." Lillian felt the tears coming. She was so sick of crying.

Mag exhaled, a sigh that filled the air with cigarette smoke. "Let me talk to him."

Relief felt like her bones were melting. Lillian had been holding herself as if waiting for a firing squad. "Anything. Tell him I'll do anything. I don't even know where he's living."

Mag looked stricken. "Oh, honey, I thought he told you. He's rented himself a little apartment over on Pinehurst."

Lillian's ears rang. *Mag already knew he'd left.* Did Mr. Pat and Margaret know, too, and snotty Frances? It made her sick to think of her in-laws talking about her.

Mag stood and drained her glass. "Let me apologize for all of us. The Hughes family can be dicey when it comes to marriage." She bent and gave Lillian a quick, fierce hug and went out the door, cigarette smoke trailing behind her.

Lillian mixed herself a double Scotch and told Bessie to feed the children.

Will came by the next day to get the last of his stuff. Lillian followed him around the room as he filled a suitcase, head still pounding from last night's excess. "Mag says you're living on Pinehurst."

No reply.

"I could use a phone number, Will, in case anything happens."

"I don't have a telephone."

"An address then."

He gave her a cold look. "You can quit sending people to change my mind."

Lillian felt her throat close. "I have to try."

He went through the kitchen on his way back to see the girls. "Something smells mighty good in here, Bessie." Teasing as if nothing had happened.

Bessie smiled her big smile, bottom teeth red from the snuff she kept tucked behind her lower lip. "Want me to make you a custard pie?"

"I'd kill for a custard pie," Will said.

Lillian would murder Bessie if she made him one.

Will headed down the hall. Lillian trailed along behind like the ghost she had become.

The girls raced from their rooms when they heard his voice. Will squatted to Maude's height and began telling them about a new case. Lillian only heard parts, something about a man trying to burn his house down with a candle.

They laughed. They always laughed. She had laughed, too, when she'd been his wife.

April said, "Daddy, you're so funny."

Lillian felt herself heating up from the inside. Every time Will showed up, the girls fell on him like he was the second coming, and forgot the hundred things she did for them every day. Helen hugged her father, giving Lillian a look over his shoulder, a look that said: this is *your* fault.

After Will left, after eating dinner and driving Bessie home, Lillian invited Maude to come and sleep with her in the big bedroom. She hated turning down only one of the twin beds and creeping in alone.

Maude kept asking Lillian questions in the dark. "Does God sleep?"

"He watches over us while we sleep."

"But what if he gets sleepy?"

"What about you getting sleepy? You have school tomorrow."

"I hate school. When I grow up, I'm going to fix people's hair the way Jo Nell does yours."

"Our family doesn't do hair."

"Why not?"

"We just don't. Go to sleep." God knows, this youngest child was the sweetest of the three, but she wasn't clever at school, not compared with her sisters, and the teachers constantly threw it in poor Maude's face. She might end up doing hair.

Mag called the next day to report what Lillian already knew. "He wants what he wants." Speaking in her throaty rasp. "He's been that way since he was little."

The stone in Lillian's chest grew heavier. "You don't think — ?" She hesitated. "Would it help if I asked his father to speak to him?"

"You can give it a try," Mag said, "but Dad tried to talk me out of leaving the colonel, and that didn't work."

It took a month for Lillian to get up the nerve. She made a batch of divinity, drove up North State Street to the big white house, and sat in the dim front parlor with Margaret and Mr. Pat. Will's father had recently undergone cataract surgery. He wore thick-lensed glasses that made his pupils look huge and dark, like a startled child. She had never thought of him as old before.

Margaret took a second piece of divinity. "You have such a wonderfully light touch with this, my dear."

Patrick refused, saying sweets made his teeth hurt. The three of them sipped icy Coca Colas from green glass bottles, the bottoms protected by stretchy knitted socks.

Lillian sat up straighter and told her story as if they knew nothing. She ended with, "I thought maybe you could talk to Will." Her face stung with the humiliation of admitting their son no longer wanted her. The only blessing being, her blazing face probably didn't show in this dark room and her voice shook only a little.

Mr. Pat cleared his throat and looked off into the middle distance. Margaret, sitting beside her on the sofa, took one of Lillian's hands in hers. The pity in that gesture was almost unbearable.

"We are so sorry, Lillian dear. We've become quite fond of you, but Mr. Hughes and I make it a practice not to interfere in our grown children's lives."

There was a pause. Lillian held her breath to keep from screaming. Each word felt like a rock thrown at her.

"We feel it's best to let them make these decisions and live with the consequences." Margaret paused. "Even when we don't agree."

Lillian said, "But—"

"I know it's hard, my dear." Margaret Hughes interrupted, now patting Lillian's hand. "But you've always been a strong young woman and you will come through this."

Mr. Pat must have spoken to his son because the next night Will telephoned Lillian. "You leave my parents out of this."

Solitude had hardened her. Or maybe it was carrying around this stone of grief. "I'll do anything, Will. I'm not proud."

"Can't you get it through your head?" His voice rose to a shout. "I've made my decision." He hung up.

Lillian sat listening to the dial tone, ears ringing, skin hot. The man could move her from heartbreak to rage in one sentence.

Another month passed. Lillian tried to reconcile herself to the empty place at the dinner table and the vacant twin bed. She found company in the afternoon bridge games and an occasional Saturday night with Avery and Alice, who didn't seem quite as eager with invitations with Will gone. Mag always welcomed her for a late afternoon drink.

The days were full enough: each weekday morning she got the children off to three different schools. She and Bessie sat at the breakfast table to plan dinner, she with coffee and a cigarette, Bessie with her snuff.

She made velveteen Christmas dresses for the four of them, Maude's red, April's green, and for Helen and herself, black. Helen was thrilled—her first black dress.

Lillian felt, if not content, resigned. Until she heard the rumor. Will Hughes was seeing someone. Hilda passed the gossip along at one of their afternoon games, and Dimple nodded: she'd heard it, too. Lillian felt like she'd stuck her finger in a wall socket. Her skin went cold, then hot, and for a few minutes she literally could not see the cards.

"Who is it?" She could barely speak.

No one knew the woman. Dimple's neighbor had spotted Will over in West Jackson at a restaurant with a strange female. Hilda said her son saw him at the state fair, getting on the Ferris wheel with a tall lady.

At the fair? Will had taken Helen and April to the fair last Saturday. It was an annual tradition. The three of them enjoyed riding things that whipped around and turned a person upside down. Will had taught the girls to close their eyes and stomp their feet to keep from being afraid.

If Hilda's son was right, Will had gone to the fair a second time with someone else. Lillian seethed, imagining the woman: tall like Sylvia and probably with big bosoms.

Mag mentioned to Lillian over Friday afternoon drinks that Will had taken her to the fair. "I'll never get on another Ferris wheel for the rest of my life. Plus, I pulled a filling eating that damn taffy."

Lillian could hardly hear for rejoicing. Mag was the tall woman at the fair. Maybe the restaurant sighting was a mistake, too. It could have been a client, though, to her knowledge, Will had never taken a female client.

Jealousy ate at her like acid. Living alone without Will she could endure, but letting another woman have him—that she couldn't. She felt perfectly capable of murder. Will had never allowed a gun in the house, but Lillian now owned a five-shot Ladysmith, a gift from James. She kept it locked in the drawer of the bedside table with the bullets stowed on her closet shelf.

She was a good shot. She'd always been a good shot. She'd grown up bird hunting on horseback with her brothers, target-shooting when there was nothing to hunt. Unlike Will, she wasn't a bit afraid of guns. She pictured herself aiming at a tall, faceless woman and blasting a hole in her chest. She saw herself in jail wearing a tacky, ill-fitting uniform, living with a bunch of lowlifes, without liquor or any possibility of being with Will again ever. She might be running out of options to get him home, but she wasn't ready to be put away.

Some nights, after the drinks and before sleep, Lillian thought of turning the gun on herself. Seeing with warm self-pity how sorry they would all be, how opinion would turn against Will for what he'd made her do. But she wouldn't be here to enjoy any of it and, besides, she was too angry to die.

69

"You should have a house," Will Hughes said.

Velma sat across from him in a restaurant on the south side of town, eating greasy fried catfish and greasier French fries. A week since the second chicken dinner and he'd asked her out again.

She swallowed and wiped her mouth before speaking. She loved catfish, but eating anything this messy in front of Will Hughes made her self-conscious. "I could never afford a house."

"I'll bet you could. In fact, I'm sure of it." Will winked. "Don't forget, I know how much you make."

Velma felt the blush start. This felt like flirting. His new attention had become an extension of their workday. The man felt lonely without his family and probably saw her as the equally solitary spinster secretary. Kindness, not courting. How horrible to assume he liked her in some new way and find oneself mistaken.

"I do something with the children on Saturday mornings and my weekly bridge game is Saturday afternoon."

Velma nodded.

"You probably go to church on Sunday mornings. That leaves Sunday afternoon for house hunting. I'll pick you up at one."

Velma opened her mouth.

Will raised a hand to get the attention of the waitress. "No objections, please. Let's remember which one of us is the boss." He winked again to show he was kidding.

Going through houses, Velma wasn't sure what to look for, and they all looked too expensive. Will had opinions. She needed a good neighborhood, and that meant North Jackson. She wanted a house that wasn't too big and didn't need fixing up. In four hours, they went through six houses. The places began to run together in Velma's head. She let herself be led through kitchens with avocado appliances. She peered inside pink and black bathrooms. Yards were considered, as were closed garages with an entry directly into the kitchen. This was essential, Will said, for her safety.

That first week he found nothing suitable. He bought Velma a ham and Swiss cheese sandwich at Primos and took her home. She would have preferred turkey, no mustard, and any cheese but Swiss, but she ate her sandwich and kept quiet.

The second Sunday, Will arrived early. They had seven houses to go through, but the third one struck him. "Look at this." He pointed out the small den. Windows on each side of a fireplace looking out on pine trees in a grassy backyard. The house had two smallish bedrooms and one bath, a tidy yellow and white kitchen, and a living room with a separate dining room. No garage, but a carport with a storage room.

"When it rains, you'd be able to get inside without getting wet," Will said. "That's important." He whispered so the realtor wouldn't know they liked the place. His mouth that close to her ear gave Velma goose bumps.

"Do you like the house?"

Velma whispered back. "Even if I did—"

Will didn't let her finish. Took her by the elbow and led her away from the agent and out to the car.

"How can I afford it?" She pictured her nest egg, the tidy sum she had put away in Deposit Guaranty Bank, month by careful month, vanishing into one unwise purchase.

"You let me figure that out." Will looked hugely pleased. He bought them another round of ham and Swiss cheese sandwiches and took her home.

That night, Velma lay in bed, unable to sleep. She would never do anything this enormous on her own. She wouldn't be in this apartment without Garnett's pushing. Will had become an unstoppable force, with a wink to cancel every doubt.

On Monday morning, he called her into his office. "I've got the figures." He pointed to a legal pad and called her around to his side of the desk.

"The house is advertised for $11,000." Will tapped the page. "At five percent interest over thirty years, with taxes and insurance, you would pay, rough guess here, about a hundred a month." He looked up. "What do you pay in rent now?"

"Seventy-five." Velma's voice grew small with apprehension. The idea of taking on a debt for thirty years felt catastrophic.

"So, twenty-five dollars more than you're paying now, but you'll build equity. Equity is a good thing, it's like money in the bank, and the interest on the loan is tax-deductible, which means you'll save there, too." He turned to face her, his face sober. "You will need to put $2,000 down."

Velma said, "That's too much."

"How much have you got saved?"

This seemed a very personal question. "One thousand, two hundred and thirty dollars."

"You won't want to use it all." He stood, pacing in front of his office couch. "I'll speak to Ted Laird at the bank and put in a word for you. You put down, say, a thousand, and I'll lend you the rest of the deposit."

"I can't let you do that." Velma was horrified. "How would I pay you back?"

"In tiny amounts over a very long time." Another wink. "That way, you'll be forever in my debt and you won't be able to leave us for another law firm."

"I'd never—" Another wink and she realized he was kidding. He loved to do that, tell some huge fib and watch her go for it like a fish after a worm. "You're so gullible," he'd say, laughing, which Velma took to mean stupid, but she did love making him laugh.

"I'm serious about the loan," Will said. "Just think about it." He waved her, along with her objections, out of his office.

In Velma's family, no one borrowed money, especially not from a bank, not after what happened during the Depression. Papa would say she had no business owning a house if she didn't have the cash to pay for it. Too many people climbed out on that limb, got foreclosed, and lost everything.

Seeing Will so happy and pleased to help her made Velma feel— she tried to think of the word—*cherished*. A new thought brought her back to reality. She stuck her head into Will's office. "There's no bus service out to that house."

He looked up. "Then I guess you'll have to learn how to drive."

"I don't have a car."

"One step at a time. We'll worry about that after you get your license."

Velma sat at her desk feeling ill. Too many decisions too fast. She was a cautious person, raised by a cautious family. A house, and now the man talked about driving? She pushed back the feeling of nausea and typed faster.

When Garnett stopped by her desk at lunchtime, Velma shook her head. "Too much to do."

She longed for Garnett's advice, but she hadn't yet told her friend about the dinners with Will, and she'd have to explain about looking at houses, not to mention the business of a car—Garnett would not approve. Garnett would say Velma was spending time with a still-married man, and mixing her personal life with work, which was never a good idea.

Back in her apartment, Velma stood in the kitchen, ironing the week's laundry and trying to collect her wits. On the farm she'd been allowed to drive the tractor, but never the truck. Driving was a man's prerogative, and here was Will, steering her through houses and talking about her buying a car. She'd end up in the poorhouse.

She sprayed a white cotton shirt to dampen it. This rush of new experiences felt terrifying, with everything tangled in Will's winks and the way she caught him looking at her. Despite the time spent on her knees at night, her feelings were not as pure as she wished, and often not even admissible. When Will Hughes looked tired, she imagined putting her arms around him, nestling his head against her breasts, resting her cheek on his head. In a thin voice, she sang along to the radio and ironed faster. *"What a friend we have in Je-sus"* Making noise like a child in the dark, to block the queer feelings.

70

November and Lillian had only one card left to play — Ernestine. She hated going to her sister, whose favors came with a lecture, frequently involving God. Be that as it may, she had run out of options. She called Faye in Canton. What did Faye think? Faye thought Ernestine could be a pure pain in the neck, but what alternative did Lillian have?

Lillian dialed Ernestine and invited her down. There was a family problem and she needed her sister's advice.

"I live to serve."

She heard the satisfaction in Ernestine's voice. There was nothing her sister enjoyed more than giving advice, which was free and didn't require a gift-wrap.

"I was planning on coming down tomorrow for supplies anyway," she said.

That was Ernestine. Two birds required to make throwing that stone worthwhile.

Now, here she sat in Lillian's living room, looking like the perfect lady, back straight, ankles crossed, sipping her tea, the kind of person whose husband never moved out.

Lillian swallowed hard and explained the problem.

A sharp intake of breath. Ernestine set her cup down and put on the face she wore to funerals, which made Lillian want to usher her out the front door.

"Was it the drinking?"

Good Lord. Would no one on this earth let a person drink in peace? The birthmark lit up and Lillian shook her head no. "He says he doesn't want to be married anymore."

"Well, that is ridiculous." Ernestine took another sip of her tea. "He can't *decide* he doesn't want to be married."

"I've gone to his parents and his sister. Leland's talked to him. Can you think of anything else?"

Ernestine thought, indicated by a stare into the middle distance. After what felt like a long silence, she sat up straighter, and put down her cup. "When in doubt, turn to the church."

Lillian felt her hopes deflate. Were they about to pray over this?

"Never underestimate the power of a man of God," Ernestine said. "I happen to know the bishop personally." She meant the Episcopal bishop. Her face wore a pleased, pursed-lipped expression.

"Will is a Methodist," Lillian said.

Ernestine held up a finger. "But the bishop knows everyone."

Lillian leaned forward. "Would he be willing to intervene?"

Another long silence while Lillian paced the floor of her mind. Ernestine was nothing if not deliberative.

"He might very well if approached in the right manner. The bishop feels as strongly as I about the sanctity of family."

Lillian exhaled in relief, too grateful to mind the pious tone.

"I will make an appointment for us," Ernestine said. "Dress down."

Lillian knew how to dress for a bishop. When Ernestine picked her up the next week, she had on her black suit with a plain white blouse and the gold bar pin. She wore closed shoes, white gloves, and a hat.

"Don't smoke," Ernestine said. "Even if he invites you to."

The bishop was a handsome man, big, with steel gray hair and a proud front. That's how Lillian described men who covered their bellies with well-fitting suits. His large, warm hands grasped hers and she felt reassured.

"Let me talk," Ernestine had said on the way downtown, and Lillian did, staring demurely at her white gloves while Ernestine told the story.

"You wish to remain married to Mr. Hughes, is that correct?" His gray gaze fixed upon her.

Lillian's eyes filled with tears. She'd found it hard to believe in herself lately, but she had enough charm left to move a bishop. "More than anything."

"Your sister says you and your husband are Methodists?"

"Galloway Memorial."

"I know Dr. Selah well. We'll put our heads together and see what we can do. Matrimony is sacred in the eyes of the church. Vows are not lightly entered into nor lightly broken."

Lillian grasped the warm hands again. "So grateful." Ducking her head modestly. "I would be forever in your debt."

Back outside, Ernestine said, "I thought that went well." Looking puff-chested and satisfied.

Let Ernestine boast. Lillian didn't care. If this worked, she would never hear another nasty word spoken about her sister. Ernestine could toot her horn until Gabriel blew his.

71

Every Tuesday and Thursday after work, a small black Ford honked in front of Velma's apartment. Time for the dreaded driving lesson. The instructor was a fierce little man with receding, slicked-back hair and bad teeth. He sat too close with his dual controls, the car stinking of stale smoke and bad aftershave.

Clutching the enormous steering wheel, pricked by the scratchy upholstery, Velma leaned close to the windshield, and tried to obey the barked instructions.

"Clutch, clutch, ease it out, girlie, no jerking. A little to the left, please. Gauge your position. Gas, more gas. Gentle, now. *Brake, brake,*" he screamed. "Don't you see that stop sign?"

She spent these hours in what she thought of afterwards as petrification. At the end of each session, she went upstairs drained, squashed, a wreck, and had to lie down with a wet washrag on her forehead, weeping a little, hating the mean, brown-toothed man.

On the third Monday after this torture began, Will paused in his dictation to ask how the driving was coming.

Velma let the frustration out. "How in the world can a person operate a brake, a clutch, an accelerator, a gear shift, and have enough brains left over to steer and remember where they're going?"

Will laughed. "That's the most words I've ever heard you say."

"You're laughing, but I'm not sure I'm smart enough to drive."

"I'm laughing because you are like a child, Velma. I'm not saying you're not smart and competent—don't give me that wounded look—

but in some ways, good ways, you're unspoiled and innocent. It's quite endearing."

Endearing. Velma pondered the word later. Your aunt could be a dear. A deer could be endearing.

At their Monday lunch together in the drugstore downstairs, Velma confided in Garnett. She admitted spending her Tuesday and Thursday afternoons learning to drive, making it sound like her idea. She loved hearing her friend laugh over the awful little man.

Garnett leaned over her toasted pimento cheese sandwich. "How come you suddenly decided to learn how to drive?"

Velma licked the cheese oozing from the cut side of her sandwich. "I'm thinking about buying a house."

Garnett's eyes widened. "A *house?*" She and Bob still rented a place near her parents.

Velma took a breath. "Don't tell anyone. It may not work out."

Garnett used her free hand to zip her lips.

"I may as well tell you everything. Mr. Hughes—Will, not Mr. Pat—offered to help. I've saved almost enough for the deposit, and he agreed to take the rest out of my paycheck a little at a time."

"You never said anything about wanting a house."

Velma recognized Garnett's tone as resentment. Single people weren't supposed to get houses ahead of a married couple.

"I never thought about it until I saw this one advertised in the paper and made a bid on it." Lies and more lies. "The loan may fall through. The bank will probably turn me down. Please don't tell anyone."

"I said I wouldn't, but I still don't get it. To own a house, you have to learn to drive?"

"The house is way out by the Deaf and Blind School. No buses."

"And that means a car?"

"A used one, I guess. I haven't figured that part out yet. I certainly won't buy a car until I get the house, but I'll have my license. I'll be ready."

Garnett gave Velma a sharp look. "You're chock full of surprises, Velma Vernon. Consider yourself lucky. Mr. Blair wouldn't help Bobby and me buy a pack of gum."

Here she sat, telling half-truths to her best friend, but the need to confide outweighed caution. "I'll probably end up broke, but at least I'll be independent. It's important when you don't have ..." She started to say *a man* "anyone, and need to make your own way." Velma heard the words and realized they were true. She *was* making herself independent—of everyone, including Will Hughes. Except it had been his idea to buy the house, and the car, and she depended on him for her job.

The day she passed her driving test and got a license, Will took her out to celebrate. Chicken cacciatore for a third time.

"Tomorrow we'll see about a car," he said.

"I really can't afford a car." Velma meant it. If the loan on the house came through, the monthly payments would be enough of a burden, since she would also be paying Will back for his portion of the down payment. "Doris drives," Velma said. "She lives with her parents out near the new house. If I pay for gas, she'll bring me to work."

Will's lips thinned in disapproval. "You did not learn to drive to let someone else drive you. And you don't want to depend on anyone as unreliable as Doris."

Acting giddy and flirtatious made you unreliable. Shyness made you endearing. Velma took note.

She found a check for seven hundred dollars on her desk the next morning, along with a note in Will's handwriting: "With gratitude for your extra efforts on the newspaper case."

She placed the check on Will's desk when she went in for dictation. "What's this?"

"Your car," he said.

"You gave me a week's bonus for working on that case."

The blue eyes turned cold. "When you're being done a favor, Miss Vernon, perhaps you shouldn't expend quite so much energy trying to undo it."

Velma's ears buzzed and she blinked back tears. She picked up the check. "I didn't mean to sound ungrateful."

Will opened his legal pad to a page of scribbled notes. "Shall we get to work?"

After the morning dictation, Velma went back to her desk, thoughts swirling. She wiped her burning eyes. Had that been a quarrel? It gave her a taste of how it felt to be on the wrong side of Will Hughes, an experience she did not wish to repeat.

By afternoon, he was back in a good humor, chortling with her over another fraudulent insurance claim.

After work, he drove her to the Chevy dealer. On the way, he told her General Motors was a dependable ride, but to pay no attention to gimmicks like Powerglide or Dynaflow. Real drivers preferred manual shift, which saved on fuel.

At the lot, he showed her the second-hand Chevrolet he had already selected. "It's in fine shape." He patted the car's white hood. "Only 20,000 miles on the odometer. Owned by an old lady who only drove it to church." The blue twinkle meant he was kidding.

The salesman handed her the keys. Velma signed over the check Will had given her that morning, which turned out to be precisely the cost of this 1950 coupe. She now owned an automobile that she had never sat inside or driven, a car she hadn't said she liked. Blue would have been her choice, if anyone wanted to know. She swallowed the mutinous thoughts. Men probably picked out cars the same way they decided what you should eat in restaurants.

Will said, "Drive me around the block so I can check you out."

She gripped the steering wheel to keep her hands from shaking.

"Don't be scared." He put a hand over hers. "Think how independent this will make you."

Exactly what Velma had said to Garnett. Her ears rang. Such a nice, warm hand. *He had touched her.*

She thought about that touch driving back to the apartment alone—driving slowly, fitfully, still a bit jerky with the clutch. Will held her hand, or covered it with his, which was almost the same. She looked at her flushed face in the rearview mirror and felt ashamed. She shouldn't let herself be touched by a married man, even a separated one, and she definitely shouldn't feel the way she did, darts and sparks down where a nice girl wouldn't feel anything. She took deep breaths and concentrated on the road. Will had covered her hand with his for two seconds. *Settle down.*

Safely parked in front of the apartment, she got out and stared at the white car. Kicked a tire the way she'd seen men do. Her car. Mama and Papa would not recognize the person she'd turned into, which was a reminder to not get proud. Upstairs, she took an aspirin, kicked off her shoes, and stretched out on the couch to recover from the drive.

To her surprise and dismay, the bid on the new house, which Will had made in her name, a full $500 under the asking price, was accepted. A month later, Will marched her down Capitol Street to Deposit Guaranty Bank. They sat across the desk from his friend, the Vice-President. When Velma picked up the pen to sign the mortgage, her hand shook so, she could barely write her name. This is this, that is that, the man said in his deep, official voice, showing her where to sign.

"Velma is our best secretary," Will said. "This is her first house."

The man gave an approving nod. "Very wise to begin building equity while you're young."

Velma wasn't sure she understood equity. A mortgage felt more like sinking under debt than building anything. Years of payments stretching ahead, thirty years of typing to pay for what she'd just signed.

When they were done and Velma was pronounced a homeowner, Will took her to the Mayflower Cafe, a noisy, narrow place where lawyers went for lunch. To everyone he knew, Will said, "You know my secretary. Velma just bought her first house."

People congratulated her. Strangers smiled. She was too nervous and excited to finish the gumbo Will ordered for her.

Ten days of packing after work and on weekends. On a Wednesday, the moving truck arrived and men carried Velma's possessions out of the familiar apartment. Watching her stuff go down the stairs, Velma felt pride at what she and the lady at furniture store had picked out. Nothing shoddy here.

She walked through the empty apartment, checking that she hadn't left anything behind. She would miss the place. She would miss the sound of the train at night. She hugged her landlady goodbye. They had lived in harmony for twelve years by leaving each other entirely alone.

She followed the van to her new address, supervised the unloading, and stood, finally, alone inside her new home, surrounded by boxes.

She walked from the yellow kitchen, through to the dining room with her mahogany table and chairs. The living room looked a little bare, with nothing but the sofa, coffee table, and one chair. She'd buy another chair if she ever again possessed two spare pennies. Her feet echoed in the wood-floored hall. She felt like a trespasser. Should she get a carpet? Velma stopped herself. She wouldn't be buying anything for a long time.

Two bedrooms, one empty, the other filled with the familiar maple furniture. She made up the bed and unpacked the ballerina light.

In the kitchen, she opened a can of vegetable soup, and heated it on the unfamiliar gas range. At the dining room table, she listened to herself swallow. Exhaustion numbed her, and she felt completely alone. Will was with his children; Garnett was with Bobby. In her old apartment, she could have walked to the bus stop and gone anywhere she wanted: taken a walk through downtown; seen a movie. Here, she was miles from everything. No Jitney Jungle up the road. She would need to get in the car to buy milk. Enough. She was no more alone than she had been yesterday. On Monday, Southern Bell would hook up her telephone. Tomorrow after church, maybe she would take a ride and explore her new neighborhood.

She turned the radio on to the gospel hour and walked through the rooms again. Everything smelled of fresh paint and damp cardboard. It had rained while the movers were unloading. Fortunately, the house came with blinds because she did not have the money to buy curtains. Walking from room to room, she closed them against the night. She locked both doors. Why did she feel so nervous? She had never felt scared in the apartment, not even after Garnett moved out. Maybe she should put an ad in the paper and find a roommate for the second bedroom. She could turn into Mrs. Moseley and serve soup and crackers every night to a stranger.

Will had told her to take two days off and get settled. He showed no interest in the move, which did not surprise Velma. When the question of new carpets arose at the firm, he said Velma should order what she liked and have them installed after work. Left to her own devices, Velma duplicated the deep wine wool of the old carpet. She wasn't sure Will even noticed until the bill came. He cared little about his surroundings or anyone else's. At home behind his desk, surrounded by legal files, in one of his starched shirts, tie firmly knotted, suit coat and hat waiting on the rack by the door—he possessed all he needed. Except for that first day in his Navy uniform, Velma had never seen Will dressed any other way.

Back at the office on Friday, Velma told Will she'd gotten pretty well moved in.

He looked up from his brief. "I'll drop by on Saturday after my bridge game and check on you."

She was too surprised to respond.

"If that's convenient," he said.

"Of course."

Sitting at her typewriter, insides buzzing like she'd swallowed bees, Velma tried to untangle her thoughts. Surely, it was reasonable for Will to want to see the house he'd talked her into buying, the house he'd paid for part of. Mrs. Evans said a good secretary kept her personal life well way from the office, and Velma obeyed this rule. A visit from the boss felt—*odd*. She flexed her fingers and told herself to stop acting like a teenager. This was not a breach of decorum. This was a boss paying a courtesy call on his secretary in her new house. She would wear flats to show she made nothing of it. She would serve lemonade.

72

November and freezing inside the house when Velma got home from the beauty parlor. She turned up the thermostat, changed into a dress and sweater, and put on ballet flats. When she heard Will's car in the driveway, her heart tried to jump out of her chest.

He rang the front bell. "Come and see," he said. "I brought you firewood." Will opened the trunk of his car, looking proud. "I had to ask around. Turns out they sell it at a nursery out on Highway 51." He carried an armload of wood through the kitchen and into the den.

Velma held the door. "That's so kind of you."

"Consider it a housewarming gift." He stacked the remaining wood against the wall of the carport. Brushed his arms to get the chips off, looking as pleased as if he'd chopped it himself. "We can have a fire."

"Want to see the house first?" Velma said.

"Sure." He followed her, nodding politely as she showed him how she'd arranged her furniture. Halfway through, she realized he'd never seen her apartment, so where things went here didn't mean much.

With the tour over, Will built a fire in the fireplace. Except for a gray shag carpet, the den was unfurnished. Velma stood back and observed, surprised that he knew how to build a fire. He'd remembered to bring kindling and newspaper. Watching with her country eyes, she decided he did a better than average job.

He helped Velma down onto the gray shag carpeting. They sat, side by side, watching the flames. She was glad her dress had a full skirt and she didn't have to worry about keeping her knees covered. Through the windows on either side of the chimney, fading light turned the pine trees into black shapes against a midnight blue sky.

"This is perfect," Will said.

Velma had opened her mouth to say, "Yes, it's very nice," when he kissed her.

She'd fantasized about kissing Will Hughes. In spite of good intentions and Biblical admonitions, she'd sat in the chair opposite, taking dictation, and imagined his lips on hers. When it actually happened, she stiffened with surprise. No one had tried to kiss her since Chalmers Root, and this was nothing like that.

Will pulled back. "Did I frighten you?"

Velma's head buzzed; her heart thudded against her ribs. She didn't have enough breath left to speak. She shook her head no.

"You have beautiful eyes," Will said.

She shook her head in denial, and he kissed her a second time.

"Like pools of clear water." He held her by the shoulders. "Like windows into your soul." He kissed her a third time.

She closed the pools of clear water and surrendered. No prayers or pleas for purity rose to block the way. Will's hands pressed her back against the rug. She was beneath him now, breathing Old Spice and Camel cigarettes, his chest heavy against hers. She felt nothing but elation—this man she adored wanted her. *Her.* Velma Vernon. His mouth was on her neck. Her body tingled and sparked. A warm hand worked its way under her skirt and up her thigh. Everywhere he touched turned to fire. He tried to get her underpants off, saying words she only half heard. She lifted her hips to help.

Dark now, with only the fire lighting the room and his body against hers. His breathing sounded desperate. He put a hand down there and Velma felt a jolt, as if she'd been shocked. This was desire. She'd read about it in novels and tried to imagine how it felt. Her skirt was up around her waist and Will pressed himself into her. Velma gasped, arching her back against the gray carpet to stop the pain. She was a country girl; she'd watched plenty of animals do it. The females usually stood stoically. She had no idea it felt like being torn in two. She held on, wondering how such a searing pressure could become exactly what she wanted. Will cried out and collapsed against her, breathing like a farm mule. He pulled away, leaving Velma empty and sticky.

Standing, he zipped his trousers. "I apologize. I did not mean for it to be like this the first time." He looked distraught. "I neglected to bring protection."

The first time? Velma let him help her up. "That's all right." *What a stupid thing to say.* Something wet ran down her leg.

"Are you okay?" He looked worried.

"Of course." Velma had no idea how she was, and she needed him out of the house to figure it out. She tried to smile as she walked him to the door

Will took her hand. "I'll see you tomorrow — I mean Monday."

"All right." She leaned against the closed door. She hadn't served the lemonade or thanked him for the wood. In the bathroom, she peeled off her clothes. The place where he'd put his thing in hurt. "Down there" and "his thing" were her only words for organs you weren't supposed to mention. Down there ached. There was blood on her leg and on her petticoat. Velma knew about bleeding the first time, but she hadn't expected it. Thought she was too old somehow, dried up. She ran warm water onto a washrag and tried to clean herself. This required more than a washrag. She filled the tub.

Sitting in hot water, she kept going over what happened — Will Hughes had made love to her. Followed by: Will Hughes is married and her boss. She'd read stories about what happened to working girls who went too far. She could be fired; she could be *pregnant.* Her heart bumped at that thought. They'd only done it once. Surely God would not punish her for one lapse.

Leave God out of this, a voice in her head said. *Was that her mother?* Velma soaped her legs and scrubbed down there. She'd finally done it. Or, to be accurate, had it done to her. There went virginity. She'd made love, had intercourse, fornicated. With that last word, she saw Papa's furious face, erased him, and pictured Will instead, his lips against her neck, saying those half-heard words about wanting her.

She had wanted him, too, all this time, and neither of them knew how the other felt. People were walking secrets.

She skipped church the next morning and cleaned the blood off the den carpet with cold water. Mama said cold water was the only thing for a bloodstain. Hard to put Mama in the same space with this particular blood. Plus, the fact of her cleaning it off a rug on the Lord's Day.

Velma tried to order her mind. There was Will and there was right. But mostly there was Will—and this host of new feelings. Still, the man was married. She longed for someone to talk to, and there was no one in the world she could confide in. She had done the unthinkable. The preacher back home said virginity was a woman's most precious possession, and Velma had given hers away to a married man. She rinsed out the skirt and blouse and hung them to dry.

After a bowl of soup that she couldn't swallow, she put on a clean nightgown and knelt beside the bed, searching through the Bible for words of comfort. Everything she read condemned her. God had withdrawn.

On Monday morning, back at the office, to which she'd driven slowly and carefully in her white car, she didn't know how to act. Her bottom ached in such an unfamiliar way she was surprised people didn't see it on her face.

Garnett stopped by her desk. "Are you okay?"

"Tired from moving," Velma lied.

"I can't wait to see the new house. Want an aspirin?"

"I just took one, thanks." Two lies in less than a minute, a sign of her fallen state.

When Will Hughes came in, he said, "Good morning" in his friendly, distracted way and went into his office. He told Velma to bring in her pad. When she was inside the door, he closed it and kissed her, leaving her pink-faced and panting.

"We shouldn't do this here." He wiped lipstick off his face with a handkerchief. "Can I come over tonight?"

She nodded, dumbstruck. They were a *we*? He wanted to keep doing it? Shame battled exhilaration.

"I'll be there at 7:00."

Seven meant after supper. Velma raced home after work, swallowed a bowl of cream of mushroom soup, took a bath, and was breathless but ready when the doorbell rang.

Inside the closed door, Will kissed her dizzy.

"Let me bring in another load of wood."

They kissed more in front of the fire. "How about we do it in a bed this time?"

He called what they did "it" too. Velma felt hypnotized by his warmth and the feel of his lips on hers. She let herself be guided down the hall by an elbow.

"I want to undress you."

Velma closed her eyes, burning with embarrassment and longing as Will unbuttoned her blouse and let her skirt fall around her ankles. When he reached to unfasten her brassiere, she trembled.

"I'm not going to hurt you."

She didn't open her eyes. He was going to do the thing he had done before, and she couldn't wait. Her best underpants, pink with white rosebuds, dropped around her ankles and Velma stepped out of them.

"Look at you," Will said.

"I can't." Velma got under the covers as fast as she could and watched Will undress. It felt like a sacrilege, as if she might be struck blind for looking. She watched the way he hung his shirt on the back of her rocker, and how carefully he folded his trousers over the arm. She closed her eyes when he began to pull down his boxers and didn't open them until she felt him beside her.

"What are you afraid of?" Will's face close to hers.

"Everything." Her heart pounded the way it had the night before, making such a racket she could hardly hear.

"You're safe with me. I remembered to bring protection tonight."

She kept her eyes closed, listening to the creak of the bed, a crackling sound, and the grunt of him pulling on what the boys in Picayune called a "sheath." He put a leg over her and began pressing himself inside. Desire returned, mixed with hurt, worse this time with the thing on. But once he got inside and moving, she felt only happiness. When he cried out, she responded with an answering joy. Was that what the books called an orgasm? She had no idea. No one in her family had ever mentioned the word. Garnett was the only married person Velma knew well, and she never talked about orgasms either. Everything she knew about sex, Velma had read in books and women's magazines, which usually wrote in vague terms about satisfying the husband. She lay there, listening to Will's breath slow. There was blame here, and sin, but she would worry about that later. Right now, all she felt was happiness.

This time he stayed put, and Velma did feel safe lying next to him in the silent and still-strange house. *Velma Vernon's head against Will Hughes' ear.* For all her fantasies, she had never imagined herself here. Except for him being married and the sin of fornication, this was everything she'd ever wanted in the world.

He sat at Velma's breakfast table the next morning—*her breakfast table*—eating corn flakes and drinking coffee as if it were the most natural thing in the world.

"Here's what we can do," Will said. "On Friday nights and some Saturday mornings, I see my kids."

Velma nodded.

"I play bridge until late on Saturday, and Sunday I usually have lunch with my parents. How about if I come over late Sunday afternoon?"

"That would be wonderful." *Would it?* Who had the space to think watching him light a Camel and sip coffee at her very own yellow Formica table?

"I'm thinking Sunday and Wednesday nights we'll spend here, and Tuesdays and Thursdays we can meet somewhere like The Rotisserie for dinner. How's that sound?"

"Terrific."

He'd planned it all, spinning out their days as if there were no end to them nor any question that they were a couple.

"I like figuring things out," Will said. "Don't you?"

"I do." Velma understood by now his need for order.

That first week, on Tuesday and Thursday, they left the office at separate times and arrived at the restaurant in separate cars. Chicken Cacciatore again, knees bumping under the table. On Wednesday and

Sunday night, they met at Velma's, had canned soup and crackers for supper, and made love.

On Friday night, Velma went with Bobby and Garnett to see *An American in Paris.*

Over hamburgers after, Garnett said, "Don't you love Leslie Caron?"

Velma nodded with her mouth full. In her head, she kept hearing, "Our Love is Here to Stay."

"Doesn't Velma look pretty tonight?" Garnett said. "She's glowing."

Bobby's turn to nod.

Velma smiled through her worry. *Something showed.*

"We've got to find you somebody," Garnett said.

On Saturday Velma cleaned the house, shopped for groceries, did the laundry, and had her hair done. On Sunday, she went to church where the very walls accused her.

She had plenty of time on the weekend to think about her predicament. She kept calling what they were doing "it" because she couldn't admit to the sin of calling it an "affair." It certainly wasn't marriage, no matter that Will Hughes claimed otherwise. "It's just like being married," he'd told her on Thursday night, "except I'm separated instead of divorced. Don't frown like that. What we're doing is not a sin."

But it was a sin. That's why he parked his car around the corner, and why she had awakened from a dead sleep last night, heart thudding, as if God had called her name. Will never mentioned getting a divorce and Velma never dared ask.

She wasn't stupid. She might be naive about things she'd never experienced, but she wasn't a dunce. Will had helped her buy this house, and the car, for his own reasons—not to build equity or assure her future—but for this—this thing they were doing. He said he wanted her be independent, but he also wanted her out of Belhaven where his sister lived. He'd picked a house three neighborhoods away from his family. A place safely distant from everyone he knew. To be secure, Will needed her to drive.

She appreciated her new house. As December grew colder, she loved the freedom of driving instead of waiting in the freezing rain for a bus. She certainly wasn't angry with Will, but she remained aware of the calculation behind the change in her circumstances. She saw him in a slightly different light. He was a man who calculated. She had benefited, but everything had been done on his terms.

Peter, Peter pumpkin eater,
Had a wife but couldn't keep her
He put her in a pumpkin shell
And there he kept her very well.

The nursery rhyme came into her head as she hung wet sheets on the line early on a cold December Saturday. She was nobody's wife, but here she was, safe inside her pumpkin. She'd taken Will's money. Did that make her a prostitute? Not if she didn't take more. Not if she paid back every penny he'd loaned her. That still left $700, the money he'd given her for the car, but she had worked terrifically hard during the newspaper case, more than a week's worth of extra hours. Rationalization, as the preacher said last Sunday, was another word for self-deception, another reason not to face God.

She raised her head to the scudding clouds. *Be grateful.* She no longer had to spend Saturdays at the laundromat. The new house came with a washing machine. More sheets to wash now that they were doing whatever this was. She did laundry twice a week. Chastity regained through clean sheets smelling of sunlight, even if Velma occasionally caught the whiff of sulfur.

Church remained difficult. Instead of a weekly haven, a coming home to God, Velma sat with her tailbone grinding into the wooden pew. Same place; different Velma. The first Sunday, looking in the mirror as she brushed her teeth, she thought her face had changed. The mirror reflected a more knowing look, something lost that could never be regained. The difference showed, but no one else appeared to notice. The church ladies treated her with the same friendly condescension. To them, she was an old maid, a young woman who went to a job instead of staying home baking and ironing. In spite of the radical change in her circumstances, Velma realized, on the outside she was still a person no one much noticed.

But she was no longer good and that bothered her. She had always tried to be a good person, and mostly succeeded. That was over. By no one's definition was she a good person now.

On Sundays past, she had lifted her face to God's light with no more on her conscience than a selfish thought or impatience over some malfunction at the office. Now, sitting in the Sunday quiet, she couldn't get her mind around what she had become. Will kept saying he was no longer married. He was separated. He said the word *separated* with emphasis, pronouncing each syllable, as if to turn it into divorce. But in the eyes of God, the man was still married. Hadn't Jesus told the much-married woman in the Bible she had no husband but the first? Will had children and a wife, Lillian, who now lived alone while Velma fornicated with her husband. She loved him too much to stop, that was the truth. On her knees, she held her love out to God each night. "Right now, he belongs to no other woman, and I love him so much."

Which wasn't enough. If she confided in the preacher, which she would never in a million years do, he would tell her she needed to give Will up for the sake of her immortal soul. Velma wasn't willing to do that, so the only alternative was to give up her soul. She had placed Will Hughes higher than God. In the eyes of the church, she was damned.

Will Hughes grew impatient if Velma shared these troubled thoughts. "Let's keep God out of this," he said. She was forced to stew alone.

On Wednesday and Sunday nights, when he pressed into her, she forgot about damnation. Tuesdays and Thursdays, joking over dinner, his knees touching hers under the table, she felt light and pretty—and so happy.

"All we've got, Velma, all anyone has, is now—this moment," Will said. It was the Thursday before Christmas. Over yet another plate of Chicken Cacciatore, he broke his rule about showing affection in public and took her hand across the table. "We're lucky."

Were they lucky to be together or lucky not to have been caught? Velma squeezed his hand and smiled.

"Merry Christmas." He pushed a small white box toward her, his blue eyes twinkling. For one crazy, breath-holding moment, Velma thought he was proposing, but the box was long, not square. She opened it to find a strand of lavender beads nestled in cotton.

"It's so pretty."

"I hope you like amethysts."

"I love them."

"I picked them out myself. The color reminded me of you."

Will never bought gifts. As one of her secretarial duties, Velma selected birthday and Christmas presents for every member of his family. For Christmas this year, she'd chosen gold charm bracelets for the girls. She had not been asked to buy anything for Lillian. Her own gift for Will, wrapped and waiting in her drawer at work, was an engraved silver letter opener. In prior years, before—Velma couldn't find a bearable word for now—they exchanged appropriately bland gifts. Last year, the florist delivered a poinsettia to Velma, and she'd given Will a leather-bound datebook.

"When I saw the necklace in the window of Bourgeois," Will said, "I thought to myself—Velma."

She could never wear this gift to work. Garnett would get more curious: a house, the car, and now a necklace. Velma fastened it around her neck and patted it. "They're lovely."

Will's eyes twinkled with the pleasure of his success.

She would wear the amethysts to church.

73

Two weeks passed and no word from the bishop. Lillian called Ernestine.

"You can't rush these things, Lillian. I suggest you try prayer."

She kept busy instead. Christmas was almost upon them and, though Lillian had always bought and wrapped the presents, decorated the house, and supervised Bessie's baking without any help from Will; doing it as a single woman felt bleak. She found herself counting the Christmas cards coming in. Fewer this year without a Mister in the house, she was sure of it. She studied how they were addressed: some to her alone (Those people knew.) Some to Mr. and Mrs. (Those didn't.) A few arrived addressed to The Hughes Family (Ambiguous).

She hadn't told anyone outside the family and her bridge circle about the separation, but in a place as hungry for gossip as northeast Jackson, that was enough. Shopping at the Jitney Jungle, Lillian questioned the sincerity of every smile. Invitations arrived for holiday gatherings, but not as many as in prior years. On Friday and Saturday nights during December, sitting at home, Lillian felt sure there were parties to which she had not been invited. No one wanted a single woman and she didn't blame them: she didn't want to be one.

Christmas must go on, and outwardly Lillian tried to behave as if nothing had changed. She chose gifts for the girls and hid them. Helen liked to sneak around finding presents, so Lillian tucked her daughter's main gift, a pink cashmere sweater set, into a drawer beneath her "gadgets," the g-strings she wore under her girdles. Helen had once spied these flesh-colored nylon crotches drying on the shower rod and gagged with disgust. She wouldn't go digging through that drawer.

Will had set up an account for Lillian at First National where he deposited her monthly allowance. She hadn't had her own account since they built the addition, and enjoyed the freedom of writing checks again. The money felt more like hers and there were no awkward questions about how she spent it.

A week before Christmas, she and Bessie began baking: fluffy white divinity and thick rich fudge; sugar cookies, date rolls, sausage balls, cheese straws laced with cayenne. The house filled with the fragrances of the holiday. Lillian rolled butterball cookies in powdered sugar and stored them in the yellow tin breadbox lined with waxed paper. She would not be taking these to the office party at Margaret and Mr. Pat's house because she wasn't invited. She wept a little at the injustice of this and wiped the tears away before Bessie noticed.

"You got sugar on your face," Bessie said.

Lillian took the girls downtown to buy gifts for their father. They chose a red and black striped tie, Old Spice Soap on a Rope, and handkerchiefs embroidered with an H. Lillian bought him nothing.

She filled bright red tins with her homemade Christmas goodies. Maude went with her to play Santa. They visited Jo Nell, who did Lillian's hair, then Hilda, Dimple and Frances, her bridge partners. They delivered a tin to Will's sister Mag, and last, to his parents. Maude acted as decoy, golden-haired and darling in her red velvet dress. Will's parents made a fuss over the child and complimented Lillian's baking, forgetting, or pretending to forget, the awkwardness of the circumstances. She might not have Will Hughes at home this Christmas, but she was still his wife. She was kin. Lillian would not let any of them forget that.

74

On Christmas Eve, Lillian drove the girls up to Creekmore. Leland and Olive were staying at the hotel for the holiday, along with James, Faye, Jimbo and his wife Kitty. and Ernestine and Knox, of course. Knox III and his wife Heather came down from Boston, and Ernestine's younger son Little Leland.

Everyone drank eggnog made from Grandma Creekmore's recipe, a concoction calling for a dozen eggs, a pint of whipping cream, and a cup of bourbon. They ate ham and spoon bread for Christmas Eve dinner and put the children to bed. Helen and young Leland were too old to believe in Santa Claus, but they pretended for the sake of April and Maude. All four were warned not to get up or even open their eyes until morning. If they did, Santa would not arrive. Knox III climbed into the attic with a string of sleigh bells and galloped up and down, pretending to be Santa's reindeer on the roof. Lillian smiled at the sound. Since her childhood, one male or another had made reindeer noises on Christmas Eve. Lillian pictured April and Maude in their room, staring wide-eyed into the dark, with April probably crying from excitement.

They put out the gifts from Santa Claus. The men assembled Maude's toy kitchen and April's bicycle, drinking and laughing while they worked. Lillian fell into bed tipsy and exhausted. In the cold little room, with the walls swirling, she admitted what a good time she was having without Will. She hadn't worried about him getting enough to eat or gotten tense when James or Leland told a joke. Best of all, no one counted her drinks, though Ernestine had given her a squinty-eyed look after three.

On Christmas morning, like all the Christmases of Lillian's childhood, she woke to see-your-breath cold, with everyone hugging and shouting, "Christmas Gift" for good luck. Presents, then a breakfast of roast quail, grits, and Lena's biscuits with wild plum jelly. A break, with the men snoring in their armchairs and the air thick with the smell of turkey stuffed with oyster dressing, roasting in the big oven. The children took their shouting out of doors.

Lillian relaxed in a chair next to the fire with her feet pulled up, holding her first drink of the day.

"Isn't it a little early for that?" Ernestine murmured in passing.

Lillian ignored her. She felt safe here, surrounded by the people she loved. This was her family and she didn't need to watch what she said or did around them. Nobody mentioned Will's absence or treated her as if she were pitiful without a husband. They cherished her for who she was, and she was enough.

75

On Christmas morning, after giving the white car a good wipe-down in the freezing carport, Velma drove to the farm.

In her mother's kitchen, the air seemed almost furry with the smells of a baking ham and two freshly made mince pies. She put down her suitcase and hugged Mama. Papa sat in his usual chair looking out of sorts. She gave him a kiss on top of his balding head.

"I'm sorry I wasn't able to come earlier. The law firm gives that party on Christmas Eve, and they don't like for us to miss it." She talked fast, hoping neither of them noticed anything different about her.

"Well, you're here now," Mama said. "And you drove down in a car of your own. I can hardly believe it." She made the familiar gesture of wiping her hands on her apron. "Give us a look at it."

Papa got up with the groan old people made when they stood. "I can't believe they pay you enough to buy a car."

Outside, their breath steamed in the cold air. "It's used," Velma said. She felt a surge of pride opening the passenger door so they could view the freshly vacuumed upholstery. "Only twenty thousand miles on the odometer when I bought it."

"A car *and* a house. Imagine." Mama sounded proud.

Papa said, "Did you have to borrow money?"

"For the house, yes." Velma kept her voice firm. "The car I paid cash for."

Papa walked around the white Chevrolet looking suspicious. He kicked a front tire. "Living pretty high on the hog up there in the city."

"I work hard and the firm pays me well." If her parents ever found out what was going on outside of work, Mama might forgive her, but Papa—never.

"Which bank gave you a loan on the house?" Papa said.

"Deposit Guaranty."

"Hope for your sake they're solid."

"Funds guaranteed by the U.S. Government. My boss, Mr. Hughes, knows the vice president."

"Government." Papa spat on the frozen ground.

Velma did not miss seeing men spit.

"Let's go inside," Mama said. "I got a ham in the oven. Aunt Orrie plans to drive over for dinner tonight. Hope you don't mind sharing the bed."

Just when she thought she'd come up in the world—another night with Aunt Orrie. "Not a bit," Velma said.

They sat down to baked ham, rice with red gravy, mashed turnips, green beans, corn bread, rolls, with pie later for dessert.

Mama smiled. "You're our guest today, Velma honey. You say the blessing."

Velma swallowed. "Thank you, Lord, for this meal. Bless those who made it and we who eat it. In Jesus' name, Amen." The words stuck in her throat.

Orrie spread butter on her roll. "Bet you don't eat like this in the city."

"Most days after work I heat up a can of soup."

"That's why you're so skinny," Orrie said.

"She looks the way girls do nowadays," Mama said. "It's the fashion."

"A strong wind could blow her over," Orrie said. "And she's got that peaked look around the eyes. They test you for tuberculosis up there?"

Velma laughed to cover what Orrie might be seeing, a loss of weight from excitement and worry. "Where are your children this Christmas, Aunt Orrie?"

"Drew Junior's driving transport for the Air Force. Couldn't get off. Ruby's training with the Army Nurse Corps. You may have heard, we're at war again."

Velma sensed reproof in her aunt's voice and ignored it. "That's wonderful training. Ruby will be able to get a job anywhere."

"*My* children have no desire to leave home." Aunt Orrie speared a green bean while delivering this thrust.

Papa cleared his throat at the head of the table. "When the time comes, I've asked young Drew to take over the farm."

Velma swallowed at the unexpected pain of this announcement. "That's nice." What—did she think Papa would leave valuable land to a single woman?

"If you'd hitched up with Chalmers back when he asked, things might be different," Papa said.

"Oh, for heaven's sake, Raymond." Mama pushed the basket of rolls towards him to shut him up. "Don't go digging up that old bone. It's Christmas. We got our girl home."

"Just saying."

Lying in the narrow bed that night, listening to Orrie snore like a rooting pig, Velma compared Christmas in her two lives: amethysts in Jackson; a hand-knit coverlet from Mama here. A jar of homemade elderberry jelly from Aunt Orrie, who instructed Velma to hold it to the light. "Like rubies," she said. "Not many can make a jelly that clear." Papa gave her a smoked ham to take home.

She'd brought them city gifts: a new leather wallet for Papa and a white wool cardigan for Mama. Orrie got Mama's second gift—a box of April Violets bath powder. Her aunt took one sniff and began coughing. "They'll think I'm a harlot."

Velma loved them dearly and their gifts were precious to her, but every word people said to her down here—not Mama, but the rest of them—made her accomplishments up in the city feel small. She hadn't done her duty by marrying Chalmers; she hadn't signed up to serve her country; she spent money on a mortgaged house and a used car, possessions a single woman neither needed nor deserved.

She moved as far away from Orrie as she could without falling out of bed. *What was Will doing right now?* Missing her, she hoped. He'd eaten Christmas dinner at his mother's. The children were at the family hotel. If she were home, she and Will could be curled up together, though he seldom spent an entire night in her bed. She decided to use work as an excuse and drive back tomorrow.

76

February: almost three months into what Velma thought of as her double life, her pretend marriage. She had been at the front desk when Lillian's brother Leland Creekmore came to see Will. She'd watched him leave, head down, bottom lip pushed out. She was there the day Mag went in and spoke to her brother. Voices were raised behind the closed door and Mag came out red-faced.

Velma worried that the heated talks might be about her, but Leland and Mag gave her a cursory nod coming and going, as if she were part of the furniture. If they had any hint of the truth, her stomach tightening at the thought, she would transform instantly from efficient secretary into home-wrecker, the office whore.

Will Hughes was in a terrible temper after his sister's visit, but did not offer an explanation, and Velma had learned not to ask questions. They went on as before, and she tried to put worry out of her mind.

Until the morning when, fingers racing over the keys, Velma looked up to see two older gentlemen come in. They had called for an appointment, so she knew who they were. The bishop was taller than the minister. Both wore clerical collars and serious expressions. She opened the door to Will's office. "Dr. Selah and Bishop Gray to see you."

Will rose with a smile, holding out his hand, but Velma noticed a wariness in his eyes. She closed the door. They were in there for over an hour, a murmur of voices, nothing loud enough to hear. They came out, bowed slightly in her direction, and left. She waited. Will did not call her in for dictation. The door remained closed.

At lunchtime, Velma and Garnett walked down Capitol Street to the cafeteria. Since buying the house, Velma saved on expenses by bringing a sandwich to work, but Garnett claimed they hardly saw each other anymore, and lunch today was her treat.

They filled their trays and found a table. Velma had chosen corn, beans and greens, trying to get in a week's worth of vegetables. Working and making time for Will, she wasn't eating properly. Mama said she looked iron poor.

Sitting at the table with Garnett, she wondered what the two churchmen wanted. Why hadn't Will Hughes called her in for dictation after they left?

"We never talk anymore," Garnett said.

Velma's guard went up. "Yes, we do."

"Not like in the old days."

She smiled at her friend, trying to remember how she'd acted before the secrets started. "I'm sorry. Buying the house and learning to drive, then Christmas. The last few months have been crazy."

"Bobby and I worry about you."

"Do you?" Was this going to be a lecture about Will Hughes?

"He thinks you spend too much time alone. I do, too."

Relieved, Velma laughed.

"Doris lives out by you, doesn't she?"

Velma nodded. "Why?"

Garnett's voice dropped to a whisper. "She drove by your house the other night and said she saw Mr. Hughes' car in your driveway."

This was it. Velma saw spots in front of her eyes. Her friend's concerned face went in and out of focus.

"Are you okay?" Garnett said.

Velma nodded, giving herself time by taking a swallow of water. She held the glass with both hands as if studying it, then carefully placed it back inside its wet circle. "I was afraid people might think something was strange." She'd worried aloud to Will, but he said he'd gotten tired of parking around the corner. There were a hundred cars in town like his, he claimed.

"You know Will Hughes." Velma kept her voice light. "Now that he's separated from his wife, he feels perfectly free to keep me working the same hours he puts in."

Garnett frowned. "He comes to your house to make you work?"

Velma nodded again. "Like he did during the newspaper case."

"Does he pay you for the extra time?"

Velma decided a little honesty wouldn't hurt. "I'll tell you the truth if you promise not to tell."

Garnett leaned closer.

"Will helped me get the loan for the house. I owe him."

"That doesn't mean he gets to take over your whole life," Garnett said.

"You're right." Velma took another swallow of water. Her hand barely shook. "I need to start having more fun."

"Time to meet Mr. Right," Garnett said. "Did you ever hear back from Harold Meeks?"

The friend of Bobby's. Velma shook her head no. "I don't think he liked me."

"Is there no one at your church?"

"No one under sixty."

They walked back to work, heads down, holding their coats closed against the wet February wind. In the park across from the office, thick gray clouds raced over the bare trees like a warning. Velma felt Garnett glancing at her and maybe not believing her.

Will wasn't in his office. Velma checked behind the door: his hat and coat were gone. He hadn't spoken of any afternoon appointments. This was Thursday, one of their nights to eat out. When he didn't reappear by 5:30, Velma drove home.

Something was wrong; she felt it in her bones. Heating a can of tomato soup, she thought of the girl she'd been nine years ago, newly arrived at Mrs. Moseley's, walking hopefully up North State Street to Baldwin Business College. Excited to start her first job and ignorant as a potato. She thought of Mr. Pat and how kind he'd been. When she pictured his face now, he looked disappointed.

On Friday, Will Hughes seemed out of sorts. There was no mention of the missed dinner. Going over corrections in a long brief, his face creased with worry. Velma knew better than to ask. He was the boss of their affair and, outside of that, he was the boss, period. When she left that evening, he was still shut inside his office.

He did not call or come by over the weekend. Her apprehension grew, along with exasperation. She realized, sitting in church on Sunday morning, the only phone number she had for Will, outside the office, was the home where he no longer lived. She would never call Lillian. The fretting stung like nettles. She told herself not to be foolish; Will was a private man. He like to keep things to himself until he got them settled in his mind. She hoped nothing was wrong with his girls. She hoped it wasn't about her. There was nowhere to turn with this anxiety. After church, she took it out on the kitchen floor, mopping and hand-waxing the green and white vinyl tiles until they reflected the ceiling light and her own pale face.

77

Lillian felt more optimistic in the new year. The girls were behaving, and she had grown accustomed to dinner without Will at the other end of the table. Helen, when she was in a good mood, replaced her father as family storyteller, doing imitations of her geometry teacher that made them choke with laughter. Lillian was able to enjoy a drink or two before dinner without being criticized, and a nightcap to help her sleep. She had a Valentine party at the Staples to look forward to and had made herself a new dress: blue silk with crystal beading around the neckline. Best of all, the troubles had caused her to lose ten pounds.

When Leland telephoned a week before the party, she had nothing more serious on her mind than which shoes to wear with the blue dress. The black alligator pumps, she thought.

"I have Will's terms."

"What terms?"

"He's willing to come back if you agree to his terms."

Heart thumping, ears ringing, Lillian sat down hard on the bed to keep from falling.

The terms arrived the next day in a large manila envelope. Leland delivered them, hardly able to look at her. He said he would be happy to return them to Will after she signed them, or not. Whatever she decided.

Inside the envelope, the pages were handwritten on sheets torn from a yellow pad like the ones Will used once to write briefs at night, in their small house on Monroe Street. During that time when they thought they would always be happy. He obviously hadn't wanted Velma or anybody else at the office to see this or he would have had it typed. It was drawn up like a legal document and titled "The Agreement."

The Agreement

This is an agreement between William Calhoun Hughes (hereafter known as WCH) and Lillian Creekmore Hughes (hereafter known as LCH), husband and wife.

WCH agrees to reside in the marital residence under the following conditions:

This is a marriage in name only. This is a marriage maintained for the sake of three underage female children, Helen, April and Maude Hughes, and under the terms stated herein.

WCH will domicile with LCH and his three female children until those children reach maturity, or LCH acts to cancel this agreement.

WCH will reside in the home, pay reasonable bills for upkeep of same, and participate with the children in family occasions and activities, so long as those do not interfere with the efficient conduct of his legal practice.

WCH will no longer be expected or required to perform other marital duties, or to show physical or verbal manifestations of affection toward LCH.

He will not attend social events with LCH unless those concern the children, the family, or his business, and do not interfere with the latter.

WCH is neither required nor expected to take trips or vacations with LCH. His leisure time is his and is not to be questioned.

Likewise, his working hours, which are and will continue to be extensive.

LCH agrees not to consume alcohol in the home when WCH is present, except during such times as WCH and LCH entertain, and then only in moderation.

LCH agrees to live within the budget set by WCH and not to request additional sums for remodeling, redecorating, travel, etc.

The undersigned WCH agrees to these terms.

The undersigned LCH agrees to these terms and is hereby notified that any abridgement nullifies the agreement.

This agreement becomes effective March 1, 1952, when WCH resumes residence in the family home at 1015 Kings Highway, Jackson, Mississippi, U.S.A.

Space for two signatures and dates.

Lillian burned with humiliation. She got up and quietly closed the door to the bedroom. She went into the bathroom, as far from Bessie as she could get, sat on the closed toilet, and read the pages through again. Odd to feel such attraction at the sight of Will's handwriting, and such revulsion at the words. The words made it plain: the man she married did not love her. He might not even like her, but he was willing to come home.

She brought the pages out of the bathroom and sat in the chair beside her bed. She lit a cigarette and read the agreement a third time, blinking through the smoke. *A marriage in name only.* The envelope had been closed with a string tie. Leland must have read this. The thought made her cringe. No wonder he wouldn't look at her.

Could she live this way, with a person who didn't care for her or wish to be with her? Will didn't say he despised her, but he might as well have.

He wanted rules. If she obeyed the rules, she got to keep the husband: his name, the house, and her position in the community. She tried to remember the last time they'd made love. He'd been gone four months and it was long before that, maybe a year. She managed to do without—What had he called it? —his "marital duties." She missed the intimacy, but had survived without being touched. For all she knew, other of her married friends might exist in similar circumstances. Hilda's husband never went out at night; Dimple's Ben had prostate trouble; Peggy's Harry refused to travel.

She loved Will Hughes and he no longer loved her. That was the plain truth of it. If she were a woman with pride or money, if she didn't have three children, if she had any way to make a living and didn't care what other people thought, things might be different. If she were ten years younger, thirty-two instead of forty-two (forty-four, but no one remembered that lie), she might be able to make another choice. But she wasn't any of those women.

She needed to look at the demands from a more positive angle. His leisure was also hers. She was free to go to parties without him, or to travel, anything she wanted and could afford. She wasn't forbidden from doing any of those things, but she reminded herself of how notoriously stingy Will could be. Like the remodeling: seven years had passed and he still begrudged the money she'd spent—enough to mention it in the agreement. Still holding the new bedroom against her, along with the bed where he no longer had to touch her.

James and Leland were around if she needed money. On her last birthday, Leland had put a piece of an oil lease in Lillian's name. This provided a tiny income of her own. A check for a hundred dollars, sometimes more, depending on the price of oil, appeared in the mail each month. Depositing it, Lillian felt almost wealthy.

If she agreed to Will's terms, no one else need know. In a year or so, their friends would forget he'd ever left. The family might remember, but if she and Will showed up together for Thanksgiving and Christmas, the separation would slip into the dustbin of their memories.

She went to the mahogany secretary in the living room and got out her pen. She took several deep breaths. This was a life-changing decision, and she might be making a terrible mistake, but she could see no other way. Her heart beat uncomfortably and her hand shook. She braced it against the surface of the desk and signed Lillian Creekmore Hughes, the writing shakier than usual. She wrote in the date, February 10, 1952, and blew the ink dry. Eighteen years ago, she'd signed a marriage certificate and here she was, agreeing to a non-marriage. She stared at the paper feeling empty, as if she'd given away a piece of herself.

Which was foolishness. She was shaky because she'd forgotten to eat. Her so-called independence had always depended on Will. She didn't want to raise these children by herself, dealing day after day with Helen's sulkiness, April's tears, and Maude hiding her vegetables. In addition, and this was the horrible truth, she still loved the man. Where there was love, surely there was hope.

Underneath the doubts, she felt an edge of excitement. Will was coming home. He might not sleep with her, but he would be in the next bed. He had agreed to stay until the children were mature. Did mature mean eighteen or twenty-one in Mississippi? She needed to look it up. Maude wouldn't be twenty-one for fourteen more years. A lot could happen in fourteen years. Her chest tightened in fear. Then what? She counted. In February 1966, Will planned to walk out again? She would be fifty-seven by then, too old to fool herself or anybody else into thinking she was worth having.

Leland came by the next day and picked up the signed document. Staring at the floor, he said, "You don't have to settle for this, Angie. You're still young. You could find somebody who'd treat you right."

She thought about that misbegotten night at the hotel. Leland meant a laughing, drinking man like Bob Bradshaw. She put a hand on her brother's cheek and felt him go rigid. A kinder person never lived, but Leland did not enjoy being touched. "You are the sweetest brother a girl could have. I wish I'd found a man like you, but I got Will Hughes, didn't I, and he has a lot of fine qualities. Loving me just doesn't happen to be one of them." Saying the words, her eyes filled with tears and her brother's face blurred.

Leland shook his head, still not looking at her. "I hate seeing you do this to yourself."

Wiping her face, Lillian laughed. "If you can find me a man as good as you, I'll break this agreement in a minute."

After her brother left, Lillian sank into the nearest chair. "For better or worse," they'd said eighteen years ago, and for better or worse now. More worse than better, but she'd made this bed and she preferred to lie in it as Mrs. Will Hughes. Being married with rules was a far better fate in 1952 Mississippi than being a divorced nobody. Better for the children, too. She smiled thinking of their glee when they heard the news: Daddy was coming home. They didn't need to know the rest.

The agreement didn't take effect until March 1. No reason not to get dressed up and have a nice time at Alice and Avery's. She might not have a husband who loved her, but she had a darling new dress.

78

Velma got to the office early on Monday morning. The door was shut, but the light was on in Will's office. She sat down and began typing the corrected brief she found on her desk. His voice came over the intercom: "Could you come in here, please?"

Opening the door, Velma tried to read his face. Everything was in place: hair combed, shirt crisp, but his eyes looked deep-set and tired.

"Close the door, please."

She sat with her pad, her body prickling with anxiety.

"I have deep feelings for you, Velma, and nothing I am about to say in any way changes that. Do you understand?"

Her dread increased.

Will shifted in his chair. "This is hard, so I might as well just come out with it. I have agreed to move back in with Lillian."

Velma felt as if she'd been dashed with cold water. Feeling left her hands and the steno pad dropped to the floor. She bent to pick it up and felt blood rushing to her face. *Do not cry.*

Will came from behind his desk and stood over her. "Nothing will change except appearances."

She kept her head down. *Do not cry.*

"Lillian has agreed to my terms. We're maintaining a marriage for the sake of the children—it's in name only. I don't love her."

She sat up and looked at him, his face as flushed as hers.

"I plan to move back next week, but Lillian and I will not be—" He hesitated. "—sleeping together."

Velma watched his lips move through the roaring in her ears. She got up without a word. The other person, the one who controlled her body, took her out to her desk, sat her down, and returned her eyes to the place on the page where she'd been typing. Was it only last week that she'd—admit it—pretended she was married to Will Hughes? He belonged to no one else, so he must be hers. Exactly like marriage except for the church part, a piece of paper and a few words.

She couldn't see to type. She got up, went to the ladies' room, locked herself in a stall, and threw up. Then she let herself cry.

Doris came in while Velma pressed cold, wet paper towels to her eyes. "Are you okay?"

"I must have eaten something bad. I got sick." Did Doris believe her? She didn't care.

Without a word to anyone, Velma did what she had never done in all her years at Hughes & Blair: she put on her coat and hat, picked up her purse, and left. Riding down the elevator, she looked at her watch, the gold-plated Bulova Will gave her after she admired it in the jeweler's window. Only nine-thirty. She got into her white car and pointed it toward her white house. Driving slowly because she was still new at it and her eyes didn't work right.

At home, she threw up for a second time, and a third, until nothing came up but the bitter acid of her own sin. She took two aspirin with swallows of warm Coke, lowered the shades, took off her shoes, and lay down on top of the cover. She got up and pulled the comforter over her, closed her eyes, and waited to die. Might as well. Everything inside already felt dead. It seemed a small matter to quit breathing and silence the torn heart that made her chest hurt worse than when she had pleurisy. She would die and go to hell where she belonged. Mama and Papa would be sad, but not if they knew the truth. She had traded her everlasting soul for sex with a married man.

Velma opened her eyes and took her Bible from the bedside table. She stared unseeingly at the pages. King James version with the words of Jesus printed in red. Given to her the Sunday before she left Picayune to keep away the bullets of sin. *Hadn't worked.* She opened it to the page for Family History. No one's name there but her own. Will

Hughes had been married when they began this abomination (the word rose unbidden), and he was still married. Nothing had changed except he was moving back home to his wife. The separation Velma had used as an excuse to give herself over to evil had ended.

What had he said? He still had deep feelings for her. Feelings didn't mean love. Neither of them ever uttered that word. Velma didn't say it because she couldn't until Will did, and Will didn't, probably because he didn't feel that way. What difference did a word make anyway: the man was married. He'd been married from the start.

Returning home, he said, for the sake of the children. It would look like a marriage, he said, but it wasn't a marriage. Surely Velma could see. But all she saw was a man who had encouraged her to sin. He was an adulterer; she was a fornicator. Ugly words for uglier deeds.

She lay under the quilt until it got dark. For all her trying, she didn't die. She got up, put on her nightgown, and turned down the bed. She did not pray, and Will Hughes did not call. Both her gods were silent.

She did not go in to work on Tuesday. She called a locksmith and had the locks changed on the front and back doors. When the phone rang, she didn't answer it. She went through the house, scrubbing everything that could be scoured with Bon Ami and the rest with Murphy's Oil Soap. Cleaning, cleaning until she caught a glimpse of her pinched face in the mirror and remembered to eat. The small collection of Will's things, a razor, a striped tie, and a pair of what he called "soft" shoes, she put in a brown paper bag and set it outside the back door.

Twilight arrived early in winter. She turned out the inside lights and closed the blinds in her bedroom. At 7:00, she heard the sound of Will trying his key at the front door. She ignored it. She heard him at the back door and sat on the bed holding onto her knees and rocking while he fumbled. He kept trying, probably thinking he had the key in wrong. A dunce when it came to mechanical things, exactly like his father. She ignored the knocks, the calling of her name, the puzzled silence. She heard his car drive away and quit rocking.

Now for the hard part—the rest of her life.

79

On Wednesday, Velma called in sick, speaking to Garnett, apologizing for not calling the day before. "Too nauseated," she claimed. Velma never got sick, so the firm couldn't fault her for missing a few days. Garnett wanted to come and bring her soup, but Velma said she thought she'd drive down to Picayune and let her mother nurse her. The phone rang as she went out the back door. Garnett must have told Will. She ignored it.

When Velma drove up to the farmhouse, Mama was on the freezing front porch, pushing a pair of wet overalls through the hand-cranked wringer. She glanced up, surprised. "Didn't expect you back so soon." She wrestled the stiff garment through, knuckles red from the strong brown soap.

The smell of that soap took Velma right back. Nine and a half years ago, she had gone down the steps of this porch with her suitcase, telling everyone goodbye, tickled to be heading off to her new life.

She tried to smile the worry off her mother's face. "They gave me a few days off." She opened her arms for a hug, feeling her mother's bones under the grey sweater, feeling the sting of her own tears.

Mama held her at arm's length. "Are you okay, girl?"

"Tired," Velma said. "Bone tired."

"Let's go sit in the kitchen where it's warm. I'll heat you a cup of cider." She put the steaming cup in front of Velma. "Seeing you drive up in that car is still a surprise."

Velma sipped and felt her eyes closing. She had hardly slept the night before. "Could I take a nap?"

"Go in our room, yours is too cold. I'll warm it up while you have a rest. Get you some extra quilts."

Velma lay in her parents' bed the way she had when she was small and sick with the croup. Warm under quilts her mother had made, comforted by the familiar smell of their pillows, she slept.

Papa didn't ask why she was there. He didn't mind listening to Velma's tales of life in the city (whistling through the space in his two front teeth when she said something that astounded him), but he never asked questions. On this trip she didn't feel like bragging.

At supper, she ate roast pork, greens, and cornbread, savoring the home-cooked food, aching for the girl she had been when she left this table, the bad choices not yet made.

In her own bed, feet warmed by a felt-wrapped brick, she felt better. These were her people and this was where she belonged. That other world was a dream she'd wandered into, and the dream had become a nightmare.

For the rest of the week, she worked in the fields with her dad, bundling straw over the soft earth where asparagus would emerge in the spring. She helped harvest the last of the winter turnips, her hands aching from the cold. In the frigid barn, she filled crates to truck down to the coast. She worked until she was too tired to feel anything but the pain of unused muscles. On Sunday she went to church, sat in the pew between her parents, and listened to the preacher talk about damnation. He asked the congregation to cast out error and temptation and be washed in the blood of the lamb. Velma closed her eyes and sensed a light moving through her, a gentle wind warming every cell of her body. When she opened her eyes, she felt cleansed. "The peace that passeth understanding," she whispered.

"Are you all right?" Mama said.

Velma squeezed her mother's arm. *Go forth and sin no more, Jesus said. She could do that. She had reached out to the Lord and He had heard her.* She was not abandoned. A sinner could be saved in spite of her sins. All she had to do was set her feet on the straight and narrow and keep them there.

At the dinner table with her parents, Velma ate fried chicken, creamed corn, biscuits, and pie made from blackberries put up last summer. The air was thick with the smell of the wood stove and good food. She closed her eyes, feeling blessed.

In the late afternoon, she packed her bag, hugged her mother, kissed Papa on top of his head, and drove back to Jackson. She had closed the door firmly on sin and chosen life instead. Anytime she felt doubt, she could go back to where she belonged.

On Monday in the office, Velma held that resolution firm as a shield. Behind his closed door, Will Hughes explained again how nothing was different. Velma watched his lips move, inhaled the faint scent of Old Spice, and continued to love him. She couldn't make herself not love him. Her body yearned, but the spirit did not weaken. When she spoke, her voice was firm. "I hear what you're saying, but it's not my way."

No, she would not go out to dinner with him. No, he could not come over. She stood tall and stiff to ward him off. "If this too difficult, perhaps I should look for work at another firm."

"Of course, you won't go to another firm." Will spoke in a choked shout, slamming his hand on his desk. Velma winced and his voice softened. "As a lawyer, you know how much I admire reason."

She nodded.

"Reason and logic say I may appear to the outside world to be married, but I am not actually married. I live at home to satisfy my family and the community, and because I love my children, but my time is my own. Lillian and I have an agreement. She understands this is a marriage in name only. As soon as Maude goes off to college, I will leave for good. You have my word."

Velma listened. When he was done, she tried to keep her voice even. "I'm sure your reasoning makes sense to you, and I don't like to go against your wishes, but in the eyes of the church you are a married man. I won't come between you and your family. It would be a sin for us—"

He broke in. "You know I don't believe in that garbage."

"But I do."

He muttered *"Christ,"* saying it like a curse. She walked out, softly closing the door behind her.

The next day, she found a small black velvet box in the drawer where she kept her purse. Earrings to match the amethyst necklace.

She took the box in with her when Will Hughes called her for dictation. "I can't accept these." She set the velvet box on his desk. "They haven't been worn. You can return them to the store."

Will glanced at and away from the box. Without comment, he flipped through the pages of the opposing side's brief. "Shall we begin?"

She took up her pad and pen. When he was done dictating, she left. The next time she went in his office, the box had disappeared.

Days passed. Will Hughes dictated and Velma typed, but the old ease between them had vanished. No more winks and grins. That was a lesson, Velma realized. Once you had s-e-x, you couldn't take three steps back into friendship. Under his eyes, she felt strange in her body, as if she'd forgotten how to walk or breathe naturally.

At the office she did her job. At home she wept and prayed. Once she had asked God to take away the lust and leave her the man. Now she prayed to be cleansed of all desire. She begged the Lord to fill the aching emptiness in her chest, and to remove the stain of sin, so she would be able to look at Will's wife and darling children without shame.

80

On the first Saturday in March, with Bessie gone for the afternoon, Lillian gathered the girls around the breakfast room table. Helen, taller now than her mother, refused to sit, looming instead, stewing with teenage impatience.

"I have good news," Lillian said. April, smaller, blonde and blue-eyed like her father, looked ready to cry. The child was nothing but nerves. Dimpled Maude, taking a cue from her older sister, appeared equally apprehensive.

"Your father is coming home."

Helen stood straighter, exhaling a puff of shock. April wept. Maude began bouncing on her fat bottom. "Daddy, Daddy, Daddy."

"When?" Helen said.

"Monday after work—and why on earth are you crying, April?" Lillian tried to keep the annoyance out of her voice.

"I'm just so happy." April blubbered.

"Well, this is exactly what I want to talk to you about." Lillian looked at each of them. "Your father is returning and I want his homecoming to be peaceful. Part of the reason he left was that he couldn't find the quiet he needed to think here at home." She ignored the pinch of guilt. This lie was in service to a cause, and it wouldn't hurt any of them to take some responsibility. "We all know how hard he works."

They nodded.

"So, we must do our best to create an atmosphere of—" She tried to find the right word. "—of harmony. Which means, no tears, darling." She took April's wet chin in her hand. "No temper tantrums." Staring pointedly at Helen. "Or sulking." She stroked Maude's blonde curls. "As for you, Miss Pris, no running up and down the hall like a wild Indian."

Maude shook her head. "No running."

April snuffled wetly, and Lillian handed her a paper napkin.

There was nothing to be done about Bessie. "Mr. Will, we been *missing* you around here." Throwing her loud voice against Will on Monday evening as if he'd risen from the dead.

"Haven't we missed him, baby?" She shouted at Maude, who fastened herself around one of Will's legs. "Daddy, Daddy, Daddy." Helen and April came running up the hall and flung themselves at him.

"Glad to see me, are you?" Will's boisterous voice.

The hero returns, Lillian thought from the sewing machine next door in Maude's room. Remembering the agreement, she let no emotion show, though her heart leapt. She stayed where she was, bent over the Singer, politely returning Will's greeting when he stuck his head in.

"Lillian."

"Will."

He went to unpack and she told the girls to wash their hands for dinner. She and Bessie had gone to some trouble over this meal. There was fried chicken with rice and gravy, green beans, a nice salad with pink grapefruit sections, a combination Will particularly enjoyed, and for dessert, his favorite: egg custard pie.

"Will, would you say the blessing?" Lillian pretended to close her eyes, but she watched him, reveling in having this man back at her table.

"Bessie, everything tastes wonderful." Will smacked his lips in appreciation. He told the girls stories about his cases, making them laugh. Lillian joined in the laughter, as if he'd meant the stories for her as well. In actuality, he had neither spoken to nor looked at her since the initial greeting.

After supper, he put his coat on and offered Bessie a ride home. Talking to Maude, who followed him carrying a picture book. "Daddy has got to go back to work."

One meal and he was gone again. Lillian made her rounds, making sure Helen was off the phone and April and Maude in bed. She took off her makeup with cold cream, patted on astringent, and moisturized her face. Put on her nightgown and bed jacket. Switched on the reading lights and turned down both beds, folding the corner of Will's sheet into an inviting triangle. She set out a clean pair of his pajamas. The *Time* magazines that had arrived since his departure were stacked on his bedside table. John Wayne grinned from the cover of the most recent, his hair combed the way Will's did his, into a little pompadour.

Nothing else to do. Not yet nine o'clock. Lillian pined for her nightly drink and resisted. She checked the doors, made sure the light was on in the carport, the back door unlocked, and climbed into bed. She read a story in *Ladies Home Journal* about a woman and her mechanic husband who adopted eight handicapped children. Better them than her.

Will came in at nine-thirty. He nodded to her, perfectly pleasant. Put his change, wallet and watch on the dresser, his hat on the closet shelf, and hung up his suit coat. Went into the bathroom with the pajamas and closed the door. Faucet running, brushing sounds, flushing noises. He came out in his robe, crawled into the far bed, and picked up the top issue of *Time*.

Lillian watched while pretending to read a piece on how to make a bunny-shaped Easter cake. She had not comprehended one word since he walked in the door.

After half an hour, Will stood, took off his robe, got back into bed, said "Good night" to the room, and switched off his light. He turned his back on her and settled the covers around his shoulders. The snoring began within minutes.

Lillian stared at his back, listening to the rattle. She had not missed that, but snoring didn't matter. Nor did the cursory greeting or refusing to look at her. He could knock down the walls with his noise. He could compliment Bessie for a meal Lillian had planned, and tell stories to the girls as if she weren't at the table. None of that mattered. He was home. She was Mrs. Will Hughes with a husband in the next bed.

81

A month passed and Velma wondered if she would ever regain the role of courteous, reserved secretary without this stiff feeling of self-consciousness.

She typed, fingers flying over the keys. The phone of her desk rang. "Hughes and Blair."

"Velma?"

She did not recognize the male voice. "This is Velma Vernon. To whom am I speaking?"

"It's Harold Meeks." He sounded apologetic. "Do you remember me?"

She had not given the man two thoughts since the night at the bowling alley. Garnett's Bobby must have asked him to call: Save the pitiful creature or she'll die a spinster. Mrs. Evans had not approved of personal phone calls at work and neither did Velma. She responded in her most professional voice. "Of course. What can I do for you?"

"Sorry to phone you at work. Would you like to go to the picture show with me on Friday night?"

Velma surprised herself by saying yes. *Why not?*

They saw *The Adventures of Annie Oakley*, which Velma found funny and blessedly distracting. Harold reached for her hand during the second half. He had a work-roughened but warm hand.

Afterwards, they sat with coffees in the cafe across the street. Harold said, "Your hands are so cold."

"I've had a hard time keeping warm lately."

"I'm glad you came tonight." He leaned closer. "I thought, you know, that first night, you must not have liked me."

Velma laughed, covering her mouth. "I was a terrible bowler, I figured you were glad to see the back of me."

"I thought *you* weren't interested."

"I'd been on a total of two dates before that night. I didn't know how to act."

"Are you more prepared now?"

It wasn't a joke, and his earnestness made Velma feel a hundred years old.

"Let's just take it one picture show at a time." She smiled to take any harshness out of the words, a big smile without the hand covering her gums.

Harold Meeks struck her as a man who wouldn't mind gums. He was kind, polite, and aside from the ink-rimmed fingernails, scrubbed and neat. He worked hard at a decent job. His light brown hair was already receding and he didn't try to comb it forward the way some did. She watched him over her coffee cup. He would make somebody an excellent husband, but in no way was he a substitute for Will Hughes.

The next weekend they double-dated with Garnett and Bobby. The weekend after that, Bobby cooked steaks behind their small house. Velma noticed Garnett's relief seeing her with Harold. Her friend was right: it was time to come to her senses.

On the fourth weekend, at the front door, Velma let Harold Meeks kiss her. On the fifth, she invited him in, gave him coffee, and, while embracing on the dusty rose sofa, allowed him to clasp a breast on top of her blouse. His breath grew harsh, but she felt nothing except a certain impatience to be alone.

When he asked her out on the seventh weekend, she made the excuse that she needed to go home to Picayune. On the eighth, she saw another movie with him, *House of Wax* this time. Afterwards, they sat opposite one another in the same coffee shop. She studied his eager face and decided to head things off.

"I know you like me, Harold, and I like you, too."

"It's more than like, Velma, I want—"

"Please don't say anymore. I enjoy having you as a friend."

"I don't want to be a friend. I want you to marry me."

Velma had to keep herself from groaning. She stared at the half-eaten hot fudge sundae in front of her and tried to think of a kind way to do this. "I can't. I am truly honored to be asked, but I can't marry anyone."

"Garnett said there might be someone else."

Garnett said? Velma kept her face bland. *She had to be guessing.* "There is no one else. I just can't. I'm sorry."

His face turned solemn. "I won't come begging again. This is it."

"I hope you'll forgive me. I never meant to make you beg."

Garnett looked distressed in the ladies' room the next Monday. "What did you do to Harold? He called Bobby."

"I told him I couldn't marry him."

"Why not? He's such a nice guy."

"Because I don't love him."

"Honestly, Velma, don't blame me if you end up an old maid."

Velma felt her throat tighten and turned away. "I promise not to blame you." This was her good friend, her best friend, and she kept lying to her. She recognized the hollow feeling: she could never be truly honest with anyone again. She had given up the privilege.

On Saturday, going through the schedule of her chores, Velma lectured herself. Harold Meeks was right: this was it. She'd had a suitor, a nice man who wasn't already married to someone else, a man who apparently cared enough to marry her, and she had turned him down. Which meant she was doing exactly what Will Hughes asked: waiting for him to be free.

I am not waiting.

She replayed what Will said. "When Maude goes off to college, I'll leave for good. You have my word." Velma had gone to Maude's christening. In her bedroom, she pulled open a bureau drawer and took out the box where she kept everything pertaining to Will Hughes: clippings from the newspaper case, his picture when he was head of the V.F.W. Here was the christening invitation, with a tiny photo. Maude got christened late because Lillian waited for Will to get home from the Navy. The child had been almost a year old. In the photograph she had beautiful blonde curls and big blue eyes, an angel. November 18, 1945. That meant Maude was now seven. In eleven years, she would go to college. In eleven years, Velma would be thirty-nine. Thirty-nine was too old for anybody to want.

Following the christening, she'd been invited to a party for the baby at Will and Lillian's new house. Lillian had tried to make Velma feel at home, asking about her job, telling her they were slave-drivers at that law firm and Velma mustn't let them work her too hard. She remembered smiling and nodding, trying to stand out of the way of this small, fast-moving woman, who had the ability to show off the baby while smoking a cigarette and holding a drink.

They drank out of sweating silver mint julep cups. Velma had never been invited to drink alcohol on a Sunday afternoon, or to drink anything out of a silver cup. The Senior Hughes did not come to the house after the church service, nor did Will's sister Frances. Possibly because of the alcohol. Mag was there, cigarette in one hand, silver cup in the other. Velma saw Will's youngest sister, the pretty one who'd divorced a pharmacist and married—was it an opera singer? A crowd of Lillian's Creekmore relatives were there. Velma couldn't keep their names straight.

She'd eaten peppery cheese straws, a thing she'd never tasted before, and which made her cough. What she remembered most was the cake. Bessie their cook had made it. Three layers of moist chocolate with a delicious fudge icing. There was coffee for those who wanted it. Velma had set aside the strong-tasting drink and poured herself a cup.

She recalled noticing that Will Hughes did the same thing men did at gatherings down in Picayune: hung out with the other men. This was years before anything happened between them.

Bessie had come out of the kitchen, a large, dark woman in a white uniform. Velma told her how good the cake was. There was a second, lighter woman in uniform. She took the baby when Lillian got tired of showing her off.

Through the whole thing, Velma felt as out of place as she had during that first Christmas party at Mr. Pat's. A gathering filled with drink and laughter and cigarette smoke, part of a life she would never know. Filled with admiration, she had watched Lillian dart here and there, serving people, refilling drinks, and talking the whole time. She was the fire at the heart of the party.

Velma closed the box and returned it to the drawer. In eleven years, Will Hughes would be fifty, too old to make changes. The only sensible solution was to live her life as if he'd never made that promise. Velma sat on the floor with her face in her hands: *I am not waiting.*

The best way to endure her present life was to pretend they had never been together. If you were chaste long enough, surely God would forgive the sin and allow the sinner to forget.

She got out her steno pad. She would make a list of the things she wanted to do as a single woman.

1. *Garden.*

She knew perfectly well how to grow things. No excuse for not making more of the yard, except all her spare time had been spent with Will Hughes.

2. *Read.*

Outside of school, she'd never read much more than the novels you rented from a rack at the drugstore. Now she had time. She would use her library card and ask one of the librarians to recommend more serious books.

3. Travel.

She'd never been anywhere except the Gulf Coast for that typing contest. She was so ignorant of the world she didn't know where she wanted to go. Will talked about Hawaii. She might go there. It would take a long time to save enough money for a trip to Hawaii, but time she had.

4. Cook.

She was a lazy cook and had no excuse. At home, she'd let Mama do it and never paid much attention. She needed to learn a few easy dishes and have more people over. She owned a nice place to entertain, thanks to Will. A wet blotch smeared the word "cook." She wiped her eyes angrily. The Lord might love a sinner, but He certainly didn't love self-pity.

What had the minister said last Sunday? If you're feeling sorry for yourself, go help someone in need. She added another item to the list:

5. Help the less fortunate.

82

Almost eight months had gone by since Will Hughes returned to his family. In the summer of 1953, during one of the hottest Julys Velma could remember, she waited, sweating through her cotton blouse, outside the minister's office at Riverside Baptist Church.

During the past months, she had worked efficiently, prayed diligently, and kept Will at a polite and professional distance. The effort was taking a toll. She found herself dragging at the end of each day, hardly able to get her clothes off at night before falling into bed. She went to a doctor. He listened, probed, and prescribed fresh air and exercise. After work each day, when the weather cooled a little, she forced herself to take a walk around the neighborhood. When that didn't help, she suspected the problem might be spiritual. This heaviness must be guilt, sin expressing itself in the flesh.

She had joined this small church when she got her own car. Riverside was newer and less prestigious than First Baptist, the enormous church she'd first attended. A one-story red brick building with a stumpy white steeple, it possessed a modest sanctuary with a piano instead of an organ. To Velma, the place felt more like home.

Sam Ray Knox was the preacher and he preferred to be addressed by all three names. "Sam Ray Knox," he'd say to men visitors, thrusting forth a small white hand. He did not shake hands with women. He was a redhead, but the color had faded.

He called her in. Sam Ray Knox would not have been Velma's first choice for counseling, but she knew no one else.

The preacher took her hand in both of his. His were warm and damp. He called her Sister Velma and led her into his private office. Paler than she and, from the soft look of him, a man who got no exercise at all, Sam Ray Knox buzzed with busy good spirits. He sat her down on the couch and sat beside her, their knees almost touching. The table in front of Velma held a Bible and a box of tissues, which felt ominous — the tissues, not the Bible.

"What can I do for you, Sister Velma?"

"You're very kind to take the time."

"Preaching is only a part of our duties. We are here primarily to bring comfort." He paused, waiting. "Guidance in whatever way we can." The hands fluttered, outlining comfort and guidance.

Velma wondered if by "we" Sam Ray Knox meant him and God. She was not accustomed to discussing personal troubles. In her family, any kind of emotional outpouring had been discouraged. There was little that couldn't be resolved by six days of physical labor, followed by hard praying on Sunday, and the occasional purge. She tried to start several times.

"Take your time, Sister Velma," Sam Ray Knox said. She heard an edge of impatience in his voice.

Staring at her hands, Velma began. "I have sinned, Reverend Knox, and now I'm sick. The doctor says nothing is physically wrong with me, so it must be the sin."

Sam Ray Knox nodded enthusiastically. "Sin can poison the body. Fill us with the devil's own bile." He stood and bent over her. "Describe the sin, Sister."

Velma's tongue stuck to the roof of her mouth. She hadn't expected to be specific. "I can't."

Sam Ray Knox's voice grew deeper. "You must. Speaking the sin is the first step to salvation. Do you not believe God sees our sins?"

She nodded.

"And am I not God's representative here on earth?"

Another miserable nod.

"Then *speak*." Shouted in a pulpit voice that made her tremble.

Velma whispered. "Fornication."

"Louder."

"Fornication." She felt her face and neck blazing.

"Name the man."

She shook her head no.

"With God as your witness." Sam Ray Knox raised a hand as if to strike her. "Name the man."

Velma wept, reached for a tissue, blew her nose, and said nothing.

Sam Ray Knox sat down heavily. "Is this man married?"

Velma nodded.

"So, you have made him into an adulterer?"

Another miserable nod. She fumbled for a second tissue. He moved the box closer.

"Are you presently—" He cleared his throat. "—in a state of sin? Are you still fornicating with this man?"

"No, sir."

"And will do it no more?"

"No, sir."

"And are you heartily sorry?"

Velma felt a wave of heat pass through her. "Yes, sir."

"Fall to your knees, Sister Velma."

She got on her knees facing the sofa.

He stood over her like an avenging angel. "Lord, look now on Velma Vernon, a sinner. She has lain with a man not her husband, Lord. She has profaned her flesh and the flesh punishes her."

A spray of spit hit Velma's bare arm. She tried not to flinch.

"We beseech Thee, Lord, to forgive her." Sam Ray Knox put a heavy hand on Velma's head. "Let Your light shine upon her once more. Let her walk clean in her days and kneel blessed in Your presence each night. You do pray, don't you, Sister Velma?"

"Yes, sir."

"Forgive her, Oh Lord."

Several pats on the head that felt like thumps.

"You may rise."

Sam Ray Knox was quite red in the face.

Velma had expected to feel cleansed, the way she had when the light passed through her at church in Picayune. But Reverend Knox made her feel dirtier. "I would like to pay you for your kindness," she said.

He nodded. "Sacrifice aids salvation. A donation to the building fund would be suitable."

Velma made out a check for a hundred dollars, every bit of her spare money for the month.

"Our sins are not washed away in a day, Sister Velma. Weekly counseling might be needed."

Velma stayed mute. God might have forgiven her, but it didn't sound as if Sam Ray Knox had. She decided to do without the weekly counseling, and maybe skip church until she could face this man without hearing his voice shouting: *fornicator, adulterer.*

83

On a Saturday night, Lillian sat at the breakfast room table smoking a cigarette and watching enviously as her daughter April, now fourteen, made her way through a dish of butter pecan ice cream. Ice cream would be just the thing to ease Lillian's stomach, if she weren't already feeling so plump. The ten pounds she'd lost while Will was away had returned in the form of fat around her middle.

Maude was in bed and Will had taken Helen, a freshly-minted high school graduate, downtown to a Golden Gloves match. At 8:30, Lillian checked herself in the bedroom mirror, smoothed her dress, and ran a comb through her hair. Will never noticed her appearance, but no sense looking sloppy.

Back in the kitchen, April licked the inside of the bowl.

"Don't put your face in the bowl, honey. Makes you look simple."

It was after nine when Helen came through the back door ahead of her father. "It was terrific." She gave her sister a pitying look. "Too bad you can't stand the sight of blood, Ape."

"Mama." April screwed up her face to cry. "Helen called me an ape."

"Please do not refer to your sister as an ape, Helen." Lillian carried the empty dish to the sink and ran water into it.

"Boxing is not for the faint of heart." Helen smirked at her younger sister. "In the last round, the winner smashed the other guy's nose. You should have seen it. Like a red sneeze."

"Mama, she's trying to make me throw up." April made a gagging sound.

"Don't make that noise, April, and enough of the gruesome descriptions, Helen." Half her time was spent issuing correctives, to little apparent effect. Will was still the fun loving, story-telling parent.

Lillian felt unreasonably irritated. She should be glad Will enjoyed taking their daughter to an event where most men took their sons. Instead, she felt a dull pain in her gut, which she named jealousy and tried to ignore. Helen's glee made Lillian want to slap her daughter's face.

Helen held her fists up, moving like a boxer. "At the slugfest we call pugilism, I was the rare female face, but not unwilling to contend."

"Enough theatrics, please." Lillian heard her voice, too sharp.

"Okay, squirts," Will said. "Back to your rooms. You were a good sport, Helen." He gave April a kiss on the head.

Will made himself a bowl of cereal, his nightly ritual. "We have one tough daughter. Nothing fazes her. Picked up the rules, understood the lingo."

Lillian smiled across the table to show how happy she was to hear this, but Will studied the back of the Corn Flakes box. He seldom looked at her, even when speaking to her, or when no one else was in the room. Lillian felt like knocking the cereal box off the table to get his attention. She took that thought back. He'd said *we*. "We have one tough daughter." They were a family again and she should be thankful. She was thankful, but she, too, liked boxing and did not mind seeing blood. He could have asked her along. Lillian pressed a hand against her stomach to quiet the gnawing. She was jealous of a seventeen-year-old.

She watched as Will picked up the bowl and drank the last of the milk.

"Almost as good as having a son, isn't it?" She didn't say it in a mean way, but this was as close to a blow as she'd dealt since his return. She held her breath, waiting to see what he'd do.

Nothing. The man might as well be deaf. He set his bowl in the sink without rinsing it and went to put on his pajamas.

84

Velma's period began a week after her visit to Sam Ray Knox. She expelled great dark clots of blood and thought they must be the visible signs of sin leaving her body. When it didn't stop after ten days, Garnett took Velma to her gynecologist, who diagnosed uterine cysts, and put her in the hospital for a partial hysterectomy. The uterus must go, but she was still a young woman—the ovaries could stay. Velma lay in the hospital bed after the operation—empty and hurting. She wouldn't have children with anyone now.

On Friday after work, Garnett and the girls came by, bringing candy and office gossip. "Will sends his best," Garnett told her. "Said he'll come see you tomorrow."

Just before noon on Saturday, Will arrived with magazines and a bunch of yellow roses—his favorite color. He'd never asked Velma what her favorite color might be—which was pink. Why was she lying here thinking selfish thoughts when the man had been kind enough to come? Will's eyes kept skipping over her as if they couldn't find a place to land. He looked terrified.

"Please sit." Velma indicated the lone chair. "I'm not contagious."

Will shook his head. "Can't. Got to get to my bridge game." He paced nervously at the foot of the bed. "Always hated hospitals. You're doing okay, right? Anything I can get you?"

"No, but thank you. I'm doing fine."

"Didn't take out anything crucial, I hope."

"Nothing that will keep me from typing." Velma meant it as a joke, but Will did not smile. She didn't know what he'd been told, but from his appalled glances at her blanket-covered body, he apparently didn't want details.

"As long as you're not going to die on me."

She laughed, which hurt the incision. "Of course not. I'll be back before you know it."

"All right then. Can't run the place without you." He gave her nearest hand a pat and fled.

Velma felt lonelier than before. She'd never seen a man so nervous. Will claimed to hate hospitals, but it felt more like he hated sick people, and this had been a female operation. Papa used to leave the room when women started talking about their parts.

She leafed through the magazines he'd brought her: *Redbook, McCall's, Ladies Home Journal.* Probably the same ones his wife read. She wondered if he treated Lillian this way when she got sick. The man was squeamish, no other word for it. Living on a farm, you got over that. Growing up in that big house of his, Will probably never saw anything born or die. Her thoughts grew kinder: he was like a child, afraid of what he didn't understand.

She reached for the bunch of yellow roses. He hadn't thought to get water and the buds were drooping. She couldn't get out of bed and hated bothering the nurse. Never mind. It was the thought that counted. The firm had paid for a private room. She should count her blessings.

From her second-floor bed, Velma watched gray clouds pile in the west. What had happened was clear: she had sinned and, as punishment, God took away the possibility of children. Will Hughes had told her how much he longed for a son. She'd fantasized that someday he would divorce Lillian and marry her. *She* would give him this dearest wish. In the fantasy, Will stood beside a hospital bed like this one, holding his son and looking proud. Velma dug her fingernails into her palms to keep from crying.

She'd been hollowed like a gourd and cleansed by the knife. It hurt like the dickens, but after Will went back to his wife, she hadn't planned on marrying anyway, so what difference did a hysterectomy make? She studied the red, fingernail-shaped dents in her palms and eased deeper into the pillows. She'd made a vow to devote herself to work. God had taken this vow seriously and removed the organ of procreation. Accepting that loss was her task now, her penance. If God could forgive her, she could forgive herself and move on. She felt her eyes closing. For once, she could sleep as long as she liked.

85

In 1954, when sued by the widow of a man who had smoked Kents, the Lorillard Cigarette Company became Will's newest client. Win or lose, the case was a triumph for the law firm, one of the first tried against a cigarette company after research showed a link between smoking and lung cancer.

"No scientific proof," Will told the family at the dinner table. "The dead man could have gotten cancer from anything. People make a choice to smoke or not. Shouldn't blame a cigarette company."

So long as doubt remained, Lillian had no intention of giving up her Lucky Strikes.

The case required trips to New York. Lillian would have liked to go along, but Will didn't offer. She couldn't remember exactly what the agreement said, but she was fairly sure begging wasn't allowed. She'd been to New York once with Ernestine for a bridge tournament, but that was before she married.

She imagined herself in the city with a different kind of man—a man like Bob Bradshaw. While he took care of business, she'd spend the day shopping at Saks and strolling Fifth Avenue. They would have a room at the Waldorf Astoria, dinner at 21, maybe go to a show. He'd take her dancing at the Rainbow Room.

Pure make-believe. She hadn't seen Bob Bradshaw in eight years and Will had not danced since the war. He cancelled their membership at the Country Club when he left for the Navy and never renewed it. A foolish expense, he said. So many decisions in those post-war months had been determined by Will's new coldness. She'd been happy to get him home in one piece and to be living in Jackson again. She wasn't about to argue about membership in a club they hadn't entered for two years.

Will's trips to New York were as brief as he could make them. If forced to spend the night, he returned to Mississippi the next day. "Glad to be out of there," he told them at Sunday dinner. New York was dangerous, dirty, and filled with communists and foreigners. No place for a Southerner.

He described the one place he did like—the Automat. You dropped a quarter in a slot, opened a glass door, and removed your own delicious slice of still-warm custard pie. Forget museums and Broadway, the Automat was the only good reason to be in Manhattan.

When he was away, like tonight, with the children in bed and Bessie gone, Lillian felt free to go into the dining room and unlock the liquor. In five minutes, she was back in bed with a bourbon and water, a cigarette, and a fresh copy of *Redbook.* The right amount of alcohol sent her floating.

Once, after the war, she had complained (before she realized how little Will cared what she thought) that his father paid him badly and he should start a law firm of his own. He told her not to speak of matters she knew nothing about. He would never leave Hughes & Blair. Odd how she recalled every criticism, but not the compliments. There had definitely been compliments.

On Monroe Street, before the children were born, Will used to come in the back door, take her by the hips, and pull her against him. Their mouths spoke about his day, but from the waist down they talked about bed.

That had been a lifetime ago: before the war, before moving to the hotel, before a third daughter and that hussy he brought home. The thought of Sylvia made the birthmark on Lillian's forehead smolder. Helen still brought her up. Remember that woman Daddy brought home after the war and her awful son? Lillian remembered all right. Will never mentioned Sylvia's name. He had a talent for shutting down unpleasant matters. "Not now," he'd say; or, "I don't wish to discuss it."

"You're doing it again."

Lillian jumped in fright. Helen stood one step up in the kitchen doorway. The girl crept around like a ghost. "Get your hair out of your eyes."

"Why do you drink by yourself? You know Daddy hates it."

"I'll thank you not to use that tone. I'm your mother."

Helen mumbled something.

Lillian sat up straighter, feeling the birthmark burn. "What did you say, young lady?"

"I said I wish you'd act more like it."

Lillian fumbled on the floor for a bedroom shoe to throw. "I wouldn't have to drink if —" She stopped.

"If what?"

"If you and your sisters behaved, if you didn't drive me crazy with your constant arguments."

Helen rolled her eyes. "I'd be out of your hair if you'd let me join the swim team this summer."

"No public pools. We've had this discussion."

"They found a cure for polio. I took the vaccine, remember?"

"They're not positive it works. I won't take the chance."

"*Mama.*"

The headache-inducing whine. "You'd be sorry if you ended up in one of those iron lungs like Lois's daughter."

"I won't end up in an iron lung."

"We're done here." Lillian picked up her magazine.

Helen slunk through the kitchen, talking over her shoulder. "I hate you."

Lillian spoke to her daughter's back. "You are why I drink." She didn't want Helen at that pool again. Last summer, she'd gone out with a lifeguard, and Lillian had discovered later the man was twenty-one years old.

Through her nightgown, she kneaded her stomach. She was getting flabby. Having a son would have made all difference. If Maude, sweet child, if Maude were Will Junior, Lillian felt pretty sure she would still be loved.

The only thing Will enjoyed about being married was her cooking, which Bessie did most of. Good food, a comfortable bed for the few hours he spent at home, shirts ironed the way he liked them. The alcohol buzz faded. Negativity had brought her down. Lillian swiped at tears with her free hand. She was not the kind of woman who sat in bed and wept alone. She was the kind of woman who marched into the dining room and got another drink. She drained the glass, rattling the ice against her nose. These were short drinks in a short glass. No way you could call these highballs.

Before the cigarette trial, Will Hughes had read the research on smoking and cancer he claimed not to believe. He won the case, but after it was over, he quit cigarettes. This came as a shock, smoking being one of the few things they enjoyed in common. He didn't tell Lillian not to smoke, thank God, but to her disgust, he replaced his Camels with cigars—fat, brown, nasty things, stinking up his clothes and car. Not that she got to ride in that car much.

86

In May of that year, fate intervened in a way Lillian could never have imagined: the Supreme Court outlawed segregation in the country's public schools. On the night of the decision, the family sat at the dining table, with Will talking to the girls while Lillian pretended to be included.

"What do you think the Brown versus Board of Education decision means?" Will enjoyed turning meals into learning opportunities: Name the eighty-two counties in Mississippi, he'd say, and April could do it; Name three Confederate generals and their most famous battles.

Helen was home after her first year of college, working in the Chancery Clerk's office for the summer. Higher education had made Lillian's oldest daughter even smugger, if that were possible. She answered with confidence. "I think it's terrific. In a hundred years we'll all have caramel-colored skin and no pimples."

Lillian coughed to disguise her shocked laugh.

Will looked startled, then angry. "I cannot believe a daughter of mine would say such a thing. Do you have any idea what caused the fall of the Roman Empire?"

Helen quit smiling. They were all wary of Will's temper. She obviously didn't know what caused the fall of Rome. Neither did Lillian.

"You'd better learn your history before you start spouting nonsense," Will said. "*Miscegenation*, that's what."

Lillian wasn't sure what miscegenation was.

Nine-year-old Maude saved her. "What's 'segination?"

"The mixing of the races." Will spat the words. "Social intermingling. That's what the Federal government is trying to force on us, and your big sister seems to think it's a fine idea."

"But, Daddy." Helen lowered her voice so Bessie, behind the swinging door in the kitchen, wouldn't hear. "It's not fair that they only get to be cooks and yard men."

Her eldest daughter looked near tears. Lillian took a bite of the perfectly fried chicken, thinking: Welcome to the club.

"Who told you life was going to be fair?" Will looked at Lillian and nodded as if to say: *Am I right?*

Surprised, Lillian nodded back and, just like that, they were on the same side against Helen.

Will had predicted integration would never happen; the high court would not dare to intervene in what was so obviously a state's right. Now that he'd been proven wrong, he leapt into battle to protect the South. Lillian felt a reflected urgency. She'd never thought one way or the other about the separation of the races. It was the way things were and the way they had always been. White people were the bosses and colored people were the help. No one she knew questioned a reality they'd all grown up with. At the hotel, she'd worked around Negroes her whole life, admiring some, despairing of others, but nobody bucked the system. The fight for what Will Hughes called "our way of life" became his cause, and Lillian happily joined the battle alongside him.

Within four months, in order to block possible integration, the Mississippi legislature passed a measure abolishing the public schools.

"Really?" Helen, home for the weekend from Ole Miss, responded with disbelief. "Mississippi would close all its schools?"

"Drastic times require drastic action," Will said. "I would take a gun and man a barricade in the street before I let my children go to school with niggers."

There was a stunned silence. Not at the absurd thought of Will with a gun, but at the sound of that forbidden word, a word no one in this house had ever uttered.

Into the echo, Helen spoke. "You told us never to say that."

"That was before," Will said. "Things are different now."

Bessie came through the door with a dish of asparagus and everyone quit talking.

Will joined the Citizens' Council, a statewide organization made up of prominent white men. The Council punished colored people who tried to speak up or register to vote by firing them, cutting off their loans, or throwing them out of their rented houses. Lillian thought this harsh, but did not open her mouth to object. Will claimed the Council did its work without violence, which made it nothing like the Ku Klux Klan. That's what Helen called it at another dinner before leaving the table crying.

When a fourteen-year-old boy was lynched in the Delta for whistling at a white woman, Lillian see-sawed between sympathy for his mother and fury. What kind of ignorant person would send a teenager raised in Chicago to Mississippi? Two white men were acquitted for mutilating and shooting the boy, then dumping his weighted body in a river.

Helen lectured the dinner table as if the family was personally responsible.

Will Hughes said, "No Chicago colored boy has any business being in the South. What was his Mama thinking?" Echoing Lillian's silent opinion and, in her mind, cementing their partnership. Integration and states' rights outranked a difficult marriage. Will Hughes might not be affectionate, but at least he spoke to her now, which gave Lillian a chest-warming joy.

Helen said, "You're both despicable. This whole state is despicable."

"I was idealistic like you at eighteen," Will Hughes said. "You will mature and see what the world is really like."

"I will *never* be like you." Helen threw down her napkin and fled. Her bedroom door slammed and Lillian smiled. Will batted his daughter's arguments away like gnats and almost every disagreement ended in tears, which meant Helen lost and Lillian won. Helen might not know how much her father despised a crying female, but Lillian did.

That night, lying in their separate beds, she spoke. "I was just thinking."

"Uh-oh," Will said.

Lillian ignored him. "Growing up, the colored people at the hotel were like extra aunts and uncles. In this house, Bessie handles every bite of food we put in our mouths. Why have we turned against them?"

Will put down his magazine. "We're not against Bessie or anyone at the hotel. We're not against progress, whatever the skin color. It's the forced mixing we're against."

Lillian's hands twisted under the bed covers. She hadn't meant to get him going.

"We give the Negroes schools," Will said. "They have the opportunity to better themselves. Separate but equal is fine, as long as it's kept separate. That's our way of life here in the South and that's what we're fighting to keep. I hope you don't go around in public spouting your nonsense."

"Of course not." Although, to Lillian, it still sounded as if Will and his cronies were against colored people. Henceforth, she would keep that opinion to herself. His new warmth depended on complete agreement.

Another dinner and the same old arguments. Helen confronted her father. "Why do you hate Negroes?"

"I don't hate them," Will said, "but I can't forget Reconstruction."

Helen's mouth opened and closed. "Reconstruction happened a hundred years ago."

"Lower your voice, please," Lillian said.

Maude sang out in a sweet, high voice. "'Red and yellow, black and white, all are precious in His sight.' That's what we sing in Sunday School."

"Very nice, honey," Lillian said.

"You're still mad about something that happened a hundred years ago?" Helen said.

"Reconstruction was a travesty to everything Southerners believe," Will said. "Maybe when you've learned some history, we can have a real discussion. Until then, I guess you'll have to keep crying."

Helen stormed out. April decided to cry, too. Lillian's middle child could weep over a broken fingernail. "Girls, please. Try not to spoil your father's dinner."

"Too late," Will said.

In the bedroom later, he put down his magazine. "Where did we go wrong? We've raised a Communist."

Lillian thrilled again at the word *we*. "She's just trying to be a rebel. She'll get over it."

She didn't want Helen to get over it. Helen was the enemy they held in common, the family traitor. She and Will were getting along better than they had in years. If this were the double bed of their early marriage, she would reach over right now and give him a reassuring pat, maybe run her hand through his hair. No, not the hair. Will didn't like anyone touching his hair, even back in the good days. The pushed together twin beds were too wide for a pat. Lillian tried to remember when they had last touched. As long as she didn't try anything physical, she could pretend Will wouldn't mind if she did. She wouldn't be able to bear it if he recoiled.

87

Lillian's bridge partners had left and Bessie had supper almost ready. Fried oysters tonight, a family favorite. Lillian cleared away the drink glasses, finishing off the icy dregs in each one. Since signing the agreement that brought Will back into his twin bed, bridge with her friends had become her chief recreation (and opportunity to drink). They gathered at one house or another three afternoons a week. Today, they'd met here, and Lillian tried to clear away all signs of their presence before Will got home from work.

Three drinks in three hours. Not bad; nothing to worry about. She bumped into a corner of the card table, straightened, and giggled. Such a fun afternoon. She'd played well. She threw out the cigarette butts and rinsed the ashtrays at the kitchen sink.

"You in my way," Bessie said.

Lillian ignored the complaint, bumping Bessie's hip with her own. With all signs of guests erased, she went to the bathroom to check her appearance. Ran a comb through her hair, rinsed her mouth with Listerine, and put on fresh lipstick. She admitted to her reflection that she primped in the dismal hope of being admired by a man who never noticed.

Helen, home from her second year at college and back at the Chancery Clerk's office, rode back and forth to work with Will. Arguing about the Negroes, Lillian hoped.

At the dinner table, her oldest daughter glowered. Lillian tried to ignore the girl, putting oysters on each plate, along with a serving of

Bessie's French fries. April said the blessing. Bessie passed the butterbeans. There was a silence.

Lillian decided to tell them about her triumph at the bridge table. Will loved bridge. "I did well today," she said. "On our last hand, we were pretty even for the day." She stopped to gather her thoughts. Stories tended to get away from her like dogs off a leash. "I led with the six of spades and had king high with five of them. Dimple took the trick with her ace. Hilda should have returned a spade, but she led with a nine of diamonds." She paused. "They got that trick with Peggy's ten, but then I took four straight spade tricks."

Helen frowned at her. What an ugly face. April stared at her plate. Only Maude seemed oblivious, eating happily around every butterbean.

"What's your point?" Will said.

Lillian flinched. His tone had not been nice. What had her point been? "They were vulnerable and I took four straight spades. Four spades. That's what happened." It didn't sound heroic. Had she left something out?

Will sat at the other end, chewing with his eyes shut. Pretending she didn't exist. Pretending he didn't live in this house. Which made Lillian furious. She tried to remember, and couldn't, if the agreement forbade getting angry. Stuff the agreement. She clanked her fork and knife against the plate. No one noticed, or they pretended not to notice, which made her want to howl.

Will left to go back to the office. Lillian stood at the dresser in her nightgown, wiping her makeup off with cold cream and tissues. The afternoon's buzz had worn off, leaving her with a sour stomach and a headache.

Helen stood in the doorway with the same unpleasant expression she'd displayed at the dinner table.

"What?" Lillian said.

"You're drinking too much."

Lillian straightened in an imitation of her sister Ernestine. "Haven't we had this conversation?"

"You slurred your words at supper."

"I most certainly did not."

"And you kept saying the thing about the spades. No wonder Daddy goes back to work every night."

Lillian took off a wedge-heeled bedroom slipper and flung it at her daughter's head.

Helen ducked.

"Do not think you can march in here and tell me what to do, young lady. Show a little respect. I get three meals a day on the table, don't I? I make those dresses you wear."

"Mama, it's almost every night."

"Your father is very disappointed in you, Helen. He thinks you're a Communist."

"He thinks you're a drunk."

Lillian trembled with fury. The girl had no idea what she put up with. "If I ever get to the point where I can't take care of this house, maybe you can talk to me about my drinking. Until then, consider it none of your business."

She longed to throw the other shoe at Helen's departing back. She blotted hot tears on the greasy tissue. In this house, Bessie was her only friend.

88

On a Friday night in June of 1955, Lillian sat propped on pillows in her twin bed, reading *Ladies' Home Journal*. Will, that distant fellow planet, lay in the other bed reading *Time*.

Helen stuck her head in the door. She looked scared.

"May we come in?"

Jack Bedford entered behind her, which made Lillian sit up straighter, pull her bed jacket closed, and take off her reading glasses. Jack was Helen's latest swoon, the young man she had raced home from Ole Miss to see every weekend during spring semester. He seemed decent enough: Georgia Tech, a Kappa Alpha like Will, had served in Korea as an Army lieutenant. Helen said he worked for a company building tract homes in northwest Jackson. Lillian did not know his people. Will had never given him more than a handshake and a, "Good to see you, son." He called every boy who showed up "son," never remembering their names.

Will gave a grunt, which Lillian interpreted as: Look at the hour. It was after nine.

"Jack has something he'd like to ask you, Daddy."

Poor Jack: tall, thin, freckled, quiet at the best of times. Lillian watched as he gathered his nerve.

"Mr. Hughes." His voice cracked and he stopped to clear his throat. "I would like to ask permission to marry your daughter."

Will stared at him for a long moment. "You're welcome to marry her," he said. "As soon as she finishes college." He put his reading glasses on and picked up his magazine.

"*Daddy*." Helen's voice went high with begging. "I can't wait two more years."

Will put down the magazine. Lillian knew how he felt about daughters. Hardly worth educating when the future held no more than marriage and motherhood. Here was Helen, a smart girl, doing exactly as he predicted. If she were a son, Will would roar a refusal, send the girl off weeping, and Will Jr. back to college with a cut in his allowance.

"Is this what you want—to quit college and get married?"

"Yes, Daddy, *please*."

"You're how old now?"

"Nineteen."

"Old enough to marry without my approval. I guess it's out of my hands."

Helen ran to the bed, gave him a kiss on the forehead, then back to hug Jack.

Lillian watched. Her oldest daughter was incandescent with happiness, practically dancing around the room. The girl had not the slightest idea what marriage entailed, and let's see how long Jack's puppy dog adoration lasted. There was a sour taste in her throat. A kinder mother might have warned her daughter, but Helen had never listened to advice.

Lillian turned her mind to the business of marriage, which improved her mood. She had once run an entire hotel; she could organize the hell out of a wedding. She would make this one into a spectacle. If Will thought she threw good dinner parties, wait until he saw what she could achieve with a real event.

"We'll make a deal," she said to Helen. "You can be engaged now, and let's plan a wedding for late next fall." Lillian turned to Jack. "Helen has never liked a boy for more than six months. You two have been dating her for what—four? If she dumps you, we'll have time to call everything off."

Jack looked visibly deflated.

"Mother, *please*," Helen said.

"The man you plan on marrying should know the truth. We'll make it the end of November to be safe." She turned her attention to the groom. "I never asked, Jack, but who are your people?"

He flushed. "We moved down here from the Delta. My dad's family owned a plantation up in Sunflower, but when the Depression hit, the bank took it. He works for the government now, grading cotton."

Just as Lillian suspected: nobodies. She patted the bed beside her.

Helen came and sat. "Can we make it a holiday wedding?"

"Thanksgiving, I think." Lillian sat straighter in the bed. "Get me the calendar from the kitchen, and a pad and pencil." Planning a wedding was like planning a war. She would be Commander in Chief.

Will went back to his magazine. Jack settled into the Windsor chair by the door, looking watchful, in case Will decided to engage him in a manly conversation. Rest easy, Lillian wanted to say. You're neither a judge nor an important politician; you're a freckled-faced contractor with your first job. My husband is not interested.

Helen studied the calendar. "Maybe the night before Thanksgiving? That way, everybody will be home from school."

"What's the date of that Wednesday?" Lillian said.

Helen checked. "November 23rd."

Lillian wrote the date at the top of the pad. "I'm thinking fall colors," she said. "Perhaps dahlias."

Helen shivered with excitement and Lillian felt her spirits rise. This event would have everything her own pokey wedding lacked. No coming down a set of corner stairs in a borrowed dress with only your family watching. She would produce a marvel. Will would balk at the cost, of course, but he'd change his mind when he realized the boost this would give his career. A first daughter marrying: every judge and lawyer he'd ever met would be invited. Will might be frugal (to put it kindly), but coming from that big house on North State Street, he wanted to be seen as first rate.

"An evening wedding," Helen said.

Lillian nodded. "Tails for the men; full-length gowns and long gloves for the girls. The altar banked with fern and white tapers." She lit a cigarette and exhaled, smoke circling her head. She pictured herself holding court at the reception in a gown of sea-foam taffeta.

Jack sat in the corner, knees together and silent. Lillian sent him a smile of approval that made his ears turn red.

Over coffee and cigarettes the following morning, Lillian worked on the list. Bessie had the day off; Will left early for the office; she was free to stay in her gown and robe as long as she liked.

There must be a party announcing the engagement. Helen needed a new dress for the newspaper photos, something to show off her dark hair. She made a small sketch: long-waist, fullness in the skirt, very rich looking.

Helen came in looking sleepy. She pointed at the drawing. "What's that?"

"An idea for your announcement dress."

"Don't I get a vote?" She flopped into a kitchen chair, looking as unpleasant as possible.

Lillian wondered if her daughter and Jack were doing it. She added a doctor's appointment to the list. Helen needed her plumbing checked out.

"I hope you're not marrying for sex," she said.

Helen looked startled. "Why?"

"When that's over, you'll have nothing."

"Is that what happened to you and Daddy?"

"I'm speaking hypothetically, and promise me you won't get pregnant and spoil my plans."

Helen rubbed the sleep out of her eyes. "Don't worry. Jack's a good boy. He believes in waiting."

Something about the way Helen said this made Lillian think her daughter did not, but she let it go. "Have you started on your invitation list?"

"I hate all these details. I only want to get married."

"There's *getting* married and there's *being* married," Lillian said. "The second lasts a lot longer. Enjoy what's left of your freedom."

"You're such a party pooper."

What did Shakespeare say about ungrateful daughters? Lillian would know if she'd had the money to finish college.

89

Through the summer, the wedding list became Lillian's diary — a place where she wrote "ungrateful wretch" in the margin when Helen turned sarcastic, and "penny-pincher," when Will's grouching over the costs grew unbearable.

She kept her head and forged ahead: On the night of November 23, 1955, Jackson, Mississippi, would watch in awe. Standing beside her in the receiving line, greeting the state's most important politicians and judges, Will would be forced to admit this was not merely a marriage of convenience, a thing he'd been dragged back into for the sake of the children. His wife, Lillian Creekmore Hughes, shared his ambitions and possessed the talent and grace to help him achieve them.

She nibbled on the pencil eraser and looked over Will's list of invitees. His secretary Velma, had put it together. The woman was quite efficient.

Her mind switched to her daughter, now working as a secretary at the advertising agency where Knox and Knox III were account executives. The girl was only nineteen. In spite of thinking she knew everything, she had no idea what it meant to move, in the space of a few words, from being Helen Creekmore Hughes to Mrs. Jackson Bedford. From that moment, as far as the public was concerned, she would possess no first name. Her children would be born to Mrs. Jackson Bedford. She would die as Mrs. Jackson Bedford. Lillian had not paused to consider this loss when she married, not that she didn't glory in being Mrs. Will Hughes.

Jack and Helen had gone downtown and chosen china and crystal patterns without asking her advice. The results were less than glorious in Lillian's opinion, but she hadn't uttered a peep. Deserved congratulations for her restraint.

Her coffee was cold. She could make another pot, but better to go work on Helen's announcement dress. Nobody in this house properly appreciated her skill. They said, "Thanks," for the new dress at Christmas, and twirled happily in front of the mirror in the ball gowns she created. But not one of them was truly grateful. She held up the bodice of Helen's dress, ecru lace over dark brown taffeta. She only needed to attach it to the taffeta skirt, fit it on Helen a last time, and mark the hem. The French lace for the bodice had cost a small fortune, but it would photograph beautifully.

At two, she drove Helen to Frances Pepper, Jackson's finest dress store. They sat in satin chairs and Frances herself brought out wedding dresses. Helen tried on a ruffled lace, made a face, and retreated to the dressing room. She came out in a puffy taffeta that made her look like a meringue. Lillian kept a neutral smile on her face, a smile that neither approved nor disapproved. To each dress, she said, "What do you think?" Helen was sure to despise anything she liked. The third dress was creamy satin with a snug lace bodice.

"I love this one," Helen said.

Lillian agreed. "I can bead the neckline if you like." Helen's face lit up. Driving home, Lillian admitted to a pleasurable surprise. The dress purchase had not been nearly as dreadful as she feared. Another task checked off the list.

The announcement dinner at the end of August came off well. Jack's parents were pretty much as Lillian expected. The father hardly spoke. The mother Ellaray (named after her own dear parents, she confided), used old-fashioned words like earbobs for earrings, and pocketbook for purse. They may have once owned a plantation and reserved box seats at the Memphis opera, as Ellaray claimed over the Charlotte Russe, but to Lillian the pair felt country as a cornfield.

Helen's engagement pictures appeared in the Jackson, Memphis, and New Orleans newspapers, on the front page of the Society section, above the fold. Lillian showed them to Will at the breakfast table and explained what an achievement this was. He nodded, but the man could not say a nice word without bringing up money. "If you look at what this wedding is costing me, that's about a thousand dollars per photograph."

On a separate list, Lillian kept the names of people who had accepted the wedding invitation, a terrific crowd so far, including several federal judges. To show off the gifts, she removed the furniture from the glassed-in porch and rented tables, covering them in white cloths with ruffled skirts, trimmed with satin ribbons and tiny wedding bells. Adorable. She loved taking people through to admire the growing stack of china, the lengthening rank of sterling silver flatware.

Helen had insisted on nine bridesmaids, which in Lillian's opinion, would make the assembly at the altar look more like a chorus line than a wedding. She kept her mouth shut, ordered enough emerald green velvet for nine long gowns, and found a dressmaker to handle the sewing.

She and Helen went to Kennningtons to pick out the wedding night peignoir. Lillian recalled, but did not mention, frightening Will practically out of the bed on their first night. Helen chose an off-white satin gown with a matching lace robe.

"They have it in white. Wouldn't you rather have the white?" she said.

"I would not."

Was this a comment on her daughter's virginity, or the lack thereof? With Helen, Lillian had never found the right time to talk about sex. At twelve, the child almost bit her nose off when she tried to talk about the monthly "curse." "They showed us a movie at school," Helen said. That was the end of that.

Lillian rented the men's tails from a shop in Memphis. Will threw a fit at the idea of wearing a long tailcoat with striped trousers, but she ignored his objections. This was a formal wedding; tails were required.

Sitting in bed with her list and Will off at the office, Lillian toted up the chores remaining. Olive and Leland had agreed to host the rehearsal dinner at Creekmore Inn. For once, Ernestine could afford to serve steak instead of chicken.

The groom's family were paying for the flowers. She'd gone over the plan with Ellaray: dahlias for the bridesmaids, yellow roses and white freesia for the bride, and yellow rosebuds for the groomsmen. Ellaray asked what color dress Lillian planned to wear. Her own was gray chiffon, which sounded a bit drab for a wedding, in Lillian's opinion. But Ellaray wore her hair an undyed iron gray, so the dress would match.

Lillian, who kept her own short curls colored a warm brown, fashioned herself a glorious full-length gown in blue-green silk taffeta. She got out of bed and rummaged through the dresser until she found the worn velvet box with Maude's pearl and gold earrings. She tried them on. Almost too precious to wear, but so becoming. She held up the bodice of her nearly finished dress, and stared at her reflection. Not bad, if she did say so herself.

A week later, Lillian drove Helen downtown to buy linens: towels and sheets for the bridal couple, everything monogrammed. On the way home, she took her hands off the steering wheel to light a cigarette. "You and Jack can have the furniture from your bedroom for your new apartment."

"Mama, watch where you're going. You almost hit those ladies."

"I didn't almost hit them and colored women aren't ladies."

Lillian ignored her daughter's indignant huffing, thinking how many good times she and Will had once shared in the bed she was giving away. She wondered if he ever thought about those nights of gin rummy, back tickling, and sex? Probably not. Men, in general, lacked reflection. "Your hope chest is now complete." Lillian picked a speck of tobacco off her tongue and allowed a moment of self-congratulation.

Helen leaned against the passenger door, still angry over the colored women. "Towels and sheets aren't my idea of a hope chest. In novels, they're filled with embroidered nightgowns and lace-trimmed petticoats."

"You could have had those," Lillian said, "if you'd bothered to learn how to sew." This was a sore point. Lillian lacked the patience to teach and Helen didn't have enough to learn.

When the bill for the linens arrived, Lillian left it on Will's dresser. She was in the kitchen, whipping meringue for a lemon pie when he came in the back door.

Silence. Then a shout over the hum of the mixer. "What is this?"

Here he came, waving the bill for the linens.

Lillian pretended ignorance. "Lemon pie."

He flapped the paper in her face.

At the stove, Bessie played deaf.

Lillian turned off the machine and ran a spatula around the meringue. "That is the bill for your daughter's linens, her hope chest. Every bride is expected to have one."

"*Two hundred dollars for sheets and towels?*" His face had turned crimson.

"She won't need to buy linens for ten years." Lillian heard a quiver of fear in her voice.

"I'm not trying to outfit her for ten years. I'm trying to get her married without going bankrupt."

He stomped off and Lillian saw Bessie's back shaking with laughter.

"You can laugh," she said. "You don't have to live with him."

Will came into the bedroom later that night with a smirk on his face. "I offered Helen three thousand dollars if she and Jack agreed to elope."

Lillian put a hand over heart, which she was sure had stopped. "You *didn't?*" Her glorious triumph wiped out in an instant. "What did she say?"

"She said, she didn't want money. She wants a wedding."

Lillian exhaled. Her daughter was no fool. Like her mother, she appreciated the value of a grand occasion.

Will climbed into bed. "Women."

She saw no need to reply.

90

Will was at the office, Helen was out with Jack, and the younger girls were asleep. Lillian poured herself a small drink and crawled into bed with the list. Plenty of time if she heard Will's car pull into the carport to slide the glass under the table. It wasn't as if he ever got close enough to smell her breath.

The wedding photographs were done. Ernestine had helped write the wedding announcement for the newspapers, and it sounded quite elegant.

Leland's wife Olive offered to buy Helen a going-away outfit and Lillian had gone with them to Gus Mayer to pick it out. Three hundred dollars for a cashmere suit, another hundred and fifty for bronze leather shoes and a matching bag, a hundred for a feathered hat. Lillian would give her eyeteeth to own such an outfit, but she'd have to be buried in it, because Will would surely murder her if she ever spent that kind of money. Olive never blinked, and Helen gushed over her aunt's generosity in a way that made Lillian want to put a finger down her throat.

On a Friday in October, Lillian dropped Helen off at a doctor's office on North State Street for her pre-marital checkup.

"I still don't see why I have to do this," Helen said.

"Every bride needs a physical." Lillian wasn't sure why. She hadn't had one before her own marriage. Her bridge friend Hilda had recommended this woman during a game. "Good to see if the machinery is working," Dimple said. The others agreed, handing around meaningful looks. "Machinery" being the unseen and unmentionable.

Helen got out of the car. "Seems ridiculous. I'm perfectly healthy."

"I'll pick you up in an hour," Lillian said.

She returned to find her daughter waiting at the curb.

Helen got into the car with a look of disbelief. "You sent me to a lunatic."

"Hilda recommended her."

"First, she put in me these horrible stirrup things with my knees up around my chin.

Get used to it, Lillian thought.

She poked around inside and said I could have a seven-pound baby."

"That's good to know, isn't it?"

"Then she gave me *this.*" Helen waved a booklet under Lillian's nose. "Here, in colorful detail, are the five venereal diseases you can contract from having sex. I'm getting married and she's talking about venereal disease."

"Does sound a bit strange." Lillian held her breath to keep from laughing.

"That's not the worst. She told me not to read the book before going out with my fiancé because I might get *aroused.*" Helen started giggling.

Lillian let it out, cackling until she coughed. "You're going to make me wreck this car."

Helen flipped through the pamphlet. "Wait until you see the pictures."

Lillian allowed herself the pleasure of this moment, laughing with her daughter the way she imagined other mothers and daughters did, the way she had laughed with Maude before her own wedding.

91

Lillian checked the final items off the list: hiring an off-duty policeman to guard the gifts during the wedding and reception. Willie, the gardener, would drive Bessie and Doreen to the church. Lillian had made arrangements for the servants to sit in the balcony. She confirmed the double ballroom at the King Edward Hotel for the reception. Decorations had been arranged and refreshments ordered: champagne and sauterne to fill the rented fountain, a crystal punch bowl and silver coffee service borrowed from Will's parents. Fruit punch and hot coffee for the non-drinkers. Helen wanted two cakes and they were ordered: the bride's white, the groom's spice.

In the final week before the wedding, Helen kept inventing catastrophes: she had a pimple; the stylist giving her a permanent had scorched her forehead; she'd lost weight and the wedding dress wouldn't fit. Maude needed to quit eating ice cream or her dress wouldn't fit either.

Lillian kept a ministerial calm, handing out salve for the pimple and the tiny burned spot, telling Bessie not to give her youngest daughter any more ice cream until after the wedding.

Lillian finished Helen's rehearsal dinner dress the night before the event: apricot *peau de soie* with a low-square neckline, fitted bodice and full skirt. "One of the best things I've ever made," she told Helen. Turning in front of the dresser mirror before the dinner, her daughter agreed.

The girl looked absolutely beautiful. All she needed was— "Why don't I lend you Maude's earrings," Lillian said. The rose gold will go perfectly with that dress." She went to retrieve the velvet box.

Helen clipped them on. "They're beautiful."

"Take good care of them. I'm wearing them tomorrow night to the wedding."

Her daughter turned her head, admiring the effect. "If I had pierced ears, you wouldn't need to worry about me losing them."

"Don't be silly. Only gypsies pierce their ears. Just be careful. Maude gave me these the night before my own wedding. They belonged to our mother." Lillian felt unexpectedly teary and left the room before Helen noticed

Will was in the bathroom shaving. Lillian stood in front of the mirror admiring the dress she had made for herself: white chiffon with a shirred neckline to show off her shoulders, which were still quite nice.

Will drove to the hotel with Lillian beside him and the two younger girls in the back. "Ridiculous to go this far for a dinner," he said. "We won't see a bite of food until 8:00."

Lillian ignored him.

Leland and Olive were not stingy. In the large dining room, tables had been arranged in a U-shape, with starched white cloths and bouquets of pale pink and white roses. Tall, creamy candles burned in Ernestine's silver candlesticks. Everything looked quite sparkling and lovely. Lillian was happy neither Will's parents nor his sister Frances had chosen to come. She had explained to them (apologetically) that champagne would be served, tonight and at the wedding reception, then let them to make the decision. Frances said she and Bill would bring her parents to the church service, but would skip the rehearsal dinner and reception.

Dinner began with gulf shrimp cocktails and moved on to filet mignon with béarnaise sauce, white asparagus, and puffed potatoes almost as good as Galatoire's. Lillian thought longingly of New Orleans. If Will were a different kind of man, she would have spent a lot more time in that city. Maybe Helen would have better luck with Jack.

Bourbon and Scotch before dinner and wine during; champagne with dessert. This was Lillian's idea of a proper party. Will rose to make a toast. "To my dear Helen and to you, Jack. May you find many years of happiness in each other's company."

Lillian half-hoped he'd say something like, "I wish for you the same happiness your mother and I have shared." A lie, maybe, but lawyers were known liars. She took a swallow of champagne and tried to listen to whatever religious tripe Ernestine offered. She didn't dare meet Faye's eyes for fear of bursting into laughter.

She ignored the slice of Baked Alaska put in front of her, preferring to take her calories in the form of alcohol. A lot of giggling from the head of the table. What was Helen up to? Lillian leaned past Leland to see. The girl could not hold her liquor, and she'd already had three glasses of champagne.

"*Helen?*" Lillian used her sternest voice. No response. In a circle of admiring groomsmen, Helen had taken off one shoe—the shoes dyed to match that gorgeous apricot dress. Faye's son Jimbo proceeded to fill it with champagne and drink from it.

What the hell? Lillian squeezed past Leland and stood over her daughter. "May I ask what you're doing?"

"Isn't it great? Just like the movies." Helen's eyes looked glassy.

"No more champagne for you, young lady. Jimbo, empty the shoe, please, and give it back. Utterly ruined now, no thanks to either of you."

Lillian went back to her place and lit a cigarette. One more day and the girl would be Jack's responsibility. She had felt such warmth toward her daughter a few hours ago, and now she wasn't sure she even liked her.

Olive leaned past Leland to ask if Lillian had enjoyed the food.

"Everything was marvelous but if I eat dessert, I'll pop out of this dress." Where was Otis with the champagne bottle? Lillian had achieved enough of a glow to carry her through to bedtime if she didn't let it wear off.

A voice close to her ear. Ernestine's younger son, little Leland "You better come outside, Aunt Lillian. Helen's trying to jump in the empty swimming pool."

Good God almighty. Lillian crushed her cigarette out and pressed past Leland again.

Down by the pool, Helen, no shoes now, teetered on the end of the diving board. "I don't want to get married." She spread her arms. "I'm going to jump."

Jack's best man Hank, edged out onto the board behind her. "You can't jump, Helen," he said. "There's no water in the pool."

"It's not empty." Drunkenly, Helen leaned over the edge and pointed to the dry leaves in the diving well.

Lillian thought she would have a heart attack. She put on her biggest voice. "Helen Creekmore Hughes, come down from there this instant."

Helen wavered, looking blearily around. Hank grabbed her waist and led her off the board.

"You should be ashamed of yourself." Lillian pulled her daughter by the arm, across the gravel driveway, up the walk, longing to slap her face. "Behaving this way in front of your family. Get in the bathroom and straighten yourself out." Lillian shoved her inside the small lavatory off the front parlor.

Helen closed the door and Lillian waited. When her daughter did not emerge, she pushed on the door, which refused to open because Helen had passed out on the floor behind it. Lillian shouted for Jack. He appeared and she said, "See if you can get her up and home." Neither Will nor his family needed to see this.

Jack squeezed inside and took Helen under the arms. "Let's go, bride."

Helen groaned.

Lillian watched as Jack half-carried, half-dragged her daughter to his pink and gray Chevrolet, freshly waxed for the wedding. The young man was showing a lot more tolerance than Lillian would have given him credit for.

"Take your time getting to the house, Jack," Lillian said. "I need to be there first to unlock the door."

She rounded up Will and the girls. If she hurried, she could get everyone in their rooms before she had to wrestle drunk Helen inside. She floored the accelerator, ignoring Will's protests.

With everyone safely behind closed bedroom doors, Lillian watched the street from the sun porch. Ten minutes later Jack's car pulled up. Between the two of them, they managed to get Helen out of the car and inside the porch door.

In the light of the sunroom, Lillian shrieked. "Look what you've done to my dress." Dark, wet splotches marred the front of the apricot *peau de soie*. Stains that would never come out.

Helen peered down at herself.

Jack looked unhappy. "Didn't mean for it to take so long. She threw up against the closed car window. I had to stop and clean it up."

"I am so sorry." Lillian gave Jack her best smile, hoping it was only the car he was upset over, not the bride. The man had been a perfect gentleman and she did not want him fleeing before the ceremony. "I apologize for my daughter, who obviously cannot hold her liquor. Thank you, Jack. I'll take over from here."

Lillian pushed and pulled Helen into her bedroom, closed the door, and stripped off the ruined dress.

Her daughter fell backward onto the bed. "I'm too drunk to get married tomorrow. Drunk people can't get married."

Lillian flopped her over, unfastened the Merry Widow, and tugged a nightgown over Helen's head. "It's too late for that kind of talk."

Look at the girl, not an ounce of fat on her. Lillian's body had once looked like this. Would she switch places, be nineteen again and getting married? No thank you, not to Jack. "If you wanted to change your mind, you should have spoken up months ago."

Helen kept her eyes closed and Lillian watched as tears slipped down the sides of her daughter's face.

"Too late for crying, young lady. Three hundred people will be at that church tomorrow night. You have nine bridesmaids in emerald green velvet and a roomful of gifts out there on the porch. Most of which you have yet to thank people for."

Helen turned her head against the sheets. "No, no, no," keeping her eyes closed. "I don't want to get married."

"This is what is known as last minute jitters." Lillian lifted her daughter's feet onto the bed. "You can get divorced next month, but

I've worked too hard to put up with this kind of silliness tonight." She reached into her pocket and pulled out a small pill. "Swallow this."

Helen opened one eye and squinted. "What is it?"

"A sleeping pill. Take it."

"Drunk people shouldn't take pills."

"I said swallow it. Sleep while you can because—" Lillian checked her watch. "In twenty-two hours, you're walking down that aisle."

Helen opened her mouth for the pill and fell back. She was unconscious before Lillian turned out the light.

What nonsense. Helen had been given plenty of time to back out of this wedding. Everything she'd said tonight was drunken raving. Lillian quietly opened the sideboard in the dining room. A drink might help her sleep. No one was awake to see.

92

The big day, and nothing would go wrong if Lillian could prevent it. Will went to the office for the morning. Lillian waited until 8:00 before going into Helen's dark bedroom and raising the blinds.

Her daughter groaned.

"Rise and shine. We've got a wedding in twelve hours."

Helen burrowed deeper. "I'm sick."

"Up, young lady. Take a look at what you did to my beautiful dress"

Helen raised her head.

The dress hung on the closet door, stains dark against the apricot silk. "Ruined," Lillian said.

Helen sat up, holding her head. "I'm sorry. I got so sick."

"You got so drunk. You cannot hold your liquor, my dear, a trait you inherited from your father, not me." Lillian folded the spoiled dress over her arm. "Get going. We have a bridesmaids' luncheon at noon."

Helen fell back onto her pillow. "I don't think I can eat."

"You can pretend to eat. Where are the earrings I lent you?"

Helen felt around for her bedroom slippers. "I'll find them."

At least she wasn't spouting more foolishness about not getting married. Lillian sat at the breakfast table with a second cup of coffee. Bessie pulled open the broiler door to check on the toast.

"Our queen bee is out of bed." Lillian rattled the pages of the newspaper. "Says here we're getting more rain today."

"Bad weather won't keep anybody away from this wedding," Bessie said.

Lillian skimmed a story about Indochina. She wished she were more interested in foreign affairs, but she wasn't. Somebody she couldn't pronounce was running South Viet Nam, and the communists were in charge of the north. Truman said the U.S. would defend any country threatened with communism. Her eyes lit on a sentence: *fathers were no longer being drafted.* Too bad that hadn't been true when Will went. Everything in her life would be different. Lillian sipped her coffee and smoked. Negroes rioting in Chicago. The South wasn't the only place with troubles.

Helen came in, barefoot and pale. "I can't find your earrings."

Lillian stood so suddenly the coffee cup rattled in its saucer. "You better not have lost them." The girl was too hung-over to see straight. Lillian went to Helen's bedroom and searched it thoroughly. Of course, her daughter would lose the one thing Lillian cared about. When had Helen ever thought about anybody but herself? Should never have loaned them to her. Back in the kitchen and filled with rage, she tried to keep her voice even. "You had them on at dinner."

Helen looked frightened. "I might have dropped them in the pool, or maybe in the toilet when I threw up. I am so sorry, Mama. I phoned but nobody at the hotel has seen them. Jack says they're not in his car."

Lillian felt capable of murder. She took a step forward. "I wish you were still small enough to beat." Helen backed away. "You are a careless, ungrateful girl."

Bessie gave a warning grunt, which Lillian ignored.

She was in Helen's face now. "Those earrings were the only thing I had left from my mother, a remembrance from my sister Maude. I asked you to be careful." She was crying now, the birthmark burning a hole in her forehead.

Maude and April came in to see what the fuss was about. Both tuned up to cry.

Helen kept her head down. She looked positively green and, for once, had nothing smart to say back. When she spoke, her voice sounded tiny. "What can I do?"

"Before or after I kill you?" Lillian shouted.

More "uh-uh" sounds from Bessie.

Lillian took a breath. "The stores open at ten. March yourself downtown and find me another pair of earrings to wear tonight."

She turned on Maude and April. "Stop that sniveling. Go take your baths and get ready for the bridesmaids' luncheon."

No earrings on earth could replace the lost ones, but this was the only punishment Lillian could think of. Murder was tempting, but she didn't want to go to jail before the wedding. She called after her oldest daughter. "Be back by eleven o'clock and use your own money."

Bessie made noises of commiseration.

"It's your fault, too," Lillian said. "Always taking her side." She went out onto the sun porch. The sterling glittered against the snowy table covers, the heavy dinner forks and knives lined up like soldiers next to stacks of Helen's ugly expensive china. Lillian felt her breath slow. Every gift was a small acknowledgment of what she'd achieved by forcing Will Hughes to come home.

An hour and a half later Helen returned. "I couldn't find anything like them."

Anger flared in Lillian's chest. "They were irreplaceable." She opened the small white box Helen offered and held up a cascade of pearls and gold.

"Are they okay?"

They were actually quite lovely, but Lillian would not give Helen that pleasure. "They will have to do, won't they?"

"I went to three different stores. I spent my last hundred dollars."

"Which in no way makes up for what you lost. Go get dressed."

Luncheon over, everyone went down for a rest. Will came home from his bridge game at five. At six-thirty, Lillian had Bessie zip her into the floor-length silk taffeta gown. This shade of sea green flattered her pale skin, as did the cowl neck. Three-quarter length sleeves hid her upper arms. She'd fitted the dress over a girdle and a Merry Widow, to flatten her stomach and give her a waist.

"Suck in," Bessie said. "Can you breathe?"

"Well enough. See how the girls are doing while I get the bride dressed."

Lillian slipped into new gold sandals and clicked down the hall. *Ouch.* Her feet would be swollen before this night was over. She'd need a visit with her podiatrist, a small man with wonderful hands whose treatments brought Lillian the only ecstasy she got nowadays. She was breathing with only the top half of her lungs, but being corseted from chest to thigh reminded her to stand straight.

In the back bedroom, Helen sat at the dresser in a lacy Merry Widow and a long half-slip. With her hair combed and makeup on, all signs of last night's debauchery had vanished. The girl glowed.

"Let's see if we can get you into this." Lillian lifted one side of the heavy satin dress so that Helen could duck under and come up into the bodice. Lillian had beaded the entire front with pearls and iridescent sequins. She helped her daughter into the tight sleeves and began buttoning the twenty-eight tiny satin-covered buttons down the back.

Helen stood facing the mirror. "The beading is so beautiful, Mama. I don't know how you do it."

"By making myself half blind," Lillian said. She stopped, realizing she'd received a compliment. "Thank you." She held the veil as Helen fastened the beaded crown onto her short brown curls. Stepping around the train, Lillian stood back to examine the results. "You never looked better." It was true.

Helen studied her reflection. "Feels like I've been run over by a truck."

There was a knock at the porch door. Lillian gave Helen a final pat. "That's Jimbo for me and your sisters. Your Uncle Leland will be here for you and your father. He's in our bedroom cursing his white tie. The off-duty policeman is in the kitchen with a piece of Bessie's cake." Lillian picked up her small gold evening bag. "Have I forgotten anything?"

Helen said, "You look beautiful, Mama."

Tell that to your father, Lillian wanted to say, but one did not involve children in marital troubles. Time enough for Helen to discover her own. She should have used these final moments to have some kind of mother-daughter talk, but Helen wasn't that kind of daughter, and Lillian hadn't forgotten the lost earrings.

"April, Maude." She shouted. "Our ride is here."

The younger girls looked precious in their long green dresses, even ten-year-old Maude, who was not growing out of her baby fat.

Lillian did a final check in the hall mirror and reminded herself to keep her chin up. When she forgot, she had as many chins as Leland.

93

In the crowded church foyer, Lillian took a professional look around. The bridesmaids' dresses were stunning. The gold dahlias they carried made a perfect contrast with the dark green velvet. The rented tails appeared to fit the groomsmen. Each wore a yellow rosebud boutonniere, looking quite handsome as they ushered guests to their seats.

A few minutes before eight, Jack's older brother led Ellaray — hair indeed a perfect match for her gray chiffon — to her place on the groom's side. It was Lillian's turn. She sucked in her stomach and lifted her chin. A hand atop Jimbo's large arm, she started down the aisle. The church was packed. Lillian felt a tingle of pride as she bestowed a smile here, a nod there. Better than she'd imagined. Settled in her place, with room for Will after he gave the bride away, she examined the décor: masses of banked ferns across the front of the sanctuary. She'd told the florist she wanted masses and that's what she'd gotten. Dozens of tall, white tapers. The effect was stunning.

Will's niece Leila stood and sang *Ave Maria*. The girl had a lovely voice and, with those black curls, an exotic look. There was a rumor she'd been adopted as a baby and Lillian wondered if there might be Jewish blood.

The organ struck up the bridal march and Helen's bridesmaids wafted by to stand in front of the groomsmen, all of whom were tall, except Ernestine's son, Knox III. He held his chin as high as Lillian's to make up for it. Backed by ferns and glowing candles, the nine girls in their green velvet were a winter fairy tale.

The organ grew louder. Helen and Will were coming. It wasn't polite for the mother of the bride to turn and stare, but Lillian savored the "Ohs" and "Ahs" as they approached. Will looked as handsome as a prince in the tails he'd fought wearing. Helen looked gorgeous. No one watching this glittering bride would believe she had been a drunk, moaning mess twenty-four hours earlier. The train of the wedding gown trailed six feet behind her and the veil floated perfectly on top of it. Will sat down. His arm felt warm next to hers, and Lillian savored this contact he couldn't avoid. She thought about reaching over to pat his hand, but if he recoiled people might see.

She hardly heard the words of the ceremony, too busy relishing the results of her hard work. Jack's brother carried the ring; Will had an envelope in his pocket with money for the minister. Helen's voice broke when she said, "Til death do us part." Lillian wondered if her daughter thought about not wanting to be married when she stumbled over those words? Did she have any idea what she was promising? She looked too caught up in her performance to take in the meaning of it. Jack was a nice enough young man, but he was no Will Hughes. His prospects, like his looks, appeared ordinary. He would never fill a church with judges and lawyers.

She glanced up at the balcony. There was Bessie, huge in her white uniform, with Doreen, and Willie in a proper white shirt. They sat next to Molly, Ellaray's cook. Olive and Leland's couple were there. She was surprised to see Ellis and his wife Gert, along with Flora May, Johnny, Preston and Savannah — everyone from the Hotel except Lena, who was too old to travel. Ernestine had said she would try and get them here. An impressive gathering and sweet of them to drive all this way. Showed respect, and a crowd of dark faces let people know you came from quality.

After the ceremony, in the ballroom of the King Edward Hotel, Lillian herded excited young people into place for photographs. That done, she arranged the receiving line. She stood at the head, then Will, Helen and Jack, and Jack's parents. The rest of the wedding party made up the tail. At her signal, a waiter flung open the double doors.

As guests came through the line, Lillian kept her head high. She was the wife of the handsome accomplished man next to her. She was the mother of this beautiful bride. Lillian whispered people's names to Will, and he greeted them graciously. He claimed to hate parties, but he could charm paint off a wall when he wanted to. The Mayor and his wife came by, Judge Mize and his wife, Judge Minor and his, the entire law firm, along with every lawyer Lillian had ever had for dinner, and many she hadn't. James and Faye came through.

Faye whispered into Lillian's ear. "A triumph, honey. The Queen of England couldn't have done it better." Lillian closed her eyes in a moment of pure happiness. Will had to realize what this meant for his own ambitions.

Here came Velma with the other secretaries. Poor girl, wearing the same unfortunate dress she'd worn to last year's Christmas party. If Will had to spend his working days with another woman, thank God he'd chosen this one. She gave Velma a particularly brilliant smile.

"Aren't you sweet to come? Yes, it was lovely. Thank you so much." She handed the secretaries down the line.

Will was kind to everyone who worked for him. It was one of the qualities Lillian most admired.

Helen cut the cake and fed Jack a bite. She stood on one of the gilded chairs and tossed her bouquet. Ten-year-old Maude jumped sideways like a fat rabbit and grabbed it out of the air. Everyone laughed and Lillian decided it was good to have a touch of humor at a formal occasion.

She pulled Helen upstairs to change into the going-away outfit and back downstairs where everyone waited outside to throw rice. The bride and groom were pelted and cheered as they pulled away in Jack's Chevrolet, with just a touch of what looked like dried throw-up on the passenger window. Helen's smile was as wide as Texas. They would be taking a late flight to New Orleans for a three-day honeymoon. Both had to be back at their jobs on Monday.

That was it. She'd done it. Lillian's feet hurt so bad she thought she might cry before she got home, but she'd pulled it off. Everyone who was anyone had come, and they all seemed to have a fine time. She went back up to the ballroom. Only stragglers left, including one of

Helen's college friends, trying to sneak out with a bottle of champagne under each arm.

"Young man."

At least he had the grace to look ashamed. "Sorry, Mrs. Hughes. Thought you were done with these."

Like hell, Lillian said to herself.

She found Maude next to a tray of dirty champagne glasses, draining them one by one. "Sweetheart." Lillian dragged her away. "You don't know whose mouth has been on those."

Maude looked at her crooked. "So good."

She was drunk, ten years old and drunk. Honestly, what next? Lillian grabbed April. "Go and find your father." She jerked Maude's arm. "Not a word out of you when we get in the car, do you understand me?"

Maude nodded mutely and let herself be pulled along.

Will would have a fit if he noticed the child's condition, and he would find a way to blame Lillian.

In the car, she tried to make cheerful conversation, keeping a hard eye on Maude in the back seat. "Wasn't it wonderful?"

Will drove, as always, well under the speed limit. He made a noncommittal noise.

April said, "I can't wait to get married."

Will groaned.

"Let's hope you manage to wait a little longer than your sister did," Lillian said.

"Don't worry." April sounded complacent. "I'm going to make my debut first."

Will groaned louder.

Shoes off, in her bed at last, Lillian's turn to groan. Her feet hurt, her back hurt, she was exhausted in every cell of her body. What she needed was a cigarette, a large bourbon and water, and somebody like Faye to gloat with.

"The happy couple must be halfway to New Orleans by now," she said to Will.

He switched off his light and turned his back. "Thank goodness that's over."

Thank goodness that's over instead of you are amazing, or what a fabulous job, or no one but you could have pulled it off. Her stomach hurt. That's what happened when she forgot to eat. She got up, plugged in the heating pad, and let its warmth soothe her belly.

She turned off her light. If Will wouldn't cooperate, she would lie here in the dark and gloat alone. The wedding had been a triumph. Faye said so. It was the event of the season. Several people going through the receiving line uttered those exact words. The entire occasion had been more splendid than even Lillian had dreamed. She'd given Will's career a boost whether he had the grace to admit it or not. Except for Maude getting drunk and that young man trying to steal champagne, everything had gone perfectly. She might never have graduated from college, but Lillian Creekmore Hughes could organize the rest of them under the table.

Will's snore ripped the silence. A hollow opened in her chest and Lillian mopped tears on an edge of the sheet. This entire magnificent evening had been done for the two of them, Helen and Will, and neither had bothered to thank her. All those months of work and here she was, sitting in the dark, celebrating alone. Will didn't care about the wedding or anything else she did. When Maude went off to college, he would leave her. She was pretty sure that's what the agreement said. She'd been stupid not to ask for a copy. Pain cut through her gut.

She slipped out of bed to swallow one of the pills the doctor prescribed for sleep, the same pill she'd given Helen last night, a hundred years ago, before her great, stupid triumph. Slumber descended like a blessing. It had been great. Will could not take that away.

94

Helen's marriage did not stop arguments over segregation at the dinner table — the only change being the addition of Jack, who listened, nodded, and appeared to agree with everyone.

In March of 1956, Will joined the Sovereignty Commission. The Citizens Council discouraged Negro advancement by economic pressure; the Sovereignty Commission, created by the state legislature, investigated everyone, colored or white, who wrote, spoke, or acted to promote racial mixing. Or that's how Will explained it.

"It's the biggest spy operation in the country," Helen said.

"Where'd you hear that?" Will looked amused. "From one of your leftie friends?"

Did Helen have leftie friends? Lillian had no idea. Nor did she know how the Sovereignty Commission went about its spying. She got most of her news second-hand from Will, who told her the most prominent men in the state supported the Commission's work. That was enough for her.

The two men who'd been acquitted of murdering Emmett Till confessed to the crime in an interview with *Look* magazine.

"They cannot be tried again." Will announced this at Sunday dinner.

"But they're guilty — they admitted it," Helen said.

"Double jeopardy," Will said. "It's the law."

"The law is as crazy as the rest of this state." Helen's eyes filled with tears. "It's not fair."

She looked to Jack for support and Lillian watched as the young man nodded sympathetically. Still besotted, more so now that Helen was pregnant.

"I don't know why you ever thought you could be a lawyer," Will said. "You can't cry in front of a judge."

The ultimate insult. Lillian waited to see what her eldest daughter would do.

April, home from her freshman year at Hollins College, broke in. "My social science professor says every woman should be able to earn her own money, even if she has to take to the streets to do it."

Maude choked on her mashed potatoes laughing.

Will's face grew red. "Is this what I'm paying good money for? Disgusting ideas like that?"

Helen looked gratified. "Good for him," she said to April.

Lillian moved the food around on her plate to make it appear she'd eaten, happy to hear them arguing. Tonight, in the privacy of their bedroom, Will might complain that he'd raised two communists. Everyone stopped talking when Bessie came through the swinging door to take away the dinner plates.

The Mississippi legislature declared the Brown decision invalid, enacting a "Resolution of Interposition" to forbid state officials from implementing integration in the schools. A few months later, in Washington, a hundred senators and congressmen introduced a "Southern Manifesto," pledging to reverse Brown and prevent the use of force to implement it.

Another Sunday dinner. "The Supreme Court may hand down a decision," Will said, "but you can't force people to go against custom and tradition." Nodding his head in satisfaction.

"A state cannot win against the federal government," Helen said. "Isn't that what the Civil War proved?"

Maude kept her head down. In her youngest daughter's eyes, her father could do no wrong.

"You just watch us," Will said.

In July, Helen gave birth to a baby boy, accomplishing what Lillian had never been able to. She saw a gleam of triumph in her daughter's eye. They named him Jackson after his father.

A month after the birth, Jack went away for two weeks of National Guard training. Helen called, crying. "I can't do this by myself. Can I move home until Jack gets back?"

Lillian said, "Of course." She did a little shuffle in her wedge-heeled bedroom slippers. The high-and-mighty daughter finally needed her. April was away at college. Lillian settled Helen and the baby in her room.

On her third night back, a much-subdued Helen watched as Lillian bent near the light, sewing a pattern of gold sequins onto a blue-green organza dance dress for April. Each sequin was topped by a gold bead to hide the needle holes. The tedious work made Lillian's eyes ache. She pulled the lamp closer.

"You're amazing, Mama," Helen said.

"Practice," Lillian said, "and strong glasses." She felt tender toward her daughter, who looked puffy and ill from motherhood. She could almost forget their quarrels, and the shoes she'd thrown at this one's head.

Helen sat on the end of the bed. "Why don't you leave him, Mama?"

The needle slipped and pricked Lillian's finger. She sucked it to ease the pain, eyes watering

"He never touches you," Helen said. "When he talks, it's to us, not you. He never says more to you than, 'Pass the salt'."

Lillian studied her eldest daughter. "You couldn't possibly understand."

"You like to drink. Daddy doesn't drink. You like parties. He never goes. You want to travel. He only wants to go fishing with his card buddies."

"I am not unhappy." Lillian felt her throat close and swallowed.

"But you're not happy either."

Lillian folded the dress. She would do no more work tonight. "Your father and I have more in common than you realize."

"You mean segregation?"

"Well, that and—"

Helen interrupted. "I see you nodding like a doll at every word that comes out of his mouth."

Lillian sat straighter. "Don't be disrespectful. Your father is doing work he deeply believes in, and I support him."

"You could find someone more like you. Somebody like Uncle Leland or Uncle James, a man wants to be with you and have fun."

"Said with all the confidence of a girl who can't manage one small baby."

"I'm serious."

Lillian leaned over and gave Helen a quick hug, more a bump of heads than a caress. "I know you are, honey, but part of the reason I've stayed is for you girls."

Helen's voice rose in exasperation. "We never asked you to stay. We want you to be happy."

Lillian felt as tired and miserable as she claimed not to be. "The part you don't understand is—I still love your father."

Helen looked disbelieving. "How can you love someone who doesn't love you back?"

Lillian swallowed hard. "You're young. You don't know what you might do." *She would not cry.* "Your father and I are married. It may not look ideal to you, but I've learned to be content. You have no idea how different our lives would be if we had divorced. Frankly, I have no desire to be a single woman in a town like Jackson."

The baby began whining and Helen left to see about him. Lillian took off her reading glasses and rubbed her eyes. She was exhausted from the strain of pretending things were fine when even her children could see they weren't. Some days she thought the strain was making her ill.

95

In September 1957, when Arkansas Governor Faubus refused to let Negroes attend Little Rock's high school, President Eisenhower sent in paratroopers to enforce the law.

"What do you think of that," Helen said to her father at dinner.

"They've turned the city into an occupied territory," Will said. "It's the darkest day for the South since Reconstruction."

Lillian listened peacefully. Let them have at it. She would be the sympathetic ear in the bedroom.

In 1959, Helen gave birth to a second child, a girl this time. Jack built them a new house in a nicer neighborhood. He had started his own business, designing and building custom houses for well-off young couples. Helen did volunteer work for the Junior League and taught Sunday school at the Episcopal Church. No one knew what went on in other people's marriages, but from what Lillian observed, Helen and Jack were fine. She gave herself credit; she had put a lot of work into raising that girl.

April transferred to the University of Oklahoma to be with her high school sweetheart. Maude remained, at sixteen, the only child left at home. Will claimed she only went to school to eat her lunch, but Lillian found her youngest the most loving of all her girls. Grades weren't everything.

Will was now working to get Ross Barnett elected governor. Barnett ran on the issue of race, campaigning with speeches like: "God made the Negro different to punish him. His forehead slants back. His nose is different. His lips are different, and his color is sure different." Lillian did not disagree, but no one with any manners would say things like that out loud.

In January, after Barnett won and was sworn into office, he invited Will to be his personal attorney. Before his rise, Ross Barnett was not the type person Lillian would choose to sit next to at a dinner party, but personal preference faded next to political power. According to Will, the entire state was under attack. Their governor was fighting integration on every front. He had chosen Lillian's husband to be at his side. She basked in that reflected glory.

Will got Helen a job that summer, working as a secretary for a few weeks in the governor's office. She and Jack still came to dinner twice a week. Bessie and Doreen took care of the babies in the kitchen. On the dining room side of the swinging door, the conversations grew more heated.

"Barnett hires convicted murderers to be his personal servants," Helen said. "If they work hard and don't slice anyone's throats while they sleep, at the end of his term he pardons them."

Will did not look up from his plate. "That is a long tradition for the governors of this state, and I consider it admirable."

"These poor women come into the office." Helen gestured to make her point. "Their husbands are in jail and they wait all day hoping to see the governor, some of them with small children. *White* women, you understand. No telling what happens to the colored ones. The governor finally agrees to see one or two, and if he's feeling generous, or maybe she's cute, he pardons the husband."

"The act of pardon is a governor's privilege," Will said.

"It feels like justice on a whim," Helen said. "And Barnett doesn't believe in women smoking." She shook her head in disbelief. "Men can smoke as much as they want, but we have to hide our cigarettes on the window ledge every time the big man steps out of his office."

"I never approved of you smoking," Will said.

"You smoke cigars," Helen said. "Mother smokes."

"It is a nasty habit."

"Barnett is a nasty bigot," Helen said.

"He's the most important man in this state." Will spoke in his enough-of-this-foolishness voice. "You should feel honored to work for him."

Under the table, Lillian pressed her hands against her aching gut. She hadn't appreciated Will's "nasty habit" remark. He was eating with his eyes closed again. Helen sent him a killing stare, which failed to penetrate his eyelids. Jack studied his food while Maude ate around her vegetables. Another delightful evening in the Hughes household.

Bessie took away the plates and passed around slices of chocolate pie. Lillian wondered how much of this talk she and Doreen heard in the kitchen and pretended to ignore.

Helen spoke into the silence. "We're having another baby."

Bessie stopped her trip around the table. "Finally, some good news."

Will opened his eyes and smiled. "Congratulations."

Jack sat straighter, looking proud.

"I hope it's another girl," Maude said.

So did Lillian. Serve Helen right for being snotty about the boy. During labor for the second child, the doctor told Lillian her daughter was using self-hypnosis and could not be disturbed. What a bunch of hooey. Maybe she would punish Helen and not go by the hospital at all for this one.

96

Will invited a federal judge and the author of an important book on race home for dinner. Lillian made sure Helen and Jack could be there. Helen might talk like a communist ("A little pink," Will described her), but she did add spark to the conversation.

Lillian set the table with Will's mother's lace cloth, the good china, and their wedding crystal. She adjusted the centerpiece, a silver bowl filled with roses from the garden. In the kitchen, the rice kept warm over hot water, the roast looked perfectly done, and the gravy was smooth and shiny.

She took a last look at herself in the bedroom mirror and lifted her head. Pretty soon she'd be all chin and no neck. She turned to the side and sucked in her stomach, flattening it with both hands. Even with a girdle, she had a hard time keeping a slim silhouette. She gave herself the lecture: stomach in, chin up, and don't take that third drink. Inside, she buzzed with anticipation. She loved having company. Around strangers, Will treated her well. She would do him proud tonight.

April was home from college. Stepping down the hall, Lillian reminded the girls to put on something nice. She heard Will open the front door.

"Lillian?' In front of company, he said her name with a lilt that made her heart sing.

"Gentlemen, my wife, Lillian."

"So happy you could join us." She gave them her best smile.

The judge was small and white-haired with a slight stoop. The author, Carleton Putnam, had an enormous forehead and worried eyes.

"Can I get you gentlemen a drink?" Lillian said.

"Scotch and water for me," the judge said.

"Alcohol is a poison," Putnam said. "I'll take seltzer if you have it. No ice." Lillian nodded. Guests who refused a drink made her suspicious.

Helen and Jack arrived. Lillian brought the tray in and passed around drinks in silver mint julep cups. She settled in a wing chair across the room from the gentlemen with her legs crossed. She still had good legs. She enjoyed watching Will charm people. The judge laughed at a joke Will told about a good lawyer knowing the law and a great lawyer knowing the judge. The strange little author drank his club soda. Lillian took tiny sips of her bourbon and water.

Bessie put avocado salads on the table and announced dinner. Lillian called down the hall for Maude and April. Will said grace, ending with: "In Christ's name, Amen." With her head bowed, Lillian experienced a moment's anxiety: Was Mr. Putnam Jewish? She should have warned Will not to mention Jesus.

"Avocado." The man stared at his salad.

"So hard to find a good one this time of year." Lillian smiled, which seemed to have no visible warming effect. She noticed Maude hiding hers under the lettuce and said nothing.

"Not native, I believe," Mr. Putnam said. He wasn't eating his either.

Bessie took away the salad plates and brought in a platter with the roast. Lillian stood to carve.

"She's better with a knife than I am," Will said. "Have to watch myself."

Everyone laughed. When Will made a flattering joke about her, Lillian's chest expanded with happiness.

"Roast beef with rice?" The author eyed his plate with doubtful eyes. "Never mind, I know what to do when I get back to the hotel."

Bessie went around the table with a serving dish of *petite pois* peas.

Will had April do her trick—reciting the names of Mississippi's eighty-two counties in alphabetical order. By the time she got to "Yazoo," the girl was pink as a baked ham.

The judge applauded.

Mr. Putnam said, "Proves my point."

"And what is that?" Helen's voice held an inappropriate edge. If Lillian could, she'd give her daughter a warning kick under the table.

"The superiority of the white race." Putnam lowered his voice in deference to the dark person now coming through the door with a basket of homemade biscuits. They all got quiet.

"Biscuits with butter?" the author said. He took one. "Never mind, I know what to do when I get back to the hotel."

"This is a real treat," the judge said.

"Have a little more of Lillian's plum jelly," Will said.

Lillian's plum jelly. She grew warm at the compliment.

"I don't know when I've had a better meal," the judge said. "Will, you're a lucky man."

"Wait until you taste Bessie's pie," Will said.

Bessie may have made that pie, but it was *her* recipe. Lillian pressed her lips into a smile and kept quiet.

Helen described a course she had taken in political science at Ole Miss.

"You get these Yankee professors and you don't know what the students are being taught," Mr. Putnam said. "Perhaps in the next five hundred million years the Negro may overtake the white race—when he has bred out his limitations—and that will be time enough to consider absorbing him into the South."

Lillian watched Helen swell with indignation.

"It's all in Mr. Putnam's book, *Race and Reason*." Will spoke up, perhaps to keep his daughter from exploding. "He brought you an autographed copy, Helen."

Lillian saw the sarcastic expression on Helen's face and was relieved when she managed to say thank you.

The room went silent while Bessie removed the dinner plates and brought in apple pie with wedges of cheddar cheese.

"Cheese with apple pie? Putnam said. "Terrible combination, but I know what to do when I get back to the hotel." His eyes bulged with concern.

Helen must have run out of patience. She leaned toward him. "I hope you don't mind me asking, but what do you do when you get back to the hotel?"

Will gave his daughter a warning look, but Mr. Putnam did not seem bothered by the question. "Bromo Seltzer."

After everyone left, Lillian noticed Helen had left behind her copy of *Race and Reason*. She flipped through it, wondering about the theories of anyone with such a sour stomach. Not that she would cross Will on this point. She loved being on his side and against their daughter.

She was in bed when he returned. "That went well." Sounding, maybe, a little loud.

Will had his back to her, untying his shoes. "Very nice." Using his calm-down voice. The company had left. He didn't need to be nice to her anymore.

"The judge seemed like an interesting man," Lillian said. "The other one was odd."

Will said, "Uh-huh." The bathroom door shut behind him.

Lillian blinked back tears. In front of company, she let herself believe the man she'd married felt proud of her and believed himself, as the judge said, a lucky man. This was the happiness trap and she fell into it every time.

97

The next morning Lillian telephoned Faye up in Canton. Whenever she needed to vent about Will, she called her sister-in-law, the only family member who sympathized without judgment.

"Will got mad at me again last night."

"Do you ever stop and think that maybe you married a man who cannot be satisfied?" Faye's voice carried an edge of impatience.

Lillian tried to sound jovial. "I keep trying, though, don't I?"

"But you never quite manage to please him, do you? And that's his power over you."

This conversation was not going the way Lillian had hoped. "It's not about power. I love him, so of course I want him to be happy."

"But he doesn't love you, isn't that what you said?"

Lillian winced. Had she told Faye that? She couldn't remember. She must have been drinking. "I shouldn't have said that. It was a long time ago."

"Darling Lillian, can't you see?" Faye sounded tired. "Will Hughes can never be pleased, and you can never stop trying to please him. So, you're stuck."

Lillian heard a sigh and ice clinking. It was only eleven in the morning. Surely Faye wasn't drinking. Probably a Coca-Cola.

"Maybe we're all stuck." Faye hung up.

Lillian sat holding the receiver. That had been a most unsatisfactory conversation. Faye wasn't herself these days.

98

June arrived, as hot and humid as always. The window air conditioners groaned with effort. Lillian set the dining room table for her Saturday afternoon canasta game. The girls had switched from bridge to canasta for the season. More people could play, and the game required so many decks of cards, they bought a machine to shuffle them.

She felt tired. The heat perhaps, or maybe she was still exhausted from giving April a wedding equal to her sister's. Her middle child, the sensible one, wisely chose to postpone marriage until after she made her debut and graduated from college. With minor alterations, April was able to wear Helen's dress. The ceremony had gone off with as much pomp as her sister's, but with fewer expectations on Lillian's part. She had learned her lesson: Will Hughes would appear, behave appropriately, grouch about the cost, and thank her for nothing.

Faye hadn't attended. James said she'd been having chronic migraines, and her back was acting up. Lillian missed Faye's compliments and the exchange of sarcastic eye rolls over Ernestine.

Maude was almost done with college down at Mississippi Southern. She would graduate next spring with a degree in elementary education. Lillian shook her head, remembering the child's earlier ambition to become a hairdresser. She'd managed to squash that, though Maude *was* good with hair. A definite talent, but a Hughes couldn't be a hairdresser. Teaching was a respected profession.

She was pleased with how the three girls had turned out. Life ran smoothly these days, in spite of — she stopped before the words "not being loved" fully formed in her head.

The phone rang in the kitchen and Lillian went through the swinging door to answer it.

James' voice sounded thick. "Faye's been shot."

Lillian went cold. She couldn't speak.

Her brother pleaded. "Did you hear me?"

"Where are you?" The phone shook in Lillian's hands. Her voice echoed oddly in her ears.

Bessie quit making tuna fish sandwiches to listen.

"Canton hospital."

"Is she going to be okay?" *Please, God.*

"No." The line went dead.

Who would shoot Faye? Faye didn't have an enemy in the world. She hardly left the house. Lillian needed to get up there fast. She dialed Peggy: "Family emergency — no time to explain. Cancel the canasta game. I'll call you later."

She grabbed her purse from the bedroom. "I've got to run up to Canton. Miss Faye's been —" Hard to say the word. "— shot."

Bessie let out a wail.

Lillian could not afford to fall apart. "Keep things together for me here, Bessie. Tell Mr. Hughes where I've gone. I'll call when I know more."

Lillian drove with the accelerator floored and her skirt hiked up over her knees.

Faye looked tiny under the hospital sheet, and so pale she was almost gray. There were tubes emerging from the bedclothes but, thankfully, the wound remained hidden. Lillian didn't think she could bear to see it. Faye's eyes were closed. Every few seconds, she twisted, as if trying to get away from the pain, and moaned.

James sat beside the bed holding one of his wife's pale and perfectly manicured hands, his face swollen from crying. Jimbo sat in a corner, head bowed.

James let Lillian hug him.

Lillian clutched her coat against her. This couldn't be happening. Faye was only sixty-one. She wasn't supposed to die for a long, long time. "What happened?" Her voice shook.

James held onto Faye as if only his grasp kept her alive. "Gunshot," he said. "Hit her stomach. Doctor says nothing they can do."

"Who shot her?"

He tilted his head, indicating the bed.

"Are you telling me she shot *herself*?" The shock of this made Lillian sway. The Faye she knew would never—

"Give Angie your chair, son."

Jimbo got up and pushed the chair toward Lillian. She sat and rested her forehead on Faye's bed, trying not to pass out.

"It's my fault." Jimbo took a ragged breath. "Mama was so happy I quit drinking and started going to church. Took me with her every time the doors opened. Then she found out I got a job running gambling at the country club."

Lillian stared at the young man looming over her. "I'm sure that's not the case." No sane person would shoot themselves over Jimbo, who'd been raising hell since he was old enough to wear long pants. Moving to the other side of the bed, Lillian took Faye's free hand— gently because of the IV. "Darling, it's Lillian. Can you hear me? Squeeze my hand if you can hear me."

No response.

"It was an accident, wasn't it, baby?" James bent and kissed the hand he held. "An accident. You didn't mean to do it, did you? Gun just went off?"

Faye groaned, a hideous sound from a place of horrible pain.

Lillian mopped tears away on the back of her free hand. "Can't they give her something?"

"They have," James said. "Can't seem to reach where it hurts." He smoothed Faye's hair.

Faye's eyes opened, blue and filled with anguish. She searched the air wildly as if looking for a way out.

"Baby, baby." James cradled her head.

Looking at the gray face, Lillian's gut clenched. This was dying, no clouds parting or angels coming to carry you home. Pain and terror.

Ernestine bustled in. "I've spoken to the minister. He tried to tell me Faye could not be buried in consecrated ground, because of—you know." Her mouth in a knowing twist.

"God, Ernestine." Lillian thought her head might blow off. "Faye's not dead. She can hear you."

"Why, hello, Lillian." Ernestine planted a kiss on her sister's cheek and gave her an appraising sniff.

A check to see if she'd been drinking. Lillian gritted her teeth.

Ernestine lowered her voice. "I explained to the man that as far as the family is concerned, this was not a suicide attempt. It was an unfortunate accident and Faye has every right to be laid to rest in the Creekmore plot."

Lillian stayed the night in Faye and James' empty house. Their housekeeper Mateel left supper in the fridge, but Lillian couldn't eat. She put her things in the guest room and telephoned Will. Hearing his reassuring voice made her start weeping again.

"Terrible business," Will said. "Give James my condolences."

Will didn't get emotional. Didn't offer to drive up, either.

"I love her so much." The weight in her chest kept Lillian from breathing right. "She's my best friend."

"I know," Will said.

He actually sounded sorry. He cared because this was her family, which meant, no matter how cold he acted, the man wasn't totally without feeling.

"James refuses to leave the hospital." Lillian made the mistake of taking of sip of the drink she'd mixed herself. Ice clinked against the glass.

Will's voice turned cold. "I'll explain to the girls."

"Tell them it was an accident. They're crazy about Faye."

"I will."

"I'll call you as soon as—" Lillian couldn't keep herself from sobbing. "—as soon as we know something."

"I'll let you get back to your nursing."

His sarcasm made Lillian cry harder. She drained the first drink and mixed herself a second. Nobody in this house cared how much she drank. She wandered from room to room. She hadn't eaten since coffee at breakfast. Food might stop the shaking. She looked at the sliced meat and salad greens under waxed paper and felt ill.

In the den, she lay on Faye's back-support lounger and stared out the big glass window as twilight settled over Canton. Part of the burning in her gut was anger. If Faye truly loved her, she wouldn't have done this to herself. She drank and wept, swiping at her wet face with the heel of her hand. Faye was the only person in the family who knew about Lillian's troubles and sympathized. Except during that last phone call. Lillian never thought to ask if Faye had troubles. Now she'd lost the chance. Here she was — feeling sorry for herself instead of Faye. The only person she could talk to about being this selfish lay unconscious in a hospital bed.

For three horrible days, Lillian, James, and Jimbo watched Faye die, spelling each other at the bedside. Lillian stayed midnight to dawn, then went back to James' house to try and sleep for a couple of hours, and to bolster herself with Mateel's bitter coffee. She had never seen anyone suffer like this. When the drugs wore off, Faye thrashed and wailed like a wounded animal. Lillian suffered with her, yelling at the nurses to bring more morphine. She'd begun by praying for Faye to live, but by the end, she begged God to let her die.

99

All of Canton came to the funeral. Sitting in the Baptist church with Will on one side and Maude on the other, Lillian felt too hollow to cry another tear. Helen and Jack sat next to Will, April and her husband in the row behind. For all her irreverence, Faye had been a devoted Baptist. Unlike James, who, according to Faye, began and would end as a heathen. Lillian watched her brother squirm, barely able to tolerate the minister's talk of hellfire and damnation. Lillian agreed. What did any of this have to do with Faye? From the set of Ernestine's jaw, she too found it distasteful. Nothing like an Episcopal funeral with its grand, solemn words from the *Book of Common Prayer*.

At the gravesite, James had to be supported by Leland, and Jimbo tried to throw himself on top of the coffin.

Back at the house, Mateel heated the casseroles people brought, and put out platters of sliced ham, warmed biscuits, and pies. Without a word, she carried away empty plates and sweating glasses, her grief evident in the thunderous looks she gave anyone who met her eyes. Helen went around crying, telling embarrassed relatives how much she loved them. James got thoroughly and deeply drunk. Lillian tried to be discreet, sipping her drink, hoping Will thought the glass in her hand was her first.

James said he'd never loved a woman the way he loved Faye and never would. He'd taken care of her in every way he knew how, except for the damned gun, and he only bought that so his baby would feel safe.

Baby was not just a nickname. James had treated Faye like a fragile doll. He tilted toward Will. "You got to treat them right, Will. You got to love them the way they deserve. Don't end up like me." He broke down again, and Lillian saw her husband attempt to back away.

James put a heavy arm on Will's shoulder, his liquored breath close, the broken blood vessels like a road map on his broad face. "I been noticing the way you treat my baby sister." The words thick with emotion and slurred by liquor.

Lillian held her breath, watching in horrified fascination.

James spoke loud enough for anyone close by to hear. "It's not right, Will. She's a little treasure, aren't you, Lillian? Come here, Angie." He put the other heavy arm around her. Lillian tried to smile but the infuriated expression on Will's face frightened her.

"You need to treat her like the jewel she is. Me and Leland hear any different, we'll have to come down there and tear you sideways from Sunday."

Will attempted to pull away from her brother's drunken grasp.

"James?" Lillian spoke in a pleading voice.

"A man needs what a man needs, we understand that, but you got to be careful, you know what I mean? Everybody heard about you and that secretary. You can't be doing that, Will. It's shitting where you work."

That secretary? Lillian's ears rang. Will had been cheating on her with a *secretary?* Which one? She ran down the list: Garnett: too nice and, besides, married. Not gawky Velma, who couldn't say boo to a turkey without turning the color of a boiled shrimp. Must be that nasty Doris, the one who dressed like a tart. Or maybe a secretary from another firm. Capitol Street swarmed with them at lunchtime.

Will managed to pull away from James' embrace. "You're drunk." He took Lillian by one arm, Maude by the other, marched them out of the house and into the car. For the twenty-five-mile drive home, he did not speak, and neither did Lillian. She glanced at Maude in the back seat, staring out the window, expressionless. Maude must have heard. So had Helen and April and most of her other relatives. Inside the car, the air felt heavy with accusation and silence.

When they were alone in their bedroom, Lillian exploded. "You had an affair with a *secretary*? That is disgusting. Which secretary?" She said the names of the women working at Hughes & Blair, stumbling in her fury. Fists clenched, holding her breath, she watched his face.

At one name, his pupils contracted and she caught an involuntary twitch. She had him, but everything inside her turned to jelly at the truth. The tall woman seen with Will in a restaurant across town — that had been Velma? That awkward, ill-dressed, country-talking nobody? Picturing their intimacy made Lillian burn and she spat the words. "You had an affair with *Velma Vernon?*"

Will turned on her, his face ugly with anger. "Do not speak her name. Don't even say it. I'm back here, aren't I? This is what you wanted. You wanted it so bad you sent half the town after me. Well, it worked. You've got me, but you are never to question me, is that understood? *Never.* And for your information, Velma will have nothing to do with me. She's a better person than either one of us." He picked up the car keys.

"Where are you going? Her voice shook with fear of his rage. It's nine at night." Was he leaving her again?

"Where I always go to get away from you — to work."

Oh, God, oh, God. When the back door slammed, Lillian crumpled onto the bed. She wanted Faye back. She wanted to erase this night and James' terrible words. If Velma wanted nothing to do with Will, that must mean he tried something and she refused him. Lillian rubbed her stomach. No wonder she ached, hearing James say that horrible stuff in front of everybody, being jerked out of Faye's house, and now this.

Faye was the only person she could speak to about what James said, but Faye was gone. And why, that's what Lillian wanted to know. Faye had everything a woman could want: money, clothes, a husband who adored her. Yet she had killed herself. Anger and grief battled inside her. If Faye were here, she would sit Lillian down and sort things out: What did she actually know? James had been very drunk and drunk men make mistakes. Will might have tried a kiss at a Christmas party and been spurned. His anger might come from being accused in public of something he'd never done.

She kneaded her aching stomach, unconvinced. Will had done something, something she must never again accuse him of. The frustration of that made her groan. Quiet or she'd wake Maude. Will despised her. She'd seen it in his face. Let him. She was not a quitter. He might try and leave her again, but she would never give him a divorce. Never.

Head up, shoulders back, and a double bourbon.

Sitting in one of the flowered chairs on the sun porch with the lights out, she traveled in memory to the little house on Monroe Street. She had not invented their happiness. Will had once adored her. He used to come in the door and kiss her before he took his coat off. Rub against her in the joy of being together again. The light in his eyes had been for her. The jokes were for her. Hard to believe now. When she watched him with their girls, Lillian saw a pale reflection of those days: the sly jokes, waiting for the girls to catch on, the shared hilarity when they did. Once, that had all been for her. In that other lifetime, Will found her amazing.

She drained her glass, letting the ice hit her nose, not bothering to wipe away the tears.

At the buffet in the dark dining room, she poured herself more bourbon. Before he left for the Navy, they had kept chickens in the back yard. Will brought in the eggs each day, as proud as if he'd laid them himself. One night, when she produced a succulent pan of chicken and dumplings from an unwanted rooster, he'd been flabbergasted.

"You *killed* a chicken?" Staring at her with a disbelief that made her laugh. He'd be surprised to know how many chicken necks she'd wrung at the hotel.

In that other lifetime, she'd been strong and independent, afraid of nothing except boredom. She had gone from being that girl to a frightened woman, watching what she said, sneaking drinks, grateful for crumbs—a smile here, a nod there. She was like one of those unwanted roosters, trying to stay on the safe side of his irritation, hoping not to get her neck wrung.

Which meant divorce. Then he'd be free to marry Velma. How could it be Velma? He was such a snob about family and his place in the community. If Will loved someone else, wouldn't it be someone smarter and at least *prettier?* Velma could never pull off a dinner party for twelve or entertain judges. She could never produce a spectacular wedding.

Lillian drained her drink and put out her cigarette, carrying the ashtray and glass to the kitchen to wash. The clock on the wall said 11:00. Will had not returned. She brushed her teeth and got into bed as if nothing had happened. As if the evil words had never been spoken. They would go on as before.

Lillian never mentioned Velma's name in Will's presence, but that didn't mean she couldn't question others. She telephoned Will's sister, whose voice got stiff and embarrassed. Lillian didn't care; she needed information. Mag said Velma was a quiet girl, very efficient, and she had never seen anything untoward. But would Mag even notice? The woman hardly stepped out of her office, hidden behind those books and enveloped in cigarette smoke. She called her brother in Canton to ask what he knew and how he'd heard it. But James got weepy over Faye and claimed not to remember anything from the night of the funeral.

When she was forced to call the office, Lillian listened for guilt in Velma's voice, but couldn't pick up a thing. The young woman continued, polite and expressionless as she'd ever been, speaking in that flat country accent.

Never mind. Lillian did not plan on giving Will the opportunity to marry anyone else.

100

The marriage went on and Lillian tried to count her blessings: Will might not love her, but he hadn't left.

In September, she lay in her gown and bed jacket, face covered in moisturizing cream, with Will in the next bed reading *Time*. The phone on Lillian's bedside table rang. A call this late could only be bad news.

Her sister Ernestine's voice sounded strained, making her harder to hear than usual.

"I can't understand you, Ernestine. Speak up."

"Knox has died."

Lillian sat straight up in bed, everything inside her pulled into a knot. "Tell me where you are and I'll come."

Will put down the magazine and took off his glasses.

"At the hospital in Canton," Ernestine said. "The ambulance brought him in and I followed, but—" Her voice faltered. "It was his heart. He was already gone."

Lillian didn't know how to comfort this sister who never required comforting and, even now, didn't sound as if she were crying.

"He went so quickly," Ernestine said.

"I'm driving up." Faye had been dead for less than three months.

"There's no need." Ernestine's voice turned practical. "I will spend the night with James. He's with me now."

"I'll be there in the morning. I'm so sorry. *Knox.* I cannot believe it."

"Neither can I." Ernestine pronounced it "nigh-ther."

Ernestine insisted on speaking in that stuck-up Yankee way even in a moment like this, as if she'd been born in London, not Way, Mississippi.

She turned to Will. "Knox died."

Will closed his magazine, looking distressed. "A good man."

"I cannot imagine how Ernestine can carry on without him. His salary kept the hotel going."

"Maybe it's time to close the place."

She felt the birthmark on her forehead fire up. Will never said a kind word about Creekmore. "You're talking about my home, which, if you remember, the State of Mississippi just declared a Heritage Site."

He clicked off his light and turned his back. "The place is a fire trap."

"Well, it's *my* fire trap."

Knox, dear Knox. Lillian switched her light off. Since the war, he and Ernestine had struggled to make a go of the place. In these more prosperous times, people preferred vacationing in New Orleans or on the Gulf Coast. The hotel sponsored beauty contests, an art colony, even rented the place out for religious revivals (With speaking in tongues, Ernestine reported). Her sister hosted anyone who could pay, including a group of drunken insurance people, who insisted on being served a backwards dinner on the front lawn (beginning with dessert and ending with soup nobody wanted).

Ernestine and Knox struggled in the same way they did everything, without raising their voices or complaining, and without drinking to forget their troubles. The hotel was still closed, preparing to open for the summer. Ernestine had been forced to deal with this death alone.

Lillian remembered the two of them in the evening, sitting at a small table in the back of the dining room, enjoying a private dinner after the last guests had eaten. She saw Knox's tired eyes and the fond way he looked at Ernestine. Had she and Will ever talked that way? They used to laugh in the old days. They played cards, argued, got tipsy, and made love, but had they ever really talked? She mainly remembered listening. Maybe she'd forgotten. Her memory was more a sieve than a sponge lately.

The next morning, Lillian drove the twenty-five miles to Canton, hugged her older sister, who did not appear to require a hug, and sat with her in what had been Faye's sunroom.

"We had dinner late," Ernestine said. "When we got back to our room, Knox complained of indigestion."

James brought out cups of his strong coffee.

"I went out to the office to get him an Alka-Seltzer. By the time I got back, he was unconscious. Doctor Durphy said it was a massive heart attack and Knox had probably died almost at once." Ernestine's cup rattled in its saucer, her only indication of distress. "There was no warning. He seemed more tired lately, but I thought it was the strain of driving back and forth to Jackson every day. I asked him to cut down, but, as he said, the bills keep coming."

"How old was Knox?" Lillian said.

"Seventy-three." Ernestine dabbed her eyes with a handkerchief.

Seventy-three and still working a full-time job at the advertising agency and another up at the hotel. Lillian put a hand over her sister's. "Tell me what I can do to help."

Ernestine's eyes filled with gratitude. "Thank you for asking."

This was how you comforted Ernestine, by offering to carry part of the load.

The funeral was held in Canton's small Episcopal church. A closed casket and no caterwauling about hell. A quiet burial in the family plot. At the graveside, Ernestine's two sons flanked her. She looked pale but steadfast in her black suit, inviting people back to the hotel after the service. There, in the parlor, the servants handed around trays of sandwiches and cups of coffee and tea. Ernestine listened patiently as her brothers talked about selling the hotel.

When they were done, Ernestine said, "I wouldn't dream of it."

"You can't run the place by yourself," Leland said.

Lillian suspected that Leland helped Ernestine in the same way he helped her—with regular infusions of cash.

"Lillian has offered to assist." Ernestine beamed at her.

Lillian meant it when she made the offer. She enjoyed the idea of a summer at the hotel, meeting new people, playing cards and drinking in the evening. The hard work would be slimming. But that would also leave Will alone with Velma, or whoever he was seeing. She couldn't take the chance.

She turned to Ernestine, shaking her head in regret. "I honestly thought I could come, but I spoke to Will. With the situation the way it is—" She nodded toward Ellis, passing a tray of cakes, to indicate the problem. "—he feels it's wiser that I stay close to home."

Will looked perplexed but did not contradict her.

Ernestine, with her perfect manners, showed no disappointment. "People count on the hotel." She spoke in a slightly louder voice. "We will carry on, won't we, Ellis?"

Ellis nodded without looking at her. "Yes, Ma'am."

If Ernestine didn't carry on, a lot of dark-skinned people would be out of a job. Lillian watched her sister's sons, short Knox III and tall "Little" Leland, both solicitous of their mother. Will watched too, probably wondering how this sister had produced two male heirs when his wife couldn't manage one. Lillian handed her cup to Ellis. *She was dying for a drink.* Money was tight, but surely Ernestine could have managed sherry.

Back in Jackson, closed in their bedroom for the night, Will said, "You can go up there and help this summer if you want."

You'd like that, wouldn't you? Lillian sat on the bed rubbing her bare arms with lotion. "I had hoped to, but Doctor O'Ferrell thinks I shouldn't take a chance with the heat." She got under the covers and turned on her side, not waiting to see if Will believed her. She spoke to the wall. "Poor Knox. Poor Ernestine."

"He was a good man."

The second time he'd said that. To be a good man was her husband's highest praise. Lying there, un-kissed and unloved, Lillian thought about her older sister, with two sons and years and years of an affectionate marriage. She envied Ernestine without wanting to be her. Ernestine didn't have enough fun. Lillian could no longer count on Will, but she had her friends.

At bridge last week, halfway through a third bourbon and water, Lillian laughed at something Dimple said and realized she was happy. This was what happiness felt like, a giddy lightness that faded when the game ended and her friends departed, leaving her to clear away the mess before Will got home. Then came supper and Will chewing at the other end of the table with his eyes shut. Some nights, neither of them uttered a word except to Bessie. Will went off to the office. By the time Lillian pulled on her nightgown, that brief blossom of happiness felt like a fantasy.

Poor Knox was dead, and here she lay, wallowing in self- pity. No sister left now except Ernestine (Olive being too kind to count). She would eat worms before confiding in Ernestine, who would advise in her poisonous soft voice to hand the matter over to God.

Lillian had switched from Episcopalian to Methodist when she married Will, whose family tree was laden with Methodist preachers and missionaries. She attended Galloway Memorial on Sunday mornings, but she'd never developed a personal relationship with God the way Ernestine claimed, where you got down on your knees and He lent an ear. Lillian believed, but God kept busy and so did she. They left one another alone.

What if Will died like Knox? That thought woke her up. She would feel horrible of course, devastated, but she would also be a widow. A widow was entirely different from a divorcee. Widows were respected, and besides, she'd have Will's money. She had no idea how much money her husband possessed, but surely enough for her to travel and buy nice clothes. When people told her how sorry they were he was gone, she would agree, remembering Will from before the war.

Who was she kidding? Lillian slumped lower on the pillow. Will wouldn't die. He didn't drink. He smoked only those nasty cigars, which he didn't inhale. Listen to him over there. Even the snoring sounded vigorous.

101

Eleven years since Will Hughes returned to his wife. Velma took her emotional temperature and decided the fever had broken. She and Will had managed to move from what she recalled as teasing boss and blushing secretary into a more professional relationship. Not that there weren't pinches of regret. These she tried to ignore and, on the whole, felt she had developed a maturity that no longer required romance outside the covers of a book.

Three men were in the office with Will. Velma recognized the managing partner from Jackson's other big law firm and the congressman from their district. She didn't recognize the third, a burly man, too big for his suit, a man with a Yankee accent.

She knew the reason for this visit. James Meredith was trying to register as the first colored student at the University of Mississippi. Governor Barnett (with Will's help) had blocked him every way from Sunday. There had been one scene in front of the TV cameras where the Governor, before handing Meredith a fancy proclamation denying him admission, glanced around the group, all white except for the young colored man, and said, "Now which one of you is Mr. Meredith?" Didn't the governor have a terrific sense of humor, the newspapers wrote the next day.

The men in Will's office had not closed the door and, as their voices grew louder, Velma quit typing to listen. The Yankee man said, "Barnett is trying to start a war over this. You've got to stop him."

She heard Will reply — quieter, soothing.

Barnett had asked all right-thinking Mississippians to go to Oxford and fight for the state's sovereign rights. He wasn't the worst. One supporter, a former general, went on the radio telling people to pack their tents and skillets and surround the campus to prevent Meredith's registration. This was not a skirmish; this was war. As the governor's personal attorney, Will went back and forth between him and the federal government, trying to keep the peace.

The words "Sovereign rights" were code for "Don't let that smart-alecky Negro register," but the Fifth Circuit in New Orleans threatened to fine Barnett ten thousand dollars for every day he delayed Meredith's registration. Ten thousand dollars of the governor's personal money. To Velma, watching from the sidelines, unless Barnett and his cronies convinced enough people to head up to Oxford and fight, the young man would be a student after all.

Hadn't the country already fought a war to settle this? In southern Mississippi where Velma was from, there hadn't been a lot of colored people, but her church preached love for all God's children, and she took that to mean not just the white ones. The hate-filled talk she overheard these days bothered her, especially coming from Will, who, outside of Mr. Pat, was still the most honorable man she knew.

More and more of the office's time was taken up by the segregation troubles. Will also represented the city of Jackson and, when the federal government ordered the public pools integrated, closed them instead. Swimming wasn't a right, it was a privilege, Will argued, and if colored people insisted on swimming with whites, that privilege could be withdrawn.

Now no one, colored or white, got to swim. Velma didn't swim, she'd never learned, but thought it a pity during these hot summers for young people not to be able to take a cooling dip unless they were rich enough to belong to a country club. Anybody could swim in the Pearl River, but the swift water was filled with snags and cottonmouths. Children drowned there every summer. On the other hand, she also thought it a shame that colored people insisted on swimming in white pools when they had a perfectly good lake of their own out by the zoo.

The phone on her desk rang. "Hughes & Blair," she said.

"The Attorney General for Mr. Will Hughes."

The Attorney General was the President's brother. Robert Kennedy was on the line. Velma could hardly speak for excitement. "Just one moment." She buzzed Will, two short and one long, meaning, Emergency. He left the men in his office and came out to take the call.

"Bobby Kennedy." Velma mouthed with her hand over the receiver.

"Yes, Mr. Attorney General," Will said.

The voice on the other end was loud and nasal. Will held the phone out from his ear and Velma picked up a broad Boston accent on the other end. "You've got to put a stop to it."

"We're trying, sir. No sir, we don't want violence either." Will gave Velma an exasperated look. "The Governor will go on the radio again this afternoon. Yes, sir, we're drafting his speech now."

The Attorney General barked something Velma didn't catch.

"Yes sir, he'll be more conciliatory this time."

Velma heard, "The President is counting on you."

Will said, "We're doing our best." He hung up.

"The President is counting on *you*." Velma spoke in wonder.

Will's expression was wry. "The President doesn't have to deal with Ross Barnett." He went back into his office and the voices rose again.

Reasoning with Barnett must not have worked. The next day, the president sent five hundred U.S. Marshalls to protect James Meredith. That night, three thousand rioters surrounded the Ole Miss campus. A journalist and a bystander were killed, and three hundred people injured. The papers called it The Battle of Oxford.

"Could have been worse." Will rushed by Velma the following morning, face grim. "Much worse."

All day, the media phoned wanting to talk to Will Hughes. Velma fielded calls from *The New York Times* and from network television. One man, impatient at not being able to understand her soft country accent, accused Velma of trying to put something over on him. She felt insulted. Everyone she'd grown up with talked this way and understood each other perfectly.

The town of Oxford was occupied by federal troops, and in spite of the chaos, Meredith did register. According to what Velma read, he peacefully attended classes, escorted by federal marshals. The university did not collapse. Ross Barnett ordered the flag in front of the governor's mansion flown at half-staff to mourn the "invasion" of his state.

The office settled back into the business of law, but the troubles simmered on. Two years after the Meredith business, the national papers phoned again. Three civil rights workers had disappeared in Neshoba County. Velma heard Will tell them that those boys were probably hiding down in Cuba. Then their bodies were dug out of an earthen dam, where they'd been buried after being shot, with the almost certain cooperation of the Neshoba County sheriff. Velma saw how upset Will got, but he told the media those boys had no business being in Mississippi in the first place. One of them had been from Meridian, but Velma did not remind him of this.

The Neshoba County murders happened during what the papers called Freedom Summer, when Negro and white volunteers flooded the state with volunteers. They were here, they claimed, to educate and register colored voters. Will's oldest daughter Helen came to the office. She and her father had a loud argument and Velma heard the young woman say, "We are the shame of the nation."

Velma quit typing to eavesdrop. "We want to go into the poorer neighborhoods and teach literacy," Helen said.

A silence, then Will Hughes' voice: "By poor do you mean colored?"

Helen's voice. "Some of them, maybe."

"I absolutely forbid it. Those neighborhoods are not safe and it is not appropriate for a white woman to be there."

"But it's where people live who need to learn to read and write."

"That's my final word." Spoken in Will Hughes' final voice. "And I will ask you, for once, not to go against my will."

Helen was a grown woman with children of her own, but here she was, still seeking approval from her father. Velma understood: Will Hughes had that kind of gravitational pull. The young woman came flying out of his office, hurling words at Velma as she left. "I hope *you* don't feel the way he does."

In truth, Velma wasn't sure how she felt except she didn't want to go against Will. Most people she knew felt the way he did—segregation was the South's way of life, and outsiders shouldn't come in trying to change things. The coloreds had been happy until these agitators worked them up. The whole business was part of a communist conspiracy. Everything about integration, according to the papers, was part of a plot to take over the country: "Better dead than Red; Love it or Leave it."

You didn't want to be caught disagreeing, so Velma listened politely when people spoke about the troubles and kept her mouth shut. At night, especially after the murders down in Neshoba County, she got on her knees and prayed for the bad times to end. God was silent.

102

In frozen January, Knox III called while Lillian enjoyed her second cup of coffee. She picked up the wall phone in the kitchen.

"The hotel caught fire," he said.

"Oh, my God."

"Gone before the fire department could get there."

"Gone? What do you mean 'gone'?"

"Burned to the ground."

"Where's Ernestine?"

"She's on the train, headed for New Orleans. I'm going to Meridian to try and catch her."

Lillian hung up and turned to Bessie. "I swear I am going to quit answering this telephone. The hotel caught fire."

Bessie's eyes got big. "Lord help us."

"Burned down before the fire department could get there."

"What'll Miss Ernestine do?"

"I have to drive up there, Bessie. You feed Mr. Hughes his supper if I don't get back."

She telephoned Will at the office.

"It was only a matter of time," he said. "The place was a fire trap."

She lost her temper, which she almost never did openly. "We're talking about my home, Will, the place where I grew up. It is all Ernestine has."

"Which doesn't change the facts."

"Knox has only been gone six months. Try and have a little compassion."

"Your sister couldn't possibly keep that place going by herself. With Knox alive, they barely broke even."

"She wasn't even there," Lillian said. "She was on her way to New Orleans."

They used to joke, back in the days when they still shared jokes, that Ernestine spent the winter visiting for free the people who paid to stay at the hotel during the summer.

Lillian met Knox III and Ernestine at the hotel. It was worse than she had pictured. Everything was gone, the family wing, Warm Part, Cold Part, Annex, even the office and Pavilion. All that remained were brick chimneys rising out of the ashes, the well house, and the swimming pool. Lillian walked through the still warm ashes, picking up bits of broken china.

Ernestine had her photograph taken by a man from *The Clarion Ledger*, standing in the ruins in her good coat and hat, next to Aladdin, the hotel collie. The photographer did not invite Lillian to be in the picture.

While Ernestine comforted the servants, telling them it wasn't their fault that the pipes froze, Lillian kept thinking of everything they'd lost: Great Aunt Thelma's crazy quilt in the hall outside the dining room; Ernestine's long strand of amber beads, each as big as a bird's egg; the enormous grand piano in the entrance hall; the family silver; Knox's architectural sketches; Karl Wolfe's portrait of Maude, the one Leland couldn't bear to look at. Every memory of her first twenty-five years, wiped away.

January had been fiercely cold. Ellis said the two guests staying for the winter had used an electric heater in their bathroom. A towel or curtain might have caught fire. No one was sure. Ellis noticed flames on the roof over the kitchen when he came back from taking Ernestine to the train. Below, in the kitchen, Johnny Tucker didn't even realize until Ellis told him. Between them, they managed to get the hoses hooked up, and then discovered the pipes were frozen. By that time, it was too late to save anything.

People cried and hugged. Lillian wept in the arms of Parthenia, Flora May, Ellis and Preston, and cried harder when she realized she would no longer see these people she had known and loved all her life.

Ernestine stayed with Knox III. They would need to find her an apartment, buy clothes, and get furniture. There was an insurance policy, but not nearly enough to rebuild. All Ernestine had left was the land.

What Lillian needed was a strong drink and somebody to share a good cry with. Somebody like Faye. After Faye's funeral, Will refused to speak to James, so she didn't see her brother as often. Jimbo said his father was dating a divorced teller at the Canton Bank. Knox was dead and now the hotel in ashes. Lillian felt life was being peeled away. She had the children, of course, but they were headed out into worlds of their own. She wanted someone to *be* a child with again, people who remembered how much she had loved pancakes, or that her other nickname was "Me, too" because of not wanting to be left out. No one remembered that long-ago Lillian.

Back in Jackson the next day, she stopped by Knox III's house for a drink. Sitting in their plain, comfortable living room, she started to cry. "I can't bear the thought of everything being lost."

Ernestine refused to join in the misery. "We must bear it and move on."

"If only the servants had thought to save something. Your jewelry or the silver."

Ernestine stood, straightening the jacket of the one good suit she had left. "They were only things, Lillian. Knox III and I plan to look at apartments tomorrow. I don't know how much I'll have, but it should be enough to rent a small place in the Belhaven district."

Lillian got up. Her sister's rising indicated either time to go or time to stop complaining. She could not imagine Ernestine reduced to a small apartment, but her sister looked steadfast. Maybe Will was right and Ernestine felt secretly relieved. Running Creekmore had been a burden she was happy to lay down. Not that she would have ever done so voluntarily. The place needed to be destroyed for her to let go.

Lillian wondered if that's how she was, desperately holding onto Will.

103

In the summer of 1963, Velma kept another of her resolutions. She marked off an area four by twelve feet in the sunniest part of the back yard, well away from the pine trees. She lifted the sod off in squares and stacked it, then dug down a good twelve inches. Should be eighteen, but she'd become a stranger to labor. Twelve inches left her with blisters. Not to mention what happened to her back and legs from the squatting.

A new neighbor had moved in next door and she saw him watching from a distance. The name on his mailbox said, "Withers," but Velma hadn't introduced herself and did not appreciate being noticed.

For the next week, she could hardly straighten from the stiffness. Will asked if she was all right. Velma suspected he never wished to hear anything less than a hundred percent, so that's the answer she gave.

In straight rows, she used string to line them up, Velma planted greens, carrots, lettuce, and onions. Too late for lettuce; it would bolt in the hot sun, but the turnip greens thrived, their dark green leaves casting shadows over the feathery carrot tops. She wished she'd thought to plant tomatoes. Next year.

This Saturday morning, she pulled weeds from around the greens, wondering what Mama and Papa would think of this effort at farming.

She stood with a grunt and noticed Mr. Withers again. Closer this time, leaning on the fence between their properties. Velma had heard from the woman on the other side that the man was a widower. Probably lonely, but the way he stared made Velma feel uneasy. If he wasn't a peeping Tom, he was the next thing. Seemed like she couldn't go in the yard to hang up clothes without him popping out his back door. She wondered if he looked in her windows at night.

He spoke. "They killed that nigger last night."

Velma had seen the paper. A man named Medgar Evers, the head of the local N.A.A.C.P., had been murdered in his driveway. "It's terrible." She spoke without looking up from her weeding.

"Got what he deserved."

Velma's back, already stiff, went rigid. "No one deserves to be murdered." She began weeding down the other side, keeping her face hidden under her hat. What a despicable person.

"Something happened to your lettuce," Mr. Withers said.

"I know."

"Ought to spray."

She didn't reply. She had no intention of spraying.

"Maybe put out some traps."

Including a big one for you.

"I could help you with that."

"No, thank you."

"Just trying to be neighborly. No need to get all high hat."

"I don't mean to be rude, Mr. Withers, but I prefer to garden in silence."

"Not right, a young woman like you living alone."

He wasn't the only one who thought that. People at church made similar comments. Velma smiled and ignored them. "I manage just fine."

"Anything could happen."

Was that a threat? "I'm not afraid. I keep a loaded gun next to my bed." This was a complete fabrication, but the words made an impression on Mr. Withers.

"A gun?"

"If so much as a branch moves outside my window—" Velma straightened her arms and made her hands into a pistol pointed at Mr. Wither's unpleasant face.

He backed away. "You better watch out. You could kill yourself in your sleep."

"Not a chance," Velma said. "I'm a country girl. I know all about guns."

Mr. Withers went inside his house, grumbling under his breath.

That should take care of any itch he had to look in her windows. Velma wished she were the kind of girl she claimed to be, like Annie Oakley in that movie. She ought to get a gun. She knew how to shoot. Maybe she would. Pretending she had a gun made her feel braver. She wasn't afraid of Mr. Withers anymore. A lesson there.

Poor Medgar Evers. She'd seen him on TV, talking about how colored and white people could live side by side. The paper said he had a wife and young children. Will didn't think colored people should be on television. He'd quit watching the Ed Sullivan Show when Mr. Sullivan kissed that colored singer Pearl Bailey, and Ed Sullivan had been his favorite show.

Velma only wanted peace. She agreed with poor dead Medgar Evers about that. Too much hate poisoned people's minds. She put away her gardening tools and went inside.

So far, she'd kept two of her resolutions. She'd joined a group at the Presbyterian church and taken up crocheting again. The nice ladies there invited her to their knitting group, but it met during the day while she was working. She looked at the pink, blue and white squares she'd made. When she had enough, she'd connect them and make a throw. It was called that because you threw it over yourself while you watched TV.

Time heals all wounds. That's what Velma told herself when the pangs of loneliness struck. Pang was a good word for it. Loneliness felt like a dagger in the chest. Not an actual dagger, she had no idea how that felt, but a stab of pain that left her aching and hollow. If she got up and kept busy, it went away.

104

To Lillian's satisfaction, the arguments over Sunday dinners went on. In June of 1963, when the local head of the N.A.A.C.P. was shot dead in his driveway, Will claimed that the organization was nothing but a tool of communism.

Helen said, "The words of a bigot."

Lillian interrupted. "Please try to respect your father when you're sitting at his table." Being married, Helen could no longer run to her room crying. She settled for stony silence, which seemed to suit everyone.

In November, an unknown assassin shot President Kennedy. Lillian found Bessie crying in front of the kitchen TV. Her own eyes stung watching poor Mrs. Kennedy in that blood-soaked pink suit, which Lillian would have taken off in two seconds.

At dinner on Sunday, Helen said the workmen remodeling their house told her Kennedy got what he deserved. "I don't think I can live in this place," she said.

Jack looked up from his slice of Sunday roast, alarmed.

Will said, "The man had a lot of wrong-headed ideas, but he didn't deserve to be shot."

Lillian admired Jackie Kennedy's funeral outfit and how straight and staunch she looked behind that black veil. It was all a terrible pity. She didn't agree with the late president's politics, but he had been such a good-looking man. Now the country had Lyndon Johnson, who looked like a hound dog. He reminded Lillian of Ross Barnett, all country joviality on the surface and probably mean as a snake underneath. Johnson's wife Lady Bird always looked a little beat down.

Helen had started back to school at a local college. Ridiculous for a married woman with three children, but Helen claimed it kept her brain from rotting. And she *was* smart—even Will's sister Frances, who was smarter than anybody, said the girl had brains. She told the family she'd signed up for a writing course with Eudora Welty. "Write about what?" Lillian wanted to know. Thinking privately, it was a good thing Miss Welty was known for the writing because no man was ever going to marry her.

Helen got pregnant again and the fourth child was a boy. She and Jack must be carrying on like rabbits. Helen named this one William Calhoun Hughes after Will, which didn't impress him one whit. No male counted except the son Lillian had failed to produce.

Word got back that Helen had been seen at Tougaloo, the Negro college, attending a Joan Baez concert. Will delegated to Lillian the job of passing along his disapproval.

"What do you mean, 'I was seen'?" Helen's voice indignant on the other end of the telephone. "Why shouldn't I be there. It was beautiful—Negro and white people linking arms and singing *We shall Overcome*. It's the way things ought to be."

There was no reasoning with the girl.

When those three young men were murdered down in Neshoba County, Will claimed that they weren't missing; they were hiding. He and Helen argued until the bodies were dug out of a landfill. Helen said, "What now? Are you going to claim they killed themselves?" Will admitted the murders were a terrible business, but things would be a lot better for everyone if these outside agitators stayed out of Mississippi. Both of them talking loud enough for Bessie to hear every word.

"Manners, please." Lillian nodded toward the kitchen.

105

Bridge this afternoon with tuna fish sandwiches and Bessie's homemade cheese straws. Lillian and her partner Peggy had won. With two and a half drinks in her, Lillian felt better than good.

Bessie moved over and made room for her to empty the ashtrays into the garbage can under the sink. Both of them had gotten heavier over the years, but Bessie had her beat by about a hundred pounds. The cook's bottom lip protruded, fat with snuff, sulking because of the extra work of a luncheon.

On the porch, Lillian wiped the drink rings off the glass-top table and shoved it back under the window. She and Will hadn't played bridge together since before the war. She'd always been the better player, and Will hadn't enjoyed being beaten by a woman. Lillian bumped the bamboo chairs into place with her hip. Will only played cards with his men friends now. She played bridge with her friends on Mondays and Wednesdays, and canasta on Saturdays. Will hinted that she should play less often and have fewer drinks, but she ignored him. They had lived with the agreement for something like fourteen years now. She no longer worried about the finer points. For a few hours on card days, people found her charming.

"Hey." Helen appeared from the hall.

"Look what the cat dragged in." The girl had gotten too thin. In Lillian's opinion, people who lost weight were usually up to something, but she kept quiet. Ten years after marrying Jack, her oldest daughter was very much her own person: Mother of four, chairman of the Junior League's Carnival Ball, her husband making good money — Lillian had no complaints.

In May, Helen had graduated from college in a robe and tassel, grinning like the cat that ate the canary. She didn't look quite so pleased today.

"I need to tell you something," Helen said.

Lillian waited. Nothing good followed a sentence like that.

"I've decided to go away for a little while."

Every muscle in Lillian's body went tense. "What do you mean 'go away'?"

"I'm worn out. I want to go somewhere different and think things over."

Alarm bells. Lillian tried to keep her voice calm. "Who are you doing this going away with and for how long?"

"Nobody, and I don't know."

"You can't just leave without telling us where you're going or when you'll be back."

"Yes, I can."

Lillian saw red. "Are you saying—" She couldn't believe the nerve of the girl. "—you want to leave your marriage?"

"For a while." Helen looked out the window and at the floor, a sure sign she was lying.

Lillian felt the birthmark on her forehead light up. "I won't let you throw away everything I worked for."

"*You* worked for?"

Not the way she'd meant it to come out, but holding a marriage together and raising the girls as if nothing were wrong had been damned hard. If Helen left Jack, instead of being the proud wife of Will Hughes, Lillian would become the mother of the woman who deserted her children.

Anger only made her oldest daughter more stubborn. Lillian took a breath. "You have a husband who loves you and four beautiful children. You have plenty of money. Don't walk away as if that's nothing. I won't let you do this to yourself."

"I came over here to tell you, not to ask permission."

When Helen was twelve, Lillian had pulled a hand back to slap her, only to have the girl grab both of her wrists. By then, she was as tall as Lillian, and stronger. Her look said: *you will never hit me again.* Today, in the face of this outrage, Lillian couldn't find the air or the words she needed. The girl was too big to beat and too stubborn to listen. She tried another tack: "What about the children? You cannot mean to leave those precious children."

"I'm not leaving them forever, and it's not as if they'll be orphans. They have their daddy and Doreen, and Jack's parents. They have you and Daddy."

Lillian realized she and Will hadn't been ideal grandparents, not the way Jack's parents were—taking the grandchildren on weekends, filling the backyard with a swing set and sandbox. Lillian was too impatient to spend a lot of time around small children, and all children made Will nervous. "Watch the corner of that table," he'd yell. "Don't let her put that in her mouth."

"What about Jack? Have you given any thought to what you're doing to him?"

"He's very sad."

"*Sad?*" Lillian stood on her tiptoes, straining to be as tall as her daughter. "I'm surprised he hasn't beaten a little sense into you. Can't you see?" Pleading now, taking Helen by her arms. "You are ruining your life?"

Helen pulled away. "I may be, but I have to go."

Lillian recognized defeat. Nothing she said had ever moved this child. It was sickening, her certainty, the blindness to consequences, believing life kept giving you choices. "You may be book smart, Helen, but you have the common sense of a flea."

Helen stared at her without speaking, the way she had as a teenager, boring a hole somewhere between Lillian's eyes.

The back door slammed. When the girls were small, the one threat that always worked was fear of their father's wrath. "You'll have to tell your father."

"I will."

From the sunroom, Lillian listened to the murmur of Helen and Will in the living room. She couldn't make out the words, but Will did not sound angry; he actually sounded sympathetic. The traitor. Will was probably envious. Maude would be twenty-one and graduating from Mississippi Southern this year. He'd said he would leave when she started college and he hadn't. Maybe the agreement meant he'd leave when she finished.

Hearing their voices, Helen explaining and Will commiserating, made Lillian want to smash something. She considered putting the heavy ashtray through the glass top of the table, except she'd be left with nowhere to play bridge and a mess. She hated her daughter for casually discarding a life she would give her eyeteeth for, and she recognized envy in the mix of feelings. She would never have that kind of nerve.

106

Helen left on the first of July and did not return. In November, Jack sued her for desertion and got custody of the children. She lived in Miami now, attending graduate school, returning every few months to see the children, her hair long and straight, wearing no makeup, handing out large helpings of liberal opinion at the dinner table. A year after the departure, she married a Jewish lawyer. Turned out, this was the man she'd left town with, a fact everyone in Jackson apparently knew before Lillian.

Outrage upon outrage. The girl had no shame. That she left for her mother. Lillian read scorn and pity behind every false smile at the grocery store. Once she'd held her head high, smiling down on less fortunate women. Since Helen ran off, she shopped early and hoped to see no one she knew. The support of her close friends was almost harder to take: "A crying shame." "Don't know how she could do that to you."

She couldn't shape her grown children's lives, but Lillian made a vow to take more control of her own. She and her bridge-playing buddies, Hilda, Dimple, and Frances, planned a trip to Mexico. Leland provided the money and Lillian lied, telling Will she'd saved it, bit by bit, out of her weekly allowance.

"I must be giving you too much," he said.

107

Being away made Lillian feel like a girl again. She forgot about Helen and Will, or any other troubles waiting at home. They had booked two rooms at the *Gran Hotel de Ciudad Mexico*. Lillian stood under the soaring stained-glass ceiling and rode the gilded elevator, amazed to be here. Mornings were spent shopping or visiting Mexico City's museums (Lillian tolerated museums only because at the end you were rewarded by a gift shop.) At the Artisans Market on the first day, she bargained in her garbled Spanish: "*Quanto est?*" They bought thin Mexican silver bracelets to remember the trip by. She posted colorful cards to April and Maude. In the afternoons, the four of them played bridge and drank fruit-flavored cocktails by the hotel pool, then napped. Each evening's dinner turned into a celebration.

The first night, they ate in one of the city's oldest restaurants, the walls colorful with paintings and posters of bullfights. Dimple reached into the centerpiece, arm tinkling with silver bracelets, and plucked out a hibiscus. "You and that red dress need a flower." She tucked it behind Lillian's ear.

Lillian took out her compact to check the effect. A scalding memory stared back: Waiting at the train station for Will to return from the war, and seeing Sylvia emerge in a red suit with a flame-colored hibiscus in her black hair. She snapped the compact shut and told her friends the story they'd never heard: about the woman Will brought home from Hawaii, with her swinging hips and big bosom. The way she'd fastened onto Lillian's husband like a leech. They were horrified and sympathetic, which was the wonderful thing about friends.

The waiter recommended *tequila sangritas*. Two tall, slim shot glasses appeared at each place, one filled with tequila, the other with a spicy tomato juice. He indicated that they should sip first from the tequila, then cool the fire with a swallow of juice.

With dinner, they ordered sangria. As an entree, the waiter suggested the restaurant's specialty, an authentic Mexican goat dish. Dimple tasted her portion and made a face. "Are we sure it's not *perro*?"

"Are you saying we're eating dog?" Hilda looked sick.

The waiter grew upset. The women assured him they were teasing, but he did not understand teasing. He fetched the chef, a round man in a towering white hat. *"No perro,"* he insisted. *"Birria, no perro,"* followed by a flood of Spanish. When both were safely out of earshot, the women fell apart laughing.

They finished the meal with a bottle of *mescal con gusano*, toasting themselves with shots of the strong, smoky stuff. At the bottom, the *maguey* worm floated like a fat, gray slug.

"Whose turn is it?" Dimple said. "Last shot has to swallow the worm."

Frances and Hilda shook their heads no. After drinking tequila and eating her first goat, Lillian felt indomitable. She threw her head back and tipped the bottle. As her friends shrieked, she let the worm slide down her throat in a final gush of liquid. She blinked from the fiery taste and tried not to retch. People at other tables cheered.

Cleaning her face that night, the room tilting around her, she laughed. "I keep seeing that poor chef's face: *'No perro, No perro.*" She and Frances fell on the bed cackling.

Lying in the dark, with a foot on the floor to keep the room from spinning, Lillian listened to Frances snore, a melody compared with Will. She felt happy. With no one around to criticize or silently judge her, she saw what a burden that had become, and how weightless and free she felt away from it.

Early morning. She awoke with a dreadful case of *tourista*.

"Probably the fruit in that sangria," Frances said. "Or that disgusting worm."

From the bathroom, Lillian groaned. "Please do not say the word worm."

Frances fetched Dimple, who had the most Spanish, and Dimple went to the *farmacia* for medicine. No one else got ill. Hilda said it must be the fresh pineapple Lillian insisted on buying from a street vendor. They had warned her.

Lillian clutched her stomach. "Who could resist?" The pineapple had been the most succulent and delicious of her life.

For two days, she thought she would die. On the third, feeling better, she joined the girls for a last evening at *Hosteria de Santo Domingo*. With another hibiscus in her hair, Lillian was able to look, without blanching, at the dishes of *Chile en Nogada* set in front of them. This was the house specialty: poblano chilies filled with ground meat, fruits, spices, and topped by a walnut cream sauce and pomegranate seeds.

"The three colors of the Mexican flag." Dimple said. "Green chili, white nut sauce, and pomegranate for red."

Everything tasted marvelous. The girls said how skinny Lillian looked and claimed they all should have gotten sick.

Last Christmas, Leland had presented her with another tiny share of an oil well. This one brought in a hundred and eighty-nine dollars a month. Together with the monthly hundred from his first gift, Lillian felt free.

The four of them talked about going to Europe next year and maybe to Japan the year after that. Will might not travel, but that didn't mean Lillian had to sit home like a sick cat. She had friends who found her cute and funny. She had places to go and money to spend. She might not have the marriage she'd imagined, but the old Lillian was still alive and well, ready to make her own happiness.

108

Christmas 1967. No more Creekmore Hotel, but the three girls were home, which gave Lillian a reason to feel festive. Helen and Eric, the Jewish lawyer she'd run away with, were staying in the back bedroom. Prepared to despise the man, Lillian instead found him charming, filled with compliments on her cooking and the comforts of the house. He called her "Lillian" and addressed Bessie as "Mrs. Johnson," a peculiarity Lillian pointedly ignored.

The grandchildren were with their father for the holidays, but Helen carried on with her laughter and stories as if she hadn't destroyed her reputation and shamed the family. April would be here for breakfast, along with small, tidy Walton, a husband who looked so much like her, they could be siblings. No children yet, but April said they were "trying," a picture Lillian would rather not entertain. Maude, darling still-plump Maude, slept in the bedroom across the hall from Helen and Eric. She planned to marry the tall country boy she'd brought home at Thanksgiving. Lillian's youngest would never fit into Helen and April's wedding gown. Lillian would need to find her something with an empire waist to disguise what lay beneath.

Christmas morning. "Christmas Gift." she shouted into the kitchen.

Bessie looked startled.

"You're supposed to say 'Christmas Gift' back," Lillian told her. For one day, please God, let them be a family.

She'd bought frozen, farm-raised quail and Bessie had arrived early to make the traditional Christmas breakfast: grits, quail with gravy, biscuits, and wild plum jelly.

"Does this mean Bessie doesn't get a Christmas?" Helen, up early and trying to cause trouble.

"Bessie will have Christmas with her nieces when she gets home tonight." Lillian spoke brightly, holding the coffee pot out to Eric. "She doesn't mind one bit — do you, Bessie?"

"No ma'am."

Not when she saw the bonus check Will had for her.

Bessie frowned at the quail, pink and naked in their Styrofoam tray. "No meat on these birds."

They did look puny compared to the ones Lillian remembered from the hotel. She got out the big skillet and used flat irons to press the birds. In the end, nothing tasted the way she remembered. Maybe it was her dicey stomach. Everyone else picked around the tiny bones with relish and sopped the gravy with Bessie's biscuits.

"With farmed birds, at least there's no birdshot to worry about," April said.

Helen announced that she'd become a vegetarian and took only grits and biscuits.

Lillian gave her daughter a sour look. Anything to be different. Breakfast over, it was present-opening time.

As it had been for years now, Will's gift to Lillian was an enormous box of chocolates.

Maude made yum sounds as Lillian unwrapped it. "Two layers."

Lillian tried to maintain her Christmas smile. Velma had been sent to buy this candy, no doubt, along with some trinket for each of the girls. Will's office wife and who knew what else. Velma also chose their birthday gifts. Lillian wasn't sure anymore if anger caused her aching gut or the other way around. She watched as the others opened her gifts: cashmere sweaters for the girls, a new uniform and orthopedic shoes for Bessie. Will made grateful noises over his tie, handkerchiefs, a leather desk set from Lillian and, from Helen, a history book he would never read. Lillian thanked April for the vase, Helen for the silk scarf, and Maude for the crystal earrings.

The day felt small and empty, with hours to go before the end. The pressure to get Christmas dinner on the table, with Will growing surlier as the clock crept past noon. Lillian in the kitchen, side-by-side with Bessie, preparing the sardine canapé appetizer, making sure the turkey was cooked through, the dressing moist, and the gravy lump-free. The side dishes: a sweet potato casserole with marshmallows, green beans with almonds, Bessie's rolls. For dessert, the two traditional cakes waited on the sideboard, chocolate and coconut. After dinner, an endless clean up. If Will refused to wait until Bessie finished the kitchen before returning to his office, Lillian would have to drive her across town.

Her stomach hurt like hell. Lillian pulled the top off her box of chocolates. What a dispiriting gift, this empty gesture from a husband who couldn't be bothered. Everyone laughed. Eric must have told a joke. Lillian missed it. Will and the new husband pretended to like each other, acting as if they hadn't been on opposing sides of practically every civil rights case in the state. *More empty gestures.*

Lillian stared at the candy, each bonbon nestled in its pleated paper. Drugstore chocolate for a wife who must pretend to be grateful. The candy's glossy brown surfaces mocked her: Eat us and get fatter; he'll like you even less. Looking at the stuff made her gut ache worse. With a sharp thumbnail, Lillian cut through the top of each chocolate, moving left to right, exposing caramel, nuts, pastel creams.

Maude's eyes grew wide. "Mama, what are you doing?"

The room grew silent.

Lillian looked up, ignoring Will's frown. He probably wondered when she'd found time to drink this early. "Seeing what's inside."

The day ended and they lay in their twin beds.

"You should have told me you didn't want candy." Will's voice sounded stiff.

"Sorry." Lillian did not make the effort to sound sincere. The heating pad wasn't helping her stomach.

"Have you been drinking?" The accusatory tone.

"No." She flipped the pages of *Redbook*. Next year she wouldn't try to make so much of Christmas. The past wasn't something you could uncork when you needed a swig of happiness.

She looked at him in the next bed, nose in *Time* magazine. Why hadn't he left her? Maude was out of school, but he showed no sign of budging. Perhaps he was content with the nice house, good meals, the wife he could ignore.

Would she mind now if he did leave? She would be fifty-nine in February, not counting the two years she'd subtracted. He'd broken her heart. Faye broke it again by killing herself. The hotel burned and Helen ran off. Lillian didn't have enough heart left to break.

109

The pain in Lillian's gut woke her. She turned the heating pad up a notch, listening to Will in the bathroom. He never whistled or sang, just went about his business: running water, scrape of razor, shower, silence, flush. She held her breath against the pain.

She would not mention it. Wait until he left and call the doctor. Will hated illness. He said the smell of a hospital made him queasy. The sick made him sick. Life came filled with things one would rather not do but did anyway. Lillian gritted her teeth.

How many years had she lived this way, with a man who didn't like her when she was well and would be repulsed by any illness? Fourteen, fifteen? She hurt too much to count. Lie here and take shallow breaths until he left for the office.

"Mama."

It was Maude, plump Maude, now almost twenty-three. She would never be as pretty as Helen or as smart as April, but she had always been Lillian's favorite.

"What, sweetie?"

"I'm heading back to Hattiesburg."

"Drive safely, darling." The pain drove a hook into Lillian's stomach and she stifled a gasp.

Will stood outside the bathroom knotting his tie.

Lillian tried to smile at her daughter. "Loved having all my girls home."

At the doctor's office, Lillian writhed under Tom Andrews's probing fingers. Her gynecologist looked worried. "I'm going to put you in the hospital for some tests. Let Jim Hodges have a look."

"Hospital?" Lillian tried to sit up. She didn't want to go in the hospital. Fear gave her chest a hollow knock. Not just a stomachache then. Jim Hodges was a surgeon.

110

On the last Saturday of 1967, Velma held her breath as she painted her toenails. She did her fingernails and toes on Saturday night, cleaning off the old polish and carefully applying a new coat for Sunday and the coming week. She found these small rituals comforting. Friday nights were for dinner or a movie with two single secretaries from another firm. Clean sheets and fresh towels on Saturday morning, plus grocery shopping for the week. She liked getting to the store before the crowds. Laundry washed and hung on the line outside unless it rained. She preferred the smell of sun-dried sheets. Church on Sunday and lunch after with a group from Sunday school. Lingerie washed and hung to dry on a folding rack in the front bathroom. Hair washed and set on Thursdays when Marie kept the Beauty Barn open late. If she slept in a hairnet, she could make it last a week.

Yesterday at lunch Garnett had looked across the drugstore table. "You get better looking every year."

Velma shook her head in denial.

"You do. You're tall and your figure is good. You have beautiful eyes and you're the sweetest person alive. Any man would be lucky to have you."

Velma took a bite of her toasted pimento cheese, refusing compliments along with the idea of a man.

She made Garnett laugh describing the men who approached her at church. "They're either fat or bald, and every one of them thinks he's Clark Gable." They got her phone number from the church directory and called asking her out. Velma never accepted, knowing as she refused, she was once again making the choice to remain single. Will Hughes had ruined her for other men.

Velma finished painting the toes on her left foot and put cotton between each one. She spent every weekday working side by side with the only man she'd ever cared for, often close enough to feel the heat of his body. To her, the feelings had become a private sacrament—eternal and everlasting, felt but unspoken. The Baptist preacher would be horrified, which was why such thoughts stayed safely inside her head, and she turned all talk of men into a joke.

Forty-three now. Maturity became her. She had learned how to dress. She bought tailored clothes, suits with soft blouses, the coats buttoning nicely over her bosom and showing off her waist. She kept her hair shorter than she'd once worn it, and used an ash brown rinse to "even it out," which was what Marie called covering the gray. Already going gray.

Mama had noticed the change. "You've turned into one of those city girls."

Thinking about Mama made the brush shake, and Velma set it back in the bottle of polish. Her mother had died last year. She did not seem sick when Velma went down the month before, but she had looked thinner, skin almost transparent, pushing away her daughter's worry and the offer of a city doctor.

"She gave out," Aunt Orrie said at the funeral. Country people didn't go to specialists for fancy operations; they gave out. Papa had passed two years before. Velma missed her father, but losing her mother was the greater sorrow, a cave in her chest that could not be filled. No farm to go back to now. True to his word, Papa had left the place to Orrie's son Drew. Drew and his wife Pearl would welcome Velma, but it wasn't home anymore. She was an orphan.

Each morning she read a page from a book of daily devotionals and at night before bed, a chapter of the Bible. She prayed for tranquility. Some nights she found herself praying to the small photograph of her mother instead of to God, asking for a comfort she couldn't name.

She had made a life of habits, moving from one small task to another — cleaning out the refrigerator on Tuesdays, doing the ironing on Thursday nights in front of the television. The days, weeks, and years flowed by, without Will of course, but also without sin. If she couldn't manage pure thoughts, good habits might get her through.

She finished painting the last toe and screwed the cap on the tiny bottle of "Love That Red." The doorbell rang. She hobbled into the living room, holding her toes up to keep the wet polish from smearing. She didn't like for the doorbell to ring at night. It had better not be that old man from next door. Velma peeked around the curtain without turning on the front porch light or the light in the hall.

Will Hughes stood on the small porch, head bent, pinching the bridge of his nose the way he did when he worried.

"Just a minute." She shouted through the door and turned on the outside light. Heart pounding, Velma jerked the cotton from between her toes, shoved on ballet flats, pulled off the nightgown, and pulled on a dress, fluffed her hair, and went to the door. He had probably given up and left.

He hadn't. "Will?"

He looked at her, frowning. "Lillian's sick."

Velma opened the door wider. "I'm so sorry." She regretted spoiling her toenails. "Come in, won't you."

He came, carrying his hat.

Hat in hand, he comes to me, Velma thought, like something out of a novel. She led him into the living room, turning on lamps. She had furnished this room with pieces she loved, adding her mother's curio cabinet after her death. She would not take him to the den, the room where they had — she closed her mind on that. "Please, sit down. Would you like a cup of coffee?"

Will shook his head and didn't sit, but paced from the coffee table with its never-lighted, pine-scented candles, to the wing chair, slipcovered in a darker shade of rosy velvet. "I don't mean sick like a cold. She's in the hospital. They're operating on Monday."

"What do the doctors say?" Velma watched him pace. "Please sit, I'm getting dizzy watching you."

He sank into the velvet chair. "I don't understand what they tell me. I hate being there—in the hospital. They say it's some kind of abdominal blockage. The operation is exploratory."

Exploratory—not a good word. Velma shook her head in sympathy.

"I called Helen and told her to come home. April is in hysterics. Maude's up from Hattiesburg." Will pinched the bridge of his nose again. He was going gray, the blond hair fading almost imperceptibly.

"Would you like a bowl of cereal?" That's what Velma ate when she couldn't think of anything else.

He looked up as if she'd offered salvation. "I would love a bowl of cereal."

Sitting in her kitchen at the yellow Formica table, eating cornflakes with a sliced banana, Velma watched Will revive.

"I feel better already." He pushed away the empty bowl. "I should go home. Thank you for putting up with my troubles."

"Anytime."

Velma saw him to the door. "Please give my best to Lillian."

He didn't take her hand. There was no offer of a kiss. They nodded at one another and she closed the door.

Back in her nightgown, she took out the polish remover and began repairing her spoiled toenails. She felt overheated. Will needed her. When trouble came, and this sounded like serious trouble, he turned to Velma. Nothing to feel guilty about. Not one thing wrong with offering comfort. Our Lord believed in comforting the sufferer. She'd done nothing but lend a sympathetic ear.

From deeper inside, a bubble of hope arose. Velma spoke to herself sternly, but the bubbles popped in her chest like champagne. No stopping it, so she got down on her knees and begged forgiveness. She stayed there until her knees felt thoroughly punished by the bare wooden floor.

111

Lillian came out of the anesthetic as if from under deep water. Peaceful down here, dark green and calm. She would have liked to stay and rest, but she sensed light above and let herself rise to meet it, noticing as she got closer to the surface the way ease and comfort fled. Something felt very wrong. She broke surface into the glare of the recovery room and saw a nurse doing something with a tube. Her body felt gripped by pain. Moving her eyeballs hurt. She must have cried out because the nurse bent closer.

"There, there, Mrs. Hughes. We're back, aren't we? Try and relax."

When Lillian opened her eyes again, they were wheeling her into a room. She saw Will talking to a doctor. Somebody somewhere was screaming, making sleep impossible.

"Can't you do something?" Will's voice. "This is terrible."

"We've given her as much morphine as we dare."

Lillian raised her head, a superhuman effort because of the pain and the noise, but she was that angry. Her voice sounded harsh. "If I don't get a drink in the next two minutes, I'm pulling every damned tube out of my body." She fell back.

A scurrying and murmuring in the room. She didn't care. She'd said her piece and she was proud of it.

"She is in withdrawal," she heard the doctor say. "You do realize your wife drinks a great deal."

Raising her head once more, Lillian looked the man in the eye, or where she supposed his eye would be if she could see straight. In her best voice, the one she saved for rude salespeople, she said, "I am *not* an alcoholic."

112

Will Hughes sat in Velma's kitchen eating corn flakes with sliced banana for the second time in a week. Velma swung between warmth at being the person he turned to, and the suspicion that he chose her because she wasn't family and would keep quiet.

Will said, "They had to give Lillian alcohol in her drip today." He paused, but Velma said nothing. "To calm her down. I'm about at the end of my rope."

"I am so sorry." He had hinted about Lillian's drinking in the days when they exchanged such intimacies, but hadn't spoken of it since. Pride, she suspected. No one in the Hughes family should have such troubles, yet here he was, at her kitchen table discussing his wife's private business. Velma changed the subject. "Are the girls still here?"

Will nodded. "Helen claims we need to get her mother psychiatric help once she's well." Worrying, he pinched the bridge of his nose. "I'm not sure Lillian is going to get well. The doctors have patched her up, but they warned it could happen again."

Velma saw him shudder. "*It.*" Lillian's actual condition remained unnamed.

"Finish your cereal," she said. On her way to the sink with her own bowl, she longed to put a hand on his shoulder, but refrained. She would neither take advantage of his troubles nor indulge in stupid fantasies. For the fourteen years since Will returned to his family, they had been boss and secretary, nothing more. Neither of them mentioned Will's promise to leave Lillian when the children were grown. The children *were* grown and he hadn't left. They exchanged no affectionate glances. There was no accidental touching. Velma made sure of it. In the face of Lillian's illness, she would not allow herself to slip into careless hope. This man suffered, and to feel anything other than pity was a sin God would not soon forget.

"At home I have a bowl of cereal every night," Will said. "Seems like the only thing that tastes right." He picked up his bowl and drank the last of the milk. "I must be reverting to childhood."

At the sink, Velma smiled. From her years of observing the lawyers at Hughes & Blair, in spite of the big voices and swaggering accomplishments, most of the men seemed like large boys.

"With the girls here," Will said, "the house sounds like a nest of magpies. They never stop talking about their mother. They go through every gory detail of the operation. 'We should do this when she's better'. 'No, she needs that.' 'How would *you* know?' April says to Helen. 'You're never here.' At the hospital today, I actually heard April tell her older sister to quit patting Lillian's hand."

Velma made a sympathetic sound.

"Helen wants to fix everything. April gets hysterical and yells. Maude cries and drinks wine."

Velma returned to the table. "Still, you're lucky to have them."

Will captured a last slice of banana with his spoon. "True." His voice sounded tired. "They spell each other at the hospital. Gives me the time to get a little work done."

Putting cream on her face before bed, Velma repeated that line: *Gives me the time to get a little work done.* She loved Will, but like Papa, he lacked empathy. When trouble came, you wanted women around.

113

Lillian knew she wasn't well. By mid-January, out of the hospital and creeping around the house to avoid jarring her stitches, she realized the old Lillian had not come home. There was a new tentativeness — a weakness she saw reflected in her eyes. In the mirror, they stared back at her from some distant place, as if they had gone ahead, and waited there for her without enthusiasm. She was thinner. That felt nice: two weeks in the hospital and down two dress sizes. Will acted sweeter, which was even nicer. He treated her as if she were a package from the butcher shop. If he didn't take care, the wrapping might split and reveal a piece of bloody meat.

Her husband belonged to the baked potato school of anatomy. Humans weren't a sack of skin filled with slimy organs. They were nice and solid, white all the way through. The sight of a bloody nose turned him faint. When Helen was five and came down with a fever, the doctor stopped by one night to give her a shot. The hypodermic needle appeared, the child screamed, and Lillian went hunting for Will to help hold Helen down. She found him hiding behind a chair in the living room.

Will's new kindness lent room for hope. Perhaps the seriousness of her illness made her seem more valuable. He'd turned generous. When she mentioned being smaller, he told her to treat herself to a couple of outfits from Frances Pepper. He had never in his life suggested Lillian spend money, which meant either she was dying or he'd changed. She found herself humming in the mornings after he left for work. Her gut still hurt, but aside from that, she felt closer to happiness.

She wore a new suit to her first card game at Dimple's house, tweed and very country chic. Everyone complimented her slim silhouette, but Lillian heard worry behind the sweet words. A bourbon and water went down okay but tasted awful. The same with lunch. She gave up on eating after a bite or two. The tuna sandwich, no matter how many times she chewed, rumbled inside as if she'd swallowed rocks. She had forgotten how much her friends chattered, gossip being more interesting than cards. A skilled and competitive bridge player, Lillian felt too tired to care. Glad to leave after two rubbers, glad to hang the new suit in the closet, and crawl between the sheets. She groaned in relief. Bessie stuck her big head around the door looking concerned.

"I'm fine, Bessie. It's good to be off my feet."

"I made you some nice boiled custard. It'll go down easy."

"Not right now but thank you. If you'll close the door, I think I'll take a nap. Give Mr. Hughes his dinner, will you?

She still drank black coffee in the mornings. It tasted foul, but she couldn't get up without it—coffee and a couple of Bufferin for her head. The only other thing that felt good, and this was crazy because she'd never liked it, was sherry: tiny sips of cheap sherry. Some days she was surprised to find she'd sipped almost an entire bottle. Will didn't notice—or pretended not to notice.

She hardly ate. When she did, she chewed every bite thirty times. That was her new rule. She would not take a chance on another blockage. She chewed until the food turned to spit and she couldn't remember what she'd put in her mouth.

So, it seemed entirely unfair to wake up one night in mid-February, clammy and sweating, her insides again gripped by pain. She tried to wait it out until daylight, but the agony was too great. Will drove her to the hospital, where she writhed on a gurney waiting for the doctor, and groaned through the prodding and tests until the blessed oblivion of anesthesia.

Hours later? Days? She lay in bed, not daring to open her eyes or move for fear of how much either might hurt. She heard the gasp of air hospital doors make when they open. Padded footsteps. Hands plumping her pillow and feeling her pulse. Lillian squinted. The woman checking the flow on her IV was not one of the younger nurses, not the one she could wheedle into fetching a cup of coffee, but the old, fat one with permed gray hair and rimless glasses over remorseless eyes. Remorseless. That was the word for this whole business.

"Mrs. Hughes. Mrs. Hughes. Time to wake up now. The doctor wants you out of bed."

What a dreadful voice, like one of those nasty little dogs. Lillian tried pretending sleep and gave up, opened her eyes and attempted a smile. Charm meant nothing to this woman. Made of stone.

"Let's try and sit up."

A rough arm under her shoulders and Lillian felt a pain so sharp, so excruciating, she was sure something inside her had torn. She screamed and the sound matched the pain.

The nurse frowned but did not relent. "The quicker we get you walking, the faster you will heal. The doctor let you sleep for forty-eight hours to get through the worst of the withdrawal."

Lillian stopped screaming. "I have no idea what you mean."

"The alcohol withdrawal, dear."

"You're talking nonsense. I've had major surgery."

"Of course, you have, and you also had the D.T.s. Don't try and play the innocent with me. I've been around drunks too long."

She took Lillian by her upper arms. "Now, let's try again."

"Take your hands off me, you ugly bitch. Don't you touch me." Lillian's voice was a hoarse command.

"We'll see about that, Missy. We'll just see."

The nurse marched out of the room and Lillian eased back down, closed her eyes, and let the pain subside.

The door opened. It was Dr. Hodges, looking harassed, followed by the bitch nurse, almost honking in triumph.

"Doctor." Lillian tried to make her smile both winning and pitiful.

He stood looking down on her, and not sympathetically. "Do I understand that you refused to obey Nurse Gordon's orders, *my* orders, and that you insulted her?

"She insulted me."

"I don't have time for this."

Jim Hodges, a man she'd known for years and had entertained in her home, a man she'd caught admiring her legs? Now, he didn't have time for her? Lillian closed her eyes and tears squeezed out the corners.

"Lillian." A gentler voice. She heard a chair scrape and he sat. "We're dealing with two serious situations here. We've repaired the latest intestinal blockage, but we don't have a lot of confidence it will hold. And," he hesitated, "there's the drinking."

"I've cut back."

"Listen to me. There's no alcohol in your system now. We've flushed it out. That's one reason you feel so bad. If you recover, you must never take another drink. Do you understand?"

"*If* I recover?" Lillian blinked.

"We're very concerned. But right now, our first job is to get you up so you can get stronger. I want you to work with the nurse, okay?"

"It hurts too much."

"Of course, it hurts. You've had abdominal surgery. But we've got to ease up on the drugs to get you going. Now be a good girl. Help us make you better."

Lillian refused to look or speak to Nurse Gordon, but she let herself be lifted and managed to take a few faltering steps. Her legs were like rubber bands. She couldn't believe they'd once supported her unaided. Back in bed, exhausted, with knives of pain slicing her abdomen, she considered that word "if." *If* she got well. She hadn't planned on dying. She was only fifty-nine. Well, sixty-one, but who remembered that lie? If she'd thought there was a chance of dying this young, she would have taken better care of herself.

The surgery did not hold. After a week and a half in the hospital, another kink, another trip to the operating room, and this time no talk of going home. Lillian thought of her insides as overcooked spaghetti. Tubes refusing to hold their hollow shape. She remembered the hogs they used to slaughter at the hotel in the fall, hung upside down, blood draining into a bucket, bellies slit, and the gray, wormy mass that spilled out, the stinking slimy mess. She could smell herself; she reeked, rotting from the inside out.

Will came by the hospital before and after work. He sat by the bed looking stricken. He asked how she felt. She always said fine. He didn't want details, and he certainly didn't want to hear any mention of hog intestines. He talked about his cases. He shared funny stories he'd once saved for the girls. It hurt to laugh, and laughing made her cough which hurt more. He told her what went on at the house and what Bessie had cooked the night before. The mention of food made Lillian wince at the pain eating might bring to her collapsing insides. When she cringed, Will got a frightened look on his face.

Some days he brought her roses from the garden, which was sweet. She didn't lack for flowers. The room filled with bouquets. Lillian sent the extras down the hall to other, more barren rooms.

Her friends came in the afternoon, sometimes singly, but frequently the whole card group, as if to include her in a game they never got around to playing. For half an hour or so, with them all in the room, interrupting each other and laughing, Lillian forgot the reason she was here. That never lasted. She'd catch their glances, eyes piercing, worried but also somehow thrilled. Looks that said, *So, you're the one, the first of us to go. Who would have thought?* Well, who would have? Certainly not Lillian, who had always felt at least twice as alive as most people: moving faster, able to smoke, drink, talk, bid a hand of bridge, and still be impatient at how slowly other people's minds worked. She watched them, joining in the laughter when she could, thinking: You too, one day.

After her friends left, she sank back in relief. Their noise masked the pain and brought the world into the hospital for an afternoon, but the visits exhausted her. Soothed by the quiet, the softness of her pillow and the nurse's injection, she let herself slide into sleep. Much of this bliss came from drugs and Lillian felt grateful for them. Delicious, delicious drugs.

The minister came by. They had a nice talk about dying. He talked. She nodded. He said she shouldn't be afraid, that all her sins were forgiven, which made Lillian smile, though not in a rude way. She felt far more sinned against than sinning. She forgave Will. Now that she lay dying, he was trying to make up for the years of neglect.

He brought Bessie by to see her. Bessie made the hospital chair squeal with her bulk and spent the visit crying and wiping her eyes with one of Will's handkerchiefs. Saying, "I don't know. I just don't know what we going to do."

Ernestine came regularly to pray over her. Lillian let her. James visited, big, awkward and helpless in his love. Leland and Olive arrived with a giant bouquet of fragrant lilies and a box of candy. Who could eat candy; who could eat? Leland said not to worry about money, which seemed amusing to Lillian since money was now the least of her concerns.

The girls were here: Helen from Florida, April from around the corner, Maude from her teaching job in Hattiesburg. They brought her lovely new nightgowns and bed jackets. After the painful sponge bath, the powder, the lotion—she let herself be done up each day in pink, blue or cream, with ribbons and lace, embellished and helpless as an overgrown baby.

Looking at her children, Lillian decided she had done the best she knew how. For all her hard work, Helen had left her husband, April appeared to be out of her mind half the time, and Maude, sweet, weepy Maude, had grown big as a sow. Lillian did not mention any of this. She had given up criticism.

She roused herself on Saturdays for the Ole Miss football game, listening on the radio or watching the television opposite the bed. Lillian adored quarterback Archie Manning. She had the nurse pin a large Archie Manning button to her bed jacket on game days. Will often watched with her. She knew a lot about football from growing up with her gambling brothers. She could sensibly discuss what had gone wrong with a play and what the coach should have done. These games cost her. She felt the strength they'd taken the next day, but they were worth it. Game day was only time she felt alive.

She was thinner than she'd ever been. Helen brought her a new dress from Frances Pepper, black silk with a white ruched collar, darling and very well made. Lillian examined the seams and the tag:

a size four, as petite as she'd always longed to be. She had April hang it on the door of the closet and showed it off to the nurses.

"You'll wear it," they said with bright, false smiles. "You'll be dancing in that dress."

No one but the minister mentioned death. Not Will or the girls, not friends or family or the doctors. To talk about death was to admit defeat. She saw the fear reflected in their eyes when they bent over the bed. The talk was of a good day or a not so good day. "She was a little better today," the nurse said, and the visitor smiled. Progress. She would perhaps be a little better the next day, too, or if not, the next. Hope ran ahead.

More and more now, she slept, rousing herself with reluctance for visitors and sometimes not bothering. The girls leaned over the bed, holding her hand, saying, "We love you, Mama." They said it over and over, as if to convince her, or to compensate for the years they hadn't loved her, or acted as if they didn't.

Even Will said it when her eyes were closed. "I love you, Lillian." Which would have been funny if she'd had the strength left to laugh. He squeezed her hand and she felt genuinely touched. She let herself believe him. Will Hughes, this husband, the man she'd sacrificed everything to be with: health, self-esteem, a life of her own. All of it foolishness when you lay here dying.

The choices she'd made, the people she'd loved or not loved enough — all that mattered less and less. She thought about death and how the body readied you for it, so that leaving seemed less fraught and more like finally being allowed to rest after a long, hard job. Not having to be responsible or bothered about anything. Not minding what you might miss because you couldn't dredge up the strength or will to think about it. She let herself sink deeper into that blissful, mindless darkness where no dreams came and nothing hurt.

114

On a Tuesday morning in late February, the phone rang while Velma timed a soft-boiled egg. The clock on the wall read 7:33. "Hello."

A muffled voice on the other end.

"Hello?"

"Lillian died this morning." She recognized Will. He sounded broken.

Velma put a hand to her throat. "I am so sorry."

"Thank you. I know—we all are." Another silence. "Would you cancel my appointments for today?"

Was he crying? He was, poor man. "Is there anything else I can do?"

"I can't think now. I'll phone you at the office later."

Velma hung the receiver on the wall and slumped into one of the yellow kitchen chairs. *Lillian was dead.* The shock of it made her feel feverish. She got up and turned the flame off under the boiling water. The last thing she wanted now was an egg. Lillian was dead. That meant—she pushed the thought away. Unforgivable. Terrible for Lillian to die so soon, and for her family. She ran cold water into a glass and drank it down. Threw it up and bent over the sink sobbing. Put the dishtowel over her mouth to muffle the sound. She was a horrible person, and God would curse her if she allowed one instant of gratification. She wasn't glad, of course she wasn't, that's why she was crying. She pressed the cool glass against the hot skin of her cheek. *Will was free.*

She mustn't assume anything. Assuming brought bad luck. For all the bowls of cereal eaten in her kitchen during the weeks of Lillian's illness, she and Will had not been intimate for fourteen years. After he told her he was going back to Lillian, they never again mentioned the future. He was free now to take a wife, but he might not choose her. Velma had become like an old pair of shoes, fine to eat cereal in, but nothing you'd want to wear out in public. Will would pick a woman with a college education, from a fine family like his own, a woman whose gums didn't show when she smiled. He might have already chosen someone.

Shame on her. Will grieved and here she sat speculating about who he'd marry. The man hadn't yet buried his first wife. Velma wet the dishtowel and pressed it against her face.

She needed to get dressed and go to work. People counted on her. She would dress soberly and show no hint of her feelings. She chose the dark gray suit and a lighter gray blouse. No jewelry today. "Clothe yourself in dust and ashes and walk in humility before the Lord." She would be God's maidservant.

She picked up her purse and car keys. She planned to be everything Will Hughes needed at this sad moment and to expect nothing. She had been living these fourteen years, not waiting. Her heart sounded in her ears — *she's dead, she's dead.*

115

On a frigid Saturday in late February, Velma attended Lillian's funeral. The service at the Methodist church felt much like Mr. Pat's and his wife Margaret's, with little resemblance to the funerals at the Baptist church outside Picayune. No audible weeping; no sermon about hell and damnation; no cake and Jell-O molds in the church hall after. The point of a city funeral must be *not* to show emotion.

At the graveside, she admired once again the Hughes' family plot. Proper people didn't buy one space in the cemetery; they bought room for everyone and put a big column in the middle with the family's name cut into stone. There was the space dug out for Lillian, with room for Will to lie beside her. Mr. Pat lay next to his wife. She still missed Mr. Pat.

Velma stood out of the way. She had perfected the art of being unobtrusive. A good secretary should be efficient and invisible. Only errors called attention to themselves.

She was tall enough to see over most heads. Will looked handsome in his dark topcoat, serious and stricken, exactly as he should. Maude: sweet, fat Maude, sobbed as if her heart had broken. Of Will's three girls, she was Velma's favorite, an open, friendly child, now woman, without a grain of snobbery. Which was more than Velma could say for the middle one, April, who, pinched and trembling, clung to her little husband. April treated Velma as if secretaries were objects to be stepped around. Helen, the oldest, did not cry. Velma didn't know what to make of Will's oldest. She acted friendly enough, but a lot went on behind that easy smile.

Greenwood was a beautiful cemetery. Velma gazed upward, past the well-kept headstones, above the twisted cedars with their rough trunks, and into the gray sky. Was Lillian there watching, or asleep inside the polished coffin waiting for Judgment Day? Velma had never been sure if your soul rose straight after you died, or if you had to stay underground until the end of days. She got the impression preachers weren't sure either, since she'd heard it both ways. She hoped Lillian wasn't watching, wasn't drifting down to read her thoughts. She wanted Will's first wife fast asleep, at peace at last. If she'd been Catholic, she would have crossed herself, which, picturing it, felt less like a holy symbol than a spell to ward off evil.

Will didn't come by the house for cereal anymore. Velma understood. He was in mourning. At work, she kept her head down and never precisely met his eye. She took dictation, maintained his calendar, handed him documents to proof or sign, and made sure everything arrived as intended. She let people into Will's office and saw them out. She did it all with decorum, Mrs. Moseley's favorite word. She had become quite good at decorum, a quality she thought the world could use more of: life in a minor key.

Out of respect for Will's loss, she did not wear bright colors. Her floral scarves stayed in the closet. She wore gray and beige, but not black, for she was not a member of the family.

Everyone treated Will with care. The man was wounded and must be allowed to mend. Everyone but Bessie, the Hughes cook. She called the office almost every day, her loud voice undiminished, giving Velma messages to pass along. "You tell Mr. Will I already ordered from the grocery once this morning, and I can't be calling them again. Tell him to stop by the store himself on the way home. I need me some lard. Not Crisco, *lard*, if he wants that sweet potato pie. I won't get to that today, tell him, but there's vanilla ice cream in the freezer for dessert. I'm leaving ham and butterbeans for his supper, and biscuits. Tell him the biscuits are in the oven."

Velma's mouth watered. She took notes in her perfect cursive and passed them along to Will without comment. In her private datebook, she copied the names of every dish Will liked: the chess pie (whatever that was), sweet potato pie, thick pork chops, stewed okra.

Jackson's widows telephoned the office, too, along with the divorcees. The town seemed suddenly crowded with loose females. Velma never put these ladies through.

"If I could just have a word." Eileen Hampton breathed through the telephone into Velma's ear.

"I'm so sorry. He's with a client."

"Well, tell him I have two tickets to the ballet? They're for tomorrow night, so I need to know if he'd like to join me."

Velma wrote another note and handed it over, smiling when she heard Will snort. She knew him so much better than these women. He would never go to the ballet. He inked a large, black "No" at the bottom and handed the note back. She called Eileen Hampton to express his regrets.

Women called with invitations to dinner, to parties, to see a play. They called to say they were bringing over casseroles or dropping by to pick up their empty dishes.

"Let me jot down what you brought," Velma said. "I know Mr. Hughes will want to thank you."

"My special oyster and spinach dish," or "My mother's fabulous mud pie." Velma passed the information along to Bessie.

"Whatever was in that dish is still in it," Bessie said on the phone. Velma liked the sound of her loud, warm voice. "Mr. Will doesn't eat nothing with a mystery inside."

Velma asked Bessie to wash the dish and set it outside. She called the lady back and said how much Mr. Hughes appreciated everyone's kindness, and the empty dish would be by the back door. She stressed the word "everyone," so no lady suffered under the misapprehension she alone offered comfort.

A month after the funeral, while she heated a bowl of chicken noodle soup for supper, Will came calling. Knocked on the front door saying he hoped he wasn't interrupting.

"Of course not." Velma felt the hateful blush rise up her neck. Every work night, as soon as she reached her bedroom, she took off her suit, heels, stockings, slip, girdle and brassiere, and put on one of her housedresses. She had two, navy with white stripes and red with black. They fit like tablecloths, touching nothing but her shoulders. Dropping one of these sacks over her head, Velma's declared the day done. She put on terrycloth slippers with foam soles and allowed her tired toes to spread luxuriously. The faded pink slippers she'd been caught in tonight needed a wash. This was not an outfit she would choose to be seen in. She wouldn't have opened the door if she'd had time to think.

"I'm just having soup." She kept elbows near her hips, pulling the navy sack in to make it look as if she had a waist.

"Soup sounds great." Will hung his topcoat on the back door hook and his suit coat over it. He loosened his tie.

Velma turned off the burner. "Let me change."

"No, no, you look fine. I barged in."

They sat, one at each end of the yellow Formica table. He talked about current cases, spooning his soup, breaking saltines into the bowl. She watched him eat and listened, keeping her arms close to her side, self-conscious about her breasts swinging loose under the cotton dress.

"How are things at home?" she asked. Her first personal question since the funeral.

Will lifted his hands in a What can you say? gesture. "Bessie takes good care of me. The girls call. It was awful right after the funeral with everyone in the house. Lillian left a will. She had my sister Mag draw it up years ago when she was still angry with Helen for running off. She left everything to the two younger girls."

Velma said, "Uh-oh."

"Exactly. Helen felt terrible being left out. Not that Lillian had much to leave, a couple of oil leases, jewelry, some furniture from her family. I explained to Helen that her mother always meant to change it, but got sick and forgot."

Velma shook her head sympathetically and carried the empty soup bowls to the sink.

"The three of them got into Lillian's jewelry box," Will said. "April decided she's the boss because she's the only one living here in town. She's telling them who can have what and Helen says, 'Who are you to say?' April says, 'The only one who cared enough about Mother to stay.' Then Maude starts crying." Will shook his head. "Terrible."

"I can imagine." Velma rinsed the soup bowls and dried her hands.

"But you know what's worse than loss?" Will Hughes spoke to her back. "Pity."

Returning to the table, Velma tried to wipe any semblance of that emotion off her face.

"It's these women, Lillian's friends." Will put on a falsetto voice. "'You poor man. You must let me do something for you.' April stops by every evening like I can't put on pajamas by myself."

"She's just worried about you."

"That, and she's the bossiest woman in Mississippi. Finished organizing her own husband, and now she wants to have a go at me." He laughed.

Velma joined in. She hadn't heard Will laugh for so long. It felt mean to talk about April, but his middle daughter probably behaved as badly as Will claimed. She got up to cut them slices of coconut cream pie. She longed to put a soothing hand on the back of Will Hughes' neck where his haircut was growing out. She did not.

The two of them weren't young anymore. There was no urgency, and Velma knew better than to hurry mourning. With Lillian gone, Will remembered everything he'd once loved about her. Death peeled away the bad parts. On his once or twice weekly visits, Velma listened. Will never asked her out to restaurants the way he had when he and Lillian were separated. Lillian had only been dead for five months. He was a recent widow and it wasn't fitting to be seen with another woman.

She hoped that was the reason. Women still called the office trying to get him to do this and that. When he left Velma's after his soup or pie, he occasionally gave her a peck on the cheek, but she never acted as if she expected one.

"Lillian could rise to the occasion." Will took a swallow of milk and cut off another forkful of the apple pie Velma served tonight. All these pies were store-bought. "I could bring the entire Mississippi Supreme Court home for dinner and everything would look perfect and taste amazing. She knew how to put people at ease."

Velma could never welcome the entire Supreme Court. She smiled at Will's stories and did not comment. Being a secretary prepared you to be an unquestioning receptacle, and she didn't mind hearing Will praise his late wife. Lillian was the mother of his children and she was dead. He sat at Velma's kitchen table now.

"You must miss her," Velma said.

Will scraped his fork around the empty plate before he spoke. "I miss the good parts. I miss the house running the way it used to." He ate the crumbs he'd collected and stared out into Velma's backyard, where she had not kept up the garden. "I'm sad for the girl I married, but Lillian drank that person away years ago. Maybe I was too hard on her."

Velma lowered her eyes and shook her head, meaning no, of course you weren't.

"But she was so stubborn. If I said to turn right, she'd go left. We were like two goats butting at each another."

Velma picked up her cue. "Instead of walking side by side."

"That's it." His blue eyes beamed. "She thought I was unfeeling, but her stubbornness made me that way."

"You never divorced."

"She wouldn't have it. She'd chosen me and by damn, it was going to be me no matter —" He stopped.

Velma waited.

"—no matter how I felt." Will stared at the table. "I laid down rules. They weren't unreasonable. I only wanted to live in peace without going bankrupt. It was her choice for us to stay together, and I'm not saying she was wrong. The girls got to grow up with a mother and father." He handed the plate to Velma. "But the thing is, Lillian found a way around every rule. Couldn't drink at night when I was home, so she drank in the afternoons. When I wouldn't travel, she went off with her friends and picked up some bug in Mexico. I'm sure that's what killed her."

Velma stood at the sink, making a mental list of rules she would not break if she ever got the chance.

"Drank her health away. But that was her choice. You can't make the fences high enough to keep a person from killing themselves."

"Or from loving you." Velma flushed at the boldness of these words. She turned on the water in the sink, loud.

"That's what Lillian said. You wonder, though. If someone really loved you, wouldn't they obey? Isn't that what marriage vows are about?"

Velma set the plates to one side and rinsed the forks. Loving Will was a lot like loving God. You had to take them both on their own terms.

"Isn't it?" Will's voice rose behind her.

Velma let the warm water run over her hands. "Of course."

116

A year after Lillian's death, on a particularly cold February evening, Will and Velma sat in her den on the black and white plaid couch Velma had chosen to match the gray shag carpet. This was the room where Will had first kissed her. He had been anything but passionate for the past twelve months.

For the first six, Velma attributed his reticence to grief, but she'd begun wondering lately if he might be one of those men who try marriage and decide they prefer living alone. He'd grown comfortable at home with Bessie cooking and the children's former nurse Doreen coming in to clean and iron his shirts. He didn't require a wife. Velma reminded herself that she, too, was content. She got to work with him all day, and they spent many evenings in comfortable companionship.

Six or seven months after Lillian died, Will admitted one night that he wouldn't object to a glass of wine. He told her he'd chosen not to drink while Lillian was alive because of her over-indulgence. Velma bought wine. With experimentation, she discovered she preferred white and Will enjoyed something sweet and purple called Manischewitz, which he liked over ice. This became their cold-weather ritual: wine and a fire in the evenings.

Tonight, the wind blew sleety rain against the glass, but inside the small paneled room, they sat, cozy as two cats. Will had kept his sports coat on. Velma's crocheted throw covered their knees; the fire crackled. They sat in silence, Will's arm around her shoulder, watching the flames.

Velma felt him stir. She leaned forward to release his arm.

"It's been a year since Lillian died," Will said.

Velma stared at the fire. "Such a sad time."

"Today ends the official mourning period."

She looked at him. "I didn't know mourning had an official end." After three years, Velma still had moments of wanting to tell Mama something, only to remember she was gone.

Will sat up straighter. "Which is why I chose tonight." He removed a small black box from an inside coat pocket.

Velma's heart staggered in her chest. All the spit in her mouth dried up. She couldn't put together one clear thought.

"To say something I've longed to say." He snapped the box open.

A diamond solitaire flashed in the firelight. Velma closed her eyes and opened them. It was still there.

"Velma Vernon, will you do me the honor of becoming my wife?"

Here came the hated blush. And tears. Velma hid her face in her hands.

"Have I waited too long? I know I'm practically an old man."

She shook her head. He was in no way an old man, but Velma felt surprised that her first response was elation, yes, but also fear. If she said yes, and of course she would, everything would change. She'd been a minor planet circling Will's sun from the edge of the solar system. She was being pulled closer.

She sat up, mopping at her face. No tears; that was one of the rules. This jumping feeling inside was probably normal.

"I thought you'd be happy." He bent to look into her face.

"I am happy."

"You don't look happy."

She tried to laugh. "That's what your father used to say whenever he did me a favor."

Will took out the clean white handkerchief he always carried.

Velma pressed it against her eyes then turned to face him. "Of course, I will be your wife. I've waited all these years to be your wife."

Will crushed her into a hug. "I would get down on my knees and do this properly, but I'm afraid I might not be able get up." He slipped the diamond on her ring finger. "I'm going to take such good care of you."

Velma held the ring toward the firelight. Fire to fire. "Can we afford a diamond this big?"

"You let me worry about money."

Velma had grown accustomed to doing her own deciding. She pushed that thought aside and leaned against Will's chest.

He folded his arms around her. "It's been a torment waiting."

She sat up and looked at him. "Then you must be awfully good at hiding torment. I thought you liked being single."

He took her face in his hands. "Surely you knew how I felt. I made you a promise that day at the office when I had to go back to Lillian. You said not to bother you again or you'd quit. I tried to respect that."

"Will, we are talking, what? Fourteen years ago."

"I've loved you every day since."

Warmth filled Velma like soup. The man was a cipher. She might as well trust him because she would certainly never know what he felt or thought. They sat with his arm around her. "Are you happy?" Velma said.

"Mmmm."

Silence as they stared at the fire. Velma's mind churned. Who should she tell first? If only Mama were here. Would they be married at his church or hers? Should she wear a long white gown or something less ostentatious, maybe a tea-length dress?

She thought she heard a snore and turned to look. Will's eyes were closed. "Are you asleep?"

He shook his head. "Must have dozed off."

"In the passion of the moment?"

He gave her a squeeze. "You're marrying an old man."

"Even if you were, you're the only man in the world I want." She held out her hand and watched the ring flash. "Mrs. Will Hughes." Her voice filled with wonder.

He gave her another squeeze. "Ready or not."

Washing her face later, Velma kept checking to see if the ring was safe on top of the closed toilet. Will had gone home to his own bed. At the door, he kissed her, but he hadn't tried to make love. Plenty of time for that, years for that. Velma wanted to call Garnett, but it was too late. If she were a different kind of person, she would shout her new status into the sleeping street. *She was betrothed.* What a wonderful word. She would become the wife of the only man she had ever loved. Her face in the mirror was flushed, her eyes feverish. Happiness made you look crazy.

She did not neglect God. She got on her knees beside the bed and thanked Him. She asked to be worthy of this man, to be like Ruth in the Bible, "Whither thou goest," a faithful companion. Lying in bed, staring up at the dark ceiling, she whispered the magic words again: "Mrs. Will Hughes."

117

Two weeks later, they sat on the couch in the den again, Will with his glass of wine, she with hers. On the television, Walter Cronkite spoke gravely of James Earl Ray pleading guilty to the murder of Martin Luther King, Jr.

"Terrible business." Will Hughes motioned for Velma to turn down the sound. "After marrying off three daughters, I hope our wedding can be a little less—"

"Ornate?"

"Exactly. A nice, quiet ceremony."

"Of course."

"In a judge's chambers."

So, neither her church nor his. There was to be no church or white dress, and no aisle to walk down. Velma recognized disappointment and let it go. "That would be fine."

"Getting married is nobody's business but ours."

By nobody, Will meant his family. He'd spent the past week telling them about the engagement and the reaction had not been one of universal joy. At work, Velma felt a distinct chill from his sister Mag, and from the nephew Owen—a you-have-stepped-out-of-your-place drop in temperature. They were perfectly civil and both congratulated her, but she noticed the difference. She had gone from being their favorite secretary and most valuable employee, to awkward pick for new family member. Which wasn't nearly as bad as the reaction from Will's daughter, April.

Will gave each of his daughters the news in a phone call: Helen and Maude congratulated him, but April, after a moment of silence, exploded. Velma did not hear this from Will, who said only, "She did not take it well."

Maude came to town and took Velma to lunch. She told her exactly what April said. "You *can't* marry her. She's nobody. She's not in our class. You could have any woman in this town and you deserve better. *We* deserve better.

Velma flushed at this. Precisely what she had thought.

"Don't give it a minute's worry." Treating the whole thing as a joke. "This is just April being April." According to Bessie, Maude said, April came to the house the morning after Will's call, interrupting breakfast, crying and storming around the kitchen. She told him marrying Velma was an insult to their mother's memory. Fooling around with a secretary had killed Lillian, according to April, and over her dead body would he bring that woman into their house.

Velma's face grew hotter.

"According to Bessie, Daddy kept saying, 'I'm sorry you feel that way' over his cold eggs. Bessie said he finally shut himself in the bathroom until she left."

Maude thought all this funny. Velma did not. Marrying Will Hughes had caused more upset than she anticipated. Forget a fancy dress, just slip away somewhere, come back married, and live happily ever after. She did not try and define what this state of happiness meant except she would be with Will. He would never have to go home to another house again.

Her own family, Aunt Orrie and her grown children, sounded thrilled. She made the mistake of telling them on a visit to Picayune that Will enjoyed an occasional glass of sweet wine, forgetting how hard-shelled the Baptists of south Mississippi could be. Not that she wasn't also a Baptist, but city Baptists didn't cast you into perdition over a glass of Manischewitz. Aunt Orrie said she expected Velma would be able to bring him back to the path after marriage. Velma said she expected so, and everyone dropped the subject. She had no intention of asking Will to give up his wine.

The only people who seemed truly happy for her were the girls at the office. They gave her a shower in the law library and took her for a celebratory lunch. They went with her to Gus Mayer, Jackson's fanciest department store, and helped pick out a wedding suit: pale blue wool with a slim skirt and a fitted jacket with a jaunty peplum. She chose a cream-colored wool hat with a jeweled crest, and black alligator pumps and a matching handbag. This was the most money Velma had ever spent on herself, but as Pauline said, "Why not? You won't be paying the mortgage for much longer."

Until that comment, Velma had not thought about giving up her house. Opening the door from the carport each evening, stepping into her cheerful yellow kitchen, kicking off her shoes and turning on the radio, had become her favorite moment of the day. Soon she would go home to Lillian's house. The idea made her feel slightly ill. Lillian might not be there, but everything in the place had belonged to her.

She pushed that fear aside. She was home now, away from the critical eyes of Will's family at the office, free to roll down her stockings and massage her aching feet. She took her wedding suit out of the Gus Mayer bag and hung it in the closet. She would not make a fuss about living in Lillian's house. Will hated fusses.

She remembered Bessie, which gave her heart a bump. She had never lived with a servant. No one in her family ever had one. Bessie was as tall as Velma and three times as wide: dark skin, a mouthful of large white teeth, booming voice. Velma could not imagine living alongside, much less supervising, a person like her.

Mayor Thompson agreed to marry them. Will named a day in March and, instead of going to work, Velma put on her new suit. Driving with Will to City Hall, she felt light-headed, as if she weren't quite inhabiting her body.

At 11:00 in the morning, with a weak spring sun outside, they were married. Will's family had not been invited because of April, so Velma didn't invite hers either. She would have liked to ask Garnett to be her maid of honor, but Will said, "Let's not." Personal business shouldn't interfere with the running of the office. The mayor's secretaries served as witnesses. Velma could hardly take in the words or her whispered responses. Will slid a plain gold band on the finger with the diamond.

The secretaries congratulated her. Mayor Thompson kissed her on the cheek, and they were back in Will's car, headed for Memphis.

They would spend one night in the Peabody Hotel and fly out the next day to Hawaii.

Hawaii. Will had surprised her the week before with this news. They would spend their honeymoon in his favorite place, an island paradise where the weather was never too hot or too cold, you walked barefoot in sugary sand, and drank rum out of a pineapple. Velma was astonished.

After that news, she and the girls spent another frenzied lunch hour looking for what the saleslady called "resort wear." Sandals, a swimsuit, sundresses, white slacks, and bright-colored shirts. Velma's savings shrank alarmingly. She kept telling herself not to worry. She had put her house on the market. When it sold, she would have the equity from that. She didn't know how money worked in married life. Will said to leave money worries to him, which made her afraid to ask.

On their wedding night in Memphis, Velma went in the bathroom to put on her gown and robe, a modest ensemble of white cotton with lace and blue ribbons. Will went in next to put on his pajamas while Velma waited stiff upright in bed. Relax. It wasn't as if they hadn't done this before. Her tongue grew too large for her mouth and her fingers and toes felt numb.

He crawled into bed beside her and put an arm around her shoulders. "We don't have to do anything if you're too tired."

"I'm not that tired." The words came out in a croak.

They slid down in the bed. Velma worried about his feet touching her cold toes, but by then he was kissing her, sliding the gown off one shoulder. Everywhere he touched turned warm and she forgot to be shy.

The next day on the airplane, her very first airplane, she tried to relax in the seat beside him.

"Happy?" Will put a hand over hers. "Hope you don't mind riding Coach."

"Of course not." Velma wasn't sure of the difference.

"Foolish to spend twice the money just to get somewhere," Will said.

"I agree." Velma closed her eyes. The years of waiting and the nights alone had been worth it. God had rewarded her patience, forgiven her early transgressions, and granted her the husband she'd prayed for. Happy as a newborn calf in the sunshine, Papa would say.

118

Hawaii was a Technicolor movie. Velma felt as if she lived inside someone else's confetti dream, accompanied by the plink of ukuleles. She couldn't seem to clear her head enough to actually see things. She blamed it on the exhaustion of working full time while getting ready for the wedding, the long trip, and her shaken nerves at his family's reaction. She found herself clinging to Will's arm, letting herself be led from one thing to another, murmuring. "Wonderful."

Meals were included in the honeymoon package. Three times a day they sat at a table for two in the windowed dining room of the Royal Hawaiian Hotel. There were uniformed waiters scurrying, a band playing, and orchids, real orchids on every table. Velma had never seen an orchid except in a corsage, and this exuberant trumpeting of color made her dizzy.

"I can't get over the flowers here," she said to Will when they sat down for yet another meal. That was the other thing. For years she'd lived on soup and sandwiches. Three meals every day left her groggy. In the afternoon, when they returned from visiting the market, watching the surfers, touring the sugar cane fields, or the Navy base, they darkened the room for a nap and made love.

Before Lillian died, when Velma was not married to Will, and lovemaking could send her straight to hell, she got so excited doing it she forgot to breathe. Strangely, now that she was a legally married lady, honeymooning in Hawaii, she could hardly wait for the act to be over so she could close her eyes and go to sleep.

She changed from slacks in the morning, to a sundress in the afternoon, and a silk gown for dinner. She hoped she wasn't disappointing Will. Waikiki Beach had left her spotted with sunburn. She felt addled by the rum and fruit Mai Tais, and bloated from unfamiliar food. It was strangely exhausting to constantly smile and make conversation with another human.

Will was kind and attentive. He bought her pearls, a double strand of genuine cultured pearls. At a luau, he showed her how to sit on the ground and eat with her fingers off banana leaves.

Velma sat with her legs bent awkwardly beneath her, pulling her skirt over her knees. "I don't recognize most of this food," she whispered to Will.

"Do what I do." He dipped two fingers into a bowl of thick purple goo.

She tried. The stuff tasted like school paste, and she spat it into her napkin.

Will shook with laughter. "What's the matter, you don't like poi? It's Hawaii's national dish."

She kept the napkin pressed against her mouth.

"You should see the look on your face," he said. "Here, have a bite of pork."

This was one of those jokes Mrs. Evans had warned Velma about when she first came to work at the firm. She'd better get used to being teased.

At Mauna Loa, they hiked together up rough black rock to peer down into a live volcano.

"Looks exactly the way I imagine hell," Velma said.

Will patted her hand. "You don't believe in a literal hell, surely?"

She didn't answer. She'd forgotten how Will Hughes felt about religion, that church was a duty and God an idea. Looking down into the red and sulfuric depths, Velma saw the damnation she had narrowly escaped through marriage.

He liked holding onto her while they went here and there, guiding her by one elbow as if she were a child who couldn't manage on her own. Velma enjoyed it, too. They had been apart for a long time. He could lead her as much as he liked.

She kept telling herself how lucky she was, and how amazing everything looked, but, inside, she was ready to go home. She sensed Will might also be worn out by this paradise he remembered from 1945. Like her, he would be happy when the week was over and they returned to their desks, their soup and sandwiches, to the busy ordinariness of work.

119

Velma had brought along a little leather-bound journal to record the biggest and most exciting trip of her life, but looking through it on the plane trip home, she found she had recorded mostly numbers: seventeen dishes at the luau; nine hula dancers; sixteen tiki torches; three leis; six miles of beaches; forty-eight steps to their room (Will believed in stairs); twelve miles up to the volcano (This adventure required a terrifying ride in a tiny plane to the Big Island); eight battleships destroyed at Pearl Harbor; six pieces of flatware at every meal.

Flying over a churning gray sea, Velma closed her eyes and said what she'd been thinking. "This has been the most amazing week of my life, but I can't wait to get back to work."

Will cleared his throat. "I've been meaning to talk to you about that."

Velma turned from the window.

"You realize of course that you can no longer be my secretary."

What was he talking about? "Whose secretary will I be?"

"No one's. You're my wife now. You're Mrs. Will Hughes."

It felt exactly like being fired. Velma's eyes stung and she swallowed to keep from crying.

He took her hand in both of his. "It wouldn't look right."

"But what am I supposed to do?" The question burst out, a question Lillian would never have needed to ask.

"Run our house. Have a wonderful dinner ready when I come home in the evening. Plant that garden you talk about. You've worked for so long, my dear. How many years has it been?" He didn't give her time to answer. "And so hard." He bent his head and murmured into her ear. "It's time I pampered you."

Velma felt choked by resentment. She wanted to say that she'd worked no longer than Will had, and he wasn't volunteering to quit. She wanted to say that work was all she knew. Hughes & Blair, with its buzz of court dates, documents in and out, cases won and lost, gossip with the girls, was the center of her existence. She couldn't imagine her life without it. She tried to keep the storm in her chest from coming out her mouth. She had promised to love and obey. That was a vow. She had begged God to give her this man. He had answered her prayer, but by taking away the other thing she loved — her job. She had once pretended to be Will's office wife. Now she was his real wife, and being Mrs. Will Hughes meant she couldn't complain about the unfairness of his decision.

"I guess I'm ready to be pampered." Inside, Velma stewed, but she let Will take her hand and returned his smile. Let him think the tears in her eyes were from joy at the gift he'd presented. Wasn't this what every good American woman longed for: the freedom to stay home?

Driving into town from Memphis, Will turned toward King's Highway instead of Old Canton Road. They were headed for his house. She wasn't ready. The thought of sleeping in Lillian's bed made Velma's mouth go dry. "Shouldn't I go home tonight and get a few things packed?"

"You are going home. Bessie's expecting us. She's got dinner ready."

She had forgotten about Bessie.

Will ushered her through the back door into the warm, fragrant kitchen. Bessie stood at the stove, enormous in her white uniform, a hand on one hip, the other stirring a pot on the stove. A black cane leaned against the cabinet next to her. Catching sight of Will and Velma, she dropped the spoon and hollered. "Look a-here, look a-here. I been wondering when you two would show up."

Velma shrank at the volume and gathered her nerve. *Begin as you mean to go on.* She walked over and shook Bessie's hand. "I'm so happy to meet you in person."

Bessie put an arm around Velma and pulled her into an enormous bosom.

Velma smelled starch and — *was that snuff?*

"We already met," Bessie said. "You admired my chocolate cake."

"That's right, at Maude's christening. I loved that cake. I hope you'll teach me how to make one."

"*Teach you?* Miss Velma, I'll make you as many of those chocolate cakes as you want."

Hardly inside the door, and already she had blundered. The woman's eyes gave away nothing and the white teeth gleamed.

"That sounds wonderful," Velma said.

"I'm starving," Will said. "Can we talk about recipes later?"

"Go on in the dining room." Bessie pointed the way. "I made you a fine wedding dinner: pork chops, spoon bread, turnip greens, and sweet potato pie."

The oval table was set with Will's place at one end and Velma's at the other, where Lillian must have sat. It felt very far away.

"Do you mind?" Velma slid her place mat and silverware around closer to Will.

"Sit anywhere you want, child." Bessie smiled, but her eyes said she did not appreciate seeing her arrangement altered. "That's where Miss Helen usually sits."

"Helen's in Florida," Will said, "and I'm sure she wouldn't mind letting the bride taking her place."

Will drank a full glass of milk with his dinner. Another thing Velma hadn't known about him. She had so much to learn. The food tasted delicious. She cleaned her plate. "Bessie, this is better than anything I ate in Hawaii."

Bessie carried the plates into the kitchen. "Everything tastes better when you in your own house." She brought back slices of sweet potato pie.

Velma considered the words. The meal was wonderful, but this did not feel like her house.

Will cut off the tip of his pie and winked at her, looking relaxed and happy to be back in familiar surroundings.

After dinner, he drove Bessie to her apartment. Left alone, Velma walked around the spotless kitchen. The speckled red Formica counters gleamed. The Percolator had been set up for their morning coffee. She examined Lillian's red and white canisters of flour, sugar, and corn meal. The stove held aluminum salt and pepper shakers and a container for bacon grease. On the wall next to the stove, a black metal matchbox holder. A brown radio on one counter, and a small television on the counter next to the Frigidaire. It had never occurred to Velma that people might watch television in the kitchen.

The whole house felt as if it were holding its breath, waiting for Lillian to return. Nervous as an intruder, Velma stepped down from the kitchen into the master bedroom. This must be the room Lillian added. Two low dressers sat against the right wall with her suitcase on top of one. She pulled open a drawer. Empty. She sniffed, inhaling a faint flowery cologne or maybe sachet. Lillian had chosen these dressers and the mirror above them, but the contents of her life had vanished. Velma opened a drawer in the left dresser and saw a row of black socks folded neatly into pairs, along with white boxer shorts, pressed and folded. *Imagine, ironing underwear.*

The long wall held twin beds under a brownish-gold leather headboard. This was where Will had slept all those years with Lillian. How would you—how did you manage—in twin beds? Maybe they didn't. She preferred to think they hadn't. Will's bedside table held a stack of *Time* magazines. In the drawer, she found a pair of the black-framed reading glasses he wore.

The drawer on the other side, her side, was as empty as the dresser. She would keep her Bible here. Underneath, on the shelf, a stack of women's magazines, the kind Velma read at the beauty parlor. She picked up a *Redbook,* the March issue, addressed to Mrs. Will Hughes. That was her now—she. Will must not have bothered to cancel Lillian's subscriptions. One wife replaced by the next with no need to change the label. Velma would have hours to read women's magazines, a realization that made her stomach go hollow.

She opened her suitcase, took out a robe and gown, and went into the bathroom. Brushing her teeth, she thought about Lillian looking into this same mirror and half-expected to see her staring back from the other side. Lillian once sat on that toilet, bathed in the tub, dried with this towel. Velma washed her face and put on moistener. When she came out, she returned the toothbrush and lotion to her suitcase as if she were a visitor and might return home tomorrow.

She took a breath, longing for her little blue bathroom and the familiar bed. Exhaling, she let it go. Folding back the beige bedspread, she crawled between Lillian's crisp white sheets. Someone had ironed these sheets and the pillowcase too. Doreen, probably. Velma had never slept on ironed sheets except in the hospital and in the hotel on her honeymoon. Quite nice, actually.

Will returned, looking pleased to see her in Lillian's bed. "Did you find everything you need? That dresser's yours and this closet." He pointed to the sliding doors on the left. He hung his suit coat on a brass valet Velma hadn't noticed and disappeared into the bathroom. Sounds of water running and the toilet flushing. Velma felt unreasonably nervous. She'd been sleeping next to this man for a week. What was she afraid of?

He emerged, face pink from hot water, turned down his bed, and plumped the pillows. Crawling in, he leaned over to kiss her. He smelled of soap and Listerine. "Want to see how this twin bed thing works?"

Velma's felt her face growing warm. She nodded.

"You pull your covers loose in the middle and I do the same to mine." They tugged. "Overlap them and, voila." His foot moved under the covers and rubbed against hers. He moved closer, straddling the crack between the beds. "I'm afraid a kiss will have to do. After a day on the plane and that drive from Memphis, I'm beat."

"Me, too." Velma settled back on her pillow, relieved. They turned out their lights. She'd never known a human who fell asleep as fast as Will Hughes. He began to snore. She hadn't realized he snored until the honeymoon. She said her prayers lying in bed, staring at the ceiling, hoping God didn't mind. She'd been doing this since they married. She didn't have the nerve yet to get on her knees in front of Will, who didn't appear to pray.

Lying in the dark, she went over the evening. She probably shouldn't have shaken Bessie's hand. She looked startled, but then she hugged Velma, so maybe the handshake had been all right. She definitely should not have asked Bessie how to make chocolate cake, and she hadn't been pleased when Velma moved her place at the table. So much to figure out.

As she fell asleep, from somewhere faint and faraway, Velma heard laughter.

120

On Saturday, Will went to the office and on to his bridge game. Velma spent the morning moving her clothes from the old house to the new. She piled dresses on the twin bed and began hanging them in the closet. Bessie stumped in on her cane, lowering herself with a groan onto Will Hughes's bed. "Me and Doreen cleaned that closet out after Miss Lillian passed." Breathing heavy.

It wasn't healthy to be that fat. Velma tried to remember Doreen from the christening, quick and light-skinned, Bessie's opposite.

"How many days does Doreen come?"

"Twice a week. Nobody cleans like Doreen, and Mr. Hughes is particular about his shirts."

Silence while Velma hung up her office suits. Might as well put those in the back.

"I don't do cleaning." Bessie said this as if warning Velma.

Bessie and Doreen. Two servants when she'd never had one. "Thank you for clearing out the closet and drawers for me."

Bessie's chuckle made her bosom heave under the white uniform. "Child, we didn't know about you back then. Couple of days after the funeral Mr. Hughes told us to clean things out. Take what we wanted and give away the rest."

How easily a wife could be erased.

"Miss Lillian was a little bitty thing," Bessie said.

"I remember." Was this a comment on Velma's larger self?

"Wore size four and a half shoes."

"Really?" Velma bent to arrange her size tens on the slanted shelf at the bottom of the closet.

"We didn't know anybody with feet that small, so we gave them to the church."

"Didn't her daughters want anything?"

"They took the jewelry. Soon as her sisters left town, Miss April came and took the mink stole and Miss Lillian's evening bags. Crying so hard she couldn't talk straight. Mr. Will can't stand that kind of carrying on."

Velma made a mental note not to carry on.

"That there's a nice dress." Bessie nodded toward the red silk Velma had bought for the honeymoon.

Velma held the dress up, looking at it. "I usually don't wear such a bright color, but my girlfriends thought, you know, Hawaii."

"Yes Ma'am, that's red."

Velma hung it in the closet.

Red and tacky.

Velma heard the words clearly. She turned to Bessie. "I beg your pardon?"

"What for?"

"I thought you said something."

"No ma'am, not me." Bessie hefted herself off the bed with the help of the cane. "I better get back to the kitchen if I want to get out of here by noon."

"Thank you for keeping me company." Velma meant it. She didn't know what to do with herself in this house.

121

Bessie had this Sunday off. Velma made breakfast for Will, feeling self-conscious in the strange kitchen. "Cereal, coffee and toast, I'm afraid," she said.

"Fine with me." Will Hughes sat across from her, wearing a wine-colored bathrobe over his blue pajamas. He looked pleased seeing her on the other side of the table.

Velma cleaned up the dishes and got ready for church, putting on her powder blue suit with the matching blouse, thinking how splendid it would feel after years of arriving alone to walk into Riverside Baptist with a handsome husband. Heads would turn. People would be amazed.

Dressed in his suit, Will stood in the kitchen holding a second cup of coffee.

"We should leave in ten minutes," she said.

"Are we riding together?"

They had never talked about whether to attend his church or hers. "We can go to Galloway Methodist if you prefer."

He put down his cup. "I have to get to the office."

"But I thought—"

"I go to the office every Sunday morning." Will picked up his briefcase and hat. "And some Sunday afternoons, if you recall." He raised his eyebrows and gave her a wink.

She did recall those Sundays when Will and Lillian were separated. He'd tell Velma they needed to deal with a pressing case.

She'd drive downtown, leaving her stockings and garter belt at home. On Sunday afternoons, they were the only people in the building. She got a jolt thinking about the black leather couch in his office, panties on the floor, skirt hiked to her waist, naked behind sticking to the leather, Will's face above hers, raw with desire. It was unfair that sinning sex was so much more fun than married sex. She had not seen that look on his face since.

"Did you pray for us back then?" Will said.

"I did." Past sins were surely forgiven by marriage, but a husband who did not attend church would not be. "Church is important to me."

"Then you should go. Pray for us both. I could use the help. We'll meet back here and I'll take you out for a nice lunch."

"I was hoping to show off my handsome husband."

His eyes went from laughing to cold. "I'm not something for you to show off."

It was as if he had slapped her.

He must have seen the shock in her face. "Sorry to sound harsh, but the office *is* my church. I'll go to yours one day, I promise—maybe on Easter."

Velma smiled to hide the hurt, put on her hat, took her purse and keys and went out the back door.

This had been their first married quarrel and it left her feeling squashed. In the car, she thought about what Will said. He was right— it had been prideful of her wanting to show him off. Not going to church together might not spoil their marriage, but she wanted to be together in heaven (whatever awkwardness this might cause with Lillian), and a non-church-going man would not be in heaven with her. She would pray for God to change Will's heart.

After a nice lunch of trout amandine and key lime pie at LeFleur's, Will suggested a drive.

"It's Sunday afternoon. I thought you'd be going back to the office."

"Now that you won't be working, we need to plan more time together. Let's take a nice ride up the Natchez Trace."

Now that you won't be working. The words pierced Velma, but it was a lovely Sunday afternoon and Will had chosen to be with her. Church might be next if she kept praying. She sat up straighter and put on a smile. "I would love that."

122

Will said Velma should continue working until she chose and trained her replacement. She interviewed candidates in the conference room, which also served as the firm's law library. A parade of young women came through, with long legs and silky hair, clutching their business school diplomas, wide-eyed, mascara-laden lashes fluttering with eagerness, bosoms heaving in their desire to be legal secretaries. Velma went through her list of questions with an imperturbable face, behind which she recalled herself at eighteen, awkward, frightened, wearing a country person's idea of city clothes.

The girls were intimidated by her. Velma watched, privately amused. Who would have guessed on the day she turned down Chalmers Root that Velma Vernon would sit here all these years later, wife of the managing partner of Hughes & Blair? Or when she stumbled through her first week at the firm behind the formidable Mrs. Evans, that she would, at least in these girls' eyes, become Mrs. Evans?

Interviewing continued for a second day. The applicant in front of Velma had on a hippy looking dress to her ankles. Her face peered out from behind curtains of hair. And was she? Velma looked again—yes, chewing gum.

"Thank you so much for coming in. We'll be in touch when we complete the interviews."

"I hope I get it." Juicy Fruit breath from across the table.

Velma stood.

"I know it would suit me. I can tell from how it smells in here—leathery with all these books." The girl pointed around the library. "You feel smarter just being in the room, don't you?"

Velma showed her out and the next candidate in, a short, serious-looking young woman with her straight hair pulled severely into a ponytail. Unadorned eyes peered nearsightedly through rimless glasses.

"I need the work. I take care of my daddy. He's disabled." She breathed through her mouth between sentences. The young woman answered the questions intelligently. She seemed like a smart girl, but Will Hughes would not like looking at that spotty skin. He wouldn't want a mouth-breather either.

Velma knew what she was looking for: Will should be well served without being tempted. When Mary Lee Caster walked in, Velma gave a mental nod: this was exactly what she'd been after. Mrs. Caster had worked as a legal secretary in Memphis. She returned to Jackson to care for her mother who had since died. She herself was a widow. Her children were grown. She exuded a quiet competence with her graying hair, nicely done around a youthful face. She wore a good suit and sensible heels. Her jewelry, a single strand of pearls against the white silk blouse, looked real. She was plump without being fat, pleasant but not flirtatious. Velma did a quick calculation. The woman appeared to be fifty, maybe fifty-five. Will was sixty-two. She would last.

Bessie made another of Will's favorite meals that night: baked ham with scalloped potatoes, green beans, cornbread, and a custard pie for dessert. At the table, with Will at the head and Velma beside him, she let him tease her.

"Not taking any chances, huh?"

Velma ignored the implication. "Mrs. Caster is experienced. You won't have to train her."

"I had my heart set on one of the young ones."

Velma felt her face growing hot before recognizing this as a joke. "You're so bad."

"I am." He said it with satisfaction. "That's why I need a good woman like you looking after me."

He stared happily down at his filled plate and Velma realized how glad he was to be back in his own house, eating Bessie's food, no longer making do with canned soup and store-bought pie in her kitchen.

A kitchen she would say a final goodbye to next week. The real estate agent they hired before leaving for Hawaii had shown the house seven times while they were away and already had an offer. Velma would miss the cheerful yellow room where she could stand over the sink eating cold pie for breakfast without anyone noticing or caring.

She and Will went through the house together, deciding what to keep. He grew impatient waiting for her to settle on whether to put the plaid sofa in storage, along with the dusty rose chair and couch. There was no room for her bedroom set or her mother's curio cabinet. They would use her dining table and chairs. The heavy mahogany oval at Will's house, along with its sideboard, had been left in Lillian's will to Maude. Velma gave the yellow Formica table and chairs to Bessie.

She became aware of qualities she could not have known at the office. Will was not sentimental. He was happy having her a part of his household, but she should fit herself around him. He wanted few changes.

A moving van took the unneeded pieces to storage and brought the rest to King's Highway. Lillian's dining room furniture went south to Maude in Perkinston. Velma hadn't met Maude's husband yet, but she looked forward to seeing more of Maude.

On a rainy day in April, Velma locked the back door of the small white house for the last time. Goodbye to evenings alone on the plaid sofa, wearing a muumuu without a brassiere, eating ice cream out of the carton while watching television. She dropped the keys off with the realtor. She wasn't sorry. She wasn't. Look what she'd gained.

On Friday night, three weeks into married life, Will drove Bessie home after dinner and went back to the office. Velma sat at the red Formica table in the still-strange kitchen and smoked, a habit she'd acquired on those Saturday nights out with the girls. She would never indulge at the office, but she enjoyed a cigarette or two at night. Will didn't seem to mind. When he was home, he joined her, puffing on the cigars he said Lillian refused to have in the house.

Starting next week, Mrs. Caster would take her place at the front desk. After twenty-nine years, Velma Vernon would no longer be part of Hughes & Blair. Farewell to being the best secretary at the firm and the fastest typist in the State of Mississippi. She comforted herself: she could always have lunch with Garnett and the other girls. Wiping away tears with a thumb, she ground the cigarette out in a brown glass ashtray. She stared at the ashtray. This must have been where Lillian sat, waiting for Will to come home, probably crying, too. She told herself to stop being silly.

The laughter again. Must be some kind of echo. Velma washed out the ashtray, singing a ragged chorus of "Down by the Riverside" to ramp up her courage. If Mama had ever been fortunate enough to have this kitchen and this house, with no farm to work, she'd have thanked her lucky stars. Which was what Velma needed to do—grow a backbone and be grateful for what she'd been given. Stop imagining things.

123

On Monday, the first morning Velma would not go to the office, she got up early and started Will Hughes's breakfast. Wearing a long, blue velour robe to symbolize her new status, she sliced a banana over his cereal. Bessie arrived, letting in a huge gust of cool, damp air, slamming the back door, rattling her purse and the large paper bag she carried. The woman was a walking thunderstorm.

"You let me do that," she said to Velma. "Sit yourself down and have some coffee."

Will came in, bathed and combed, smelling of Old Spice. He looked at Velma with pleasure. "Don't you look comfortable?"

"Morning Mr. Will." Bessie gave out with one of her big laughs. "Miss Velma here was trying to fix your breakfast. I told her to move over and let me do my job."

Will kissed the top of Velma's head. "Between us, Bessie, we got to teach her how to be spoiled."

Velma tried to look pleased. She knew she should feel grateful, and kept waiting to feel it. At her goodbye luncheon, the girls at the office had been positively pea-colored with envy: a handsome husband, a big house, a full-time cook. "La-tee-da," Doris said. Even Pauline, who was kinder, called Velma the lady of the manor. Here she was, first day running the manor, with no idea what to do.

Will finished his scrambled eggs and waited for his coffee to cool. He smiled over the newspaper at Velma "I like seeing you at my table. What do you plan to do with yourself?"

That was the question. She had worked for thirty years. She had no idea how women who did not work filled their days. "I thought I'd look around and get to know the house."

"Sounds like an excellent idea." Will disappeared behind the paper and Velma pretended to read another section. She spotted a photograph of Mayor Alan Thompson, the man who'd married them, cutting a ribbon in front of a new gas company. She showed it to Will.

"Our new client." He finished his coffee and gave Velma a kiss. "You two have fun. Don't work her too hard, Bessie."

Mississippi Valley Gas, a major new client for Hughes & Blair, but Velma would have nothing to do with that. She sat as long as she could over a second cup of coffee. She had never lived in a house with a colored person, and now she and Bessie would share these rooms from early morning to after the dishes got washed at night.

Lillian had known exactly what to do. Maybe it was knowledge you were born with if your family had servants. The very word was foreign. The janitor at the law office was colored; the elevator operator was colored. Velma knew how say hello and be pleasant, but she wasn't sure how to spend hours together. What did you talk about? What was *okay* to talk about?

She watched Bessie rinsing dishes, humming, comfortable in her skin. Look at that skin. She was at least as old as Velma and not a crease. Her cheeks gleamed like polished wood.

Bessie cocked her head. "What you looking at?"

"I didn't mean to stare." Velma felt heat creep up her neck. Colored people didn't blush either, or else it didn't show. "I was thinking how nice your skin is, the way it shines."

"Vaseline, baby, else I'd be ashy."

"Ashy?"

"You never heard of ashy? Walk down Farish Street one day and look at some of them no-accounts. You'll see you some gray skin. You got to rub Vaseline on you." Bessie demonstrated, rubbing a soapy hand down one large arm. "Takes away the ashy. Makes you shine." She grinned. "Taught you something, didn't I?"

Velma thought about Vaseline. "Isn't it sticky?"

"Not if you rub it in good. White people get ashy, too, but you don't see it on white skin."

Velma summoned her nerve. "I never lived in a house with—I never had anyone—"

"Never had you any help?" Bessie opened her mouth and let out a laugh so loud it was almost scary.

Velma nodded.

"You'll get used to it. I never met a white person who didn't. You tell me what you want. I do it. That's how it works.

"What if I don't know what to tell you?"

"I'll explain things as we go along." Bessie went back to the slow washing of dishes. "You plan on giving bridge lunches?"

"I don't play bridge."

"Then I expect we going to be good friends." Another booming laugh. "I used to get my lip out over Miss Lillian's bridge lunches—barely get done with the washing up before time to serve supper. Worked me nearly to death and not a dime extra."

Velma didn't know what to say.

Bessie gave her a shrewd look. "Hope you don't mind me watching my soaps in the afternoon?"

Velma glanced at the small television. "Of course not. Whatever you're used to."

"You and me going to get along just fine," Bessie said. "I can tell." She bent over a tablet, scribbling. "Making my grocery list. You got a car." She gave Velma a conspiratory smile. "I won't be needing to phone it in and getting that sad looking lettuce."

"Is that what you've been doing?"

"Yes, Ma'am. I don't drive. Been ordering groceries over the phone ever since Miss Lillian passed."

Velma's mood brightened. She had a task. She would get dressed and go to the grocery store. She showered, putting on the slacks and blouse she'd saved for weekends when she worked.

When she worked. How could she not work? Work was her brain, her heart, her being. Fingers flying over the keys, sharp eyes proofing the briefs, making sure the office boys got documents filed before deadlines, keeping Will on schedule. Mary Lee Caster was sitting in her chair doing that right now. Velma's eyes stung. She blinked and swallowed. She was married to Will Hughes. She ought to be thanking the good Lord, not carrying on like a schoolgirl. She might not be at the office, but she would spend every night in a bed beside him.

She'd decided to enjoy the freedom two beds allowed. She had never spent a night with anyone except Garnett, if you didn't count squeezing in with Aunt Orrie on holidays. Until the honeymoon, she hadn't realized how loud Will Hughes snored. Velma's solution was to wait until he fell asleep, quietly open her bedside drawer, and slip in earplugs. That reduced him to a rumble. This maneuver would not be as easy if they slept in the same bed.

"See if you can make out my bad writing." She and Bessie went over the list. They were having fried chicken, rice with gravy, and green beans for supper. "What kind of salad you want with that?" Bessie said.

Velma had no idea. "Lettuce?"

Bessie gave a rumbling chuckle. "Mr. Will usually likes a little something on his lettuce."

Velma tried to think.

Bessie waited and when Velma offered nothing, said: "Maybe some pink grapefruit sections with the poppy seed dressing."

Thank God for this woman. "That sounds perfect." Velma added grapefruit to the list. "Do I need to buy a bottle of dressing?"

"No, baby. We make our dressing and I got everything I need. What you want for dessert?"

"Do we have dessert every night?"

"Every night. Mr. Will wouldn't think it was dinner if something sweet didn't show up at the end."

Silence while Velma scoured her head for what Will Hughes might want.

"You could pick up a carton of vanilla ice cream," Bessie said. "When we don't have a homemade dessert, he'll eat that."

Velma added ice cream and put on her coat. She tucked the list into her purse. She had a project, and if she shopped carefully, it might take most of the morning. She'd only have to think of a way to fill the afternoon.

"Don't be gone too long," Bessie said. "I like to soak my chicken in milk before I fry it."

An hour later Velma returned, arms filled with brown bags, feeling accomplished.

Bessie unpacked. "Next time, don't be buying this cut up chicken. A whole hen is cheaper and I can chop one up easy." She held up the vanilla ice cream. "Not the brand Mr. Will likes, but he won't see the carton, so I expect he won't know the difference." Velma felt chastised.

That task done, she needed to find another one. Maybe she would rearrange things, make the house feel more like her own. She walked into the living room, a nice enough space, but a little plain. She would never have chosen that dark green paper or covered the furniture in shades of beige and cream. Bright cushions might help. Everything looked so symmetrical: a chair to the left of the fireplace, a chair to the right. She picked up one of the two ugly vases balancing one another at either end of the mantel, moved them together on the left. Stood back to observe the effect.

Put them back, bitch.

Velma flinched. The voice she'd heard in the bedroom. Nobody else in the house except Bessie, who had the television going in the kitchen, but the words had been as clear as if someone stood behind her.

She didn't believe in ghosts, but this wasn't the first time. Back in her old house, every now and then, she thought she heard her name called. "Velma" — plain as day. She had the notion it might be God trying to get her attention, but she never got up the nerve to answer, "Yes, Lord?" the way people did in the Bible. She just held still, waiting for instructions, which failed to arrive, and decided it must be a phantom noise, like the shapes that darted at the corner of your eye and vanished when you turned to look.

This voice was like that, clear but internal, and the Lord wouldn't call you a bitch. Velma picked up one of the vases and moved it back to its original spot on the other end of the mantel.

Keep your hands off my things, the voice said.

Lillian. Velma fled to the kitchen and dropped trembling into one of the plastic-cushioned chrome chairs.

"You shaking," Bessie said.

"Got a funny feeling," Velma said. "Thought I'd better sit down."

"Uh-oh," Bessie said. "Is somebody expecting?"

"Lord, no." Velma decided to confide. "I had an operation. You don't need to worry about that."

"Good," Bessie said. "I'm too old to be chasing a baby."

Things got worse. If Velma went out to pick Will Hughes roses to take to the office, the voice said, *Cut lower on the stem, idiot.* When she helped Bessie by setting the table, the voice said, *Salad fork on the outside. Were you raised in a barn?*

She and Will started to make love one night and she heard a nasty chuckle. Velma froze, which made Will say, "What's wrong?" She tried to laugh the fear away and ended up crying. Will got a worried look on his face. The poor man must think he'd married a crazy woman.

She began going out in the afternoons to get away from the voice. She strolled Capitol Street or went to a movie. She didn't mention the voice to Will, but one day at lunch with Garnett, back at their old table in the drugstore in the office building, she described what was happening.

"But you don't believe in ghosts," Garnett said.

"Not really."

"You're probably hearing things because you're nervous being around her stuff. It's perfectly natural."

"But I can hear her so plainly."

"Like you said, the voice is inside your head, so you're not really hearing Lillian. No one is there."

"I'm sure you're right." Velma stared at the marks Garnett's teeth left in her grilled cheese sandwich. "But the voice corrected me about how to put forks on the table. I didn't know salad forks went on the outside, so how could I make that up?" Velma put down her spoon. She was too upset for tomato soup.

Garnett took one of Velma's hands. "Look at you, you're shaking. You probably read about table settings in a magazine and forgot. You're going to make yourself sick if you keep this up. You have to tell Will."

"I can't. He'll think I'm crazy."

"Well then, tell him you need to move. Tell him you can't be comfortable in a house filled with another woman's memories."

Driving home, Velma tried to picture herself doing that. Moving made sense, but a change that big wasn't likely. From what she'd seen of Will Hughes over thirty years of working with him and three months of marriage, he opposed anything that disturbed his routine. The physical world should stay in place so he could devote his energy to the law. And Velma also knew, if she were being honest, most of what Will liked about her was her agreeableness. Secretaries did as they were told, and she had brought that habit into her marriage.

124

On a warm Saturday night in June that first year, Velma and Will went to Paul and Angie McNamara's to barbecue steaks. Paul was a new partner in the firm. He'd been in the oil and gas business first and gone to law school late, joining the firm while Velma still worked there. Will took to him right away. He was older than the other associates and he'd been a Navy man, too. Velma watched her husband now, accepting a second bourbon and water from Angie, laughing aloud at something Paul said. Watching the steaks sizzle as if he knew one iota about barbecuing.

Their friends' house backed onto a small lake. Sitting outside in the evening air after dinner, Will took Velma's hand. "This is nice."

She said, "Beautiful." She loved being away from the house on Kings Highway. The voice never followed.

"Something about being on the water," Will said.

"So peaceful," Velma said.

"I always did want to live on a lake."

She turned to him. "Me, too."

Paul reappeared carrying a tray of brownies topped with vanilla ice cream, one of Will's favorite desserts. "Well, why don't you?" he said.

Velma cut off a corner of her brownie and scooped up a bite of ice cream. "We were just dreaming."

Paul pointed to the house next door. "The Magees plan on moving to the Gulf Coast to be nearer their daughter."

Velma felt a flicker of hope.

Angie arrived with cups and a pot of Sanka. "Oh, do it, Will. Wouldn't it be fun, Velma, living next door to each other?"

"It would," Velma said. "I would love that."

"Buy it, Will." Angie poured his coffee. "You probably have shoe boxes full of cash under the bed."

Beside her, Velma felt Will stiffen.

"What makes you think that?" he said.

He hated for people to talk about money. He'd told Velma it was nobody's business how much he had or didn't have. Hope faded. On the drive home he was quiet and Velma did not mention the house on the lake.

In bed, she reached up and switched off her light. "They're a fun couple."

She heard Will yawn in the dark. "Yep."

Silly bitch, the voice said.

Velma put in her earplugs.

Those won't keep me out, the voice said.

Maybe not, but they reduced the haranguing to an almost inaudible buzz.

125

February blew in with gray skies and sleety rain. Velma had been married to Will Hughes for a year. She had mastered the house routine, if not the voice. Every other weekend, Bessie got Saturday afternoon and Sunday off. On Sunday morning, Velma fixed Will's breakfast.

He doesn't like his orange juice in that glass.

You call that a scrambled egg?

Get out of my chair.

Without Bessie around, the voice turned meaner. Velma moved to another side of the table.

Will looked up from his newspaper. "What's wrong?"

"Nothing. I got in the mood to sit in a different chair."

"You're looking tired," Will said. "Are you getting enough sleep?"

She wasn't. Lillian had begun appearing in her dreams. In one, she sat on Velma's head like a great pillow. Velma struggled. "I can't breathe." Lillian's laughter smothered her choked cries. She woke to find herself deep under the covers gasping for air.

Oddly, on the two Sundays Bessie came to cook a midday meal, Lillian left her alone. She was replaced by April and her silent husband Walton, who never missed one of Bessie's days.

On this second Sunday in February, the four of them sat in the living room waiting to be called to dinner. April pointed to one of the bright sofa cushions Velma had added. "Mother never believed in color accents. She felt people provided the color."

"Is that right?" Velma's naturally soft voice sank to a whisper around this daughter. She sensed a seething anger in April, most of it directed at her. And why? It wasn't as if she'd killed Lillian. If Velma disappeared, the girl's mother would not come back.

Will's middle daughter strolled around the living room, picking up objects Velma had moved and returning them to their original positions. Velma sat on the couch, gritting her teeth, keeping a pleasant, closed-lip smile.

In the dining room, Velma kept her place next to Will and let April have Lillian's old seat. Examining the table, April said, "Mother saved this crocheted lace cloth for very special occasions. It's quite fragile."

"I didn't realize," Velma regretted the apologetic note in her voice.

"And, how could you?" April at her most syrupy.

In her lap, Velma wrung her napkin's neck. Of course, the country bumpkin didn't recognize fine things. She was too stupid to use Lillian's possessions. She didn't have the class or education to live in this house and she shouldn't be sleeping in the bed next to April's father.

"I'm sorry to see Mother's holly doing so poorly." April directed this remark to Will, as if Velma, who had put together the flower arrangement, weren't there.

"It looks fine to me." Will winked, signaling to Velma that she should not take any of this seriously.

Bessie brought out the salads. April took a bite and made a face. "Mother's boiled dressing doesn't taste the way it used to."

The plates came out with their servings of roast beef, rice and gravy. April said, "I so admired the way Mother used to carve at the table."

During dessert, she took a bite and put down her fork. "I swear, since Mother died, Bessie cannot make a decent chocolate cake. This one is dry as dust."

Out of sight under the table, Velma murdered her napkin again.

Will protested gently and April's husband agreed, defending Bessie, pretending the insults weren't directed at Velma—a woman who'd needed to go out and work for a living, and therefore didn't know fine cooking from a pot bottom.

Between the bites of cake she managed to get down, April turned to Velma, squinting with inquisitiveness. "What do you find to do with yourself now that you're not Daddy's secretary?"

Daddy's secretary. Velma stuttered making up things. "I've been going through closets and rearranging the pantry."

Velma stood at the door with Will, watching April and Walton drive away. "She hates me."

He pulled Velma close "That's just April. She likes to lord it over people. Don't take it personally."

No offer of an afternoon drive today. He was headed to the office where Velma longed to follow. She called out the back door. "Anytime you need extra help."

"You stay here and rest," Will said.

Velma went back through April's remarks, getting angry all over again. Will's daughter acted as if there were some magic to Lillian. She prepared nothing herself, but her mere presence in the kitchen guaranteed better results. Which might be true. Velma had the recipes, written in Lillian's flowery script, but she had no idea if they were coming out right or how to improve them. What made a cake dry? She left the cooking entirely up to Bessie.

With the dishes put away and the precious tablecloth soaking in cold water, Velma drove Bessie home. "You can sit here up front with me, you know," she said.

"Thank you kindly, but I'm comfortable back here."

"That was a great meal, Bessie. You did us proud."

"I do my best. Some people just never satisfied."

Silence. Were they both thinking about April?

She pulled up in front of Bessie's apartment.

Bessie leaned forward and patted Velma's shoulder. "Don't pay Miss April no mind. She always got a bee in her bonnet. Been that way since she was a little girl. You keep doing things the way you like them."

Weak, wretched tears. Velma swiped them away. "Thank you, Bessie." You probably weren't supposed to weep in front of a servant—Lillian wouldn't—but Bessie's kindness felt like a salve.

"And you got nothing to cry over." Bessie said. "You doing fine."

As soon as Velma walked inside the empty house, as if waiting, the voice started.

The roast was overcooked.

Not enough salt in the gravy.

Too much vinegar in the salad dressing.

The cake was terrible. Bessie's over-beating it.

If Garnett was right and the voice was only in her head, it sure knew a lot more than Velma did. She turned the radio up, but the voice crawled like a worm inside the music.

You will die, the voice said, *trying to please him.*

126

Velma made an appointment to speak to the minister about the problem. This was not the same man she'd gone to see years ago, crippled with guilt over sleeping with Will. That man had moved on, replaced by a large, confident, red-faced preacher named Russell Hanks, better at talking to a crowd than being stuck with a single troubled parishioner. Velma felt his misery and described the voice as briefly as she could.

"It's Satan." Reverend Hanks gave a thump to the coffee table between them. "Whoever it sounds like in your head, it's Satan. It's always Satan." Two more thumps. "The devil can take on any voice. Sly as a serpent. You must cast him out, Sister Velma. When he begins to speak, fall to your knees and say, 'Out, out, foul demon.'"

This did not sound like a practical solution, but Velma thanked him, made a donation to the building fund, and left.

When she was alone in the house and Lillian started up, Velma whispered, "Out, out."

The voice laughed in her ear. *Can you tell how bored Will is with you?*

It always sounded a little drunk. Did ghosts drink?

She wondered if Will was bored. She was a dull person, duller now than when she worked. She did not have interesting stories when he came home from the office, but then she had never been that person. Her role was to laugh at Will and be his number one fan. She didn't want to ask him if Lillian was right. She suspected nothing bored a man quicker than being asked if he was bored. And if he said yes, what could she do — take French lessons?

Maude tried to come up once a month on one of the weekends Bessie didn't work. For Velma, her arrival was like a party, and a reprieve, since the voice went quiet in the presence of Will's youngest daughter. Maude slept in Helen's old room. They made Will take them out to eat, and April was not invited.

On this April Sunday afternoon, with Will at the office, Velma and Maude sat at the kitchen table. Maude had arrived with two bottles of her new favorite wine, white zinfandel, which was actually a nice pink color. "From the grape skins," Maude said.

Velma took a sip. "Sweet," she said.

"Fruity." Maude corrected.

"It's very nice." Velma described the way April had acted at Sunday dinner.

Maude nodded. "She's always thought she was better than the rest of us."

They tipped their cigarettes into the brown glass ashtray. Velma's mama wouldn't recognize this daughter, drinking and smoking on a Sunday.

"I know this sounds peculiar." Velma refilled their glasses. "I keep thinking I hear your mother's voice."

"Me, too." Maude leaned over the table, eyes alight. "Does she fuss at you? That's what she does to me."

"So, you don't think it's crazy?"

"You're living in her house. You're sleeping in her bed. Of course, you hear her. I'm a hundred and fifty miles south and she manages to find me. 'Don't gobble your food, Maude.' 'Eat your vegetables.' 'Hunger is your friend.'" Maude mashed her cigarette out. She smoked only about half of each one. "Just tell her to shut up. That's what I do."

A wave of relief passed through Velma. Maude didn't think it odd that her dead mother spoke. She liked the idea of telling Lillian to shut up better than yelling, "Out, foul demon."

Maude flicked her lighter and lit another Pall Mall. "Did I tell you what my crazy husband does on weekends?

Velma hadn't yet met Lyle, who was a professor of history at a junior college in Perkinston.

"Re-enacting," Maude said.

Velma frowned. "I've never heard of it."

"You dress up in Confederate uniforms and act out Civil War battles."

"My word." He sounded like an idiot.

"It's just play-acting." Maude got up to empty the ashtray. "There's another whole bunch in Yankee uniforms."

Maude was getting heavier, but in Velma's eyes her extra pounds equaled good cheer. April's skinniness only made her meaner.

The light outside faded: another weekend over. Maude gathered her things. "It's a long ride home."

Velma gave her a squeeze. "As long as I get to have you, you tell Lyle he can play-act as many battles as he wants."

Civil War reenactments—my word. Some people did not have enough to do. Getting to know Bessie had made Velma rethink the Civil War. She'd been taught to revere it as the South's tragic lost cause—brave southern rebels outnumbered by cruel northern aggressors. But as far as she could see, it had been about keeping colored people slaves. When she brought the subject up with Will, he said, no, it was about state's rights, the same rights that were being trampled today by the Supreme Court and the Voting Rights Act. He got so wrought up, Velma decided not to mention it again. Except it did seem to her that sitting in the kitchen talking to Bessie *was* integration and, day-to-day, about the only fun Velma had.

The next time the voice started, Velma said "Shut up," before it got the second word out. She kept at it. The voice did not give up, but talking back helped, and it certainly improved her mood.

At dinner one night a few weeks later, Will told Velma about a new case: a man tried to burn up his house and possessions to collect on the insurance. He was seen throwing a flaming skillet into his convertible parked outside. He claimed he was only trying to get the flames out of the house, but the insurance examiners found a scorched pot on what was left of a leather couch, and a second skillet on the man's bed.

Bessie, who'd been passing the peas, started laughing.

"A flaming skillet?" Tears squeezed out of her eyes; the gigantic bosoms shook. She froze in place, her large body quivering, helpless with laughter.

"Grab the peas," Will said. Velma did, and Will helped Bessie into the kitchen and got her down onto a chair. Velma heard her wheezing with glee through the dining room door.

Will returned, whispering. "That happened once when the children were small. Bessie started laughing at one of my stories and fell on the dining room floor. None of us could get her up. Lillian had to call the fire department."

Putting away the clean dishes after Bessie left that night, Velma started giggling. What if she'd done what the preacher said: fallen to her knees when Lillian started her insults, and hollered: "Out, out foul demon." They would never have gotten Bessie off the floor.

Another month passed, and Velma managed, taking Maude's advice, to keep Lillian's voice under control. She spent her afternoons in the kitchen with Bessie watching soap operas. She'd gotten caught up in *Days of Our Lives* and *The Guiding Light*. Lillian never interrupted, and Velma and Bessie discussed the characters' entanglements as if they were real people. Bessie said Miss Lillian used to spend most afternoons playing bridge, so Velma pictured her off somewhere enjoying a ghostly game.

Mornings were for grocery shopping. Afternoons they spent in kitchen chairs watching the small TV, Bessie's bottom lip fat with snuff, which she spat discreetly into an empty Red Seal tin. At night in bed, Velma wore earplugs.

Between the distractions and the earplugs, she was able to cut Lillian to one or two hateful comments a day. On Saturdays, Velma shopped and went to a movie with Garnett, or with another secretary if Garnett couldn't come.

Sunday afternoons were the hardest. Will frequently returned to the office after lunch, so Velma took to walking. She headed up Kings Highway to the Fondren Shopping Center and came back home through Woodland Hills. She liked looking in the store windows and noticing what people did with their yards. No one else walked except a few Negro servants trudging toward home. People driving by in cars looked at Velma curiously. She didn't care. Lillian's voice never accompanied her outside the house. When she got home, head cleared and legs tired, she took a hot bath in the hall bathroom (another place Lillian did not enter). She powdered and put on fresh clothes. By this time, Will had returned.

"You smell so good," he'd said last Sunday, arms around her, nose in her hair.

Velma rested her head against his cheek. "Ham sandwiches for supper?" There were few problems a good secretary couldn't figure a way around.

In spite of Lillian's taunts, in spite of not knowing what to do with herself for whole chunks of the day, when Velma made up Will's bed and caught a whiff of Old Spice or, passing his framed photograph in the living room, recalled the way those eyes softened when he looked at her, such an overwhelming happiness overtook her, she had to stop and take a breath. Whenever she got bored or down, or missed the office so much she wanted to scream, she reminded herself that God had given Velma Vernon, His unworthy servant, the man she wanted most in the world.

127

On the Sundays Bessie didn't come, Velma and Will often ate lunch at Will's favorite restaurant, LeFleur's. They sat at the same table each Sunday, waited on by his chosen waitress, a small, fast-moving woman who managed to combine deference with flirtation. Velma faced the wall because Will enjoyed being able to survey the room. Every Sunday, he ordered an identical meal for the two of them: trout almondine, puffed potatoes, an oily salad, and key lime pie. Today, Velma took a breath and said she believed she'd try the chicken instead.

Will looked astonished. "You don't like the trout?"

"I love the trout, but I think today I'll have roast chicken for a change." She smiled at the waitress, pleased with this tiny step into independence. The chicken actually wasn't as tasty as the trout, but that wasn't the point.

On Sunday afternoons, if Will didn't go to the office, they took a drive. This was the sole change marriage had made in his schedule. Two weeks before, they'd driven over to Vicksburg to see the National cemetery. Riding through the park-like acres, where seventeen thousand dead Yankee soldiers lay buried, Will said, "If only we'd had better generals." Velma nodded, but what she felt was pity. So much wasted youth.

The country was now ten years into another war in faraway Viet Nam, with thirty thousand American boys dead and no telling how many Vietnamese. Two students had been shot for protesting the war right here in Jackson. A week earlier, in Washington DC, over two-hundred thousand marched in protest of the war. Will sat in front of the television looking disgusted. He said they must be liberals and probably communists. This required no response and Velma kept her thoughts on war's terrible waste to herself.

Today, Will drove out Old Canton Road and pulled into the driveway next door to the McNamaras.

"Are we visiting Paul and Angie?" Velma hated showing up unannounced. "Their house is one driveway over."

"I know. What do you think of this one?'

"This house?" She stared at it. "It's nice."

"Let's walk around." He got out.

"This is private property, Will. The owners may be at home."

"Won't hurt to look. Paul says they've already moved to the Gulf Coast."

Will crossed the front lawn and Velma followed. He stopped to examine the brickwork. She had to smile. The man was helpless around a house, unskilled and unwilling. Will Hughes literally could not hang a picture.

"Looks in good shape," he said.

"Very sturdy." Actually, Velma found it ugly, low and sprawling with blood-colored brick up to the windows and white siding above. Not nearly as homey as their gray-shingled bungalow. From the front, with all the shades down, the house appeared to have closed its eyes against busy Old Canton Road.

They walked around back. Traffic noise from the street faded. When you got back here, the world out front ceased to exist. Being on a lake made all the difference. Really more of a large pond to Velma's country eyes, but lovely, with a little island in the middle and woods behind.

Will walked her around the perimeter. The water looked dark green. A concrete walk led from the bank to a grassy island in the middle. On the far side, a forest of pines hid the houses beyond. Heading back to the house, they crossed an earthen dam. Will held her hand. It tickled Velma that he thought her fragile. He'd never seen her digging turnips.

"It's a man-made lake." He sounded as if he were apologizing. A gray rowboat rested on the bank. The long, low house looked more attractive from this angle. A screened porch stretched across the back. Velma spotted a row of rocking chairs. The two houses had the lake to themselves, a private world.

They strolled back up the hill. "That screened porch could be closed in," Will said.

"I guess it could."

"With maybe a fireplace like the one you had at your old house."

"A fireplace is always nice." Her house had been sold and the proceeds banked. "For your future," Will Hughes said, as if he wouldn't be here. She missed every one of her small rooms. At Will's house, she found herself sitting on the edge of chairs like a temporary occupant, which was probably what Lillian's voice had in mind.

"What do you think?" Will said.

She must have lost track of the conversation. "It's a nice place."

"I thought you'd say that."

Silence. This must be what novels meant by a pregnant pause.

Will said, "So I bought it."

Her brain scrambled to make sense of what she'd heard and when she did, her body burned with shock. "You *bought* it?"

"I knew you'd be pleased."

Velma wasn't sure if that's what you called this feeling. She took a calming breath. "What's it like inside?" Her chest felt tight. He'd done this enormous thing without talking to her, gone and bought a house. Not a car, which was bad enough, but a whole house. What kind of man bought a house without showing it to his wife?

Will appeared confused by the question. "I haven't been inside yet. Didn't think that was necessary. The real estate lady told me it has three bedrooms and the right number of baths, and the price seemed fair. I figured we could change anything we didn't like."

Velma tried to sort the pain of being excluded from the pleasure of leaving Lillian behind on King's Highway. Will did not enjoy being crossed, and she'd already declined the fish. She spoke in the gentlest way possible. "We could have talked."

He frowned. "I thought we did—that night at Angie and Paul's. You said you liked the idea of living on the water."

She felt lightheaded. This was incredible and so like a man—no—so like Will Hughes. One dinner, weeks ago, where she'd agreed it would be fun to live next door to Paul and Angie and, without another word, he buys the house next door. She tried to laugh off her exasperation. "Can we go inside now?"

Will said, "I don't have a key yet. We'll be able to see it after the closing next week."

"I can't believe you did this." This was at least true.

He gripped her hand looking pleased. "I wanted to surprise you"

Well, he'd succeeded in doing that and she'd probably feel joyful when she got over the shock. A house was the biggest thing a couple could own and he'd chosen one without her.

"We'll be next door to our friends and I can fish in the lake." He sounded as excited as a kid.

Driving home, Velma began to think clearly again. The new house would be hers, not Lillian's. She took a deep breath. If she didn't like the interior, she could paint and wallpaper. She would be able to get her furniture out of storage. Lillian's voice didn't follow her to the grocery or the beauty parlor. With any luck, it wouldn't follow them to the new house. She reached over and patted Will's arm. "You are an astonishing man."

He smiled without taking his eyes off the road. "I like making you happy." That night, holding hands across the divide (the name Will had given the crack between the twin beds), they discussed the move. Will told her to take whatever she liked from this house and get rid of the rest. They decided to keep the twin beds with the single headboard. Will liked his space and, after thirty years of sleeping alone, Velma enjoyed the solitude. After a few minutes of snuggling across the divide, it was nice to retreat and don earplugs. When, on some nights, the noise of his snoring penetrated even these, she put a pillow over her head.

Will had wakened one morning to find Velma with her head sandwiched between two pillows. "You'll smother."

"It's cozy," Velma said. She never mentioned the snoring.

Maude was not so polite. During one monthly visit, she spoke up at Sunday lunch. "Daddy, you *snore*."

Will looked down his nose at his youngest daughter. "I don't think so."

"Like a broken-down freight train." Maude imitated him roaring and stopping, roaring and stopping. "I don't see how Velma stands it."

Velma smiled and said she wasn't bothered, didn't even hear it.

Will was vehement in his denials.

Lying in bed on this night, owner — half-owner — of a house she had yet to see, holding hands with Will across the divide, Velma heard Lillian's voice buzzing angrily. But that's all it was, a buzz. She kissed Will good night, put in her earplugs, and fell asleep.

128

Escrow closed on the Old Canton Road house and Velma got inside. It was larger than Lillian's house: three roomy bedrooms, two and half baths, a large kitchen; a living and dining room separated by a brick fireplace, a paneled den on the lake side and the big screened porch along the back. She didn't particularly care for the yellowish-green color of the living and dining room walls, and she would definitely get rid of that rooster wallpaper in the kitchen, but it was a good, solid house, and it was hers—no part of it had ever belonged to Lillian.

She drove Bessie over to see it.

Getting herself through the back door with the help of her cane, Bessie looked around. "Nice big kitchen. Look at that fine rooster wallpaper. Plenty of room for us to put our TV on that counter yonder." She pointed to the right of the sink. "And see this empty space by the dining room door? I'll get you to buy me a chest freezer."

Velma walked her down the hall, past the pink half bath, the blue full bath, through the master bedroom to a white bath. "A lot of tile to clean," Bessie said. "Doreen's back won't appreciate that."

"Mr. Hughes never told me he was buying a house," Velma said. "Bought it without ever seeing the inside." She had not admitted her dismay aloud until now, and she felt ashamed.

"Mens." Bessie said the word as if you couldn't expect more of that peculiar half of humanity. She stood on the screened porch. "That's a fine lake out there. Get me a cane pole and I bet I can catch us some supper."

Will called to tell the children about the new house.

Velma heard April's voice coming through the receiver like an angry wasp.

When he hung up, she asked innocently. "What did she say?"

"April can't believe we bought a house without telling her. Can't believe I would sell her mother's home." He mimicked April's disapproving tone. "'The place where we all grew up, a place filled with our family's memories.' There's more, but you get the drift."

Velma added this to her store of grievances against Will's middle daughter: April had spoiled their engagement, yet managed to get insulted at not being invited to the wedding. She resented Will's taking Velma to Hawaii, where "Mother always wanted to go." She made fun of Velma's decorating, criticized her cooking, and now begrudged them a house. April needed a good shaking.

129

They had lived in the new house for two months. Lillian's voice had not followed and Velma grew serene without the disparaging buzz. She and Will walked around the lake at sunset. They cooked out with Angie and Paul. She loved being surrounded by her own things. She hadn't dared to bring the ballerina lamp into the master bedroom, satisfied to visit it in the back guest room.

At breakfast one morning in August, Will Hughes peered around the edge of his newspaper. "Fall's coming soon. Be good to get that screened porch closed in before winter."

"It would." This was the second time he'd mentioned closing the porch and Velma realized she was supposed to make it happen. The only builder she knew was Helen's ex-husband Jack. Helen had left him to run off with a civil rights lawyer, but he was almost kin. She called.

Jack sounded kind on the telephone and came over that very afternoon. He shook his head at the old screened porch, saying things about thrust and support. He asked what they had in mind. Velma described the fireplace in her old den with windows on either side. She said Will wanted to be able to watch television and look out at the lake at the same time. Jack took measurements and said he would come back with a drawing.

She was able to report progress to Will that night over dinner and the smile he gave her, his obvious excitement, made Velma feel she didn't need a heaven.

Jack returned to meet with them both, spreading a blueprint out on the dining room table. Velma couldn't make heads or tails of it, but Will listened and looked wise. They walked outside and studied the rusting screened porch. Jack talked about the steel beam they needed to span the length so no columns would break the view. Will made knowing noises, though Velma suspected he understood no more than she.

"This would be the fireplace." Jack stepped it off. "And on either side, floor-to-ceiling windows." He stepped those off. "Room for a couch here." They stood in front of the hypothetical couch. "A couple of easy chairs. Television here." Jack walked to the left. "Plenty of room up at that end for a small dining table." Did they want exposed beams? Indirect lighting?

Velma felt dizzy at the choices. They sat down in the living room with cups of coffee and Jack talked about the cost. He said a number that made Velma almost topple off the couch—fifty thousand dollars.

Will coughed.

"That includes a separate air conditioning system. We would basically tear out the old porch and start from scratch. We'll need to raise the slab, so you won't have to step down from the den or kitchen."

Fifty thousand dollars. Almost five times what Velma had paid for an entire house. She looked at Will, waiting for him to say no.

"I think we can manage that." Will studied the plans. "Why don't you tell me what you need for a deposit and we'll call it a deal."

They shook hands. Jack said he'd have to get engineered drawings and a permit, but his men could probably begin demolition within the month.

When he was gone, Velma took Will by both hands. "Can we afford fifty thousand dollars?"

"Don't you worry about that," he said. "I'm going to give you the best closed-in porch a wife ever had."

At the office, Will used to complain when Lillian wanted to slipcover a couch. He was doing well now, but Velma had no idea how much money they had. He never talked about what he earned. Any discussion of money was considered bad taste and a proper woman shouldn't be curious. The children were grown and gone. Will was on the board at Deposit Guaranty Bank and had taken on another big client, the Mississippi Power Company.

Velma knew of these triumphs, but nothing about the money involved. He gave her a generous monthly allowance and she had a household checking account. She kept careful track of expenditures in her yearbook, putting a mark by each entry when a check cleared. There was always more than enough in the account to cover the bills. She'd known more about his assets when she worked for him than she did now as his wife.

"Don't bother your head," Will said, acting as if this were a compliment and her mind were a room he didn't want to over-furnish.

Sitting on the screened back porch the next day, rocking, watching the reflection of clouds racing across the green water of the lake, Velma thought how funny men were, the way they had to excuse giving themselves a treat by claiming it was for you. *Fifty thousand dollars.* Her parents must be rolling in their graves.

April got wind of the plans (Doreen cleaned for her, too.) She called her father, questioning the decision. She came by the next Saturday with Walton. Will walked them around, describing what was to be done and how fine it would be to sit in front of his fire watching color television, with birds at the feeders outside and a view of the lake.

April got Velma alone in the kitchen and asked how much all this was going to cost. Startled by the bluntness of the question, Velma blurted out the number. The rage in the young woman's eyes made her wish she hadn't. April marched into the living room and confronted Will. "Do you really think you ought to be spending that kind of money at your age?"

People tended to act cautious around April, who could switch from pleasant and soft-voiced to red-faced and screaming in about two seconds.

Will showed no outward anger, but Velma heard it in the way his voice flattened. "It is nobody's business how I spend my money."

April must have heard it, too, because she didn't say another word.

Velma apologized to Will after they left. "I never should have told her."

"Are you familiar with the word harridan?" Will said.

Velma shook her head no.

"Well, I have raised one."

Harridan. Velma reminded herself to look it up.

Workers arrived the next week and began demolishing the screen porch. Velma never saw anything go down so fast, almost as if it had never been real. She gave the rockers away, one to Bessie, one to Doreen, and one to Abe, who rode a mower over the big lawn each week.

Having a construction crew around was almost as good as having a job. They arrived at seven, so Velma needed to be up and dressed early. She made coffee for them in the morning and offered mugs of ice water in the afternoons. They were nice men, jokey around her and Bessie, working men like the ones she'd grown up with. She felt easy in their company.

Big lumber trucks pulled into the driveway. One exciting day, cement mixers arrived and poured gray slush that hardened into their new slab.

Each evening, she and Will walked around the job and Velma explained what had been accomplished that day and what could be expected the next. She was, she realized one morning, standing in the hall bathroom putting on lipstick at 6:45 am, happier than she'd been since she left the office. She felt useful and a part of something. She had to stop and chide herself. Being married to Will was happiness enough, especially after spending her entire youth waiting for the opportunity. Being right here when he got home, running his house, keeping him content should be plenty.

Framed walls went up and, one day, a crane lowered the big steel support beam into place. A crane in their very own driveway. Velma and Bessie were beside themselves. The roof went on, the huge windows were installed. Brick masons arrived and built the fireplace in a day. The electricians did their mysterious work and the sheet-rockers covered it up. Velma enjoyed a dizzying three months and then it was done. The painters came and went. Jack made his final inspection, and the new room stood ready for Velma to decorate.

She missed the rough company of the carpenters, but she busied herself taking care of the interior. Even now, after spending an enormous sum building the place, Will refused to hold back. "Do it up the way you want."

Velma chose pale blue carpeting (blue being Will's favorite color), a darker blue sofa and armchairs, a nice mahogany coffee table, matching end tables, tall brass lamps, and a small round dining table with four chairs for the space nearest the kitchen.

When it was finished, on a night in early November, with everything still smelling of paint and new carpet, they built a fire. It was not actually cold enough for a fire and the new room had its own central heat.

"Turn the air conditioning on," Will said. "Make it cold."

She did. They sat on the couch, him with his Manischewitz, her with a glass of white zinfandel, watching the evening news while the fire crackled and dusk fell over the lake.

"This is something," Will said. "Isn't this something?"

Basking in the warmth of his pleasure, Velma had to agree. This was something.

130

By Christmas of 1979, Velma had been Mrs. Will Hughes for ten years. Her waist had thickened, which she blamed on Bessie's desserts. Will claimed he couldn't see a bit of difference.

She decorated the house for the holidays: a large tree in the living room, a wreath on the front door, pine boughs on the mantel. On Christmas Eve, she and Will hosted the law firm party. Carolers from the firm sang. Velma served the same finger food Lillian once made: cheese straws, sausage balls, butterball cookies. She made a batch of Lillian's thick, rich eggnog. She wore a new black velvet dress with the gold and pearl necklace and earrings Will had given her the previous Christmas. Circulating, more relaxed than she could have imagined back in her office days, Velma caught Will's eye. He winked, happy with her and the festivities.

The next day, she presided over Christmas dinner for Will's children and Lillian's side of the family. Ernestine, Leland, and Olive still attended holiday meals.

Bessie made turkey and Lillian's stuffing, rice and giblet gravy, peas with button mushrooms, and yeast rolls. These were served with butter and homemade jelly, which Velma could make as well as Lillian, thanks to those long-ago summers with Mama. For dessert, Bessie's layer cakes waited on the sideboard: three layers of chocolate and three of coconut.

This year Velma felt fortunate: April had not so far thrown a temper fit and left the table, which she'd done the year before; Helen's new husband did not stand up and chant a loud Hebrew blessing the way he'd done last Easter, startling them out of their reverence.

Velma sat at the head of the table observing the family. She felt a certain distance from them, but not in a negative way. They tended not to see her and when she chose to stay silent, no one noticed.

"Pass the jelly, would you, Olive?" Ernestine turned to Velma. "Did Bessie make this? It's delicious."

"I made it," Velma said.

"We didn't know you could cook," April said.

Helen spoke. "What do you think they do for food when Bessie's not here?"

"Velma is a wonderful cook." Maude to the defense.

She wasn't a wonderful cook. She kept a notebook filled with recipes she had clipped from magazines, but noticed Will did not take to new dishes.

"You don't have to stick to Mama's menu for Christmas and Easter," Maude said.

"I don't mind," Velma said. In truth, she had no better alternatives and dreaded what April might say if she did change the menu.

"It's important to maintain family traditions." April looked around the table for consent.

"I agree," Velma said. But April had turned away to listen to Leland who was speaking to Eric.

"I just read a history of the Jews," Leland said. "I never realized how much you people suffered."

Helen guffawed.

"Very kind of you to take an interest," Eric said.

Velma saw Will frown. Dinner conversation should not be religious or political, especially not with his civil rights lawyer son-in-law present.

She rang the bell and asked Bessie to bring more hot rolls. They were such talkers in this family, interrupting and speaking over one another. By the time everyone left and Will drove Bessie home, Velma needed to lie down with a damp cloth over her eyes. She no longer got anxious around Will's family, but the commotion wore her out.

131

Maude still visited once a month. Will went to bed before 9:00, or fell asleep in bed watching an Atlanta Braves baseball game. This allowed Velma and Maude to stay up as late as they liked, sitting at the kitchen table, sipping zinfandel and smoking.

For a treat, Velma had ordered a set of balloon-shaped wine glasses with tall pastel stems.

"Pretty." Maude turned the green stem of her glass. "Tell me about how you and Daddy fell in love."

"I told you that story."

"Tell me again."

"The war ended. Your father walked in the door of the law office in his white uniform. I took one look and that was it."

Maude took a deep breath. "How old were you?"

Velma thought. "I started at the firm when I was eighteen. I must have been twenty."

Maude looked envious.

"I felt bad about, you know, your mother, but I never—I never loved anyone else." Velma traced the pattern in the red Formica with a finger. "So, I waited." She left out the part when she hadn't waited.

"It's the best love story ever." Maude tapped the ash from her cigarette. "And don't feel bad about Mother. They were never right for each other. Mama drank, to escape I guess, and Daddy hated that. A lot of nights, by suppertime, she couldn't get her words out right."

Velma remembered Will talking about it.

"Daddy wasn't happy. He used to sit at his end of the table chewing with his eyes shut, like he didn't want to be there." Maude topped off their glasses. "He's happier with you than I've ever seen him."

Hearing this made sparklers fire off in Velma's chest. It might be the wine. Maude went through glass after glass and Velma sipped. Too much wine left her muzzy-headed. They emptied two bottles in an evening. Maude never seemed to get drunk, just happy, and there was the fun of going out for groceries the next day and stopping by the liquor store for replacements.

Maude had grown heavier with the years. She had always been plump, but now you'd honestly have to call her fat. Velma never said a word. She adored Will's youngest daughter. Maude could get as big as she liked.

"Don't you get bored sitting here at home?" Maude poured the last of the bottle in her glass.

"I do miss the excitement of the office," Velma said. "Don't tell your father I said that. It would hurt his feelings."

"I won't."

"Bessie and I keep each other company and we have our soaps in the afternoons. We love all the incest and amnesia and stolen inheritances. Stuff you couldn't stand in real people."

"Which reminds me," Maude said. "Guess what Lyle started collecting?"

Velma tried: "Books about the civil war?"

"He's got those. Worse."

"What?"

"Nazi memorabilia."

"Goodness." Velma was genuinely shocked. Maude's tall, skinny husband came for holiday dinners and Velma found him unexceptional. She did wonder if Maude had married him because he was the only one who asked. Lyle reminded her a little of Chalmers Root, that same country roughness with a bit of a pumpkin head.

Isn't that horrible?" Maude said. "Next, he'll be bringing home a lampshade made of human skin."

"He would never."

Maude nodded over the top of her glass. "I wouldn't put it past him. The man is in love with war. He told me the other night, that in World History, he spends one day on Pax Romana. And that's how he pronounces it. Pax, like it rhymes with axe."

Velma wasn't sure what Pax Romana was and made a mental note to look it up.

Maude looked around the kitchen. "What do you and Daddy do with yourselves when we're not around?"

"If the weather is nice, most Saturdays we cook out with Angie and Paul." Velma ground her cigarette into the glass ashtray and got up to empty it. "Weekdays, I do the grocery shopping and get my hair done. Sundays, I go to church by myself. I wish you'd speak to your father about that."

Maude shook her head. "Not me. I'm the sweet, agreeable daughter. Get Helen to talk to him."

"Helen doesn't go to church either. And besides, your father loves you best."

Maude turned pink at the compliment and lit another cigarette. "I doubt that, and he definitely doesn't like anyone telling him what to do." She flipped through the pile of catalogs that had arrived that day in the mail.

"I love going through those," Velma said. "I order treats for your dad and me. Last month, I got us soup from France —"

"Which I'll bet he didn't eat," Maude said.

"He did taste it, and he likes the coffee I get from California. Fun having packages arrive. Gives Bessie and me something to look forward to."

Maude gave her a quizzical look. "Don't you get lonely?"

"Me? Never. Though I will admit —" Velma leaned closer and lowered her voice. " —your father does love work. Goes to the office five days a week and some nights. Back there most Saturday and Sunday mornings."

"Same thing when Mama was alive," Maude said. "Do we have any more wine?"

Velma threw away the empty and got another bottle from the refrigerator. "When he's home, though, he listens when I talk."

Maude unscrewed the cap and filled their glasses. "What do you talk about?"

"If I'm starting a new afghan, I ask his opinion about colors. If I'm thinking of trying of a new recipe, I read the ingredients to see if he'll like it."

"Don't let him treat you the way he treated Mother."

"Oh, honey, you see him. He's sweet as pie to me."

Silence while Maude downed her wine and Velma pretended to drink hers. "Once I would have known about every case he's working on," Velma said. "That's the part I miss."

"He never should have made you stop working," Maude said. "You two could have been like Nick and Nora Charles in those old movies."

"That's not your father's idea of a wife, I'm afraid." Velma carried Maude's empty glass and her full one to the sink.

Don't let him treat you the way he treated Mother. The difference being, Velma reminded herself after Maude went to bed, Will Hughes loved her. When she caught his eye, she saw the affection. The way he looked at her made her insides dissolve. Lillian might have been first, but Velma was the one he loved.

132

A week later, Velma woke to a loud knock on the back door. What on earth? She checked the clock on her table—10:30 pm. Will Hughes snored on, undisturbed. She got out of bed, put on her robe, and crept into the kitchen. The knocking grew louder. Without turning on the light, Velma parted the curtain overlooking the driveway and saw April's station wagon. *Good grief.* She switched on the light and unlocked the back door.

April stood there as if it were noon. "May I come in?"

"Of course." Velma opened the door wider. "Is anything wrong?"

"I thought I'd stop by for a chat. That's what you do with Maude, right?"

How did she know? "Sit down, won't you. Can I get you anything—coffee, tea?"

"Wine if you've got it."

Velma poured two glasses of zinfandel and joined April at the table.

The young woman looked squinty-eyed with worry. Her hands shook. She pulled the brown glass ashtray to the center of the table and fished in her purse for cigarettes. "Want one?"

"Not just now," Velma said. "Is everything okay?"

"You won't repeat what I tell you?"

"Not if you don't want me to."

"Especially not to Daddy." April took a deep drag of the cigarette.

"Of course not."

"I really can't stand being married to Walton anymore." She rolled the cigarette against the ashtray's edge until a cylinder of gray ash broke off. "Some days I dislike him so much I'm afraid I may push him down the stairs."

Velma felt wary of the sudden confidences, but she couldn't think of a reason not to listen. "That must be a terrible feeling."

"I should have married Nick Greener."

"Who is Nick Greener?"

"He was my high school boyfriend." April stared at the floor. "The only man I ever loved, and now he's single and lives around the corner." She inhaled with what sounded like a sob. "I realize what a mistake I made marrying Walton, and then doubled it by having a child. He and Margaret are driving me to an early grave. I'll never get a chance to be with Nick Greener."

The girl was insane. Velma pressed her lips together in sympathy.

"You make one bad choice," April said, "two, counting Margaret, and your life is over. I pretend everything is perfect and I do try to keep a nice home. Everyone thinks I have the perfect husband, and aren't we lucky to have this darling child?" Her voice grew shrill. "But it's not like that at all. Most of the time, it's *horrible.*"

What was the treatment for hysterics? Velma couldn't think. Instead, she got up and closed the door between the kitchen and den. "Don't want to wake your father."

April sobbed into her hands. "I hate everything about my life."

Psychiatrists said such wise things in the soap operas. Velma wished she could remember what they were. "I am so sorry." She got up and fetched the box of tissues.

April gave her a disgusted look.

What had she said wrong?

"You couldn't possibly understand. Nothing's ever happened to you." April stopped to drink. "Bessie and all the relatives think Margaret's such an angel. We never told you, did we, about how she crawled out of her crib — her *crib* — one night when she was two? Went downstairs, pulled a chair up to the refrigerator, and opened the freezer to get herself a popsicle. In the middle of the night when we're all asleep. Left the freezer door open and everything inside spoiled."

"Oh my," Velma said.

April nodded, pouring herself more wine. "That's not the worst. The next year, she did it again. Crept downstairs while we were asleep and turned on the stove burners. No flame—just gas. If Walton hadn't smelled it, we could have been blown to smithereens."

"That's frightening."

"You're telling me. All before the child turned four." April ground out one cigarette and lit another. "So, we put a lock on the outside of her bedroom door. Walton didn't want to, but I said we'd never be able to sleep if we didn't. When Margaret realized she was locked in, she went crazy. Screaming like a banshee, flinging stuff at the door. Walton wanted to let her out, but I wouldn't let him. We just laid in bed listening. It went on for hours. Neither one of us slept."

"What did you do then?"

"We took her to a doctor who told us Margaret was a sensitive child with anger issues. As if we didn't know that. I began sleeping in the room with her, which seemed to calm her down. I would know if she got up and we didn't have to lock the door. When she turned eight, she told me I could go back to my room." April emptied her glass and peered into the empty bottle.

"Sounds like a brilliant solution." Velma took the hint and got another bottle of wine out of the refrigerator.

"Except now she hates us both, especially me. And Walton won't hear a word against her. If Margaret throws a fit, and she throws a few, he wants to know what *I* did to trigger it. If we catch her lying, he says *I* gave her no choice." April put down her glass. Her mouth trembled. "Walton says Margaret is the way she is because she has an unstable mother."

Which sounded reasonable. "You poor dear." Velma patted April's hand and pushed the tissue box closer.

April stood, blew her nose hard, and glared at Velma. "The only thing worse than what I'm going through is your pity." She put her cigarettes in her purse and left.

Not so much as a thank you. Watching the car back down the drive, Velma felt used. April was not well. One wrong word and she jumped on you like a viper. Even her driving looked angry.

The next morning at breakfast, Velma spoke to Will Hughes behind his newspaper. "Your daughter April dropped by last night after you went to bed."

He lowered the paper looking pleased. "Did she?"

The next time April and her family came for Sunday dinner, Will's daughter treated her as if the late night confession had never happened. Daring Velma with her accusing eyes to mention it.

The visits continued, as did April's strange behavior. Every three or four months, Velma heard the late-night pounding. Each occasion went much the same: complaints about Walton and Margaret, along with April's longing for the high school boyfriend. Velma refrained from touching her step-daughter again, and tried to limit her responses to sympathetic sounds. These nights were not enjoyable, and Velma woke the next day feeling exhausted. But, aggravated as she got with April's odd behavior, Velma felt a great pity for the young woman, who was so obviously miserable.

She reported each visit to Will Hughes. "I'm glad you're becoming friends," he said. Just like a man not to ask what you talked about. Velma would not have called this friendship. She felt more like a vessel April poured herself into. She never repeated a word to Maude.

One night, April arrived more distraught than usual. Unable to sit at the kitchen table, she paced, wine in one hand, cigarette in the other. "This was Mama's ashtray." She ground the cigarette out in the brown glass dish.

Velma kept her voice neutral. "I thought it might be."

"A lot of the stuff you use is Mama's."

Here we go. Velma responded with a pleasant smile.

"But she never had a ring like that." Pointing to Velma's diamond.

Velma resisted the impulse to turn the ring around. What a rotten little apple this one was.

"May I take a bath?"

The clock on the wall read 11:00 pm. There was no limit to the girl's nerve. "You want a bath now?"

"Unless someone else is using the tub?"

Velma recognized the sarcasm and ignored it. "Of course, if that's what you'd like." April followed her into the blue bathroom and watched, hand on hip, as Velma turned on the spigots and got out a clean towel.

"Let me know if there's anything else you need," Velma said.

"More wine would be nice." April handed her the empty goblet.

There was a limit to hospitality, but Velma refilled the glass. "Here you go."

April was already in the tub, naked as a jaybird. Velma tried to keep her eyes on the blue tiled wall.

"You can close the door on your way out."

And you can go straight to the dickens.

Velma sat in the kitchen, tapping her feet with nervousness. Everybody else in Jackson was home in bed and she'd be there too, if she trusted April as far as she could throw her.

After forty-five minutes the young woman came through, fully dressed and as breezy as her name. She put the empty glass on the table. "Ta." A flutter of her hand and out the back door.

Ta? Next time, Velma would let the girl knock until the house fell down. She'd tell Maude, too.

On Maude's next visit, she did.

"Oh my gosh," Maude said. "Things must be worse than I thought." She made Velma get the calendar and they went over the dates of April's visits. "Walton told me April has been diagnosed as bipolar," Maude said.

Velma made a mental note to look that up.

"He usually calls me after April has a breakdown. That's when he has to put her in the hospital. Looks like she comes here before each one. She's coming here when she's most manic."

Another word to look up. "I did wonder," Velma said, "because the next time she came for Sunday dinner, she acted cold and standoffish, as if we never sat at this table."

Maude nodded. "She calls me some nights, talking fast, crying, sounding crazy. Coming into a breakdown is the only time April can be honest. Walton puts her in the hospital, they drug her back into whatever's considered normal, and she's back to her mean, perfect self. If I ask her about anything she said on the phone, like how unhappy she is, she claims I made it up and nothing's ever been wrong."

Velma repeated the stories April told about Margaret.

Maude said, "The girl will probably end up in prison and April in an insane asylum." She got up to pour them more wine. "I blame it on the South. Walton won't get April any real help because a good southern man shouldn't have a crazy wife. Instead, we all have to pretend she's fine, and hope for the best until the next breakdown."

Personally, Velma felt none of these north Jackson women worked hard enough. On the farm after a hard day, nobody had the energy left to go crazy.

133

Spring 1980, their tenth Easter together, or maybe the eleventh. Velma tried to count while she screwed on the amethyst earrings. In the mirror, she watched Will knot his tie. He hadn't been himself lately. Twice he'd come home early from the office complaining of dizziness. She'd tried to persuade him to see a doctor, but he disliked doctors almost as much as hospitals.

And, indeed, he seemed better than fine this Easter morning. How handsome he looked in his new suit, a beige linen she'd picked out. Before they married, he'd worn only dark gray or navy, but Velma encouraged lighter colors for spring and summer. They showed off his hair, which was slowly turning white.

She fastened the amethyst necklace over her good blue silk. She certainly wasn't the girl she'd been in 1945, but her hair looked nice. She'd gotten it cut into a halo around her face and colored a warm brown. Good thing she was tall; height helped disguise the weight she'd gained.

Will said, "You're as lovely as the first day I met you."

She ducked her head at the compliment. The nice thing about men: they didn't notice change. She would give God special thanks tonight for her good fortune.

Divorce was the big news this Easter. Helen had divorced husband number two, the civil rights lawyer. Velma wasn't sure why, but Maude said he cheated on her. Helen wasted no time in replacing him, and had arrived for the holiday with a new man. Barry Klein was short and muscular, with a head of thick black curls. Will's oldest acted as if a second divorce were nothing worth discussing. She spent the weekend telling them funny stories about Florida, making her Daddy laugh.

"Barry's bathroom used to be a bomb shelter," she said. "The walls are two feet thick and there's a crank for pumping in air. The downside? It's filled with green mold." Laughter. "Flying roaches appear every month on the night of the full moon. I stand on the bed squashing them with a magazine." Ha-ha-ha.

Guests began arriving for Easter lunch. From the dining room, Velma overheard someone in the kitchen, noisily lifting pot lids.

Bessie's voice. "Miss April, don't be messing with my business."

April said something about the table setting. Velma wondered where she'd gone wrong this time. She never quite managed to rise to Lillian's standards.

April's voice grew sharper. "Margaret, sit up straight. You're going to end up with a hump. And you'll give yourself permanent wrinkles from that frowning, young lady."

Silence, followed by a chorus of relieved laughter. April must have left the room.

Velma walked in the kitchen to find granddaughter Margaret happily chatting with Bessie and Doreen while eating the first of two hamburgers cooked especially for her. Like her Aunt Maude, she refused all vegetables. It showed. She was a very large thirteen-year-old. Velma didn't blame her. Fat probably served as a bulwark against her mother's moods.

An enormous chunk of Bessie's three-layer chocolate cake appeared. Margaret picked up her fork.

Velma and Will worried aloud about April, who appeared to grow stranger with each year. Velma wondered if their concern weren't a kind of secret pleasure: a situation providing endless speculation, about which they could do nothing. That was certainly the satisfaction Velma got from these family gatherings, observation followed by dissection, first with Will, and more thoroughly with Maude.

Everyone had gathered in the lake room.

Will stuck his head in the kitchen. "Are you hiding?"

"Coming," Velma said.

Ernestine must have arrived. Nobody got under Will's skin like Lillian's older sister.

"There you are," Ernestine said, emphasizing the "there" as if Velma had been discovered under the couch.

The room echoed with voices. Helen told Leland and Olive a Florida story, while her four children, stiff and darling in their Easter finery, drank Coca-Colas and poked one another. Helen's new boyfriend leaned against a wall at the far end of the room, smiling uneasily. Velma tried to remember his name.

Maude had not yet emerged from the blue bathroom. Her daily beauty ritual took at least an hour. Velma thought it was cute the way she stood at the mirror, makeup case spilling foundation, lipstick, mascara, hairspray, foam rollers, and a curling iron. Staring intently at her reflection over the roar of the hair dryer. The results were worth the fuss: she appeared with dramatically painted eyes, a scarlet mouth, her blonde hair sculptured. The whole business drove Will crazy, but Velma found the transformation astonishing. Maude might be fat, but she knew how to put herself together better than anyone else in the family. She confided once to Velma that she always wanted to be a hairdresser.

Velma watched as Will ducked away from Ernestine and headed down the hall. She heard him knock on the bathroom door and order Maude out, and Maude's derisive laughter. Those two tickled her, Will's endless teasing and Maude's mock dismay.

April tapped Velma from behind, making her jump. "I don't see the swan salt and pepper shakers. Mother always put them on the table at Easter."

Velma tried to think where the swans might be. This was haughty April. She hadn't come for a night visit in weeks.

"They're Lenox china," April said. "If you're not going to use them, I'd be happy to take them off your hands."

"Let me check." Velma fled to the kitchen and poured herself a glass of wine. Bessie rested her elbows on the counter while she shaped yeast rolls for their second rise.

Velma said, "Everything all right in here?

"Everything be all right," Bessie said, "if folks stop sticking their noses in my business." She got touchy on holidays.

"What can I do to help?"

"Keep Miss April out of my way."

Doreen had the ironing board up, giving the napkins a final touch. Her laughter mixed with Margaret's.

Ernestine came into the kitchen, standing a little too close for Velma's comfort. "Are those real?" She touched Velma's amethyst necklace and didn't wait for an answer. "Will is an extremely generous man. Not all wives are treated so well."

Was she comparing her to Lillian? Velma took a step away from the prying hand. "Thank you."

Ernestine went on. "Or equally."

The woman was impossible, but Ernestine smiled so sweetly Velma decided she must have misunderstood.

Maude saved her, coming up behind. "Look at you, Aunt Ernestine. You always dress so artistically." Code for, why don't you take off a couple of those gypsy necklaces?

"Darling girl." Ernestine held Maude at arm's length. "Such a lovely face. You would be a knockout if you could only —" Ernestine's voice drifted into a knowing silence.

Maude gave her a deadly smile. "I must take after Uncle Leland." Ernestine depended on her brother's generosity. With the hotel gone, she lived frugally in a tiny apartment, taking her daily exercise in borrowed swimming pools.

Ernestine moved on to the chocolate and coconut cakes. "Bessie, these look marvelous." With a finger, she scooped a bit of icing into her mouth. "Fresh coconut. How glorious."

"Don't be messing with my cakes." Bessie's voice held a threat, and Ernestine departed for the lake room.

"Somebody needs to give that woman a good smack." Maude refilled her wine glass.

Will Hughes' voice called them outside. "Who's ready to hunt Easter eggs?"

They gathered in the carport. "All the eggs are between here and the lake," he said. "Nothing past that dogwood on the right or the stone wall on the left. There are three dozen eggs." He paused for dramatic effect. "Thirty-four of them will make good egg salad." Chuckles. "But two are special — a silver one worth twenty dollars, and a gold worth fifty." Sounds of awe. "On your mark, get set — hunt."

Helen's children ran screaming onto the lawn with Margaret close behind. Ernestine and April followed, stabbing through the soft ground in their high heels. Using her cane, Bessie limped after them. April might have to be sedated if Bessie found that fifty-dollar egg.

Will called. "Bessie, how are we ever going to get dinner on the table if you're out here —"

In her head, Velma finished the sentence: "hunting Easter eggs?" But Will said no more and she turned to see why. She saw him leaning against the house with a wondering stare on his face. In the background, the children ran and hollered, but for Velma the world went quiet.

Will began sliding down the wall.

Velma had never liked that blood-colored brick and look at the way it was rucking up the back of Will's new suit coat.

She opened her mouth to scream. No sound emerged. She tried to run. Her legs refused to move. Noise and laughter all around and not one person paying attention to Will.

Except Helen. Velma watched as his oldest daughter grabbed Will by one arm and stopped the downward slide. "Daddy, are you okay?" She called for Maude take his other arm.

Will said nothing. His face, his dear face, blank.

Helen yelled at Walton. "Something's wrong. We've got to get Daddy to the hospital. You drive. We'll take Velma's car."

"Where are the keys?" Walton said.

Maude answered. "On the wall in the kitchen, under the phone."

With Walton's help, Helen and Maude got Will into the back seat of the station wagon. They got in on either side and, between them, managed to keep Will upright.

Walton jumped in the driver's seat.

The ignorant shouting continued, and Velma tried again to make her legs move. *God, don't let Will die.*

"Telephone Baptist Hospital." Helen yelled to the boyfriend, who looked startled to be addressed. "The number is over the telephone. Tell them we're bringing in Will Hughes."

Helen turned to Velma. "Hurry. Get in front."

As if summoned, Velma's legs obeyed and she found herself in the front seat.

"Go, Walton." Helen's voice arrived with a strange echo.

They went screeching down the driveway. Velma turned to face the back seat. "Will honey, Will?" Dazed by dread. Words like sand.

Propped between his two daughters, Will Hughes stared ahead in bewilderment and remained silent.

Walton drove fast. In the front seat, Velma began crying and tried not to.

"It's going to be fine," Maude said. "Isn't it, Daddy? Everything's going to be fine."

Velma wiped her face. "Say something, Will, please."

His eyes were open, but he looked right through her and did not utter a sound.

134

Nothing would ever be fine again. Alone that first night, Velma clutched a pillow to her stomach, feeling the emptiness of Will's bed. The doctors said he had suffered a massive stroke. He couldn't move his arm or leg, nothing on his right side. His mouth drooped and he couldn't speak.

They moved him into intensive care. Velma was allowed in for ten minutes each hour. When Will first saw her face, he became agitated and began to make noises. Nonsense noises, but he made them looking demandingly at her, his eyes hard, as if Velma knew the answer and could right this thing that had gone so terribly wrong.

Frightened, Velma said, "I'm sorry, Will, but I can't understand what you're saying." He got more aggravated and the noises grew louder.

"Aphasia," the doctor said, a hand on Velma's elbow for comfort. "Braca's aphasia. He understands what we're saying, and in his head his speech sounds normal to him. Gibberish to us, but he hears words."

Words. Velma wiped her eyes on the hem of her pillowcase. She had never longed so desperately for words. She remembered how much she'd looked forward to talking to Will after the party.

He wasn't one of those men who went on and on. They spent hours in companionable near silence, Velma embroidering initials on linen napkins for the girls for next Christmas while Will watched *Ironside,* seeing the same shows two and three times, getting as big a kick out of the solution the third time as he had the first.

He used to say, "This is my favorite kind of evening, just the two of us." She always answered, "Mine, too." They smiled at one another as if possessing the world's best secret.

Would they still watch *Ironside*? Would he be able to walk? Velma didn't cry in front of Will, but here in her bed, alone in the house, she sobbed into her pillow. It was so cruel, so unfair for everything to change. One moment, they were laughing at Ernestine and April stomping around the lawn, and the next—It didn't seem possible for a man like Will to be felled so suddenly. Anger went through her like a hot flash. What kind of God would let this happen? Followed almost immediately by regret—The God of Job, that's who. She begged His pardon.

To never speak. The doctors didn't say "Never." They said, "Speech Therapy." Velma couldn't imagine how a therapist could straighten out Will's poor tangled mind, teach him to make the words come out right. And he had such a beautiful speaking voice. In court he used it as a tool, catching a lying witness in a net of words. She had watched him almost hypnotize a jury.

A sudden and horrible thought: this meant he could never practice law again. And he must know that. That's what caused the furious look in his eyes. Never again to stand in front of a judge, painting word pictures. Never again to lead a jury as if he held them on a leash.

She cried harder, and when she ran out of tears and could only gasp, she got on her knees beside the bed. "You gave him to me, Lord. You answered my deepest prayer, and now I understand. You meant me to care for him, and I will, I promise. Just let him live." She crawled back into bed feeling no less despairing but cleansed of selfishness.

That's what she told Maude when she asked how Velma would manage after Will came home from the hospital. "I promised to love him through sickness and health, and that's what I will do."

135

Ten days after the stroke, Will returned home. Velma sat at the breakfast table next to him. A chair had been removed so the wheelchair could roll into his accustomed place. She felt nervous and couldn't quit playing with her silverware.

"Ain't this fine." Bessie's too-big voice rolled over them. "We going to have us a *good* time." From the stove, scrambling an egg for Will, she threw frightened, wide-eyed looks at Velma. Echoing what Velma felt: What are we supposed to do now?

This was a whole new world and, in it, Will had to do everything with his left hand. Velma watched, agonized, as he tried to catch a piece of sliced peach with his spoon. When he did manage, as often as not, the slice slipped off halfway to his mouth. When he did get a piece in his mouth, he could only chew on his left side. This gave his face an odd hitching rhythm. He had to keep mopping with a napkin at the juice that dribbled from the paralyzed right side.

She wanted to put her face in her hands and weep. She wanted to take that spoon and feed him, then wipe his mouth properly. But the lady at the hospital said not to help. Will needed to learn to do things on his own.

Chasing the last few bites of peach around the bowl, she saw from Will's eyes how angry this new helplessness made him. She had folded the newspaper and put it on the table next to his left side, but he barely glanced at the headlines. Velma wondered if he could still read. She needed to ask the therapist. Thoughts chased themselves around her head and she had to remind herself to take a bite of toast and stop staring.

Bessie picked up his empty bowl and put down a plate of soft scrambled eggs. "There you go, Mr. Will. Cooked just the way you like them."

Will made appreciative noises to show how good the eggs looked. He tried with his awkward left hand to get a bite onto the fork and deliver it to his mouth.

Velma couldn't watch anymore. He had spilled food down the front of his bathrobe and pajamas. She needed to find a solution, something like a bib, but not so insulting.

Aphasia. The nurse had given her a pamphlet. Aphasia meant you couldn't speak; the part of your brain controlling speech was injured. Speech was on the left side of the brain. She studied the diagram showing the inside of the head. A little round area of the cauliflower-shaped brain was colored gray to show Will's injury. He had non-fluent aphasia. Some people got the injury in another spot and talked all the time, but didn't make sense. Will figured out he was speaking gibberish and went quiet. But those other people never understood and never shut up. If she had a choice, Velma preferred Will's stuttering attempts.

He tried to get something out. "I want—I want—" She saw the cords of his neck strain to make the words.

"What do you want, Will? More coffee?"

He shook his head.

"Something else to eat?"

That wasn't it. She tried again. "Is it anything about food?"

A negative shake.

"Are you trying to tell me you're finished, ready to go back to your room?"

No, no, no. The shakes got more vigorous.

"Do you want me to call someone?"

He gave her the most exasperated look she'd yet received and thumped the newspaper with his good hand.

"Do you want me to find something in the newspaper?"

Yes, he nodded, rolling his eyes like—*finally.*

"Anything in the front section?"

Another disgusted roll of the eyes.

Velma didn't have anywhere to be. She could go through this paper page by page. When she got to the television schedule, he thumped and nodded.

"I want—"

"Something on television." She ran her hand down the page. "*Ironsides*?"

"I-don't-think-so."

I-don't-think-so, each word brought laboriously forth, meant no, but she was getting warm and Will wasn't looking at her with the angry eyes anymore. She ran her finger further down. "Baseball? Are you asking if the Braves are playing tonight?"

A thump and a deep relieved exhalation.

She checked. "Sorry, no game tonight."

He gave her an exaggeratedly dejected look and motioned to be rolled back to his room.

Be patient. Everyone in this house had to learn patience. Along with everything else that had to be learned: how to get Will from the wheelchair into bed and back to the chair without forgetting the small things, like lifting the paralyzed right foot onto the footrest so it wouldn't drag. Remembering to set the chair's brake.

Unlike most men, Will had never cared for showers. He preferred a nice hot bath. Drilling through the blue tile in the hall bathroom, men from the medical supply store installed a heavy, stainless-steel contraption above the tub. Using a crank, Velma and Doreen were able to move Will from the wheelchair into a large canvas swing, swing it slowly over the tub, and crank him down into the warm water. Velma trembled operating the thing, terribly afraid of doing something wrong and hurting him worse.

She saw his shame at being handled this way, the two of them looking at him and touching his naked helpless body. Before the stroke, he'd been a modest man, preferring to dress and undress in the bathroom. Velma felt for that lost dignity, but everyone had to get used to the new ways—including Will. She bought him a voluminous hooded terrycloth robe to wear when he came out of the tub. He rode to his room in the wheelchair, looking, Velma told him, like a Roman emperor.

He insisted on being helped to the toilet and left alone with the door firmly closed until he called. He was able to stand on his good leg, prop against the sink each morning, and shave himself. Watching through the partially opened door, Velma thought it a harrowing business with that left hand, even using a safety razor. He learned to comb his hair left-handed, still particular about the slant of that pompadour.

None of his office clothes worked. Velma bought him slacks with elastic at the waist, easy to pull on, and long-sleeved shirts meant to be worn outside the pants. She got him a set in blue and one in beige.

His right shoe needed a built-in brace, designed to hold the paralyzed foot erect. This required new shoes. The children had given him many pairs of pajamas over the years, most of which he'd never worn. Doreen put them through the washer over and over, trying to make them as soft as the old pajamas he preferred.

In bed at night, lying beside Will, listening to him snore, Velma wept with exhaustion. Had there really been days when she wandered these rooms wondering what to do with the hours?

136

June now. Caring for Will, learning the necessary tasks, and doing them well enough to make him feel less helpless, had turned into a consuming labor. Before the stroke, Velma feared being useless; now she felt thoroughly used. Used to the bone.

"Don't wear yourself out," Maude said. She'd driven up for the weekend. They sat in their favorite spot at the breakfast room table with balloon glasses of white zinfandel and the shared ashtray.

People were considerate, calling to ask after Will, coming by, bringing gifts. Velma thought some days if she didn't die from taking care of him, the kindness might kill her. She didn't mean Maude. The nights they spent drinking, smoking, and gossiping became her chief entertainment. Tonight, they spoke again of April. They never tired of April.

"She's always treated me like some lower form of life." Maude blew a cloud of cigarette smoke toward the ceiling.

"She hasn't been to see your daddy since he got home from the hospital," Velma said.

"You must miss those corrective visits."

"Not much, but your daddy must wonder. She came to the hospital that first day after you left. We sat outside intensive care because they only let people in one at a time. When it was April's turn, I heard her in there hollering. The nurse asked her to leave. Out she came, steam practically coming out of her ears, telling them what they ought to be doing and which doctor they should have called. I just lost it."

Maude's eyebrows went up. "*You* lost it?"

"I told her she was making things worse and if she couldn't sit down and be pleasant, she'd better leave."

"I'd have paid a lot of money to hear that."

"She stormed out so fast her heels sounded like gunfire. We haven't seen her since."

"Easier taking care of Daddy without her, I imagine." Maude poured them more wine. "She phoned me down in Picayune to say how mad she was that we didn't bother taking her the day Daddy had the stroke."

"He might have been dying," Velma said. "We couldn't wait."

Maude snickered. "She was halfway down to the lake with Ernestine, heel-deep in that grass. Ready to knock her aunt over for a chance at that gold egg."

"Seems like a hundred years ago." Velma felt a catch in her throat and stopped to swallow. "Will looked so handsome that day in his new suit. Remember how he started fussing at Bessie for not getting lunch on the table. The last clear words he ever spoke."

Maude put a hand over Velma's. "He was just joking with her, the way he always does." She squeezed Velma's hand. "He's never been as happy as he is married to you."

"Was." Velma blew her nose on a tissue. "He is not happy now."

"You'll figure out a way."

Would she? There were days when Velma doubted either one of them would ever be happy again. "I guess I ought to call April and apologize, but honestly, I can hardly find the time to brush my teeth, much less tend to hurt feelings."

Maude emptied the last of the bottle into her glass. "Don't you dare apologize. Somebody needs to put April in her place." She grinned at Velma. "Me and Helen are too scared to do it." She picked up the empty bottle. "Should I open another?"

"I don't need another drop," Velma said. "I won't be able to get out of bed tomorrow."

Having thoroughly done April, Maude began on Ernestine. They loved doing Ernestine.

"Who does she think she is?" Maude got another bottle of zinfandel from the refrigerator, opened it, and settled back in the chair. "Have you ever seen that disgusting demitasse cup she carries around in her purse?"

Velma shook her head, pouring herself an inch of wine.

"At the end of a restaurant meal, she takes out a coffee-stained handkerchief, unwraps her little cup, and says to the waiter: 'Would you be good enough to fill this for me, young man?' Trying get a free cup of coffee. She is the cheapest person I have ever met."

Velma tried to be charitable. "She doesn't have much money."

"She was the same way before the hotel burned," Maude said. "Giving us a piece of her 'art' (Maude made finger quotes) every Christmas. Wrapped in used paper. Anybody else would have been embarrassed."

Velma lowered her head, laughing. "We got a lumpy clay duck last year."

"We got an angel."

They shook their heads over things that couldn't be changed.

Only with Maude could Velma be honest about Will. With everyone else, even Bessie, she kept her brave face on and said how much progress he'd made. And yes, wasn't it grand the way he took it. They were all coping nicely, thank you. But with Maude, she told the truth.

"Will screams at me. Roars when he can't make me understand."

Maude frowned. "But you know what he's saying most of the time?"

"I've figured out a few things. Not nearly enough. Imagine how it must feel—that good brain trapped inside his head. He's as smart as ever and can't speak a word of it. It's a wonder the man doesn't go mad."

Maude blinked back tears. "It's so unfair."

Velma pushed the box of tissues toward her and watched as Maude blotted without ruining her mascara.

"What are you doing to take care of yourself?"

Velma leaned her head against the kitchen's rooster wallpaper. "I get my hair done. I try and go to church when I can."

"I hope Daddy knows how lucky he is to have you."

"Neither one of us feels very lucky these days." Velma lowered her voice. "He gets so down. People from the office came by in the beginning, telling him about cases, but they don't visit much anymore, and he feels it. It's hard to go from being managing partner to staring out a window at a bird feeder."

"But it's also hard talking to a person who can't talk back."

Velma leaned forward. "I understand that it makes people uncomfortable, but if they knew how much seeing people means to him. The trouble comes when they say something interesting about a new case, or a case Will worked on, and he wants to comment. He starts stuttering and counting, you've seen him." She held out her fingers. "'One, two, three, four.' Doesn't make sense to the men from the office, and when they don't understand, Will gets agitated and tries harder. The harder he tries, the less he's able to communicate. Whoever's visiting panics and hollers for me to come tell them what he means."

"Which you do," Maude said.

"About half the time."

A month later on a Saturday, Maude sat at the breakfast table again, this time with Velma and Will. She kept twisting her hands.

Velma put a hand over the girl's, stilling them. "What's going on?"

Maude looked frightened. Her voice came out small. "I want a divorce."

Will Hughes looked up sharply. "I-don't-think-so." Meaning: no.

Maude began crying. "I'm sorry, Daddy, but I don't love Lyle anymore and he doesn't love me. I hate my teaching job. I got a really good offer from a company in Dallas." The words spilled out without room for interruption. Maude's face had turned quite red.

Will started counting on his fingers, his face furiously disapproving. "One-two-three-four." All the reasons this was a bad idea.

Velma patted his good arm, trying to quiet him. "Will, at least listen."

Maude took a breath. "It's a good job—in data management."

Will shook his head; he'd never heard of data management.

"It's a coming field and Electronic Data Management, the company that offered me the job, is a leader. They'll pay me more than twice what I make teaching and I'll get to travel—showing bank personnel how to operate the new technology." She used her napkin to mop the tears. "I know you don't like to see anyone cry, but I can't help it. I hate it when you get mad at me."

Velma stepped in. "Your daddy isn't mad at you. The idea of change is harder as we get older, that's all." Will gave her a furious look, which she pretended not to see. "Your plans sound splendid. Do you good to see other parts of the country, won't it, Will?" He started to harrumph and she spoke over him. "We're sorry to hear your marriage didn't work out, honey, but when that happens, it's probably easier not to stay in a small town like Perkinston." She got up. "That's a lot of excitement for one morning. Who needs a fresh cup of coffee?"

Maude turned out to be good at her new job, receiving two promotions in six months. Living in Dallas meant she couldn't visit as often, but when she came, Velma celebrated. She had Bessie make Maude's favorite spaghetti, with the onion, celery and green pepper chopped so fine Maude couldn't spot them. For dessert, Maude loved Bessie's lemon meringue pie.

After Velma put Will to bed, the women settled at the kitchen table. "Your daddy may not be able to say it, but we're both real proud of you," Velma said.

"Daddy isn't. He'd rather see me stuck here in Mississippi with a terrible husband and a lousy job."

"He's just trying to protect you."

"I feel like I'm always disappointing him."

Velma took both of Maude's hands. "That's not true, honey. He loves you to death, all you girls, but you especially."

Maude got the wine out and filled two glasses. "*You're* the one he loves."

Velma blinked away tears and Maude pushed the tissues closer.

"Without speech and half-paralyzed," Velma said, "he's still the most wonderful man I've ever known."

They sat in silence, smoking and sipping the fruity white wine, having comforted each other once again.

137

Every Tuesday and Thursday, Will went to speech therapy at a clinic on Woodrow Wilson Drive. Velma organized the entire day around this appointment.

After breakfast, Will must be bathed, but not dressed, not yet. He liked to have his morning nap first, so Velma got him into a fresh pair of pajamas. At eleven, when he woke, she put on his street clothes, not a suit, not for speech therapy. Bessie made him a light lunch, a sandwich or soup. Velma had begun using Lillian's large white damask dinner napkins as bibs. She tucked one into his shirt collar and put a face towel in his lap. That way, no food fell onto his clothes. He liked to have a second cloth napkin to wipe the paralyzed side of his mouth. He was self-conscious about the droop and dabbed his lips after every bite.

In July, on one of the speech therapy days, April surprised them with a visit. Velma felt her body tense at the sight of her. "Look, Will. It's April come to see you." She stretched her lips into a smile. "Nice of you to drop by."

Will looked pleased.

"How are you, Daddy?"

"Fine," he said.

April turned to Velma with her eyebrows up. "I thought you said he couldn't talk."

"He can say a few words. 'Fine' means he's happy to see you."

April stared at Will. Today's lunch was Bessie's thick vegetable soup, which he enjoyed but had a hard time managing "Those are Mother's good napkins."

Velma took a moment to swallow what she wanted to say, which was: *They're mine now.* "Yes."

"We save those for holidays."

"Now we use them every day." After the incident in the hospital, she no longer had the time or patience to let April lord over her.

April watched her father wipe soup off his chin. "The reason we save them is so they won't get stained and ruined." She spoke slowly as if Velma were a dim child.

"Doreen soaks the stains out and starches them up the way your daddy likes." Doreen now came three days a week to help Velma with bathing Will and to do the ironing.

"I hope you know what you're doing," April said. "You can't find napkins like that anymore." She bent and planted a dry peck on Will's good cheek. "I won't stay, but you look good, Daddy."

The room expanded with her departure. April did not look well to Velma, hair uncombed and skirt wrinkled, and she hadn't stayed long enough to have any real conversation with her father. But at least she'd come.

On speech therapy days, there was no time for the afternoon nap Will enjoyed. After lunch, Velma rolled the wheelchair out to the carport, got him in the front seat of the station wagon, put the collapsed chair in back, and drove to the Rehab Center.

Speech therapy included talking and writing. Velma didn't care for the therapist, young and far too perky for her taste. She spoke to Will as if he were a seven-year-old instead of one of the most brilliant minds in the State of Mississippi.

"Now hon, say 'Open.'"

"Open."

"Door."

"Door," Will repeated.

"Say, 'Open the door.'"

"Open door."

And on it went. Will tolerated this treatment, but Velma could see he got no pleasure from it. The therapist had him copy what she wrote on a big-lined tablet like the ones first graders used. Will did his best with his left hand, slowly forming the letters.

When Velma had papers for him to sign, like the Power of Attorney that let her handle their finances, she wrote his signature and placed it above the line where he was to write. Will imitated what he saw, letter by letter, with no indication that he recognized the result as his own name.

After sounding things out for an hour, Velma got him back in the car and they drove home. Since the accident, he'd become more anxious about cars and traffic. He didn't like for Velma to drive on the expressway. If she tried, he looked frightened and began pointing and making disapproving noises. She took the slower back streets instead. If she drove one mile over thirty, he started again with the noises, pointing at the speedometer until she slowed.

It took a long time to get back inside the house. She had to lift the wheelchair out, set it up, make sure the brake was on, help Will stand, then sit, lift his bad foot onto the footrest, release the brake, and finally wheel him into the kitchen. Her shoulders ached after these sessions.

Mondays and Wednesdays were for physical therapy. This therapist, Dee-Dee, came to the house. Will loved Dee-Dee. Everything coming out of her mouth, even curse words, made him laugh. Up and down the hall they went, Will with his walker and, as he got stronger, a cane. He complained all the way, and Dee-Dee gave back as good as she got.

"Keep on fussing, Mr. Hughes. Just keep it up and I'll have to show your wife how to give you a spanking. I *know* how to spank a man."

Will giggled, looking deliciously horrified. Up and down the hall again.

Dee-Dee showed Velma how to exercise Will's paralyzed arm. "Got to do it. Don't care how much he howls. Stop that, Mr. Hughes. You'd scare a cat. Don't be shaking your head at me."

Will wept with laughter.

"Move it around like this from the shoulder." Dee-Dee showed her. "Then the elbow, now the wrist. Make him straighten those fingers and move them."

"Ow-ow-ow-ow-ow." Will hollered, genuinely in pain.

"I know it hurts, sweetie, but you don't want to let these muscles atrophy. See that? See what this hand is trying to do? That's what we've got to prevent."

Will's right hand had curled into a claw. Velma noticed he'd begun keeping it in his lap where he thought she couldn't see.

After an hour of physical therapy, Dee-Dee stayed for a drink in the lake room. She liked her bourbon neat. She told them stories about her love life, stories filled with honky-tonks and tattooed men on motorcycles.

Will made his "tut" noises, shaking his head in disbelief. Velma sipped her zinfandel, giggling over Dee-Dee's wild life, enjoying seeing Will so tickled. Happiest two hours of the week.

Dee-Dee left, reminding Velma to do the exercises every day. Velma tried. Will must not trust her because he made her walk next to him, with Bessie coming along behind, pushing the wheelchair in case he fell backwards. Velma tried doing the arm exercises, but the first time Will wailed, she quit. She couldn't stand hurting him.

Back from Dallas for a visit, Maude asked if Velma was jealous of the way Will and Dee-Dee carried on.

Velma shook her head. "Your daddy enjoys a pretty woman, always has, especially a bad-mouthed one like Dee-Dee. Forbidden fruit. I'd let her move in if it kept him laughing."

138

In 1980, two changes took place, two rays of sunshine in a sea of gray. The first happened about six months after the stroke. Will now felt more like himself, not a sick man anymore, just a crippled one. Bessie and Doreen worked weekends, swapping off with one another. Velma couldn't handle Will by herself.

On this Sunday, sitting at the breakfast table, Velma asked her weekly favor. "Would you mind if I left you home with Bessie for a couple of hours while I go to church?" Usually he nodded and said, "I-think-so," meaning go ahead.

Today he pointed to himself and then at her.

At first, she didn't understand. "You want to go?"

He nodded.

"With me—to church?"

Another nod.

Velma leapt up. "Bessie. Help me get Mr. Hughes into his suit." Her heart swelled so, she thought it might pop out of her chest. "We're going to church."

During the first ten years of their marriage, Will had accompanied Velma to Riverside Baptist at Christmas and occasionally for Easter. Today she pushed his chair into the sanctuary feeling proud. The head usher held the door. This was Mr. Will Hughes, one of the best and best-known lawyers in the State of Mississippi. Will looked handsome in the navy suit he'd once worn to court. She'd had to buy him clip-on ties, which he made a face at, but she didn't know how to do a man's tie and he couldn't tie it. His white-gold hair was combed into a perfect pompadour. He sat straight in the chair, head high. To Velma he looked taller than any man in the room.

She sat on the end of a row, Will's wheelchair in the aisle next to her. She could hardly pay attention to the service for watching him. He bowed his head in prayer, listened intently to the sermon, nodded a couple of times as if he agreed, and chuckled once at the minister's joke. A pale sort of joke, Velma thought privately, but she loved seeing Will laugh.

When the collection plate came around, Will insisted on reaching inside his coat pocket for his wallet. She took out a bill and he put it in the plate.

The preacher stood outside. "Such an honor, Mr. Hughes." Wringing Will's left hand. Other parishioners crowded around.

Will nodded. "Fine. Fine."

Driving home, Velma asked shyly. "Did you enjoy it?"

He nodded. "I-think-so."

This was one of his half dozen utterances. "I-don't-think-so" meant no. "I-don't-know" meant he wasn't sure, but probably not. "I-think-so" meant yes.

Every Sunday, if Will felt up to it, Velma helped him into his suit and drove them to church. She put the pledge envelope in his suit coat pocket so he could put it in the plate himself. He was the man and he wanted to handle the money.

After church, they occasionally went out to lunch. Will liked a new place on the reservoir called Cock of the Walk. Everything on the menu came fried, even the dill pickles. Will got a kick out of the waiters. If you ordered corn bread, they brought it to the table in a cast iron skillet, and tossed it high in the air, catching it in the skillet on the way down. Each time, Will laughed like it was the first time he'd seen that trick. Velma got indigestion after every meal.

He'd become sweeter since the stroke. Not that Will Hughes hadn't been considerate before, but he was a serious man and usually distracted by work. Once, long before the accident, when Helen came home, she asked Velma if her father was mad at her—he was so quiet. Velma reassured her. "Honey, men don't talk."

Now, here he was, and he really didn't talk. But he was so attentive and appreciative of every little thing. He still got frustrated when Velma failed to understand what he wanted, but she'd grown better at deciphering, and he'd grown more patient. Before the stroke, she'd never seen him cry; now he wept easily. Laughing made him cry. Anything sad on TV made them both cry. At night, praying silently in the next bed, Velma thanked God for the laughter and the tears, and for bringing him back to the church. No matter what happened, they would be together in heaven.

139

By 1988, eight years after the stroke, they were thoroughly settled into their new and narrower life. Velma told Maude she enjoyed taking care of people. She might do it as a job after, God forbid, Will passed.

But the work told on her. Each day, she lifted Will in and out bed, in and out of his clothes, the wheelchair, the car, and twice a week, in and out of the cursed bathtub sling. He was heavier than before the accident, a combination of Bessie's good cooking and inactivity. She was, too. They joked about it.

At night, when she finally stretched out next to her snoring husband, her body ached with exhaustion.

Will liked to rise early, so Velma was up and going from seven in the morning to nine at night. Not that she didn't enjoy keeping busy: she was born to do this work. God had blessed her with the patience for it—if only she didn't get so tired. It showed. She caught glimpses of herself in the little time she had to get dressed. Circles under her eyes, face pale and puffy. Caretaking had made her old.

There was something else, a thing Velma admitted to no one, not even Maude. No matter what she did for Will or how well she cared for him, underneath his kindness and consideration, Will was sad. Why wouldn't he be? In an instant he'd gone from managing partner of a prestigious law firm, to a voiceless cripple, from one of the most respected men in the state, to forgotten. She didn't blame him for feeling sad, and she worked hard to find ways to distract him.

Once a week, she drove him to the Farmer's Market. Marcy, the young woman at the stall where Velma liked to shop, was a talented flirt. She came right to Will's car window in her farmer overalls and yellow pigtails, leaning in far enough to show him a little cleavage along with her best peaches and fattest ears of corn. For those few moments, he turned into the old Will, pointing to this or that, smiling with delight, paying with his left hand from the bills Velma put in his shirt pocket before they left home.

If he felt like an outing, Velma took him to the Dairy Queen for an afternoon treat. He enjoyed something called a Blizzard, a milkshake made with soft ice cream and chopped Oreo cookies. Sipping that cold, sweet mess, he shook his head with pleasure. "Umm-umm." A blizzard could cheer him up for an hour.

But too often, when perhaps he thought no one could see, Velma caught a look of terrible sadness on his face, a bereavement nothing she did erased. She thought it must be his loss of the law, the thing he loved most, the talent that had made him who he was. Before the accident, Velma couldn't have told you where the law stopped and Will Hughes began. The two were inseparable and, losing the law, he lost the biggest part of himself. He might have legal thoughts, but he could never again speak them. When young Owen took over as Managing Partner, he'd come for a visit and talk about the firm. Velma watched as Will strained to get his own ideas out. Owen got a stricken look trying to guess what his uncle wanted: Is it this? Is it that? Are you saying this? Velma struggled to translate and everyone ended up exasperated. Will got really down after these visits.

"I know." Velma sat on the couch next to his chair one afternoon after Owen left. "I know how hard it is."

He gave her a look so terrible it made her weep. Then he began crying. They sat mopping at their tears until Will patted her knee. "Baci." That was his pet name for her and for anyone he loved. His way of telling her things would be okay. Velma went and got them two glasses of wine.

Maude flew in for her monthly visit from Dallas. She witnessed one of these crying episodes and pulled Velma aside. "You can't keep going like this. You're both depressed. You need to get medication."

Velma shook her head. "Will won't take it. He hates doctors and he already questions every pill."

"Then lie," Maude said. "Tell him it's something to make him stronger."

Velma went to see Will's doctor the next week. He listened while she described their lives. He wrote Will a prescription and another one for Velma. "It's not going to make everything okay," he said, "but it might prop you up."

Will stared at the new tablet in his pill dish and pointed. Every morning, he took a vitamin and a baby aspirin to keep his blood thin. He made a huge face swallowing these, along with a tablespoon of fiber grains to prevent constipation. He took huge gulps of orange juice to wash everything down.

"The doctor says it's a vitamin to make us feel better, being indoors all the time the way we are." Velma couldn't believe the ease with which she uttered this falsehood. "He gave me the same thing." She showed him.

Will gave her a suspicious look, as if to say, "What are you trying to pull?" But he swallowed the new pill along with the others.

A week or so passed. Nothing you could put a finger on changed, but it was as if a gray blanket gradually lifted, until one morning, awakening, Velma lay next to Will thinking through her day, and realized she felt happy. Maybe happy was too strong a word. She felt content. She actually looked forward to breakfast and pushing Will's chair out to the driveway so he could wave at the traffic going by on Old Canton Road.

April, impatient April, who now dropped by once a week, disapproved of this pastime. She said it looked common for a person of her father's stature to be waving at strangers, but Will enjoyed sitting at the top of the driveway and giving a rather kingly gesture to passing cars. People waved back, which felt almost like having company.

Neither of them had cried for ten days. Will wasn't so much cheerful as resigned. The downside—having gained resignation, he refused to continue speech therapy. A waste of time he let Velma know with a disgusted face. He still wanted Dee-Dee to come and do physical therapy, but that was mostly for the laughs. He did not practice between her visits and refused to let Velma touch his bad arm. The right hand closed permanently into a claw. He kept it in his lap, hidden under a small towel.

140

Looking back, Velma thought of these as the golden days. They went to church, ate fried catfish at Cock of the Walk, and sipped Blizzard milkshakes. They went to the Farmers Market, buying peaches and strawberries in season, melons, corn, greens, lady peas, fat white onions with green stalks, bunches of fresh spinach, dirt clinging to their roots. They bought so much that Bessie and Doreen had to take half of it home.

At night they watched TV together, a baseball game if one was on. Will wore his Atlanta Braves cap and, to make Velma laugh, groaned loudly whenever a Braves player struck out. Sitting together, Will in his wheelchair, her close by on the sofa, he would reach with his good hand and touch her softly on the cheek. Her tears were not from sadness. They gazed into each other's eyes and laughed at the miracle of still being here, and at the ridiculousness of finding themselves in this shape. "Baci," he'd say, squeezing her hand with his good one.

Velma looked the word "baci" up in the back of the big dictionary. It meant "kisses" in Italian, but for Will it meant dear one. In spring, looking out the big windows at the lake, they marveled at the dogwood and redbud trees in blossom. In the fall, she wheeled him around behind the garage to gaze in wonder at the golden maple.

Once winter arrived, Velma built huge fires. Will loved a good fire. Once a month or so, her cousin Drew came up from Picayune with his wife Pearl. Velma and Will laughed after these visits at the way they carefully hid all signs of alcohol. Velma found it difficult to believe she had ever been part of this strict family. Pearl seemed to disapprove of the house, with rooms nobody used, and the big lawn where nothing edible grew. She disapproved of Bessie, too. No one in the Vernon family had ever needed the help of a colored servant.

Once, when the two appeared earlier than expected, Will had to hide his glass of Manischewitz under the towel he used to cover the paralyzed hand. After Drew and Pearl left, he wept with laughter, indicating to Velma how he'd kept the wine balanced between his legs.

"If it had spilled, they would have thought you wet yourself," Velma said.

Will agreed, shaking with mirth, wiping his eyes on the handkerchief he kept in his shirt pocket.

Velma bought a small table and put it next to where Will parked his wheelchair. On it, she sat a framed photograph of the family, taken the Easter after Will's stroke: she and Will in the center with the children and grandchildren around them and the lake in the background. A glass of wine fit perfectly behind the frame. During Drew and Pearl's next visit, Will kept rolling his eyes at Velma and towards the photograph. Velma got tickled and Pearl looked suspicious.

On one visit, cousin Drew, who was clever with his hands, brought Will a new squirrel feeder. Long spikes had been set into a circle of wood, like the blades of a windmill. He nailed this to a pine tree outside lake room window where Will liked to sit. On each spike, Drew impaled a cob of dry corn coated in peanut butter. When a squirrel tried to eat, the wheel went flying around and the squirrel with it. At the sight of this, Will laughed until he cried. Velma gave her shy, silent cousin a big hug of thanks. This toy added a new destination to their list of outings. Once a month, they took a trip to the feed store in south Jackson to pick up a sack of dried corncobs.

141

On December 1, Velma paid the bills and made her last entries in the datebook for 1989. The holidays loomed and she felt too worn out to go through the fuss. She needed what Papa used to call a tonic. Not that she had time to be sick. Except for taking Will on afternoon excursions, going to the grocery store, church, and getting her hair done, she rarely left the house. Thirteen years next May since Will had his stroke. Hard to believe.

At the beauty salon that Friday, Sally's hands gently massaged shampoo into Velma's scalp. Tears slipped out the corners of Velma's eyes. She apologized, saying she couldn't imagine what had gotten into her. But she suspected it was Sally's touch, which felt kind and loving. She missed having someone care for her. On hair-washing day at the farm, Mama used to rinse Velma's soapy hair with water from the rain barrel. Nothing made hair squeak like rainwater. She missed her mother's hands.

Velma had skipped her physical last year and the year before that. When a reminder came in the mail, she called and made an appointment.

"Maybe you can give me something for being so tired," she said.

Standing over her, Dr. Baker asked how long since her last physical.

"I honestly can't remember."

He consulted the chart. "Five years."

"That long?" Velma hated these exams. She stared at the ceiling with her feet in the stirrups and tried to think about something else.

"You really need to take better care of yourself."

She told him about Will and said she didn't have five minutes to think about herself from one month to the next.

He was doing a breast exam now, fussing at her while his fingers palpated, moving her breast around like a piece of dough. Since she wasn't dough, and these were her private parts, Velma focused on counting the ceiling tiles.

"If you don't take care of yourself, how can you take care of anyone else?"

Which made sense, but didn't answer the question of where she was supposed to find the extra hours.

"I don't like what I'm feeling here." Dr. Baker had a hand on the underside of her left breast.

Velma brought her eyes from the ceiling to meet his for one panicked exchange.

"Let's get you a mammogram."

Velma dutifully scheduled the test and went, dreading it because she hated the process, dreading this one more.

The technician kept a bland face.

Velma spoke up after the left breast was done. "See anything?"

"I just take the pictures." The young woman went about her business of squash, click, release on the right breast. "The doctor will speak to you when we're done."

Velma clutched the too-short gown and waited in a room with other women, trying unsuccessfully to read *Ladies Home Journal.*

The doctor called her name, a man Velma had never laid eyes on before. She followed him into a small room and climbed up on the table. He palpated her breasts some more.

"Do you do self-exams regularly?"

"Yes," Velma lied. She did not touch her breasts more than was required for washing and, now that Will no longer touched them, her breasts went largely ignored. It was not that Will couldn't have caressed her with his good hand, but they had come to a silent agreement to let go of that part of their lives. They gave each other affectionate pats and kisses, but Velma was wary of hurting his paralyzed right side and they no longer attempted intercourse.

"Didn't you feel this?" The doctor raised her hand with his, placed it on her lower left breast, and moved it.

She felt—what? She wasn't sure, but nodded obediently.

"I want to do a biopsy, and if the results are," he hesitated, "positive, we may need to think about a mastectomy."

Velma's felt the room tilt. A ringing in her ears over-rode his voice. "Are you saying I might have—" She could hardly bear to say the word. "—*cancer?*"

"Let's not jump to conclusions yet."

She didn't tell Will a thing until after the biopsy results were in.

She waited until supper was over and Bessie was gone for the day. During a commercial in the Braves game, she muted the TV. "I have to have an operation."

Will's eyes widened in alarm.

Velma started crying. "I'm sorry, I promised myself I wouldn't cry. It's cancer. They have to take off my breast."

Will began weeping. He clasped her hand. "Baci, baci."

"Aren't we a pair?" Velma mopped at her tears and Will got his handkerchief out to wipe his. "I'll get Maude to come and stay with you while I'm in the hospital." The commercial over, she turned the sound of the game back on.

Maude was there when Velma woke from the anesthetic, her left side flat and padded, and hurting, hurting, hurting. Sweet Maude.

"They say they got it," Maude said. "They took some lymph nodes, too, and they want you to have radiation."

Maude brought Will to see her, carrying a bunch of yellow roses in his lap, rolling his chair as close to the bed as he could. They stared into one another's eyes while Maude did the talking.

"Doesn't she look good?"

Will nodded. "Fine, fine."

Velma knew she didn't look anything close to good, but she saw that for Will, her appearance didn't matter. What they loved about one another was under the skin and had no bearing on legs that worked or having two breasts.

She did the radiation. She went to physical therapy to learn to move her left arm properly. She hurt and was too weak to wheel Will by herself, so she hired Flora May. Flora May and her husband Johnny had worked at Creekmore Inn, but moved to Jackson after the place burned. When Lillian was alive, Flora May used to come to the Kings Highway house to help with the sewing. Flora May, Bessie, and Doreen spelled each other, spending nights in the guest room. Will had a bell by his bed and one in the lake room. If he rang, someone came. He sat himself up in bed at night and peed into a urinal. Sometimes he missed a little and the pale blue carpet grew stained from that and the brown medicine he used for his toe fungus.

The best times were lying in bed next each other, teeth brushed, tucked in, having safely made it through another day. Will reached across the divide between the twin beds and clasped Velma's hand in his cool, dry one.

"Aren't we a pair?" she said.

He chuckled into the dark.

142

A year later, the doctors took Velma's second breast. She did her crying privately. Getting dressed, her flat, sunken chest seemed to her a visible proof of defeat. She had a prosthetic brassiere, but it weighed a ton and she only wore it for church and company.

She began reading the Bible more. She increased their pledge to the church without telling Will. She suspected the cancer was God's way of punishing her for the original sin of loving Will while he was still married. She'd thought, by marrying him, she had erased that blight, but she'd been wrong.

Velma remembered Maude telling her how April carried on when the two of them got engaged, saying the thought of him marrying his secretary made her sick to her stomach. Velma must have made God sick too, and now he was returning the favor. She did not share these thoughts with Will.

For months she felt too weak to go to church. On Sundays, she and Will watched a televised service out of Fort Lauderdale. Will nodded and pointed his finger at the screen, agreeing with the preacher.

Velma nodded back, but found her mind wandering. She had never planned on dying before Will, thinking she would care for him until he died and then, perhaps, use her skills to care for others. But cancer had opened the door to another room. What would become of Will if she died first? He couldn't live in this house alone, and she couldn't bear the thought of him in one of those homes where no one knew how he liked his egg, or that he needed a face towel to cover the withered hand. No one else would take the time to translate his garbled words. He would live with his good mind trapped in a silent body and not a soul around to care. Worrying kept her awake.

Velma's minister visited now that they couldn't get to church. He knelt next to Will's chair and prayed: "Lord, lift these burdens from your servants, Will and Velma." She didn't know if he expected the burden to be lifted by a miracle, like a cure for cancer, or maybe Will regaining his speech, or by both of them dying. She did know the motive for these frequent calls: her ever-larger pledge. She was not a fool. But she was afraid of dying, and kneeling with this man of God next to Will's chair comforted her.

Aside from prayer, her comforts arrived by mail order. She eagerly awaited the mailman and the day's catalogs. To make up for not going out, she ordered monogrammed stationery from Neiman-Marcus for each of the girls; triple-milled soap from France; big tins of flavored popcorn. When the packages arrived, it felt like Christmas. The mailman's white truck or the big brown UPS truck pulled up the driveway. "He's here," Bessie sang out. Velma, Bessie, and Flora May gathered around that day's surprises like children.

143

In June, the cancer returned, this time in Velma's ovaries. A different cancer, the doctor said, not connected to the breast cancer, which made not one bit of sense to Velma. She had another operation and the doctors once more claimed to have gotten it all. Maude came to stay while Velma recuperated.

From the hospital bed, Velma looked up at Maude's round, sweet face. "I'm worried you'll lose your job taking so much time off?"

"They're very flexible," Maude said. "Besides, I'm so good they couldn't get along without me." She traveled all over the South now, teaching bank employees how to use the new data systems. She'd been promoted again and bought herself a darling house—she showed Velma photographs. She also owned a tiny, bright blue convertible and had joined a club where people with the same car raced on weekends. It sounded like an exciting life, and Velma felt bad taking Maude away from it. But not bad enough to give up her company.

When she returned home after this third operation, Velma watched Maude with her glasses of wine. Did they notice the drinking at work? Maybe she only drank at home. Velma had given up smoking and wine tasted horrible, but when she had the strength, she joined Maude at the kitchen table.

"April came by this week," Velma said.

"What's she up to now?" Maude tapped her cigarette on the edge of the brown glass ashtray, dislodging a cylinder of ash.

"Fidgety, bossy, making your father nervous. She likes to tell us what we're doing wrong. Bessie doesn't keep the kitchen clean enough. Doreen lets stuff pile up on the closet floors. We don't need Flora May, who only sits around entertaining the others when they should be working. By the time she leaves, we all feel worse about ourselves."

"I hope you pretend to be deaf." Maude refilled her glass with zinfandel. "April's been trying to make me feel lower than a snake since the day I was born."

When Maude left, Helen flew in from Florida. She had turned into a health enthusiast since her last visit, and arrived with bags of brown rice and organic oatmeal. She cooked up batches of gluey stuff, claiming miraculous benefits. Bessie rolled her eyes and Velma tried not to smile. After she left, they threw the bags out.

Helen lived a thousand miles away; April's moods changed from one visit to the next; Maude was the only daughter Velma could count on.

Three months later, both Helen and Maude flew in for the weekend. Helen went to bed early. Velma sat with Maude in the kitchen.

Bald and exhausted from chemo, Velma spoke. "If I die—"

"You're not going to die."

"If I do, you've got to promise me something."

"Anything." Maude said.

"You'll take care of your daddy. You won't let anyone put him in a home." Watching Maude's face, Velma saw the answer she prayed for.

"I won't."

She was such a good girl. "Promise me."

Maude's blue eyes filled with tears. "I promise."

Velma took a deep breath, satisfied. "Of all you girls, you were always the one."

"But you're not going to die."

"One more thing."

"Okay."

"When the time comes, I want you to sing."

Maude shook her head. "Smoking ruined my voice."

"I don't care. You know the song I like."

"The lullaby?" Maude sang softly so as not to wake Will or Helen.

Skeeters are a hummin'
On the honeysuckle vine
Sleep Kentucky Babe!

"That's the one. Do you promise?"

"Promise." Maude wiped her eyes and blew her nose on a tissue.

Helen came in, rubbing her eyes. "Are you two still up?"

"Velma thinks she's going to die," Maude said.

Helen stood behind her stepmother with her hands on Velma's shoulders.

"You can't die, Velma. We couldn't do without you."

Helen had no idea how heavy those hands were. Velma tried not to wince. "You know what I'm most afraid of?"

Both girls said, "What?"

Velma almost laughed. Helen said the word as if, whatever it was, she would vanquish it with seaweed powder. "I'm afraid of going through the Valley of the Shadow of Death."

Helen dropped into a chair, putting her face close to Velma's. "Don't be afraid. With Daddy's stroke and your cancer, you've already been through that valley."

Velma shook her head. Helen hadn't set foot in a church since she left Mississippi. She couldn't possibly understand how the Lord rebukes a sinner.

144

In November of 1991, the cancer returned for a fourth time. Velma felt too worn out to care. The chemo had taken her hair and brought it back brown and curly. She was hollow-chested from the double mastectomy. In the mirror, her skin looked yellow. Will Hughes wore a look of permanent worry.

She went into the hospital for another operation. The cancer had moved to her liver. The doctors pretty much opened her, took a look, and sewed her up again. Velma was too sick to know. She was in ICU and hooked up to a respirator.

When she could talk again, she described to Maude what she'd seen. "People were murdered around me. They carried the bodies out at night when no one could see."

Maude held her hand and smiled. "Those were intensive care nightmares. The sedation they use causes them."

She had the sweetest smile.

Back at home, Velma spent her days in a big armchair in the lake room, a chair she'd bought for Will. It had a motor that lifted him to standing and sat him down again, but she was the one who needed lifting now. Will sat beside her in his wheelchair holding her hand. She looked out the window at the wind blowing the trees around the lake and the birds at the feeder. She waited to die.

One day, while Will napped, she had Maude bring her jewelry and they divided everything into envelopes with the girls' names on them. Velma told Maude she wanted to be buried next to her parents down in Picayune. "I know it'll make trouble for everyone, traveling that far, but I don't feel easy lying next to Lillian." She gave Maude a list of the hymns she liked.

Maude wept and wrote everything down. "You can't die, Velma. Daddy won't be able to stand it."

Velma didn't bother to argue. She saw death at the end of the road and she was tired. "Your daddy will stand it because you'll be here to help him." Reminding Maude of her promise.

"Of course, I will."

The girl cried so easily. All her feelings right there on the surface, waiting to be hurt. She saw the way Maude drank to cover the pain of being fat, of being called dumb by April, of being treated her whole life as the least of three.

Maude brought in hospice. Velma was only vaguely aware of the woman—a sweet black face near hers, kind hands asking her to turn this way and that, a warm cloth. Was there anything nicer than a warm cloth and soft hands massaging lotion into your skin? There was pain. Velma sensed it, crouched in her gut like a tiger, but the lady had a bottle of blue liquid, and it only took a sip to quiet the beast. Maude fed it to her from a spoon, and when Velma could no longer open her mouth, with a dropper.

Will was always beside her. Velma wondered when he ate or slept, because every time she opened her eyes, there he was, holding her hand, smiling into her eyes with the deepest, sweetest love. Velma tried to smile back. She hoped he knew she didn't regret one thing. That she loved him with all her heart and always had. Will's big chair tilted almost flat, as comfortable as a bed. She couldn't see the lake now. The light was too bright and she had to keep her eyes closed. But she knew it was out there, the same way she knew the fire was going, crackling and snapping with a comforting sound.

April arrived. Velma heard her in the kitchen objecting. "I find it horrific that you have her sitting in that chair, dying in front of everybody." She couldn't hear Maude's answer, but the back door slammed.

She liked it here in the lake room. The bedroom felt too dark, and too far away from Bessie rattling dishes at the sink and the clunk of the iron as Doreen did Will's shirts. From the kitchen, she heard Flora May's sweet voice rising and falling with a story, followed by laughter. All this came and went like waves on a shore. She had meant to see more of the ocean.

It was as if life—the life where Velma needed to do things—became a receding shore. Remembered fondly, but the ship she rode now sailed her out of sight of land. No telling what she looked like. Like death warmed over, no doubt. This thought rose out of her blue dream like a fish to bite her. Vanity, the last vice.

Helen arrived with her children. Velma liked the sound of them talking. She remembered now: Helen's daughter had given birth. She'd brought the baby boy to meet his great grandmother, a sweet tiny bundle, just beginning. The voices rose and faded around her. She felt Will's hand warm in hers, and heard Maude singing close to her ear. Such a pretty voice.

Skeeters are a hummin'
On the honeysuckle vine
Sleep Kentucky Babe!

Sandman is a comin'
To this little child of mine
Sleep Kentucky Babe!

Silvery moon a shinin'
On the heavens up above
Boblink is pinin'
For his little lady love

You are mighty lucky
Babe of old Kentucky
Close your eyes in sleep

145

On a bright, cold December day, Maude wept into an already soggy tissue. Helen stood beside her, tearless. Maude never understood how her oldest sister kept from crying when there was so much to cry about. Their father, for instance, who'd had to be carried in his wheelchair to the graveside because the chair refused to roll on the patchy frozen grass. Picked up by the two large men in work clothes, now standing by with shovels waiting to fill Velma's grave.

The funeral had been in Jackson at Riverside Baptist, but Velma wanted to be buried here, almost two hundred miles south, in this hard, wind-swept earth outside her country church. "At home," she'd called it. "Back at home."

So here they were, except for April, who'd showed her displeasure with the arrangements by sitting at the back of the church during the service instead of with the family and leaving before it was over.

April had been angry since Maude called to tell her Velma had died. She'd come banging through the back door to find her stepmother still reclining in the big chair surrounded by Helen and her children.

"This is indecent." April sat down hard on the couch, sucking the air out of the room, which, until that moment, had been filled with sweet sorrow, everyone glad Velma had been able to take her last breaths in the midst of life, surrounded by people who loved her.

April folded her arms and announced herself ready to make "the arrangements." Discovering Velma had planned her own funeral, down to the flowers on the casket, the suit she wanted to wear, and the hymns to be sung, Will's middle daughter rose to her full five foot two inches. "Then what the hell do you need me for?"

She stormed out, slamming the back door hard enough to rattle the kitchen windows. Storming being her specialty, Maude thought. April had refused to go to Picayune for the burial.

Thank God for small favors. Maude mopped away more tears. Helen passed her a fresh tissue. At least they hadn't been subjected to two hundred miles of angry April. Maude had attempted to smoke through a two-inch crack in the driver's window, while Will Hughes made slow-down noises from the passenger seat and Helen coughed from the back to remind them of her asthma. April's presence would have been the final nail.

They huddled, shivering under the funeral home's green tent. This was the homeliest cemetery Maude had ever seen. Not a single tree, just raw pastureland with gravestones here and there, and faded plastic flowers. The minister got up, a tall, raw-boned man, his features as harsh as the wind cutting across this field. He opened his mouth and lit into them. Maude was so surprised, she quit crying.

"Do you think you will escape the fires of Hell? *Wrong*. Damnation awaits every sinner who has not been born anew to our lord Jesus Christ. *Born anew*." He looked up at the empty sky and down into the freshly dug grave. His eye passed over each member of the family. "None can escape His wrath. The day will come, and soon, when *you* – " He screamed the word "you" making Maude jump. "*You* will lay here, all your earthly pleasures gone, awaiting the judgment of the Lord."

"Lie." Helen muttered out of the side of her mouth. "Not lay."

Maude felt a bubble of laughter rise and swallowed hard.

"Are you ready?" The man shouted. The cold had painted hard patches of red on his cheeks. "That's what I'm asking. Are you ready like Sister Velma to face the Lord on that fateful day?"

Maude blanked him out. She stared at his moving lips and closed her ears. When it was over and they were back inside the low, echoing room that served as a parish hall, Helen leaned in close. "Have you ever heard such crap?" At that moment, Maude loved her oldest sister.

The ladies of the church provided a feast: great bowls of shivering Jell-O in rainbow colors, with canned fruit salad floating inside like planets; pigs in a blanket; coleslaw; macaroni and cheese. Everything preternaturally bright under the fluorescent lights.

Will greeted everyone with his good left hand, saying, "Fine, fine," which meant Hello and Thank you for coming, the things that Maude, standing beside him, actually said. She could do this all day and night, but she would kill for a glass of wine and a cigarette.

Headed back to Jackson, Will gestured back at the cemetery and then to himself, counting. "One-two-three-four-five."

"What are you saying, Daddy?"

He pointed back and to himself again.

"Are you saying you want to be buried down there with Velma?" Maude said.

He relaxed. "I-think-so." Meaning, yes.

Maude looked at Helen in the rearview mirror. Helen rolled her eyes.

"Are you sure?"

He got agitated and spoke louder. "I-think-so."

"If that's what you want," Maude said. "Your word is our command."

He quieted. She and Helen talked about how nice the funeral had been, how kind of all those people to come. How sweet the ladies of the church were to make the food. Will nodded approvingly. One of the effects of his stroke was a desire for everything to be pleasant. Like the song said, he did not want to hear no bad news.

146

Maude waited until her father went down for a late nap before pouring a glass of wine and collapsing at the kitchen table, giggling with Helen over the awful preacher and the terrible food.

"Pigs in a blanket," Helen said.

"My favorite was the Jell-O. Now we'll have to go back again with Daddy."

"He'll be dead," Helen said. "We could just bury him in Greenwood Cemetery next to Mother."

"And have him come back and haunt me? I don't think so." Maude poured herself another glass of wine and dumped the empty bottle into the garbage.

Getting a glass of water, Helen opened the metal can with a foot and peered inside. "That's four bottles since I got here. Aren't you drinking an awful lot?"

As soon as Maude decided she liked Helen, her sister ruined it by saying something like this. She suppressed a desire to kick Helen's shin when she sat down. "It's the stress," she said. "Velma being sick and taking care of Daddy. When things settle down, I'll cut back." *As soon as I get you on a plane to Florida, what I do will be none of your damned business.*

"Before I forget." Maude got up and returned carrying a fat envelope. "Velma wanted you to have this."

Helen opened it. Inside were the amethyst necklace and earrings, Will's long-ago gift to Velma. "Oh, my gosh."

"She picked them out for you."

"What a sweet person."

Maude made a come-with-me gesture. "Let me show you something else." In the living room, she got on her knees, trying not to grunt at the effort in front of her skinnier sister. She pulled open the bottom drawer of the secretary and took out a large cardboard box. "This is Velma's."

Helen sat on the floor beside her. The box contained newspaper clippings about every honor Will Hughes had ever received, from being president of the local VFW in the '40s to arguing a case before the Supreme Court; graduation and marriage announcements for the three of them; birth announcements for Helen's children; faded clippings of Helen chairing various Junior League committees; April's debutante picture, invitations to every wedding, shower, and christening.

"Isn't this something?" Maude said.

"It's as if all these years Velma shared our lives," Helen said, "but off to the side. I had no idea."

"She was waiting for Daddy." Maude closed the box. "Velma told me it was worth the wait. She said God finally gave him to her and that she wouldn't have changed a thing."

"Poor Mother."

Maude felt her throat tightening. "Yes."

"She had a choice," Helen said. "I asked her once why she didn't leave him and she said she stayed for us."

Maude mopped tears. "After you and April got married, the three of us sat alone at that dinner table. A lot of nights no one said a word."

Helen followed Maude back into the kitchen. "God, that sounds dreadful."

"Don't sit." Maude opened the back door. "Help me bring the tree inside."

"We're having a tree?"

"We always have a Christmas tree."

"But we just buried Velma."

"I'm trying to keep things normal." Maude grabbed one end of the tree. "Daddy likes to see a lighted tree. He enjoys sitting around it on Christmas morning to open presents."

"I don't think he'll be much in the mood for Christmas this year."

"None of us are. You grab the other end and hold the door open."

Between them, they wrestled the tree through the kitchen and into the living room. "I'll find the stand," Maude said. "I think it's out in the storage room."

When the tree stood firmly in front of the big windows, more or less vertical, Maude brought in a stack of dusty boxes. "The decorations."

Helen poured a pitcher of water into the tree stand. "I have to fly home on the twenty-ninth. When are you heading back to Texas?"

Maude untangled strings of lights without looking at her sister. "I'm not."

Helen stood very still. "You're not going home?"

Climbing on the stepstool, Maude began stringing lights around the top of the tree.

"What are you saying, Maude?" The big sister voice.

"Plug these in, would you? I want to make sure they work before I do any more." The strings of lights blinked cheerfully and Maude kept clipping them onto branches. "You can start putting the balls on. Make sure they all have hangers."

"I'm not moving until you explain."

"I promised Velma to stay and take care of Daddy. I said I wouldn't let him be put in a home."

Helen said, "You can't stay here."

Maude reminded herself that she was a grown woman. Helen could no longer tell her what to do.

"Daddy may live a long time." Helen slipped slightly rusted metal hangers through rings on a box of red Christmas balls. "I can't stand by and watch the same thing happen to you."

Maude climbed down off the stepstool for a swallow of wine. "What are we talking about now?"

"What happened to Mama and Velma."

Maude said, "I'm taking care of Daddy, not marrying him."

"Don't be dense. They both died for love of him."

"That's ridiculous." Maude wound the lights lower. "Mama picked up a bug in Mexico."

"She died because he made her life miserable."

What a crock. Finished with the lights, Maude took two red balls and climbed back on the stepstool. "You said yourself—Mama chose to stay."

"Be careful up there," Helen said.

"Or what? I'll fall and you'll have to call the fire department?" Maude glanced at her sister and both of them burst into laughter. Maude managed to climb down and they sat on the sofa to recover. "Bessie on the floor."

Laughing too hard to speak, Helen gasped. "Daddy didn't want Mama to bother the firemen."

Maude wiped her eyes. "God, no. Bessie could live on that dining room floor before he'd disturb a public servant."

Another fit of shaking, hiccupping glee.

"Took two big firemen to get her up." Maude looked at her sister, which was enough to set them off again. Helen's face grew red.

They wept now, eyes and noses running. Helen, coughing from her asthma, brought the box of tissues from the kitchen. They wiped and blew.

"That felt good," Maude got back up on the stepstool.

Helen handed her sister more red balls. "All I'm saying is, look at the life Mama had. Daddy never touched her. She lived on bourbon and Bufferin. I read that withdrawal of affection can make you sick."

Maude moved the stool to the other side of the tree. "You read too much."

"Then there's Velma."

"*Velma?*" Maude quit her decorating and stared at her sister. "I never saw two people so happy."

Helen said, "Nursing Daddy seven days a week made her sick."

"She was glad to be here for him. She told me so."

"Wore herself out."

"She said it was God's will." Maude leaned back to study her spacing. "What she was put on earth to do."

Helen started with a box of green balls. "What about waiting all those years, never marrying?

"That was her choice."

"That's what I'm trying to say." Helen's voice rose. "Mama made the choice to stay married and Velma made the choice to wait, and those choices killed them. I don't want you to make the same mistake."

Silence. Helen was giving her a pointed look. This must be where Maude was supposed to say, *You're right. I'll put Daddy in a nursing home and go back to Dallas tomorrow.* She tried to keep the impatience out of her voice. "Eventually, we all die of something."

"Which doesn't mean you have to die doing what Mama and Velma did—devoting love and time and attention to a man incapable of returning it."

"Are you saying Daddy doesn't love us?" Maude was thoroughly sick of this conversation. "Hand me a few of the green balls."

"Of course not." Helen passed the balls up. "But can't you see what he did to all of us?"

Maude stared down at her sister. "Supported us. Sent us to college."

"I don't mean the money part. I'm talking about actually caring who we were or what we wanted. To him, we are merely females. Women should keep quiet and not cause trouble."

Maude tried not to smile. "Like you?"

Helen looked uncomfortable. "I probably ran off so I could finally stop trying to please him."

"You left to please yourself. Don't blame Daddy."

Silence. "You're right," Helen said finally.

Maude hung the last of the green balls, feeling guilty for being mean.

Helen said, "There's a box of gold ones. Want those, too?"

Maude came down off the stool and stood back to look at the tree. "Yeah, let's gussy this thing up."

"But Daddy did squash Mother's dream, remember?"

All Maude wanted to remember was where she'd left her wine glass.

"When she wanted to open a dress shop."

"It wasn't a dress shop. Get hangers on those last Christmas balls."

Helen obeyed. "You know what I'm talking about—a shop for making custom clothes."

"Mother said it didn't work because she couldn't sew fast enough."

"Daddy laughed at her."

"He did not." Maude studied the tree. "We need more stuff around the bottom."

"He pooh-poohed the idea and when it failed, he was like, 'Come on home where you belong, Lillian.'"

"He never said anything like that."

"He didn't have to." Helen began hanging gold balls around the bottom. "Every glance said it. Even his pity felt condescending. He treated her like a five-year-old whose lemonade stand flopped."

Maude took a break, found her wine glass, and emptied it. "Exactly what is your point?" She swapped half of Helen's gold balls for green and red ones.

"He did the same thing to all of us. We spent our entire lives trying to earn his love, when loving a woman wasn't anything he cared about. We were supposed to love and admire *him*."

Maude rummaged in the bottom of a cardboard box. "Look. An unopened box of ice cycles. Let's hang these and call ourselves done." *And maybe you'll stop talking and I can open a new bottle of wine.*

Helen began hanging the silver strands. "For Daddy, women were pleasant enough to have around, as long as our needs didn't get in the way of what he really cared about: the law, his reputation, success."

Maude glanced at her sister and saw frustration. She must have stewed over this for years. "You make him sound horrible. Everyone adored Daddy."

"Of course, they did. He was brilliant and funny, a charming human being when he wanted to charm. None of us could get enough of him and we were always hoping to get more. Lear could only dream of such daughters."

"Who?"

"King Lear."

Show off, Maude thought.

Helen stood on tiptoe to reach the higher branches. "If I got all A's, if April recited the Mississippi counties, if Mama baked him a perfect chocolate angel food cake, maybe then he would love us. When you dedicate your whole life to the pursuit of something that doesn't exist, can't exist, and even if it did exist, there's no way you can have it—that's tragic."

"Sounds like a theory from one of your textbooks." Maude lit a cigarette and stood back looking at the finished tree. "What do you think?"

"For a funeral tree, it's not bad."

"I think it looks very festive. We deserve a reward." They returned to the kitchen and Maude got out a new bottle. "You'd be a lot more fun if you drank."

Helen shrugged. "Wine turns my face red and makes my nose run."

Maude sat with her glass refilled and a fresh cigarette. "I'm sorry you have those bad feelings about Daddy."

Helen let out an annoyed puff of air. "And I'm sorry you pretend Mother didn't drink herself to death because he quit loving her. Which I happen to know because he told me. He said he quit loving her after she got the hysterectomy."

Maude comforted herself with a generous swallow of wine. "I don't believe that."

"Because you're a good person and you think the best of everyone."

Maude gazed at her sister. "Are you trying to make me sound stupid?"

Helen ignored her. "Then he went and did the same thing to Velma."

"That's crazy. Velma adored Daddy and he adored her."

"She was better at getting whatever love he had to give, I'll grant you that. Do you know why?" Helen waited.

Maude took a drag of her cigarette and said nothing.

"Because Velma never asked for anything in return. She was like the moon reflecting his sun."

"Now you're making her sound stupid." The wine wasn't helping and Maude was sick of this conversation.

Helen dumped the ashtray in the garbage, went to the sink, and began washing it. Was this a hint for Maude to stop smoking?

Helen wiped the ashtray dry. "Velma was certainly not stupid. She was the fastest typist in the State of Mississippi. She could take dictation quicker than a court stenographer. As Daddy's secretary, she got to be part of what he cared about most." She plunked the ashtray back on the table. "Then he made her give that up."

"To be his wife."

"You think she felt fulfilled sitting around this house in her bathrobe watching soap operas with Bessie?"

Maude ground a cigarette out in the clean ashtray and lit another one. "Not all women have big dreams."

Helen coughed pointedly at the smoke. "After the stroke, she destroyed her own health taking care of him."

"Caretaking doesn't give you cancer." Maude emptied her glass and poured herself another. "Isn't this beside the point? Velma and Mother are both dead."

Helen flung out her hands in exasperation. "Daddy's not dead and I don't want him killing you."

Maude said nothing.

Helen got up and paced. "Here's what I'm afraid of. You leave your job in Dallas, give up your house, your friends, everything you love, and move back here for Daddy—"

"That will kill me?"

Helen made a shrugging, helpless gesture: "Indirectly, yes."

Maude smashed the life out of another half-smoked cigarette. "I don't mean to sound unkind, but you're not going to change my mind. I promised Velma."

"Velma's dead."

"You want me to put him in a home?"

Helen couldn't meet her eyes. "No."

"Are you planning on moving back to take care of him?"

"You know I can't." Helen stared around the kitchen as if an answer might appear. "April lives right here in town. She could look in on him."

"Our dear sister, the one so filled with rage she couldn't sit through Velma's funeral? You want to leave Daddy in her loving hands?"

Helen shook her head, finally quiet. Maude made wet circles on the table with the base of her wine glass. In the sea of her sister's harangue, the word "indirectly" stood out. Helen meant her drinking.

Helen leaned closer. "I don't mean you're not capable of doing it, but I'm worried about what living here will do to you."

"I hear you," Maude said. That's how the business psychology books advised responding when you wanted to crown the other person with a bottle of zinfandel.

"I hope so." Helen got up. "If you insist on having Christmas, I'll go and wrap presents."

Maude spoke to her sister's departing back. "Tell you what—if you find me on the floor in an alcoholic coma, you are welcome to say, 'I told you so'."

No response. Maude refilled her glass. Swallow the anger. Everyone thought she was sweet because she smiled a lot. When you were fat, you had to be twice as agreeable and three times as smart.

She propped her feet on a chair and studied the now-yellowed rooster wallpaper. Velma disliked it, but never replaced it because Bessie loved it so. The chest freezer Velma bought looked big enough to hold a body. Her dead body, according to Helen. Out in the carport, Velma's old station wagon waited, faded and ugly, but roomy enough for the wheelchair.

Maude pictured her kitchen in Texas, Delph blue and white, a fragrant jasmine covering the pergola between the house and garage — a garage where her Miata convertible waited, polished and buffed, the perfect shade of sapphire blue. With her white blonde hair, she looked dashing in that car; she *felt* dashing driving it. She thought of her Dallas friends, who would continue gathering for weekend races, with drinking and dinner after. All without her. Her chest constricted. Deep breath. Plenty of time to cry after she got Helen out of the house.

147

Three months later, Maude and Will Hughes sat at the breakfast table on a Tuesday morning. Day by day, she had mastered the routine.

"Want me to get those grapefruit sections out for you, Daddy?"

Will shook his head and struggled on one-handed.

"Does it have enough sugar?"

"I-think-so."

"Bessie is scrambling you an egg, aren't you, Bessie?"

"This is one fine egg." Bessie put it down in front of him.

Will nodded in satisfaction and picked up his fork.

Maude sipped a can of Dr. Pepper and smoked, her thoughts as dark as her drink.

Will Hughes pointed to the can and frowned.

"I can't help it. This is what I like for breakfast."

He took a spoonful of fiber grains and spit a few at her.

"Ow." Maude jumped when they hit her cheek, startled. She reacted the same way every morning "You are a no-good rascal." This was one of Will's favorite tricks. He wiped away tears of laughter.

When he'd drunk the last of his cold milky coffee, Maude rolled her father down the hall and settled him in bed for a morning nap. Back in the kitchen, she sat at the table and lit another cigarette.

"I got my grocery list ready," Bessie said.

"I'll go in a while."

"You and me both know you don't leave this house without your makeup, and that takes an hour. The store will get crowded and I need to start on my smothered chicken."

Maude walked out into the bright spring morning. The sun made her blink back tears. She hadn't told anyone about the call from Dallas. Her time was up. Unless she returned by the end of this week, the company would be forced to make her temporary leave permanent and hire a replacement. In other words, she was fired. She should put the house on the market. Without a job, she didn't need a house in Dallas. Carting her father and his wheelchair around, she didn't need a blue Miata either.

She straightened her shoulders and got in the driver's seat of the station wagon. It wasn't as if she had a choice. She would focus on the positive. All her life, she had been the dumb daughter, the fat daughter. Now she could be first.

She would think of fun new things for them to do together. She wondered if her daddy liked movies. Why was she crying? Love was better than a job, no matter how good she was at it and how hard she'd worked to get into management.

On the way back from the grocery, she stopped at the liquor store and bought six bottles of zinfandel. She would hide four of them in the storeroom. Helen thought she was so clever, counting those empties in the trash. Maude snorted remembering. She had put two more in the outside garbage without her sister noticing. Besides, Helen was back in Florida. Maude didn't need to sneak around. Doreen, Bessie, and Flora May wouldn't say a word and her father couldn't.

Sitting on the couch next to her father's chair after dinner, she pretended to watch the screen. Was it baseball season already? Maybe Spring training. Maude drank her wine and smoked.

Atlanta's third batter struck out. Will Hughes groaned and gave her arm a poke.

Maude tried to pay attention. "What a bunch of bums."

She slipped into the kitchen. She could refill a wine glass without a soul noticing. She was a ghost on wheels, downing a third glass while everyone thought she still sipped the first. Bessie's ride had come, and the kitchen sat empty. The dishwasher groaned like someone inside was dying. She needed to call about that tomorrow. From the lake room, she heard a triumphant shout. Atlanta must have gotten an out. She checked her face in the mirror over the dining room buffet. Her roots needed a touch-up. Smile could use a touch-up, too. She wiped lipstick off a tooth.

When she got back, she'd missed an inning and Atlanta was at bat again. "That went fast."

Will tried to tell her. "One-two-three-four." Holding up four fingers.

"Atlanta struck out all three batters?"

"I-think-so." He pointed at the couch for her to sit.

The first Atlanta batter hit a double. Loud cheers from the crowd.

"Good work, huh, Daddy? I guess they aren't bums after all."

"Baci." He gave her arm a pat.

He was happy to have her in Velma's spot on the couch, a woman to pat. Maude swallowed hard. She would not cry. "You're a no-good rascal."

"I-don't-think-so," Will said.

He couldn't do his part of the joke anymore. When he could talk, they used to yell it at each other: "You're a no-good rascal." "No, *you're* the no-good rascal."

Maude leaned back against the cushions. She was close to the pink haze, a zone the color of zinfandel, the perfect amount of wine to make another evening bearable.

This was more important than a job or a darling house. She planned to be everything Will Hughes wanted in a companion, the voice that made him smile first thing in the morning and the last person he saw at night. She would keep him cheerful and help him get over the grief of losing Velma. Cook him his favorite dishes. She was a better cook than Velma and wouldn't go all brown rice on him like Helen. Maude blotted a tear with the back of one finger and took another swallow of wine. Outside, the last light turned the sky a deep purple. The pines behind the lake made a black silhouette. No use crying over things that couldn't be helped. Being here was a gift. She would be the last best person for Will Hughes. The one he loved.

Acknowledgments

This book is pure invention, except for the parts that are true. I have changed the names of fine, decent people because I don't want to embarrass them or their descendants. I have kept the names of public figures and a few beloved servants, who never received enough recognition. The historical events happened. In between, I made a lot of stuff up.

A huge thank you to my writing group—Ginny Rorby, Katherine Brown, Kate Erickson, Amie McGee, Ginny Reed, Lynn Courtney, and Nona Smith. They read and re-read these chapters. Without their encouragement and laughter, I could not have gone on. Special thanks to Susan Bono, Clay Craig, Nona Smith, and Henri Bensussen, for editing and proof reading. Gratitude to the folks at Black Rose Writing, who have been nothing but responsive and helpful. Last, but never least, a big hug for my husband Les Cizek, who patiently puts up with the hours—nay, years—I spend staring at the computer.

About the Author

Raised in the South during the civil rights struggles, Norma Watkins is the author of two memoirs: *The Last Resort, Taking the Mississippi Cure* (2011), which won a gold medal for best nonfiction published in the South by an independent press; and *That Woman from Mississippi* (2017). She lives in northern California with her woodworker husband and two cats.

Note from the Author

Word-of-mouth is crucial for any author to succeed. If you enjoyed *In Common*, please leave a review online — anywhere you are able. Even if it's just a sentence or two. It would make all the difference and would be very much appreciated.

Thanks!
Norma Watkins

We hope you enjoyed reading this title from:

BLACK ROSE
writing™

www.blackrosewriting.com

Subscribe to our mailing list – *The Rosevine* – and receive **FREE** books,
daily deals, and stay current with news about upcoming
releases and our hottest authors.
Scan the QR code below to sign up.

Already a subscriber? Please accept a sincere thank you for being a fan of
Black Rose Writing authors.

View other Black Rose Writing titles at
www.blackrosewriting.com/books and use promo code
PRINT to receive a **20% discount** when purchasing.

9 781684 339235